In Your Dreams!

In Your Dreams!

An Unlikely Later-in-Life Love Story

DANA MICHAELS

IN YOUR DREAMS!

ISBN 979-8-9855619-1-3

Copyright © 2022 by Dana Michaels
Published by Michaels Media
7551 Freeport Blvd. #1023
Sacramento, CA 95832-1001

Also available in electronic edition
ASIN B09T928PDN

DEDICATION

To my late cousin, Katherine Picone Hertz, who died with her husband, Eric Hertz, when their plane crashed off the coast of New Zealand in 2013.

And

To those of my family, friends, and colleagues who encouraged me to take a chance and do something I never thought I could. Thank you.

TABLE OF CONTENTS

Chapter 1: Award Dreams

Between the unsettling darkness and stench of rotting fish, no one in his right mind would come down to the old South London docks in the middle of the night. Nigel Stone stood under the one weak, flickering security light, anxiously glancing around the muddy beach and warehouses.

Tired and impatient, he checked the time, then pulled his scarf tighter for warmth. Every new sound got his attention. As he walked slowly toward the car park and weighed the risk of giving up, his foot caught on something. A less athletic man would have fallen flat on his face. He bent over to look more closely at the mass on the dock... then wished he hadn't.

The body on the ground had been beaten so severely, both arms and legs were broken and twisted in ways that turned Nigel's stomach. Blood pooled around the victim's head, bashed to an unrecognizable state. The short hair and size of the body suggested it belonged to a man. The reporter feared this was his informant as he looked around, pulled his mobile out, and rang Scotland Yard.

"Cut!" a woman shouted. Bright lights flooded the set and the *Nigel Stone* television crew began moving. Jamie Knight dropped his Nigel Stone persona as easily as he'd take off Nigel's distinctive jacket and reached down to help the man who played the dead body.

"Damn, 'at concrete's cold," the stunt actor said in his Cockney dialect. "Can I borrow some o' your fans to warm me up?"

"Help yourself... if they'll get near you, looking like that." Jamie waved to a dozen teenaged girls crowding the yellow "Do Not Cross" tape surrounding the TV production set. He had mixed emotions about them.

Fans were a performer's bread-and-butter. They could propel an actor's career into better roles, higher salaries, and greater status. And audience attention could be addicting. On the other hand, a serious actor wouldn't want to be equated with a flash-in-the-pan teen idol.

"That's a' they care 'bout, i'n it? 'ow good lookin' a bloke is?" the stunt man asked.

"Oh, no. They also like money, status..." And nattering about who's wearing which designer's frock to the next ball.

The actors paused and looked toward the director. Then Jamie continued. "You must get your share, when you're not covered in stage blood and twisted into a knot."

"Ay, bein' double-jointed is fun. Not that you need it. Bet they 'ave to pay you more to play Nigel now, eh?"

Jamie's portrayal of the seductive reporter-writer had earned him a small but growing British fan base. The first season had drawn such a large audience, he and his co-stars had received offers for other plum roles and at least one BBC executive had feared some might leave the show.

Jamie hadn't asked for more money, but it had come, with more freedom to choose roles that appealed to him. He had hoped to achieve that status much earlier, but reaching it by his forty-third year was still satisfying.

"They pay me enough. And I enjoy this show and crew." He nodded at the girls again. "As for that lot, they're nice kids, but most of them are underage, under-educated, overweight, and over-made-up, with nothing better to do." He grinned at the stunt actor. "You're welcome to them."

The director interrupted from across the set. "Okay, we have it. Thank you, Jamie. Thank you, Dev."

The next morning, Jamie twiddled a pen as he sat on a black leather sofa, feeling at-home in his agent's office. He had known its spartan furniture and white walls covered in eight-by-tens of famous clients since childhood, when Victor Harrington, a top rep in an international agency, had been his mother's agent. She had been one of Britain's busiest stage and TV actresses, and Jamie had known, even then, he wanted to be an actor, too. Victor had recognized the boy's talent early on and signed him when he was sixteen.

After earning bachelor's and master's degrees in the performing arts—with honors—Jamie had won modeling jobs, bit parts in British theatre, then radio and television adverts, which eventually led to voice-over work and minor roles in telly and film. While he wasn't yet famous, he had earned respect in the business by the time producers cast him as the lead in *Nigel Stone*. That role had made him popular in the U.K., but he still wasn't well-known elsewhere.

Victor leaned over his uncluttered modular desk, scanning a commercial voice-over contract for Jamie. "I don't see a problem with this," the balding man said as he took his reading glasses off. "They're just protecting themselves from prima donnas."

"Good," Jamie said. "Is that donation ready for the Women's Resource Center?"

Victor pulled a check from a drawer and set it on the desk for Jamie to sign. "I still think a £5,000 donation to Cancer Research UK would do more for your image."

"It's not about my image. I want to help battered women and rape victims." Jamie's grandmother once confided that a theatre producer had assaulted his mum when she was a young, aspiring actress. She had never spoken of it, but her reaction to any talk of sexual harassment had suggested she knew the subject personally.

Victor sighed and put the signed check into an envelope. "They'll have it tomorrow." Clearly, he believed charity was nothing more than a publicity tactic.

3

"Good." Jamie returned to the sofa and opened his iPad. "Could we go over my schedule? Danny's a good P.A., but I'd hate to appear unreliable if something fell through the cracks."

"Your Personal Assistant isn't perfect? I warned you about employing your cousin," Victor sneered as he opened Jamie's calendar on the computer. "On we go. The Prince's Trust is Wednesday. Who are you taking?"

Jamie scowled. "Beatrice Aylesworth... the blueblood Mum wants me to marry."

"Better her than a commoner—if you had to marry. It never hurts to be seen with nobility. But stay single; it's better for your career."

Victor itemized Jamie's busy schedule, including an event he wished he could skip. Friday night, they would smuggle him into a VIP preview of the new Nigel Stone exhibit at the London Museum to surprise the guests.

"Do I really have to go to that? Those things are dull as ditchwater. And the so-called VIPs...." He rolled his eyes. "Plenty of other *Nigel* people will be there."

"You do," Victor snapped. "This may get you in the Society pages, as well as Entertainment. You can never get too much press. It'd be better if fifty hyperventilating girls show up, but the museum don't want to pay for extra security. Remember, they and the BBC want your appearance to be a surprise, so not a word to anyone."

"I know." Jamie sighed and flopped back onto the sofa. "But will it help me win an Academy Award®?"

Victor peered at him over his glasses. "Don't hold your breath. The odds are a million to one for anyone, and you're not even a likely candidate. You're a decent actor, Jamie, but you're forty-three, just did your first starring telly credit, and still haven't got one in a film. Keep doing your best, but don't expect to ever have an Oscar® on your mantle."

Jamie flattened his mouth, gazed out the window and shook his head. What kind of agent spurns his client's desire to be the best? He would win one or die trying.

Victor took his glasses off and gave his client a stern look. "You've been pushing yourself awfully hard. Hell, I don't think you've taken a proper holiday since drama school. What's it been... fifteen years?"

Pleased with himself for being a model of health and fitness, Jamie beamed and lifted his chin slightly to the right. After winning many a school track meet, he still ran and had the sinewy body of a marathoner. Paired with his six-foot height and fairly good looks, he could appear quite striking.

Victor seemed to recognize Jamie's self-satisfied look. "I know you're in better shape than most of us." He patted his corpulent stomach. "But even you have your limits. Take a break before they release *First Impressions*. We can't have you getting sick and losing work."

"I'm fine." Jamie put the iPad in his briefcase. "You should come out and run with Peter Li and me." *As if that'll ever happen!*

"Right... in your dreams." Victor stood up and extended his right hand—Jamie's cue to leave.

The talent agency staff watched Jamie on his way out of the offices. He smiled, acknowledged them all, and wished he knew whether they liked him for who he was, personally, or just because he was an actor who earned a good income.

Chapter 2: Dream Trip

Katerina Mancini looked at her watch. Where was Barbara? Their international flight would leave in less than two hours, and they should have checked their baggage an hour ago. There was a long line to the check-in counter and they still had to go through security. If her sister wasn't there in the next fifteen minutes, Kat would proceed without her. She stepped into the line, figuring it would take at least that long to reach the front.

Her older sister—personal chef for a wealthy winemaking family—was always late. Today it was especially irritating since Barbara was Kat's guest on a five-day trip to London. That she had won it didn't make the second ticket any less valuable than if she had paid for it.

If only one of her friends could have gotten away that week, or she had a boyfriend or husband to go with her. She checked the time again and twisted her watch back and forth.

Rising on her toes, she looked toward the airport entrance, hoping to see Barbara. No joy, as a colleague liked to say. Well, Barb wasn't going to screw up Kat's first trip to England—the nation that gave us The Beatles, Yorkshire pudding, some of her ancestors, and excellent public television shows.

Many were on the *Paragon Theatre* anthology, which had held annual sweepstakes the past few winters. Kat entered every year, assuming she would never win the trip and tour of London filming locations. She had always wanted to go there, and still couldn't believe someone had pulled her entry from the tens of thousands they received.

When she was eleventh in line, Kat heard her name. Finally. Barbara rushed to duck under the barrier cord and join her, ignoring a few dirty looks from people in line behind her.

"Sorry I'm late. You wouldn't believe the traffic."

Kat forced a smile. "Glad you could make it."

An hour into the long flight, Barbara asked, "What's on the tour again?"

"Interesting places where they shoot some *Paragon Theatre* shows, a new Nigel Stone exhibit at a museum, and the BBC studios."

That TV season, *Paragon Theatre* had acquired a new BBC program about the popular fictional reporter Nigel Stone. Kat liked it and had read all about the production when it began.

"Hmm." Barbara looked and sounded as unenthusiastic as anyone could.

"Look, I know you don't care about TV production..." *or anything else I do.*

"And you still do? Why? You haven't worked in it for years."

"And I miss it. I'm excited about this." Kat paused and looked at her hands in her lap. "But since I'll probably never get to work in TV again, I interviewed for that public affairs promotion I told you about."

Kat had been a public affairs officer for fourteen years at the California Department of Wildlife and was popular among journalists and colleagues who believed the public deserved honest, accurate information. In recent years she had applied for better-paying jobs when they opened but had been passed over for younger applicants every time. When a senior public affairs officer retired recently, Kat volunteered to do half of his work—in addition to her own—hoping to get his job.

"How did you do?" Barbara asked.

"I don't know. Job interviews make me nervous and my mind goes blank."

"You seem fine in news interviews."

"That's different. It's easy to talk about wildlife and the good work our staff does. In job interviews, you need to brag about yourself, and I can't do that."

"You shouldn't be nervous. You already have a good job. It's not like you're still a starving production assistant and desperate for a livable income."

"I will be, if I can't earn more before I'm retirement age. I don't want to wind up living in a grungy little room in a slum, eating dog food when I'm old." The bitterness that came with knowing she was sure to face old age alone came through in her voice.

After a few minutes of silence Barbara said, "Maybe you'll meet a nice man in England."

"Yeah, right... as if *that* would last." Looking out the window, she paused. "I lost the love lottery. Not buying any more tickets to disappointment."

"Oh, don't give up on all men. You just don't believe in yourself anymore. Stop putting yourself down. There must be someone out there for you."

"At fifty-three? Fat chance."

"Gloria Steinem was over fifty the first time she married."

"Gloria Steinem is rich, successful, and better looking than I am. And it didn't last. I will not let myself fall in love so a man can dump me for some deferential bimbo, again."

The previous night—as she'd microwaved a frozen dinner and eaten alone—the idea of meeting a nice guy on the trip had crossed Kat's mind, too. She'd dismissed it. The fact that she had reached AARP age without ever marrying

9

made her uncharacteristically insecure about romantic relationships.

By her early forties, she had suffered a broken heart and the depression that followed so many times, she just stopped acting available. A forty-foot wall around her heart saved it from being broken. But it also closed the door to something she wouldn't admit to anyone that she wanted: to be married, share life's ups and downs, and grow old with a respectable man who loved her as much as she loved him.

Chapter 3: Museum Piece

London turned out to be as exciting as—and far more crowded than—Kat and Barbara had imagined. The second day of their BBC-led tour ended at the London Museum, a sleek, modern building in what locals called "The City"—the historic financial district once surrounded by a wall the Romans built in the year 200 AD.

The museum would soon open a Nigel Stone exhibit. As a teenager, Kat had enjoyed reading author B.J. Bixby's early twentieth-century novels featuring the handsome, clever newspaper reporter. Now, more than ninety years of books, movies, and TV shows about the character and artifacts from Bixby's life filled a great hall the size of a house as well as the surrounding corridors.

Because of the new BBC-TV series based on the books, the tour included a VIP preview of the exhibit—with about one hundred other "VIPs." Kat inhaled the mouth-watering aroma of savory appetizers that were so plentiful, they replaced dinner. Conversing with *Nigel Stone's* producer, director, production designer, and others who worked on the show took her back to the excitement of her younger days, when she worked in TV production.

By eight o'clock the crowd had thinned. Museum staff herded the twenty-nine remaining guests into a room that had a stage, a large screen, and theatre seating. There, future visitors would watch film and video clips from old Nigel Stone movies and TV shows, and interviews with the people who had made them. Kat and Barbara sat with Doug and Lisa Tomlinson, a couple touring with them, having won the Canadian version of the *Paragon Theatre* sweepstakes.

Upon hearing the *Nigel Stone* TV theme, most people stopped talking, and the room erupted with unexpected cheers and applause as actor Jamie Knight, who played the title character, bounded in and onto the small stage. Organizers had said he wouldn't be there. The clapping continued as people held smartphones high to photograph the actor.

Lisa jumped up and down like a hysterical teenager within arm's reach of her favorite rock star. Obviously far beyond adolescence, she looked ridiculous. Parts of her nearly fell out of her low-cut, tight-fitting red dress with a side-slit up to her hip. Doug—who looked old enough to be her father—seemed blasé about it.

Appearing as if he had stepped off the cover of *GQ* magazine, Jamie bowed. "Thank you. Thank you all for coming to celebrate the amazing work of B.J. Bixby and those who built upon her creations. And thank you for supporting British literature and *Nigel Stone*."

Scenes from the show played on a screen behind him as he spoke eloquently about the production and cast. He told some funny and embarrassing stories about the other actors, followed with generous praise for everyone who worked on the show.

Because of his reputation as a shallow, skirt-chasing Casanova, Kat wasn't a fan. Still, he had an unusual yet pleasant smile and intense blue eyes she couldn't stop admiring, although the Nigel in her adolescent imagination had been more handsome. "So... His pasty white complexion on the show must be make-up," Kat remarked. "But this slicked-back, 1930s mobster hairstyle sucks. The longer Nigel Stone style is much more attractive."

"No hairstyle could make him attractive," Barbara said with an expression that reflected her distaste. "He's a good actor, but not good looking."

"Mmm... He looks okay to me. Too bad he's a sexist jerk."

After thanking the attendees again, Jamie stepped off the stage and out to the spacious exhibit hall, followed by the guests. He glided around the room, politely meeting everyone, flirting with the prettiest women. The charming actor's conversations were brief and superficial—especially with star-struck Lisa, who fawned over him.

Kat didn't get infatuated with actors, having worked around many in Hollywood. And men like Jamie, who never let themselves be seen with average-looking women like her, didn't deserve her respect. When he shook her hand, a twinge of excitement surprised her. That made her feel stupid, but she couldn't deny a physical attraction to the much younger man. Must have been charisma.

* * *

As Jamie dutifully met each guest, a few made it clear they were his for the taking. Actors had a name for people who wanted to sleep with them because they were famous: "star collectors." Although he wasn't a star—yet—sometimes he would go for it.

But he preferred the company of people who realized actors experienced the same feelings, challenges, and problems everyone else did, plus the difficulties that came with fame. But dating those women probably wouldn't help a guy win awards or make Hollywood's A-List—Jamie's lifelong ambition.

After his perfunctory interactions with the guests, he joined his producer and director. "Is there anyone else here I have to meet?"

"I don't think you *have* to meet anyone," Margaret Chamberlain, the show's director, assured him. "But I rather liked the American who won the BBC-*Paragon* sweepstakes. She's worked in telly and was quite interested in our production."

"Humph." Jamie wasn't interested.

Producer Neil Tennison added, "Odd, too... she didn't ask much about the cast, and didn't even mention you."

That got Jamie's attention. Most women were more interested in him—and other actors—than in the show. "Sorry?"

"That's right," Margaret replied. "She wanted to hear how production had changed since she left Hollywood and to meet Rob Sharretts and talk about music." Grinning, she gently poked Jamie's side. "For once, it wasn't all about you!"

Feeling slighted, Jamie glanced around the room. "Which one is she?"

"I don't see her," Margaret said. "She may have left. She's about your age, my height, with short brown hair, in a blue blouse and a black jacket. Not your type, though."

"What do you mean?"

"She doesn't look like a model."

"Well, that's not... Was she with anyone?"

"Not when she spoke to us," Neil said, "but she likely came with the other *Paragon Theatre* winners Iris Cavanaugh brought."

Was she the rather nonchalant American? There was something about her...

* * *

Barbara yawned as she and Kat walked through the nearly deserted hall displays. "I wish we could leave. Have you seen Iris?" Iris Cavanaugh was a former BBC writer who now did promotional projects. The older woman with short gray hair was their daily guide and their ride back to the hotel.

"Not lately." Kat glanced up and down the hallway. "You want to go sit down?"

From behind them, a warm baritone voice said, "There's a bench over there."

Kat turned to see Jamie Knight again—alone.

"Enjoying the exhibit?" he asked. His posture was less formal than when they first spoke, but he still kept more than enough personal space between himself and the women.

"Yes," Kat said. "Someone did a nice job cleaning up the audio on those early films."

Barbara yawned again and went to sit on the bench.

Jamie ignored Barbara's indifference and surprised Kat by strolling past some displays and chatting with her. She was glad he didn't wear cologne. An asthma attack here would have been embarrassing.

"What's your name, again? Where are you from?" he asked.

"Katerina Mancini, Northern California."

"I'm in Los Angeles fairly often but haven't seen much of the north. A friend once drove me up to Big Sur, though. That's magnificent. Do you live around there?"

"Yeah, right... In my dreams!" She instantly regretted using such a sarcastic tone. How could he know her income? "I'd love to, but I could never afford the central coast."

As they walked past photos from his show, Jamie asked, "What do you think of it?"

"What?"

"Our show." He looked at Kat as if to ask, what else would I care about?

"I like it. The stories are well written, the photography and other production elements are first class, and I love the music." After a silent moment, she added, "And the cast is good, but you already know that."

Jamie smiled. "Thank you. How do you know about production values?"

"I used to work in TV."

"Oh? Where?"

"L.A., Sacramento, and Alaska. I loved the creativity; it made work fun." Kat missed broadcasting, and Jamie's interest made her feel good, as if she still had one foot "in the club."

"What do you do, now?"

"Media relations and writing public information for the California Department of Wildlife."

"Oh. Do you have game wardens there? I'm playing one in Africa next month."

"No kidding," Kat said. "If you'd like to talk to a real warden—"

"Thanks, but a warden from Kenya is advising the writers, and he'll be on-set during the shoot."

Jamie turned back toward Neil and Margaret in the adjacent room. Kat followed his gaze. Neil gestured to him. "Excuse me."

He dashed back to his colleagues. The man had serious charisma. And such a clear, rich voice. "That was interesting." She walked toward Barbara, resting on the bench. "I guess he didn't want to waste time on someone who's worked in the sausage factory."

"What?"

"TV—someone who knows how they make shows."

"He's just marketing," Barbara said, giving her younger sister a critical eye as she got up and they walked toward the last displays. "You should recognize that."

Her remark reminded Kat of their mother, a chronic pessimist who would insult people. Then—if someone called her on it—pretend she was kidding.

"You're a little old to be flirting with him."

"I wasn't flirting." Kat turned to her, scowling.

Barbara clucked in disgust. "He probably thinks you're his age. Remember, you don't look fifty-three. If you could see yourself..."

"Bullshit. I don't flirt with anyone. And I'd have to be a masochist to flirt with an actor—especially one with *his* reputation." She paused. "But I'd like to hear more from anyone working on the show. I miss the fun, creative people who make TV and films."

Some of Kat's current colleagues were fun, and some were creative, but opportunities to be either at work were rare. Writing and speaking for a government agency was "just the facts." And in a state office, she had gotten in trouble for the sort of wisecracks that made broadcasters laugh.

As she and Barbara reached the end of the displays, Jamie reappeared, looking even more relaxed this time. "Well, now that you've seen the whole exhibit," he asked, "what do you think?"

Barbara heaved a sigh and said, "It's nice." Her tone said, "I'm bored." She walked away, Kat guessed, to ask Iris if they could leave.

Kat wouldn't have been rude even if the exhibit hadn't been impressive. "So, Jamie, were you a Nigel Stone fan before you got the role?"

"I liked the stories, but I wasn't a fan-boy. Our producer, Neil, was." Jamie paused and looked at her for a moment. "He said you're the *Paragon Theatre* winner."

"Yes," Kat admitted, looking down. Great. A contestant. *Now he'll think I'm pathetic.*

"Congratulations. How is the tour?"

"Fun. We visited some of your locations today."

Barbara returned alone, looking disappointed. "No Iris," she said.

Jamie then said something neither Kat nor Barbara could have expected. "I hope you won't think me too forward, but since this is winding down, would you ladies like to go out for a drink?"

The question stunned both women, but Barbara reacted quickly. "No, thank you. We have an early start tomorrow."

Surprised, Kat pinched her eyebrows together as she looked at Barbara and considered arguing but decided against it. "I would, but..." She shrugged her shoulders and glared at her sister. "Thanks. Nice of you to ask." She seldom drank and didn't like bars, but she was flattered and wanted to talk more with him. He had become more interesting as the evening progressed, and she sensed he might not be his public image.

"Oh, come on," Jamie addressed Kat. "Your friend may be tired, but you're wide awake. Come and see some of London's real night life. You won't see it on a tour."

His invitation puzzled Kat. Why would an actor like him ask someone like her out? "She's my sister. Where can we go that fans won't hassle you?"

"A private club."

With an accusatory expression, Barbara asked, "*Your* place?"

Jamie raised his eyebrows and blinked at her. "No. The Huntington Club in Chelsea. I don't take people I don't know well to my home."

"Well... you're right," Kat admitted. "I'm not tired. If you'll take me back to the hotel when I am..."

Always the older sister—and a mother—Barbara shifted into her bossy parent mode. "You can't just go off on your own, Kat. We agreed to a schedule."

"Oh, stop it. I'm not going to disrupt the schedule."

"Right, then." Jamie smiled and turned to Barbara. "I promise not to keep her out too late."

Barbara's attempt to control Kat was pointless. She hadn't let anyone tell her what to do for decades. And now she could see another side of London.

Iris and the Tomlinsons came around a corner, and Lisa's eyes nearly popped out of her head. Her long, straight blonde locks flying behind her, she rushed to Jamie, gushing about his acting, how wonderful and handsome he was, and how excited she was to be so close to him.

As Jamie recognized the obsessive fan in the provocative dress, his mouth went flat. His eyes no longer sparkled the way they had a few minutes earlier. He stiffened his posture and appeared less accessible, crossing his arms and glancing away, as if looking for an escape route. Each time Lisa moved toward him, he stepped back, always keeping at least two feet away from her.

Kat had to stifle a laugh.

Doug all but ignored Lisa. Earlier, he and Kat had discussed the radio commercials he produced, some voiced by famous actors. He would have heard what they thought of fans who throw themselves at performers, and it wasn't pretty.

When Lisa had Jamie backed up to a wall, Iris announced it was time to leave and started toward the stairway. Lisa turned to look at her. Seizing the opportunity to escape, Jamie darted to the space between Kat and Barbara. The six of them headed downstairs to the lobby, with Lisa chattering at Jamie from behind. A stocky man who had followed him all evening now followed her.

Outside the glass entry, two paparazzi were skulking. "Oh, dear," Iris said, turning to Jamie, their likely quarry. "Twitter, no doubt."

"It's okay. I'll stop for a few pictures, then we'll be off." The photographers didn't wait for him to accommodate them. Their flashes turned night into day, impairing everyone's vision. Lisa tried to position herself near Jamie to be in his pictures. She so reveled in the attention Doug had to pull her away from the actor.

Jamie stopped and with tired patience in his voice said, "Hi, guys."

About five yards away, Kat blinked the sparkling dots from her vision. This must get old. As the flashes persisted and her companions walked away, she turned to Barbara. "See you later."

Iris gave her a critical look. "What are you doing? Come on, then!"

Before Kat could speak, Jamie turned to Iris and said, "She's coming with me. Don't worry, I'll get her back to you before she turns into a pumpkin."

Lisa stopped dead in her tracks, and her jaw dropped. "What the hell?" she shouted. "She's going with *him*?" Pink-faced—clearly embarrassed by her outburst—Doug took her arm and pulled her toward the car park as she stared at Jamie in disbelief.

Jamie turned to Kat and nodded toward a waiting SUV. The camera flashes continued as they walked and he put his hand on her back. She rarely liked to be touched by people she didn't know well, but this time it felt like security.

One photographer yelled, "Who's your date tonight, Jamie?"

Jamie ignored him.

Chapter 4: A London Knight Out

As they rode away, Jamie took a good look at his passenger. Margaret was wrong. Kat *was* pretty—simply not made-up, coiffed, and costumed like an actor. And her voice, a bit lower than most women's, was calming, like the gentle purr of a contented cat. "Is the tart in the sketty red dress with you?" he asked.

"No. She and her husband won the sweeps in Canada; we're all with Iris."

"That's her husband? I thought he was her father."

Kat snickered.

"So... is this your first trip to Britain?" Jamie asked.

"No, I've visited Scotland. But this is the first time I've been able to see London."

"What took you to Scotland?"

"Midland Air." Kat smiled and air-drummed a rim-shot. "Sorry. Your setup was too good to resist."

Jamie chuckled. Comic lines from a woman he'd just met... *Clever... might be fun.* Usually ladies were reserved at first, as though afraid if they said the wrong thing, he'd push them out at the next red light. He liked her confident manner but hoped that wasn't the tip of an iceberg, American arrogance.

After a pause, she said, "I'm part-Scottish, always wanted to go there, and had a chance to tour with Ed Miller, a Scottish folksinger. Have you heard him?"

"If I have, I didn't know it."

* * *

In Chelsea, the SUV pulled up to an Edwardian-era building. The understated entry displayed only the name "Huntington Club" in twelve-inch brass letters on the wall near double doors. A doorman greeted Jamie by name and nodded to Kat. He reminded her of a janitor who'd given her a contemptuous look as she sat on an executive producer's sofa, after-hours at The Burbank Studios, decades earlier.

Mellow jazz played at a low volume in a large room that resembled an upscale—but not techno-modern—nightclub. Plush, cozy booths lined three walls, and there appeared to be another room beyond. Jamie waved at someone as he headed for a booth at the far wall. The subdued, red-tinted lighting made it hard to identify someone from across the room unless you knew his or her profile well—good for people who want to be recognizable to their friends but unnoticed by strangers.

Tables filled most of the space, but the club didn't seem very busy for a Friday night. Kat felt out-of-place in such an exclusive establishment. Although she had spent more money than she liked to for her black trousers and blazer, royal blue silk blouse and almost-flats that hurt her feet, the outfit still lacked the sophistication of what other women there wore. Underdressed—as usual.

"I like to meet friends here." Jamie pointed to a corner. "Sometimes they have live music on a small stage over there."

Kat jumped on the opportunity to discuss one of her favorite topics. "What kind of music do you like?"

"Mostly rock, but it depends on the situation and who I'm with."

An attractive young server approached. "Hello, Mr. Knight. What would you like?"

Jamie directed the question to his guest. "Kat?"

She tried to remember the few drinks she liked that didn't have silly names or come with a tiny umbrella stuck in a piece of fruit. "Do you have Amaretto?"

"Of course." The server turned to Jamie.

"A glass of 2008 Monticello cabernet, please." He turned back to Kat. "So..." His voice trailed off, as though he had forgotten what they were talking about.

"Music," Kat reminded him. "You like rock, but not always. What else?"

"Oh... pop, going back to the 1940s... sometimes jazz... and some 'world' music. What about you? Being a Californian, I presume you like the Beach Boys?"

Kat smiled. "Of course. I love rock 'n roll oldies, especially from the sixties, but not hard rock or punk. And I like traditional Scottish fiddle and pipe tunes."

"Bagpipes?" He cringed, as if she'd said, 'fingernails on a blackboard.' "Why?"

"I play with a group of Scottish fiddlers."

"You play the violin?"

"No, I back-up the fiddlers on rhythm guitar. And I play in a quartet with small pipes, fiddle, and bodhrán. How 'bout you? Do you play anything?"

"Football." He grinned. "I learned to play the piano—a little—in school, but I couldn't play anything now." He seemed pensive for a moment.

The server delivered their drinks, and Kat raised her glass. "Slainthe!"

She asked Jamie about growing up in London, his travels, and his family. His mother was an actor, and his father was a judge. He didn't volunteer much, and what he did talk about, Kat probably could've found on the internet if she'd wanted to.

"I love London," he said. "It's the greatest city in the world."

The more they talked, the more she liked him, despite his reputation as a ladies' man. She could see how he charmed women into sleeping with him. His private persona was attractive, and she caught herself squeezing her thighs together more than once.

When Jamie had nearly finished his wine, the server came back and asked if they'd like another. Kat had been nursing the Amaretto. "No, thank you."

"Drink up," Jamie urged. "You're not driving anywhere tonight, are you?"

"Not if you're taking me home. Not home... but, um, you know... I mean, to the hotel," she stammered, "my hotel... where my sister is." With her eyes closed and a nervous laugh, she shook her head. "Thanks, Jamie, but if I drink up, I'll have trouble walking straight."

Jamie appeared to enjoy her embarrassment about where he would take her "home," as he turned and quietly spoke to the server. Turning back to Kat, he grinned. "So, you're a cheap date?"

"Afraid so; and not one who's fun when she's plastered. I hardly ever drink, so it doesn't take much to make me want to go take a nap."

He chuckled. "When's the last time you truly had one over the eight?"

"Been drunk? Not since a radio station promotion, years ago. My program director had to drive me home and pour me into my apartment. The next two days were hell. Worst shows of my career." She shook her head at the memory.

"Radio?"

"I was a disc jockey, then."

"You were?" Jamie shifted in his seat and faced her more directly, as though she just became more interesting. "But you're not now?"

"No." She smiled, but her eyes didn't.

"What kind of music?"

"Adult Contemporary and Oldies. I started as a newscaster, but after Congress deregulated broadcasting, news jobs disappeared. I stuck with music after that."

The server returned with two drinks. Kat looked at them, then at Jamie, and raised one eyebrow, as if to remind him she had said "no."

Jamie pressed on. "Where were you on the radio?"

"L.A., San Francisco, Sacramento... where my career died." Her shoulders dropped slightly.

"It died? How?" Jamie's expression suggested he couldn't imagine how that would feel, although as an actor, he had to know the insecurity that came with being "talent."

"Some bad choices and sexism in the business, and I was sick of being paid less than the guys—"

"Pay inequity is rubbish."

"Thank you. And they always assigned women to the worst shifts. I gave up, took a civil service exam, and was lucky enough to find a state job I could do well."

"A government radio station?" Jamie asked.

"I wish. No, I'm only on now when they interview me as a spokesperson for the state."

Jamie's interest in her flattered Kat, who found him quite likeable as the evening went on. But she didn't like talking about herself. She leaned forward. "Someone said you do a lot for charities and non-profit groups. Do you ever get involved with environment or animal issues?"

He pumped his eyebrows and joked, "I've been *called* an animal. I hosted a charity event once for Cool to Be Kind, an organization in Bath that promotes kindness to animals. But I'm more concerned with human problems, like incurable diseases and violence. Most of my charities address those issues. Do you ever get involved with those?"

"Well, I support cancer research and a rape crisis center. I've worked for women's rights and environmental protection, because if we destroy all our ecosystems, everyone will be toast. But my heart is in making the world a better place for animals, because people have abused them forever. And, of course, I support public radio and television."

"Think they checked your pedigree before they awarded you the trip?"

"Probably. I would if I were in charge." She paused to sip her drink. "I admire you for using your good fortune to help others. I wish more people would do that."

Within an hour, Kat was so comfortable with Jamie, he actually seemed kind of sexy. No wonder half the pretty women in London have slept with him.

Twice that evening, people who passed their booth said hello to Jamie and took a good long look at his companion. What were they thinking?

* * *

Like most singles his age, Jamie had been in many romantic relationships, but each had left him feeling used for his status or money. No one outside his inner circle would ever know how sensitive he was. He no longer trusted women with his heart.

His publicist and Victor had pushed him to behave like a randy playboy, to obtain frequent coverage by the entertainment media. It worked and earned him a reputation for short-lived relationships. He would have felt guilty about it, if he didn't think the women only wanted to be seen with a posh actor—not necessarily him.

Humble about his growing popularity, success, and income, he wanted to be liked for his intelligence and for being an honorable man—not for his family's money or because he was an actor. But his advisors said those qualities wouldn't help him reach his goals—Hollywood's A-List and an Academy Award.

Jamie and Kat were clearly enjoying each other's company. He asked her about the TV productions she had worked on, California, and environmental issues. She was knowledgeable without being a know-it-all. They had enough in common to make conversation easy and enough divergent pursuits to make each other interesting. They even shared some political and philosophical values, and politely discussed opposing viewpoints. She wasn't flirting. Instead, she made him feel like an old friend. He liked that.

Kat wasn't as thin, pretty, or stylish as the women Jamie dated, but something about her made him want to touch her. Was it her ash-brown hair? Or her sense of humor? The amusing one-liners she delivered with surprising alacrity made it hard not to laugh. Unlike many women he knew, she didn't seem to want anything, and was agreeable without being a pushover.

When she got too sleepy to hide it, he said, "I'd better get you back to your hotel before your sister worries." It would have been impolite to tell her she looked tired.

"As much as I hate to, I probably should call it a night." She tried to hide a yawn in a smile. "I've enjoyed spending this time with you, Jamie. May I pay for the drinks?"

He balked for a second, then arched one eyebrow at the credit card Kat held out. What kind of woman goes out with a posh man, then offers to pay? "No, thank you. I've got it." He gestured for her to put it away and was pleased when she glowered in annoyance.

Kat wobbled a little on the way out, appearing slightly off-balance. *Seriously? Buzzed on two little glasses of Amaretto?*

Jamie's throat felt dry as they waited in the club entry for his driver. He didn't want the evening to end. "Would you like to go to my place for a nightcap?"

Kat blinked and stepped back, as if he had suddenly become dangerous. "Uh, no, thank you. I really do have to get up early tomorrow. Besides, I wouldn't feel comfortable in that situation. You know your reputation." Her cheeks turned pink, and she looked away.

Jamie's lips parted, but no words came out. Before he could think of the right comeback, the black SUV pulled up, so he just opened the door for her. "Hi, David. We're taking Kat to the Radisson Blu Edwardian."

An uncomfortable silence filled the air for several minutes and an unpleasant feeling from adolescence swept over him, as if a girl he liked at school had rejected him again. He caught her glancing at him, then quickly away, so he broke the ice. "How long will you be in London?"

"Until Monday." Kat smiled. Perhaps she wasn't bothered by his invitation.

"Where else does your tour go?" he asked.

"Tomorrow we're behind the scenes at Whittaker's, and Sunday to Woburn Abbey." She paused. "Thank you for taking me to your club. I can't tell you how much I've enjoyed this evening."

"Sure, you can. You're a publicist, aren't you?"

She chuckled and glanced out the window, then at her hands in her lap. "Yes. I enjoyed the museum and talking with you the last few hours." She looked up at him. "Even though you tried to get me drunk."

"The thought never crossed my mind." Jamie grinned at her. "I didn't want to get stuck at the museum all night but wasn't ready to go home. It's been a nice evening. Thanks for trusting a guy you didn't know." *Up to a point, anyway...*

As the SUV approached her hotel's front entry, Kat thanked David for the ride, thanked Jamie again, wished him continued success, and handed him her state business card.

"If you ever need information about California's ecosystems or want to visit a wildlife area when you're there, I'd be glad to help."

He inspected the card, then slipped it into his jacket pocket. "You never know where work may take you," he said noncommittally while walking her to the front entry. "Enjoy the rest of your holiday."

They shook hands, said goodnight, and he opened the hotel door for her. As he got back into the SUV, he looked back and saw her turn to watch him leave. He sighed.

"Who was that?" David asked.

"Someone I met at the museum."

"Hmm."

"What?" Jamie asked.

"She's not your usual type. You usually snag a real stunner."

"Yeah, and I'm usually disappointed. I love the beauties, and they're good for my image. But sometimes I want to talk with someone who can hold up her end of a conversation that isn't useless gossip. And that lady can." He read her card again. A second phone number was hand-written on the back. Did she write that for him?

"Well, she's not a munter," David observed. "Just not up to your usual standards."

"It was just drinks and conversation, David. I'm not going to marry her." Jamie gazed at the city lights, diffused by mist.

His standards? Maybe that's why he had only fallen for women who used him. He had been admiring the dust jackets instead of reading the books.

At home, he typed the web address for the California Department of Wildlife and searched the site for Kat Mancini. The results page showed news releases and *Outdoor California* magazine articles with her byline. A Google search brought up more magazine stories, news clips quoting her, and a 1998 story about her as the new deejay at a radio station.

Most of the images showed her in a CDW uniform—like a cute cop. But in a few, she was on a stage playing guitar, singing, or holding a mic and wearing a radio station jacket. The evening was better than he had expected. Except... she turned him down. Why? No one says 'no' anymore.

Jamie's star was rising. He had fans throughout Britain, steady work, could buy almost anything he wanted and sleep with any woman. But his personal life seemed empty. He thought about the ex-girlfriends he had been serious about and the pain he'd felt when he realized they had never loved him. Why had he not seen that until after they'd left for someone richer or more famous?

Surely after he made the A-List, he would find someone as interesting as Kat and as pretty as Leigh—his girlfriend while they attended the University of Warwick, then the Royal Academy of Dramatic Art. But career-driven, Jamie had neglected her and had been stunned when she accepted another Bob Penrose, another friend's proposal.

He put Kat's business card in an old carved teak box with others. *Damn, I'm getting a stiffy, thinking about someone who said 'no.' What is wrong with me?*

Chapter 5: Tartan & Tweed

No... Please... It couldn't be time to get up yet. Kat had to drag herself out of bed on Saturday. She wanted to tell Barbara about her conversations with Jamie, but her sister wasn't interested. Barbara got up early, hardly spoke, and left for breakfast by herself, while Kat dressed and followed fifteen minutes later. *This must be punishment for going off on my own.*

Iris, Barbara, and the Tomlinsons were in the lobby when she got there. Lisa wanted to know where Kat and Jamie went and what they did the night before, and the interrogation continued even as they ran through a downpour to the minivan.

Finally, Doug intervened. "Lisa, give her a break!"

Kat appreciated Doug's mediation. She was about to tell Lisa to leave her alone and was so tired, she might not have been tactful. In the van, she closed her eyes and let her mind wander back to the previous evening.

She had liked Jamie Knight's acting, didn't like what she had read about him, then warmed to his personality last night. Had she insulted him with her response to his invitation to his home? That was the right choice, regardless of his intentions. But what had she missed?

The group's behind-the-scenes tour of Whittaker's Department Store, setting of the series, *One For the Money,* was perfect for a cold rainy day.

That evening, Iris took them to Tartan & Tweed, a large Celtic-themed pub, where the aromas of ale, whisky, and fried "pub grub" wafted through the air. Harps, leeks, tartan plaids, bagpipes, thistles, and red dragons—traditional Irish,

Scottish, and Welsh symbols—decorated the interior. On a riser-stage at one end of the long room, three young men played lively music on fiddle, acoustic guitar, bouzouki, bodhrán, and small pipes.

When the trio took a break, Kat noticed Iris chatting at the bar with the fiddler, who took a mischievous grin and three pints to his mates. Back onstage, he announced, "I hear there's an American in the hoose tonight who plays guitar in a Scottish group there. How'd ye like tae hear 'im play wi' us?"

A few people in the pub clapped unenthusiastically.

Iris shouted toward the stage, "Not him. *HER!*" and pointed at Kat.

"What?" Kat scowled at Iris. Had she set her up? That took a lot of nerve. Iris couldn't know whether she played well enough to perform here, or if she'd even want to.

The fiddler looked surprised, too. Humiliating a lady probably wasn't as much fun as showing a bloke who was boss. But he didn't rescind the invitation.

"Oh, no," Kat protested. "I am *not* getting up on stage and trying to play music I haven't rehearsed, on someone else's guitar, with musicians I don't know."

But people were encouraging the anonymous Yankee to be a good sport. Lisa, Doug and Iris urged her to do it. Barbara was silent.

Kat didn't think she could play well under those circumstances. But she couldn't think of a polite way to refuse and didn't want to seem like "The Ugly American." A buzz filled the room as she maneuvered around tables toward the stage, terribly self-conscious.

To the band she said, "Listen, I don't know what she told you, but I don't play professionally. You don't really want an amateur sitting-in, do you?"

The guy holding the small pipes gave the fiddler a look that suggested he should let her off the hook. But the fiddler seemed committed, probably even more certain a "girl" couldn't keep up with them. "Aye, lass. Ye'll be fine." The guitarist held a weathered 6-string out to Kat. She took the guitar and a pick, and the guitarist picked up a bouzouki. By the time they began playing, the crowd had grown larger and noisier. To Kat, that was a good thing. Playing someone else's guitar was challenging, but she played reasonably well once she got used to it. With any luck, the band and patrons' conversations would drown out her inevitable mistakes. She pasted on a performer's happy face to hide her self-doubt.

Scottish fiddle and pipe tunes are short, so bands string complementary tunes together to make five-to-ten-minute sets. The first was familiar: *The Wee Man From South Uist, The High Ride,* and *Kenny Gilles of Portnalong.* The next set was a short one she'd played with the Sacramento Scottish Fiddlers.

That bolstered her confidence, but the sets got tougher. One included an up-tempo tune with fast chord changes. She knew it well, but they played it faster than her group did, and she cringed when she failed to make three chord changes quickly enough.

Some sets included tunes she had never heard, and sometimes the fiddler turned his back to her when he told his mates what they would play next. Kat couldn't hear him and suspected he did it intentionally to make it impossible for her to start playing at the same time they did, in the correct key. But she had a good ear and faked it fairly well.

She couldn't identify the key in one tune, so she drummed on the guitar's face. When they played her favorite set, she shined, grinning from ear to ear. The bouzouki player even aimed his instrument's neck at her, and she aimed back, adding a wee bit of choreography.

A little-known, difficult tune ended the set. Thank God Scottish fiddler John Taylor had taught it to her. But Kat hadn't played it often and struggled to keep up with the trio.

Still, when the song ended, people gave them an enthusiastic round of applause, much to her relief.

Someone sent a round of drinks to Iris's table, and while embarrassed by all the attention, Kat felt both good and humbled. She needed to expand her repertoire.

Barbara acted like a different person. Beaming at her sister, she said, "I had no idea you played that well. When did you get so good?"

"About twenty years ago," Kat replied, dryly. *If you had ever come to see me...*

"Well, I'm proud of you." Barbara hugged her. She had never seen Kat perform, even though she had been playing and singing in public since the 1970s.

Everyone at their table would have been shocked—and Kat might have been too self-conscious to play well—if they had known who else had come to Tartan & Tweed that night. Three locals at the far end of the bar had come to hear live, traditional Scottish music for the first time, because one of them had spent the previous evening with a lady whose enthusiasm for it piqued his curiosity. He kept a low profile for his own reasons, but when he recognized the tourist the band had tried to embarrass, he especially didn't want *her* to see him.

Chapter 6: Woburn Abbey

Sunday, the last day of the tour, Iris drove her guests north to Woburn Abbey for a private tour and lunch hosted by the Duchess of Bedford. It was the setting for *Bedford Manor,* a popular BBC-*Paragon Theatre* costume drama. The vast acreage en route to the stately old manor house could have been the template for fairy tales. Green hills, oak woodlands, deer in the meadow... just add one knight in shining armor and a damsel in distress...

"Look at all the deer!" Lisa exclaimed.

"Yes," Iris said. "Woburn Abbey's Deer Park is the largest conservation area in Europe—three-thousand acres. Those are our native red deer, but about a hundred years ago, the duke brought other species to the estate. He had a keen interest in wildlife."

Inside the abbey, Kat detected a musty scent she had noticed in other very old buildings. The group joined nine other people in a crowded sitting room to wait for a tour guide. Since this tour was only for guests of the BBC, Leanne Robeson, one of the supporting actors in *Bedford Manor,* led it. As she guided them through the ancient abbey, she told its genuine history and that of the Russell family, who had occupied it for centuries. Most of the tourists seemed more interested in Leanne and the TV show than reality.

Barbara was most interested in the extensive art collection, which included the 1588 Armada Portrait of Elizabeth I. The Holland Library got Kat's attention. "Hey, they have Audubon's *Birds of America* here," she said with surprise.

"Yes," said Leanne. "Some of the world's first ecological experiments were done in the abbey's gardens."

After walking around the building for nearly two hours, the visitors entered a formal dining room every one of them had seen on the TV program. Staff would serve lunch amid the meticulously maintained antique furnishings, as they would have served nobility one hundred years earlier.

As they gathered around a long, formal dining table, a tall, slender man quietly slipped into the dining room. Kat and Barbara—with their backs to the door—didn't notice him until he said hello. The sound of Jamie Knight's voice startled Kat, who had assumed she would never see him again. She couldn't stop the broad smile that forced its way onto her face until Barbara asked him, "What are YOU doing here?"

"They postponed the work I had scheduled for today," he replied. "I've never been inside this abbey, and since it's become world famous, thought I'd crash the tour." He was joking, and later explained that he had received permission to join them.

While dressed more casually than he had been at the museum, Jamie still appeared more concerned with fashion than anyone else there. At the table, He pulled a heavy chair out for Barbara then another for Kat, and as she sat down, he touched the back of her shoulder. A sensuous shiver slid across and down her back.

"It's nice to see you again," she said.

Lisa Tomlinson batted her eyelashes at the actor from across the table. Jamie nodded to her and pivoted his attention elsewhere.

He would have been the center of attention had he not deflected it skillfully by asking everyone except Kat about themselves and their impressions of the abbey.

When he did speak with her, he seemed more distant than he had been two nights earlier. She didn't think herself important to anyone and assumed his coolness was because she had refused his "nightcap" invitation. Yet, twice during lunch, Jamie's leg pressed hers. He didn't acknowledge it or even look at her when he did it. Was he doing that intentionally or just hogging the leg-room?

After lunch, Jamie joined the group for the rest of the tour, seeming to avoid Kat and Barbara. Doug had to pull Lisa from his side more than once to give others a chance to talk with him as they walked around the manor house.

Outside, Leanne introduced Mr. Hoffman. "He has supervised the gardeners for twenty-nine years and will show you the formal gardens and the kitchen garden."

While traversing some distance between two gardens, Jamie slowed to walk with Kat, alone at the back of the group. "Hi," she said as they strolled along a path of small gray pebbles. "Did you notice the wildflowers on the hill back there?"

"Yes... quite striking." After a long silence he said, "I went out with friends to hear some live music last night."

"Oh? What kind?" Kat zipped her jacket as the cool wind picked up speed.

"Scottish." He said it nonchalantly, as though it had nothing to do with their Friday night conversation.

Kat stood straighter. "Instrumental or vocal?"

"Instrumental. A trio."

"What did you think? Were they good?"

Jamie continued gazing straight ahead as they walked. "Yeah..." He paused, then added, "until they got some American tourist up to play with them." He turned to Kat with a big smile and twinkling eyes, apparently expecting her to laugh. Instead, she froze, as if he had told her she had cancer.

Kat gasped. She must have been that incompetent tourist! She pressed her arms tightly against her quivering stomach. Her back muscles felt like a wave was rolling up under them, and a lump filled her throat. Had people been complimenting her musicianship all these years, just to be nice?

She glanced at Jamie, turned away, and swallowed hard. How embarrassing. To know someone in an audience thought she didn't play well enough to be on stage was...

"Kat, I'm kidding. You were brilliant! Did you think I was serious?"

She didn't know Jamie well enough to know whether he was joking, or trying to back-pedal criticism, as her mother sometimes did. "I... I know I made a lot of mistakes..."

"If you did, I didn't hear them." He put his hand on her shoulder. "I'm sorry. Come on... you must know you play well. Didn't you hear the applause? No one would have cheered if it had gone pear-shaped. And I would never say anything like that to someone who really *had* played badly."

She took a deep breath and finally managed to speak a barely audible, "Really?"

He looked perplexed. "Yes, really."

"Which?"

"What?"

"My playing... was..."

"You were GOOD! My god, how could you think you weren't? Or that I would say you had no talent if you really didn't? That would be terribly unkind."

Kat closed her eyes for a moment and took another deep breath, which helped. But she couldn't look at him.

"Music isn't just a hobby, Jamie, it's my life. It's part of who I am. I know I didn't play my best, but... to think I played badly in front of an audience..." Her failure to recognize sarcasm embarrassed her. "I didn't realize you were teasing me." The fact that he *would* irritated her. "Come to think of it, you don't know me well enough to tease me about my music. Do you poke sticks at animals, too?"

Jamie raised his eyebrows. "No, I don't poke animals. Well, maybe those little dogs some women carry in their handbags... but only if they're wearing diamond collars." He grinned, as if joking would help, then scanned the path ahead of them. The tour group had disappeared. "We'd better catch up before we're missed."

"Oh, I'm pretty sure *you're* missed, already." Kat took a deep breath. "And with both of us out of sight, Lisa's probably having kittens." She finally laughed when Jamie did. His laugh was infectious and made her feel good.

The pair hurried up the path. The tour hadn't gone far, so it didn't take long to sneak up behind the group—as quietly as one can sneak on pea gravel. One of the two people who turned around was Lisa. If looks could kill, Kat would have died on the spot. Barbara gave the dawdlers a brief, admonishing glare.

Facing them, Mr. Hoffman didn't miss a beat as he talked about a bloody battle that had taken place a few hundred years ago in the vast, green meadow behind him.

As the tour ended in front of the abbey, Jamie turned to Kat and Barbara. "May I take you back to your hotel?"

"No!" Iris's voice was loud and firm as she strode toward the trio. "I'm responsible for these people, Jamie, and the BBC would have my head if anything happened to them on some unauthorized side tour."

Lisa smirked, obviously pleased.

Kat turned to Jamie. "Nice of you to offer." His continued kindness toward her sister, who had repeatedly been rude to him, impressed her.

"How long will you be here?" he asked, as if seeking another chance to get together.

"We leave tomorrow. I wish I could stay longer." Her shoulders fell as she looked at the landscape once more.

"Pity," he said. "Well, I hope we made a good impression on you, and you'll come back." He extended his right hand as if to shake, but instead held Kat's hand in both of his. They were pleasantly warm and comforting. "Have a safe trip home."

People said that all the time, but Jamie's voice and eyes conveyed such sincerity she wanted to believe he meant it. "Thank you, Jamie. Keep breaking a leg... and... try not to poke anyone." She smiled and got into Iris's minivan.

As Iris got into the minivan, she gave Kat a look she couldn't interpret. Was Iris annoyed? Did she think Kat was a troublemaker? Or wonder why Jamie Knight kept trying to separate her from the herd? That was a good question.

On the drive back to the hotel, Lisa babbled about Jamie while everyone else talked about their favorite parts of the estate and asked questions they hadn't thought of earlier. The natural colors of the English countryside seemed warmer in the afternoon light than they had that morning.

At the hotel, Iris turned to her guests. "Enjoy your last evening in London. I'll pick you up tomorrow morning at seven-thirty sharp."

Kat and Barbara went for a fish and chips dinner—their last chance to "go local." Afterward, Barbara returned to their room to pack.

Kat wanted to stroll along the Thames one last time. Between scattered clouds, the half-moon shone a silvery strip on the river. She leaned on the cold steel railing and felt lost in life. Despite a fairly successful radio career, a few years in TV production, and multiple awards won in state service, she didn't feel successful.

The time she had spent with Jamie revived good feelings she hadn't known in a long time and fond memories of being in love, years earlier. Had she been wrong to pursue a career when her boyfriend wanted to settle down with her? What would life be like now if she had chosen marriage at twenty-six? Now it was too late.

Feeling empty inside, all she could do was gaze at the shimmering water as though something she longed for would rise up from it, if only she stared at it long enough.

Chapter 7: Tally Home

Monday morning was cold, gloomy. Dark gray clouds threatened a downpour to match Kat's feelings about leaving Britain. She wanted to do and see more there. She and Barbara met Iris in the hotel lobby before the Tomlinsons did.

Iris used their time alone to tell Kat about the rarity of Jamie Knight's invitation. "I've never seen a well-known actor invite a civilian stranger out."

While Kat appreciated that, she made sure Iris wouldn't think that was the only thing she would remember.

At crowded London Heathrow International Airport, the Canadians and Californians recounted the tour while waiting in a long line to check-in. Moments after the Tomlinsons stepped away from the ticket counter, an ear-piercing alarm went off near the luggage scanner. Everyone within earshot turned to look, and most stopped talking.

Kat couldn't hear the conversation between airport security and a ticketing clerk, but when the clerk pointed toward them, the security agent marched over and asked, "Who is Lisa Tomlinson?"

"I am!" Lisa stated, with her hands on her hips and head held up defiantly. Kat expected her to add, *Who wants to know?*

With an authoritative tone, the agent ordered, "Come with me, please," and led Lisa toward an x-ray station. Doug followed. Barbara and Kat stayed close enough to see what would happen next and assist the couple if needed.

"Something in your suitcase set off the alarm," the agent said. "What are you transporting that could have caused that?"

"How should I know what sets off your stupid alarm?" Lisa folded her arms across her chest.

A security guard stood nearby as the agent waved a metal-detecting wand around Lisa's enormous suitcase. Inconclusive. Another agent—wearing latex gloves—opened the case and gingerly rummaged through the contents.

He gave the other agent a look of disgust and with his thumb and forefinger, pulled out and held up a large, buzzing vibrator. The items shifting around it must have turned it on, setting off the alarm. Everyone nearby—except the agents, Lisa and Doug—laughed hysterically as an indignant Lisa looked around with arms akimbo, repeatedly saying, "So?"

"Poor Doug," Kat said as she and Barbara settled into their seats on the plane, still laughing. "Have you ever seen anyone's face that red? I've got to post that scene on Facebook."

"Are you kidding?" Barbara asked. "It's already been tweeted around the world."

Two meowing "fur children" and the familiar fragrance of canned cat food greeted Kat as she dragged her suitcase from the garage into her kitchen. Her heart warmed at the sight of her little family.

"Hello, sweethearts." She picked up Kellye, then Jeremy, for hugs and pets. "Oh, I've missed you, too."

The cats followed her around as she opened windows. Kellye the Abyssinian's meow was clearly one of complaint. "I know, I'm your servant, not supposed to go away. But Jo took good care of you and now I'm all yours again."

Her elderly neighbor and closest friend, Jo Evans, was an ideal pet-sitter. Yet from the moment Kat walked in, the cats wouldn't leave her side. When she fell asleep on the sofa, they made themselves comfortable on top of her so she couldn't get away again.

The next day, she spent two hours telling her eighty-seven-year-old mother, Lidia, about the trip. Dementia had forced Lidia, who had always been independent, to live in a skilled nursing facility. Hers was nice, brightly lit, always spotless, and the staff were compassionate and patient professionals. But because she couldn't leave her floor of the building without an escort, she called it "prison."

When her mother said she hadn't noticed Kat's week-long absence, her heart sank. Often Lidia claimed no one had visited her in months, even though Kat visited her nearly every day. Seeing her mother's mind and body deteriorate forced her to blink back tears.

Knowing how easily depression could overtake Lidia, Kat always tried to be upbeat and optimistic when visiting. That was hard sometimes, especially when her mother called her "Barbara." Barbara didn't live far away, but she only visited their mother three or four times a year.

Lidia gazed out the window while Kat showed her pictures of London—until she pulled out one of Jamie, downloaded from the internet. Lidia's eyes lit up. "Oh, you should marry him." Annoyed and amused at the same time, Kat had to laugh. Typical mother—couldn't remember much of anything except her youngest daughter's deficiency for having never married. "Yeah, right, Mom... in my dreams." *Maybe if I were younger, better-looking, and he wasn't a male slut.*

Grinning and talking a-mile-a-minute over lunch the next day, Kat told her colleague and good friend—Molly McKenna—about her trip. A dark-haired beauty whose personality lit up their office, Molly managed media relations, supervising three other public affairs officers.

"You're kidding," Molly exclaimed. "You had a date with the actor you tease Keith's daughter about? Was he nice?"

"Yes, and friendlier than I would have expected. I don't know why he asked *me* out, and I wouldn't call it a date. I doubt *he* considered it a date."

"Why?"

"Seriously? I'm nine or ten years older than he is. I'm not pretty, fashionable, wealthy or powerful. There is nothing about me that would attract a man like him."

"Kat, stop putting yourself down—"

"I'm not putting myself down. I'm realistic. The odds of someone like Jamie Knight falling for me—or any of us—are slim and none."

"Okay, the odds are against it. But it's not impossible. And he's not *that* famous. I'd never heard of him until you mentioned him. Maybe he's tired of fame-seekers. Maybe he saw you as the respectable, self-sufficient woman you are. And he probably thinks you're his age."

"Not likely. Still, I wish I had a picture of us at his club. I mean, something that wouldn't make me look like a fangirl."

"Why? You'll never see him again."

"I still don't want to look like a groupie." *Especially to a guy who turns me on.*

A week later, their Deputy Director, Susan Treister—a political appointee at least fifteen years younger than Kat—threw cold water on her high spirits. For several years, she had enjoyed being "the voice of CDW," recording all the agency's public service announcements and narrating most of their videos. Now, Susan wanted her to recruit a celebrity to be the department's voice—as a volunteer.

Kat was furious, especially after learning Susan only wanted that because she had heard someone in the Governor's Office brag about getting Rob Lowe to do a TV commercial for another state agency. Political hacks, competing for the Governor's favor.

"It wasn't enough to pass me over for promotion again. Now she's taking away my favorite task—the one that allows me to still qualify as talent," she complained to Molly. She couldn't express her anger to many people—especially not the one who could do anything about it. "Why? What did I do to tick her off? And what makes her think anyone who's famous and really good will do free voice work for the state?"

"Who knows?" Molly asked. "I'm sorry. I know you love narrating things, and you've done a great job—"

"Even worse, she's making me find my own replacement and figure out how to get SAG-AFTRA to allow it."

"SAG-AFTRA?"

"The talent union: Screen Actors Guild-American Federation of Television and Radio Artists. I used to be a member."

"Oh. How do you get a union to let celebrities volunteer?"

"No idea. And when I ask, I hope they tell me celebrities don't do freebies for the government!"

Chapter 8: Jamie's Summer

In June, Jamie Knight shot the exteriors for his next film—*The Ivory Reel*—on location in Africa's Democratic Republic of Congo. He loved to travel, meet new people, and experience different cultures around the world. But this film had exhausted him. He was glad to get home in time for his birthday, June thirtieth.

His parents hosted a small party at their home in Hampstead with five of Jamie's closest friends, including Leigh and Bob Penrose. His mother also invited the posh beauty she wanted him to marry—Beatrice Aylesworth, who insisted everyone call her "Trissy."

Peter Li, an independent film producer who had been Jamie's friend since adolescence, whispered, "I thought you didn't like Trissy."

"I don't," Jamie said under his breath. "Her parents and mine are old friends, so I have to tolerate her and be polite."

Bob stepped in close to Jamie. "You've known her a long time?"

"As long as I can remember. She always imagined we would marry when we grew up, but I told her that's not going to happen. Mum keeps pushing her at me, hoping I'd rather marry a blueblood than someone I respect. But vain, self-centered people like Trissy repel me. I wouldn't have her as a girlfriend, much less a wife."

Jamie wanted—someday—to share his life with an equal partner whose interests, ethics, and I.Q. were similar to his, not a manipulator who judged people by their ancestry, bank accounts, and designer wardrobes.

Because her family had Royal connections, Victor insisted he accept her occasional invitations to high-society functions, such as the Queen's annual spring garden party, where such qualities were prized. He said the publicity made it appear the Royals and "Upper-Crust" approved of Jamie. "It's one thing to go to the palace with her, for the publicity. Otherwise, I avoid her. Now she keeps trying to pull me away to be alone with her, and that's the last place I want to be," he added.

"Ah, not to worry; we'll stop that," Peter said with a reassuring smile.

Jamie's friends monopolized him—and Trissy—all evening so she couldn't corner him. She tried to follow him to the loo, but Leigh intervened. Jamie could see his mum was not pleased, but she couldn't make a fuss in front of guests.

Bob and Leigh, Jamie's friends since university, stayed late until Trissy finally left. "Thanks," Jamie sighed. "I owe you." He appreciated his parents' generosity, but not the presence of a guest he would never have invited.

Jamie's two weeks at home flew by, and he squeezed in a few dates before he had to go to Los Angeles for an audition. The ladies were all pretty, and photos of him with them appeared in the tabloids. But since none of them paid attention to current events, they couldn't discuss things that interested him. Every subject he brought up, from poverty in the country where he had been filming to Scotland's Independence Vote, exceeded their sphere of knowledge—or interest.

After dinner in London's West End theatre district, Jamie rushed one wannabe actress home for a quick shag and left early. He couldn't stand another hour of listening to her prattle on about "Yves Saint Laurent vs Versace." The bimbo buffet was boring him to death. *I'd rather be at home, reading a book. Or with someone interesting... like Katerina.*

In Los Angeles to read for a supporting role in a big studio film, Jamie stayed with his closest American friend, Bill Bleuchel, a movie location scout he had known eight years. Bill lived alone in a comfortable old four-bedroom home in the Hollywood Hills. Relaxing in the warm sun by the pool on his last afternoon there, Jamie told him about the Californian he had met in May.

"Running around with a dozen women isn't doing it for me anymore. My agent says it keeps me in the press, and I need that to get Hollywood's attention. But I'd rather spend my time with one or two intelligent, well-informed women who aren't needy... who like me for who I am—not my job or my net worth."

"It's about time, kid. You're what... forty-four, now? You know anyone like that?"

"Yeah, a couple. That lady in Sacramento keeps coming to mind. I've thought about calling her... brought her business card. But I'm not sure she likes me."

"Go for it and find out," Bill said. "If she's as smart as you say, she won't think you're hot for her, just because you called to say hi."

* * *

Kat stood in her bedroom, stripping off her wet clothes after cleaning the swimming pool filters, when the phone rang. Caller I.D. displayed a Los Angeles area code. She hesitated—probably another political robo-call. But she had friends in L.A., so...

"Hello, Kat? This is Jamie Knight."

The caller's voice sounded like Jamie. If it was, she wouldn't want him to think she knew his voice, so she pretended to not recognize him.

Kat laughed. "Yeah, right. And I'm Barbra Streisand." She let her voice drip with sarcasm and amusement. The caller didn't respond. "Come on... who is it, really?"

"It's Jamie. I'm in Los Angeles and thought I'd ring you."

It *was* him. "Really?"

"Yes." He laughed. "I'll prove it. When you were in London, I took you to the Huntington Club and we talked about music, amongst other things. When I asked you what took you to Scotland, you said 'Midland Air.' That was a good comeback, worthy of a deejay. Then you got a little tipsy on two small glasses of Amaretto."

"Oh, my god!" Kat gasped. "I didn't tell anyone *that*. Jamie, I'm sorry."

"It's all right."

"You have a good memory. What are you doing in L.A.?"

"Reading for a part. I saw you a couple of nights ago on the news... about someone shooting an endangered animal?"

"You're kidding. In England?"

"No, here," Jamie said. "I'm staying with a friend who had the telly on. He didn't believe me when I said I knew you."

"That's funny. People wouldn't believe me if I said I knew *you*."

"Touché."

"What are you auditioning for?"

"A rom-com. I liked the script they sent, but now they've changed it, and what I read today wasn't as appealing. But some of these things get re-written several times before they approve the final script."

"How can you decide whether you want a part if they keep changing it?"

"If they offer it to me, my agent will write an escape clause in the contract, in case the final script is rubbish. I've never seen one that bad, but it's good to anticipate any possibility."

"Good thinking," she said. "Good luck, if you want it."

"Thanks. What are you doing these days? Playing in pubs or at Highland Games?"

"No, our Games were in April. There are only a couple places here that have what they call 'Celtic music nights,' and it's always Irish music. Hardly anyone knows traditional Scottish tunes. The next gig I know of will be a Tartan Ball for the local Caledonian Club in October."

"Ooh... I'll bet you like that one... all those men in kilts?" Jamie teased.

"Mmm... some of them." Kat's cheeks were warming up, and she was glad he couldn't see her, probably blushing.

"Are you working on anything right now?"

"Yes. We did the Africa shoot, and next week we start on interior scenes at Pinewood—one of the big studios in London."

"Did you enjoy playing a game warden?"

"Yeah, but it was grueling, physically. Those guys have one tough job. Listen, I have to go now. I may be back in a couple months, but don't know whether I'll have any free time. I'll call you if I can, but mostly I wanted to say hi, and you looked good on telly."

"Thanks, Jamie. I'm sorry I didn't recognize your voice, but... I never expected to hear from you... since you think I have no talent."

"Sorry? Oh, right... the pub. I told you I was kidding."

"Yeah, I know. Now I'm kidding *you*."

"I see. Well... nice talking with you—for a moment. Take care."

And he was gone.

* * *

Jamie smiled at Bill after hanging up, then studied Kat's card again.

"Well?" Bill asked. "What do you think?"

"I like her. I forgot how much I enjoyed talking with her. Trouble is, she's in Northern California and I'm in London, most of the time."

"Yeah, but you're here a lot, too. And Sacramento is only an hour's flight from Burbank. I'm just saying..."

Back in London, Jamie shot interior scenes for *The Ivory Reel*. In his trailer while stagehands changed a set, he reviewed his lines for the next scene when Leigh Penrose phoned and invited him to dinner the next week.

"Sure, love to," Jamie said. "What's the occasion?"

"Nothing. We haven't seen you in a while and want to hear more about your time in Africa. People kept interrupting at your birthday."

"Oh, sure. I have some good stories for you. Hey, you know the woman I met at the museum in May—the one from California?"

"No. What about her?"

"I saw her on the news in L.A. and realized... I've been subconsciously comparing the women I date to *her*."

"Why?"

"Kat knew something about a lot of subjects and was more interesting than most. She asked intelligent questions about my experiences, she listened, and was nice to everyone we encountered—even a woman who was quite boorish to her. She's worked in telly, so I could talk about work without having to explain everything. And this is the kicker: she didn't ask about my love life and turned down an invitation to go home with me."

"Sorry? Someone said *no*?" Leigh laughed. "Smart girl. Must be a stunner."

"No, she's ordinary as white bread on the outside, but inside... Why can't I meet women with personalities like that around here?"

"Because you only talk to young stunners. Why was this L.A. woman in the news?"

"She's a spokesperson for the wildlife ministry. I'm thinking of keeping in touch."

"Well then, you should. Maybe next time you'll score. Must go now. See you next Tuesday."

Jamie leaned back in his chair. That evening with Kat was nice. Her voice on the phone was nice... *Next time I'm in California...* He closed his eyes, lost in reverie, until a production assistant knocked on the trailer door. Back to the set.

Chapter 9: Find Your Heart in San Francisco

Every September, Kat, Molly, and Janet Raffety—leader of the Sacramento Scottish Fiddlers Kat played guitar with—drove to the Sierra Nevada foothills for a weekend Celtic Festival that featured outstanding Scottish, Irish, Welsh, and English musicians.

As Kat prepared for the day, Jamie Knight called again.

"I'm in L.A., going to San Francisco to see some family friends, and I'd like to take them someplace nice for dinner. You lived there, didn't you? Know some good restaurants?"

"I did, twenty years ago. Don't you have wi-fi?" She scanned a bookcase for the San Francisco AAA tour book. "The Ghirardelli Chocolate Factory was my favorite."

"That doesn't sound like a dinner place. Maybe dessert..."

"If you like Cantonese, there's Great Eastern in Chinatown. If not, you can't go wrong at the Fairmont Hotel or the restaurant atop the Mark Hopkins Hotel."

"Have you eaten there?"

"Yes. The 'Top of the Mark' fed us when I worked a telethon they hosted. The food was even better than the view. How long will you be in The City?"

"Until Thursday." He paused. "What are you doing on Wednesday?"

"Working."

"Want to come and do something with me? Maybe show me some places the locals go?"

It took a moment for the invitation to sink in; like what? "Um... Okay. I could use a day off. But I'll have to ask my boss. Can I let you know, Monday?"

"Sure. I'll ring you Monday afternoon."

Why would he want to see *her* while visiting friends? The doorbell jerked her back to reality. Good thing Molly and Janet were late.

All Monday afternoon, Kat expected Jamie's call. By 8:45—long past afternoon—he must have forgotten her or changed his mind. *Inconsiderate men... never call when they say they will.*

When he finally called at 9:55, she said, "Afternoon ended four hours ago."

"I'm sorry. We were out on a fishing boat and my mobile battery died. We just got home." He paused, but she said nothing. "Can you come, Wednesday?"

Kat was annoyed. *Why should I? Was his the only phone on the boat?* "Will you really *be* there?" This time Jamie didn't respond; she had made her point. "Yes, Ron gave me the day off. Where should I pick you up?"

Driving to San Francisco wasn't one of Kat's favorite activities. The population in the Bay Area had exploded and traffic jams had become the norm rather than the exception.

Having grown up there and worked in The City, she used to know San Francisco well. Her father had lived there, but after he died, she'd had little reason to drive at least two hours to be where traffic and parking were twin nightmares. She had only gone back for the occasional date or work event, so had to use the web to see what had survived the Great Recession. And what activities would Jamie enjoy?

As she drove up Broadway, things were so different Kat felt like an outsider. The neighborhood had deteriorated. Nothing looked familiar except the old vertical marquee for the Condor Club, San Francisco's first topless bar. Its lights formed the tackiest thing on the street—a gaudy outline of its famous stripper, Carol Doda. Only the receding fog matched her memories until she reached the Marina District, where her father and step-mother had lived.

At Jamie's friends' apartment building, she pressed the button next to the name "Whittingham." The voice of an English woman, with the raspy quality that often comes with age, said "Hello" from the little speaker.

An obnoxious buzz blasted from above the front door, identical to the one at her father's apartment. The heavy door and long, dimly lit lobby seemed eerily familiar. Off-white stucco walls and well-worn, dark green carpet that continued up the stairs at the far end, a white plaster bench, a mirror on the wall behind it, and the comforting sound of a small water fountain reminded her of Dad's building. It even smelled like his—an odd combination of dust, mold, newspapers, and all the foods cooked in the apartments.

As she climbed the second flight of stairs, a familiar voice gave her a chill. "Katerina, you made it," Jamie exclaimed, as though he hadn't been sure she would find the place. He leaned over a white wooden railing, wearing stonewashed jeans, a royal blue T-shirt, and white running shoes. "How was the drive?"

"Nostalgic," Kat replied. Jamie's hair was longer than it had been in May, falling over his forehead and ears. He was much more attractive this way. He reached out to take her right hand as if to shake it, but instead clasped it gently in both of his, the way he had at Woburn Abbey.

His soft hands and firm but gentle grip were comforting. If he had been a doctor, he'd have a good bedside manner... Kat quickly shut-down the images *that* notion spawned. Now she was glad she had come. "By the way, my friends call me Kat."

"It's nice to see you, Kat. Come in."

This apartment, too, reminded her of her father's, but here the aroma of freshly baked scones welcomed her. Much nicer than Dad's disgusting cigars. Jamie led her down a short hallway into the living room, where a much older woman with short gray hair watered potted plants near windows facing the street.

"Nellie, I'd like you to meet Katerina Mancini. Kat, this is Nell Whittingham. She and her husband are old friends of my family."

"It's a pleasure to meet you." Kat smiled and extended her hand.

Nell's hand was warm. She had a kind, welcoming face. "It's nice to meet you, too, dear. Did you come from the East Bay?"

"A bit farther east—Sacramento."

"You drove all that way just to see our little Jamie?"

The six-foot man winced at being called little. "Why? How far *is* it?"

"About a hundred miles, I think," Nell replied, turning to Kat for confirmation.

Jamie gave her an apologetic look. "Really? I didn't realize it was that far."

"It's all right. I wouldn't want to drive it every week, but once in a while is okay. I grew up in the Bay Area, and I miss it."

"Didn't you tell me someone in your family lives nearby?" Jamie asked.

"My father and step-mother used to live three blocks from here."

"Jamie says you work with animals," Nell said.

"Sort of," Kat replied. "I work for the State Department of Wildlife. The scientists and wildlife officers get to work with animals. I work with *them*."

A look of recognition came over Nell's face. "Were you on telly recently?"

"Yes. I did a lot of interviews about a poaching case last month."

Jamie checked his watch. "Well, shall we go?"

"Oh, I'm sorry Albert wasn't here to meet you," Nell said. "He went out for his morning walk to feed the ducks at the pond."

Jamie moved toward the door. "Maybe when we come back..."

"Don't forget your jacket," Nell said.

Jamie gave Kat a look that seemed to say, "just like Mum."

"It gets cold here when the afternoon fog comes in," Nell admonished.

As if obeying an order, Jamie left the room and quickly came back holding a lightweight black jacket and a "bucket hat," the heavy cotton type older men wore at fishing piers.

"What time will you be back?" Nell asked.

"Oh, I don't know," Jamie replied. "Let's play it by ear."

Kat couldn't resist. "Like some guitar-picking tourist?"

He bent his knees and pointed at her. "Yeah, like that."

Nell gave them a quizzical look and asked Jamie, "Shall I plan on you tonight?" Then she turned to Kat. "Will you join us for dinner?"

That put Kat on the spot. Not knowing what he had in mind for the day, and not wanting to make any assumptions, she waffled. "Whatever Jamie wants to do... I'm only his tour guide." She hated sounding wishy-washy, but she couldn't assume he'd want her to stick around. And she didn't want to stay late. Once, while driving home from Dad's, she got so sleepy she could hardly keep her eyes open. Nearly falling asleep at the wheel had taught her a frightening lesson.

"May I call later and let you know?" Jamie asked.

"That's fine. Call if you're not back by four-thirty, so I know how to lay the table." As Nell watched them head downstairs, she called out, "Have fun, you two!"

59

Chapter 10: Jamie By the Bay

The fog had burned off by the time Jamie walked outside with Kat, and both welcomed the sun's warmth. As they headed toward her car, Jamie noticed she wore the same dolphin necklace and earrings she wore in London. He pulled some large, dark sunglasses out of his pocket.

"Al and Nellie are dear friends," he said. "They went to University with my parents."

"Man, a lifelong friendship like that is priceless. Some friends I've known since high school meet for annual jam sessions, and they're a blast. I hope we never stop." With an impish grin Kat added, "We plan to annoy young people by playing sixties rock n' roll, really loud."

"Like the Rolling Stones?"

"Yeah. That reminds me... I'm sorry *Nigel Stone* didn't win an Emmy®."

"Oh, well..." Jamie shrugged. "We didn't expect to. We're not that well known in The States. The show has a fairly small audience here."

"Hmm... I guess that's why, when they announced the nominations, Yahoo tweeted your name and asked, 'Anyone know who he is?' That was rude. I wished I had a Twitter account, so I could tell them."

Jamie looked at her. Nice to know she would defend someone who'd been slighted. "You're not on Twitter?"

"No. It might be fun to follow some people, but I have enough trouble keeping up with email and checking Facebook once a week. I don't have time for it. Besides, no one would care what I think about anything."

"Me neither. You can't do everything that's available these days. You'd get nothing important done, like work. Speaking of which, we finally got *First Impressions, Last Rites* in the can. I thought we'd never finish that film."

"What's it about?" Kat asked.

"It's a violent thriller, featuring a crooked D. I.— detective inspector. I play his partner."

"Oh. I'm sorry. I don't like violent movies. But I hope it's successful for your sake."

Jamie looked at her for a moment and blinked, not sure how to respond. "Thanks. No one has ever wished my film success while telling me she wouldn't go see it."

"Sorry, but there's so much violence in the world, it's not entertaining to me." As they approached Kat's Prius, she asked, "So, where are we going? What do you want to do?"

Jamie noticed an old, rust-colored, domed structure down the street. "What's that?"

"The Palace of Fine Arts. That's where the lagoon is. Do you see, uh...? What's Nell's husband's name?"

"Albert. I don't see him. Shall we have a look?" The park-like setting created an oasis of green in the midst of city concrete. "This is a palace?" he asked.

"Not exactly. The City built it for the 1915 Pan-American International Exposition. In fact," she reached out and gestured from one end of the neighborhood to the other, "they built the whole Marina District on landfill for that. This was all water, before."

"Is it still used for anything?"

"Yeah, they have they have lectures and public meetings in a theater over there."

"Do you ever attend live theatre?"

"Not as often as I'd like. But if you ever do a play here, I'll come see it."

"Would you?" he asked. "What if I do one in L.A.?"

"That depends... You offering airfare and tickets?" Kat grinned and raised her eyebrows to show she was kidding.

"I'd like to, but that'd be difficult, expensive, and depend on the time of year."

"What does the time of year have to do with it?"

"From December to the end of April, I'm swamped. Can't do anything."

"How so?" he asked.

"That's tax season, the most important time to promote the Voluntary Tax Contribution Funds I told you about. I'm also playing at Burns Suppers, and publicizing and rehearsing for the Sacramento Scottish Games. No time for anything else until May."

A pair of swans floated on the lagoon. "Well, I don't see Al. What do you like to do when you're here?"

"I told you." She gave him a wicked grin. "Ghirardelli Chocolate Factory."

Jamie wanted to grab and squeeze her for being a wise-guy, the way he would with Leigh Penrose. But he didn't know Kat well enough for that. "You're funny. What else?"

"Dad and I used to watch sailboats and wind-surfers from Marina Green. Fort Point, under the south end of the Golden Gate Bridge, might be interesting. Pier 39... She paused. "No, I don't know what's there anymore, and it's too touristy for you."

"I don't mind touristy," he said.

"You want to be mobbed by fans and spend all day posing for pictures with them?"

"Well, that's flattering, and I don't mind posing for pictures, but not being mobbed. There's a fine line between audience appreciation—which I appreciate—and obsession—which I don't. Do you really think anyone here would recognize me?"

"Oh, yeah. I'd like to think San Franciscans would be cool about it, but I could be wrong... and I don't know about tourists. It's your call, how much risk you want to take."

"Risk?" Jamie laughed. "You make it sound as if my life is in danger. Are you this protective of all your friends?"

"No... only the good-looking, rich, famous ones who attract love-sick girls with wild fantasies and no respect for an entertainer's right to have a private life."

Jamie chuckled. "Thanks, but I'm not that famous... or rich. You have *many* good-looking, rich, famous friends?"

"Not now, but I used to. Remember, I worked in Hollywood before I went over to The Dark Side."

"The Dark Side? Were you an extra in *Star Wars*?"

Kat laughed. "No. When people leave the newsroom to be government media flacks, they say we've gone to 'the Dark Side.' Anyway, I've known entertainers who were stalked by fans. Most were friendly folks who just wanted to meet people they admired, but you never know when one will turn out to be crazy. Ever see *Play Misty For Me*?"

Jamie nodded, amused by his new friend's concern. "What else could we do?"

"How about Golden Gate Park? There's a planetarium, aquarium, and a natural history museum. If you're into art, you might like the de Young Museum."

Jamie pondered the possibilities. "Those all sound good. Where's the place to watch wind-surfers?"

Kat pointed north. "This way; we can walk." After passing several apartment buildings in silence, she said, "Hey, I wanted to ask you... the guy following you around at the London Museum... was he a bodyguard?"

"Yes. The BBC sent him. I didn't think it necessary, but they're rather protective of actors with leading roles in their shows. It'd cost them a few quid if Miss Marple couldn't work because an overzealous fan tackled her." That image made them both laugh.

"You looked like you could've fought off anyone at the museum that night."

Jamie faced straight ahead. "Oh, I don't know. I couldn't resist you." *Oh, shit. I shouldn't have said that.*

"Yeah, right," she replied with unmistakable sarcasm in both her voice and the look she gave him. "You probably figured I was safe because I didn't ask for your autograph, a picture, or gush about how wonderful you are. But thanks; I'll take the compliment."

Surprised by her response, Jamie exhaled relief. She must not have heard the attraction in his voice. Good. He'd have time to get to know her better.

The wind and the scent of salt water grew stronger as they got close to the bay. Colorful kites flew over the Marina Green while a family tried to keep their picnic from blowing away.

Jamie and Kat gazed at Alcatraz and Marin County across the white-capped bay. The air smelled clean and the warm sun felt good. Occasionally, powerful gusts of wind blew a light, salty mist on their faces.

Leaning on a cold metal railing, they watched wind-surfers and sailboats. Terns and gulls called to each other overhead, while pelicans begged scraps from anglers. Brightly colored sails made the boats stand out on the brownish-green water, and when the strong wind pushed sails nearly horizontal, Jamie feared the boats would capsize.

"Aren't there sharks out there?" he asked, after a wind-surfer got dunked.

"Yep. Mostly small leopard sharks. They're as afraid of us as we are of them. White sharks are rarely ever seen in the bay. They seem to prefer the deeper waters—and surfers— outside The Gate."

* * *

The water glistened in the late morning sun that lit the orange Golden Gate Bridge against a pale blue sky. Multi-million-dollar recreational vessels, berthed at the nearby yacht clubs, caught Jamie's eye.

Following his gaze, Kat asked, "How was your fishing trip yesterday?"

"Beautiful. Until the water got rough beyond the bridge and made everyone sick. Then it got smoother as we moved farther offshore and got our sea legs."

"Catch anything?"

"No. But Al and some other people did. I got some reading in, after the initial excitement wore off. A half-day would've been long enough for me." He paused and scanned the area. "Want to go to that place under the bridge?"

"Okay. But it's not walking distance—at least not for me."

On their way back to Kat's car, Jamie asked, "Don't you walk much?"

"Probably not as much as you do; London is laid-out for walking. Most of California was designed for driving. I walk for exercise with friends at work, but I wrecked my knees, backpacking when I was sixteen, so I don't push them."

Kat smiled as she turned onto Marina Boulevard with the actor in her car. Then she noticed him staring at a pretty blonde crossing the street. Her smile disappeared.

The parking area was nearly empty at Fort Point National Historic Site. "This is different," Jamie observed, gazing up at the underside of the Golden Gate Bridge. "I never thought about standing under it. And look at these old cannons."

Nearing the door to the building, Kat stopped. "Oh, crap. It's closed today. I'm sorry."

"That's all right. The postcard view is out here." He took in San Francisco Bay, Alcatraz and Angel islands, and rocky Marin Headlands across the strait. The traffic rumbled above them, waves crashed below, and seabirds cried from all around.

Kat pulled her phone from her purse. "Let me take a picture of you with the underside of the bridge in the background. You can send it to your parents."

Jamie laughed at her. "My parents don't want another picture of me. They say my picture appears in too many places as it is. But if you want one, go ahead."

"Oh, of course." She put her left hand over her eyes and shook her head. "Sorry; for a moment I forgot you're an actor."

That seemed to please Jamie. "Let me take one of you."

As he pulled his phone out, she started to protest, then remembered that Janet had told her to stop doing that. Apparently, not everyone believed her self-deprecating humor was honest humility. She just shut up and posed. *With the wind blowing my hair all over the place, I must look like Bellatrix Lestrange, minus the makeup.*

They enjoyed the view a few minutes longer, then strolled back to Kat's car. "Are you hungry?" she asked. "What do you feel like for lunch?"

After opening the car door, he contemplated the bay before getting in. "I've heard the local crab is superb here."

"Unfortunately, it's out of season. September and October are the only two months you can't get fresh crab, even from Oregon or Washington."

"Sorry? You can't get crabs anywhere?"

"Not the kind you *want.*"

Jamie did a double-take and snickered. "Damn. Well, next time."

"It you're in the mood for seafood, I know a good restaurant, not far from here."

As Kat drove up Lombard Street, Jamie spotted a parking space.

"Good eyes," she said. "You win."

"Win... what?" he asked, giving her a tentative look.

"Lunch. You win lunch, on me."

"I'd rather have lunch on a table," he quipped, as she parallel parked in one move.

"Well, if you insist. But I'm buying, this time. Anything you want."

Jamie looked surprised. "No, you're not."

She started to argue, but he held his hand up to her. "No, Kat. It would be wrong for me to let you buy me lunch. Especially since you're doing me a favor, driving such a distance and being a delightful guide."

Kat scanned the area outside the car to see if many people were around. "You want to take your hat? In case you need to... uh... hide?"

"No, I don't like that hat. And I haven't caused a riot, yet." He grinned. "You'll rescue me if I get into trouble, won't you?"

Obviously, he was being facetious. Kat didn't look like a helpless weakling, but no one would mistake her for a bodyguard, either. She could only rip someone's head off verbally, and she had worked hard to subdue that skill.

"Absolutely." In her best tough-guy cartoon-character voice, she added, "Stick with me, kid, and no one'll touch you."

Chapter 11: Golden Gate Park

The restaurant wasn't crowded, even at lunchtime. The hostess looked Jamie over, the way one might appraise a thoroughbred.

She said nothing, but if she didn't recognize him, the waiter did. After introducing himself, the college-aged redhead said, "Forgive me, but you look familiar. Are you an actor?"

Jamie looked down for a moment. "Yes. Have you seen *Nigel Stone*?"

"Oh, yeah. Good show. What brings you to San Francisco?"

"Visiting friends," Jamie replied, smiling at Kat.

After they ordered, she quietly asked him, "How much you want to bet he'll tell the kitchen staff you're here, and they'll each find a reason to come out to see you?"

"Oh, I don't know..." Jamie seemed a little embarrassed. "It's flattering. Nice to know people like your work... as long as they let you get on with your life."

Sure enough, four people came out of the kitchen—one at a time—and cleared a table or went to the hostess stand for a moment, peering at the couple as unobtrusively as they could. Jamie focused on Kat. It didn't seem to bother him, but being watched made her self-conscious.

As they walked back to Kat's car, she asked, "What do you want to see in Golden Gate Park?"

"How about the museum?"

"Art or natural science?"

"Art. I studied it at university and love it. What about you?"

"I like both," she lied. Science appealed to her more than art, but this day was for him. Besides, she might appreciate art when accompanied by someone who understood it. And—to her surprise—she enjoyed hanging out with him, talking about whatever came up.

She reached across Jamie's lap to take her AAA map of San Francisco from the glove compartment. "I think I remember how to get there, but let's make sure."

"You still use *maps*?" Jamie asked, as though she held an abacus. "Doesn't this environmental wonder have a navigation system?"

"Not for the price the dealer wanted. Besides, I like maps." As she opened it she added, "And if you insult my car again, you can *walk* back to Nell's."

Jamie turned away and tried to stifle a laugh.

Kat focused on the map. "Okay, I'm going to take you through the Presidio. It's all that's left of the pine and redwood forest that was here before the Spaniards invaded. It used to be an Army base, but now other organizations rent the old buildings, including LucasFilm and the San Francisco Film Society."

"LucasFilm?" Jamie asked as Kat pulled the car onto the street. "I thought that was on a ranch."

"Skywalker Ranch. I don't know why George moved it down here. Want to stop and ask?" She grinned, handed her passenger the map, and drove west as he folded it— incorrectly—and stuffed it into the glove compartment. *Figures... men never ask for directions; why would they know how to fold maps?*

"If you're on a first-name basis with him, sure. You didn't tell me you were friends."

"Isn't he *your* friend?" she joked. Neither knew the famous writer-director, but it wouldn't have surprised Kat if Jamie had met him at some show business function.

He sighed. "Oh, well... Maybe someday."

"Right. After you read for *Star Wars Episode 46*. Now, we need to visualize a good parking space near the museum."

"You know, nav systems can tell you where there's parking, too," Jamie informed her. "When were you on the radio, here?"

"Mmm... When I was between twenty-six and thirty."

"And you played music?"

"Rock 'n roll oldies on KYA and Top-40 on KYUU. Unfortunately, they're both gone."

"Where'd they go?" he joked.

"To hell, like most good stations." She wasn't joking.

"Did you have to be careful where you went, to avoid being mobbed by your fans?"

Was he being condescending, or teasing her again? "My fans? People who listened to me weren't *my* fans. They listened for the music more than the jocks. I'm sure they forgot me, years ago, and wouldn't give a rat's—I mean, a hoot, now."

Jamie laughed aloud at her. "Are you trying not to swear around me?"

"Yeah. Some people think poorly of women who swear."

"You'd have to do something worse than swear to make me think less of you." He reached over and touched her shoulder. "Kat, don't worry about what I think. Just be yourself. If I didn't already like and trust you, I wouldn't be alone with you in your car."

Of course, he was right. His warm hand felt good. So did hearing him say he liked her. She was enjoying his company so much, she forgot he was a womanizer. "Okay," she said, softly. "I'm sorry."

"And stop apologizing—"

"Oh, crap." Kat hit the steering wheel with her palm. "What is wrong with me?"

"What's the matter?" Jamie turned his head in all directions, looking for the problem.

71

"I should have asked you this morning. Have you ever been here, before?"

"Oh... well... to visit the Whittinghams..."

Damn. She had been treating him like a first-time visitor, and none of this was new.

"...and clubbing once, with a couple of friends," he continued. "You know... loud music, dancing, and flirting with women none of us would ever see again?" He gave her a knowing smile, as though she must go flirt with strangers in nightclubs, too.

"But you haven't seen any of this by day? I don't want to drag you around to places you've already been."

"Well, I'm not *in* drag... and so far your ideas have been more appealing than nightclubs. If you suggest a place I've been and didn't like enough to go back, I'll let you know."

"Okay. And thank you for not being in drag. If you were, I'd have to take you to the Castro District, where they would *really* appreciate you."

Grinning, he lightly swatted her thigh, indicating he knew the Castro was San Francisco's famous gay community.

"This is beautiful," he remarked as they drove through the Presidio. "A forest in the city."

In Golden Gate Park, leaves rustled underfoot and the distant sound of reggae music accompanied the pair as they walked toward the buildings on the Music Concourse. The large lawn they crossed didn't appear to be suffering from California's three-year-old drought.

"This would be a lovely place to run every day," Jamie noted.

"Yeah. I wonder if the fog keeps the grass green." Kat looked at it carefully. "We could use some in the Central Valley. We haven't watered our lawns in more than a year."

Inside the museum, Jamie enthusiastically showed his knowledge of art history, telling Kat things that weren't on any of the displays. She expected him to know a lot about

European art, but he surprised her with expertise in works from New Guinea and Africa, too.

She hadn't studied art and knew little about it, so only mentioned that she liked certain pieces. The nudes made her uncomfortable. As they meandered through the museum, a few people looked as if they recognized Jamie, but no one bothered him.

Time flew by that afternoon. Kat checked her watch. "Remember, Nell wanted you to call her if we weren't back by four-thirty."

"Do you want to leave?" he asked, looking at his watch.

"No, that's up to you. I just don't want your friends to worry. And there's something I want to show you before we go."

"What?"

"A surprise."

"All right. Will you join us for dinner?"

That was a tough decision. She was enjoying Jamie's company, but didn't want to intrude on their evening. This would be his last night here, and the Whittinghams may want him to themselves. They probably didn't see him often.

"I'd like to, but I think I'd better head home before it gets too late."

"Too late for what? You won't turn into a pumpkin, will you?"

Kat laughed at the Cinderella reference. Didn't he use that in London? "Yeah, my evil step-sisters will lock me out. Too late to get home safely and then get up for work at five-thirty, tomorrow. A long stretch of I-80 is boring enough for me to fall asleep when I'm tired."

"That's not good," he said. "How long does it take to get there?"

"Two hours, in good traffic."

"Em, isn't the traffic usually bad, this time of day?"

Kat looked at her watch again. "Oh, god, yes. It'll take an hour just to get across the bridge, now. Shit!" As soon as she said it, she put her hand to her mouth.

Jamie laughed, pulled her hand away from her face, and held onto it. "Then the decision is made. You're staying for dinner with us." His expression suggested he wasn't just being polite.

Kat waved one hand in front of her. "No... I don't want to impose..."

"You're not imposing," he insisted. "Nellie loves entertaining. She always cooks too much food, and Al wants to meet you. They'd probably like to know someone in Sacramento, in case they ever go there and need directions. Besides, I want you to stay."

That made her feel better about it. She was surprised by how much she enjoyed his company, considering their vastly different lives and the ten years between them.

Jamie got out his mobile to call Nell. "How long will your surprise take?"

"We'll be back in the car within half an hour. Give us another half-hour to get back, if traffic's bad."

After the call, Jamie said, "Al says there's a collision on the Bay Bridge and it'll take you all night to get across it. Unless you spend the night here."

Kat's pelvic muscles tightened spontaneously. "Oh, no..."

"Don't worry. Al is prone to hyperbole. They'll have traffic reports on the radio, won't they? We can listen on our way home... I mean to the apartment. Al and Nellie's apartment. You know what I mean." Jamie seemed a little flustered, in an endearing way. "Now, what's your surprise?"

"We need to go to the Hamon Tower." On the way, Kat dreaded the traffic hell that awaited her. The elevator doors opened to reveal a glass-enclosed observation deck, high above Golden Gate Park.

"Oh, my God!" he exclaimed. "This is brilliant!"

Kat enjoyed both Jamie's pleasure and the 360-degree view of the city. They could see Sutro Hill and the broadcast tower that San Francisco Chronicle columnist Herb Caen had called the world's largest roach clip. With his phone, Jamie took pictures of the Transamerica Pyramid and the top of the one Golden Gate Bridge tower visible through the incoming fog. A wall of fog rolling in from the Pacific blocked the view west.

"I'm sorry we didn't come up here, earlier," she said. "I forgot about the fog."

"We'll have to come back someday," he said.

Kat pretended to believe him. *Yeah, right... as if I'll be your "San Francisco treat" next year...*

On their way back to the car, a trio of teenaged girls recognized Jamie and came over to check him out. Their flirting, giggling, and babbling about how much they loved him reminded Kat of Lisa Tomlinson in London. She tried not to roll her eyes.

Jamie posed for pictures with them and after a few minutes, said, "You'll have to excuse us; my friend and I are expected elsewhere." He took Kat's hand and they walked away. Until then, the girls had ignored Kat. Now they glared at her as though she was dragging him away from them against his will. Had she acted that stupid when she was a teenager?

Neither spoke until they approached Kat's car—still holding hands—when she said, "There are other places you might like, but it would take days to see them."

"I can imagine," Jamie said, looking at the surrounding community. "Great cities like this have so many interesting things to see, you'd need weeks to take them in, and still wouldn't see everything. That's frustrating when you're shooting a film on location. You never have enough free time while you're there to fully experience a city and its culture. When you get a day off, you're so tired you stay in your room, sleep, and prepare for your next scene. Then, soon as you finish, you have to rush home to another commitment."

"I've wondered about that," Kat said as they got into the car. "Do you think you'll ever shoot a film here?"

Jamie thought for a moment. "It's an expensive place to film. But you never know. I'm sure I'll come back for my own reasons."

Chapter 12: Invitation From a Scout

At Sacramento's Capitol park, people ate lunch on the lawns amid trees from around the world, read, and many walked and ran around the perimeter.

Eating their brown-bag lunches there, Kat told Molly about her day in San Francisco with Jamie. Molly's optimistic imagination went to work. "Ooh, he must like you."

"Yeah, right," Kat sneered. "Men like him weren't interested in me, even when I was his age. He just wanted to get out of his elderly friends' apartment and spend the day with a safe local he knew who had a car."

"I don't think so," Molly countered. "He could have hired a professional tour guide or asked anyone, but he called you. What if he's interested in you?"

"It's tempting, but if he is, he's out of luck. I've never liked bed-hoppers, and I'm not setting myself up to get left behind, again—even if he *is* attractive and fairly successful. Besides, he lives five-thousand miles away. Better to not get attached in the first place."

"Are you attached?"

"Hell, no. Attracted? Sure. He's charming, intelligent, generous, and sexy. But he's a playboy—a heartache looking for a place to happen, and I'm not going to let him happen to me."

"Is it hard to enjoy going out with Dennis, after Jamie?"

"Dennis who?" Kat joked. She occasionally went out with one of the Scottish fiddlers she backed-up on guitar. Fifteen years her senior, he looked old enough to be her father and was smitten with her. She liked him as a fellow musician and friend, but wasn't attracted to him.

"Yeah. Jamie's a casual acquaintance, but he's much more interesting than Dennis, and not hinting that he's hot for me every time I see him."

"If he ever does, and you don't take advantage of it, you're an idiot."

* * *

In London's Marylebone neighborhood, Jamie caught up with Leigh over lunch in a small restaurant their friends frequented.

"So you saw that woman you liked in California?" Leigh asked. "How was that?"

"Nice. She drove a hundred miles each way to spend the day with me in San Francisco."

"Really? She must fancy you. What did you do with her?"

"We watched wind-surfers, then spent the afternoon at a museum. She's a character... and you know what surprised me?"

Her eyes animated, Leigh leaned forward with elbows on the table and rested her chin on her knuckles. "What?"

"She momentarily forgot I'm an actor. I could be a taxi driver for all she cares. She acted like I was just a friend who wanted to see her city... except for being concerned that fans might recognize me and mob us. That became a running joke—that she would protect me."

"*She'd* protect *you*? How? Is she built like a footballer? Or does she carry a gun, like in Texas?"

"Neither. It was a laugh. She's a little thing—comes up to here on me." Jamie held his hand near his chin. "And she's more soft than muscular."

"Oh?" Leigh raised her eyebrows and smiled. "You've taken the next step?"

"Merely a hug. It felt good, and not just physically. I felt... I don't know... comfortable when I held her. I sensed that she had no expectations of me. Usually when I hug women, they think we're about to jump into bed."

"Isn't that usually the case?"

Jamie looked down at his plate, then at Leigh, wishing he hadn't taken their young love for granted. "It used to be fun, but now it's only to stay in the public eye." He looked down again and slowly shook his head.

"You mean in the gossip pages. It's about time you woke up, Jamie. Bob and I wondered when you would. This American did it for you, eh? What's her name?"

"Kat. Katerina. She makes me feel like a regular guy. Reminds me of you, in some ways..." Jamie's voice trailed off as he gazed out the restaurant window and recalled their college days, when he loved Leigh. Regret filled his heart.

Leigh reached across the table to put her hand on his. "Jamie, it never would have worked. You were only interested in your career, and I needed someone whose fondest desire was to have a good life with me. I couldn't play second-fiddle to fame. But you know I'll always love you, too. You'll always be my other best friend—next to Bob."

Jamie broke eye contact again, remembering how he lost her to a man who put her first in his life.

"Okay, so you went to a museum?" Leigh got the conversation back on track.

"Yes. By the time we left, the traffic was dreadful, and I talked her into staying for dinner with me at the Whittinghams."

"You had to talk her into having dinner with you? That's hard to believe."

"Nell invited her that morning, but Kat didn't want to impose, and planned to go straight home. She's very considerate... doesn't want to inconvenience anyone, wants to pay her own way—and mine, too."

"Is she rich?"

Jamie laughed. "No. She does P.R. for the government. Probably makes just enough to live comfortably. And she's frugal... uses maps rather than pay for a navigation system when she bought her car. Oh, and it's a hybrid that gets fifty miles-per-gallon."

"Environmentalist?"

"Very much so," Jamie said, sitting straighter with increasing enthusiasm. "And a musician. She plays guitar with Scottish groups, and she's good."

"Jamie, I've never seen you this excited about a lady," Leigh said. "You're keen as mustard! You going to see her again?"

"Next time I'm in California. I don't know how... but I like her, Leigh. I want to get to know her better. If she's everything she seems... who knows?"

In late September, *First Impressions, Last Rites* opened in Britain, and Jamie talked it up in promotional interviews on every medium known to man.

"It's exhausting," he told his father on the phone. "Judy and I ride around, run into a building, chat about the film, run back out to the car, David drives us to another building, and we do it again—over and over."

"Well, you wanted the acting life and Judy's a clever publicist," Reggie Knight said. "You could have followed in my footsteps instead of your mum's."

"Wait, Dad. I'm not complaining. I wouldn't trade my life for anyone's. I only wanted to explain why I haven't called lately. Next month, we do it all over again in New York."

"Well, the film is exciting, and we saw some of the programs. Maggie shocked us when we saw her on *The One Show*. What did she do to her face?"

Jamie sighed. "Cosmetic surgery. Remember how obsessed she was with her looks? I guess she was so afraid of aging, when she turned forty she tried to preempt it."

"But why? She was a lovely girl when she lived with you. She couldn't have gone to the dogs that quickly."

"She was always afraid she would. Now her agent gets her on those 'Whatever Happened To...' programmes, hoping it'll lead to work. God, I'm glad I ended that."

"She's not pretty anymore. Dreadful—like a plastic bowl, melted in the microwave. But you were very good. I want you to know that. We'll see you at dinner, Sunday."

That evening, as Jamie relaxed at home and read a script by the fire, Bill Bleuchel called from Los Angeles. "I'm going to Lake Tahoe next month to check out some locations. If you can get away from the promo circus between release dates, why don't you fly out and join me? Tahoe is amazing in winter."

"I'd love to ski there. But do they have any snow? I mean, with the drought..."

"Probably not enough for skiing. The entire west coast has dried up. But check the trail cameras on the Northstar website. Even if you can't ski, you could hike, bike, or do your Christmas shopping there. Buy stuff you'd never find in London, or even on the web... no paparazzi."

Jamie opened the planner on his tablet. "That'd be nice. I don't know why those parasites bother with me."

"You give 'em material the tabloids pay for."

"They should be in Liberia, documenting the Ebola epidemic. How long will you be at Lake Tahoe?"

"About a week. I'll be driving all over the Tahoe Basin. I can rent a cabin as close to a town or as isolated as you want."

"Sounds fun, as long as it's not *too* isolated. I don't want to end up like the Donner Party."

"Hey, Richard Donner throws fabulous parties."

Jamie groaned at the lame Hollywood director joke as Bill continued. "Seriously, you're not that well-known here. And at Tahoe, the stars are the Olympic athletes who go there to practice and show off."

"When are you going?"

"October 13th or 14th. I need to see some places between L.A. and San Francisco for another film, then stop in The City to see Dad before heading to the mountains. You fly into SFO, I'll pick you up and take you back."

"Sounds nice," Jamie said. "I could use some down time in a quiet place, and *First Impressions* opens there on the 24th."

"Perfect. I'll take you back to L.A. in plenty of time for the talk shows. I might be able to stay a couple days longer, if you want," Bill added. "Or... maybe that lady you know up north would take you to the airport after I leave."

"I'd like that, but slow down, Cupid. Send me the date I should arrive, and I'll text you as soon as I'm sure no one has scheduled something I don't know about."

"All right. We'll have a blast. Catch you later."

Jamie went into his kitchen and stood, looking out the window. People raved about Lake Tahoe, and film of it looked fantastic. A high-elevation Alpine lake that straddles two states—one an environmental leader and the other a place where almost anything is legal...

A long, busy period of movie releases followed by awards season was about to start for most popular actors. He had to fly to California anyway, the next week. But did he really want to spend another—how many hours on the road with Bill? He'd be working most of the time, so Jamie would have some quiet time alone.

On the other hand, he could be alone in his own house and save the money and time. But here, he'd be subject to family and friends' requests. *Maybe if I can do it in peace...*

Kat's trip to London had been short like that. He enjoyed the day he spent with her in September. And he was still subconsciously making comparisons every time he took someone else out. Kat was fun and easy-going. Bill would like her; her sense of humor was a lot like his. And he could provide a second opinion of her.

Talking with Leigh the next day, Jamie wondered aloud whether Kat would want to see him again.

"Probably," Leigh replied, "don't they all?"

"Most, but I can't assume. She's not like most of the women I've known. Maybe she was just being nice."

"If she didn't like you, she wouldn't have driven that far to see you. Couldn't she easily have said she had to work?"

"I suppose. Nell and Al liked her, too," Jamie recalled. "She showed genuine interest in them, and everything but sports. If she faked that, she should be an actor. But what if she's busy when we're there?"

"Well, it wouldn't hurt to call."

"Maybe we should drop in and surprise her... see her 'habitat.' If she's out, we can leave Bill's number. That might be better. Put the ball in her court and see if she responds."

"Will you invite her to the mountains with you?" Leigh flashed a knowing grin at him.

"You mean... to spend the night? I'd like to. But she doesn't act like she's attracted to me, nor seem the type to go for a one-night stand. And I haven't decided whether to pursue a long-term relationship with her."

Later, Jamie searched Facebook and found three women named "Katerina Mancini." They weren't all spelled the same, but some might have been typos. The two in California were forty-two and fifty-four, if one could believe the sources.

Having seen all kinds of incorrect "facts" about himself on the web, Jamie never assumed that everything posted about others was accurate. Why don't they let the public see their pictures? *She couldn't be fifty-four, but she might be the forty-two-year-old... or neither of them.*

Looking for information about her online made him feel sneaky. He could have asked Danny to research her, but didn't want his cousin to know he was interested in an American. The temptation to mention it to someone else in the family might be hard to resist, and since his mother wanted him to marry Trissy Aylesworth... *Hah—in her dreams!*

With help from his manager and Danny, Jamie rescheduled some activities so he could disappear for a week in the High Sierra.

Victor praised him for taking a break. "Even a physically fit man like you can push yourself too far. You don't have to be old, fat, and lazy to get sick."

"If I ever get fat or lazy, just shoot me!"

Chapter 13: Sacramento Surprise

The October sun shone through a tall, narrow window in Kat's small office in Sacramento. Books about animals, plants and ecosystems, a dictionary, thesaurus, *Elements of Style*, and the *Associated Press Stylebook* crowded a metal shelf above her computer.

Wearing her usual blue jeans, white Nikes, and a turquoise polo shirt, Kat negotiated the price of airtime on the phone with a network executive. Publicity campaigns to raise money for the California Sea Otter Fund and the Rare and Endangered Species Fund were her biggest—and most challenging—projects each year. The challenge? Figuring out how to reach the twenty million Californians who filed income tax returns, with an advertising budget that wouldn't have much impact in even *one* of the state's fourteen media markets.

"Corliss, you know I hate to ask for favors, but the 2015 tax season will be critical, since I had no money to advertise, *this* year. It's October, and we still haven't received the minimum donations either fund needs to survive." Her voice reflected her passion for protecting animals.

"You will, but it would be nice to reach it earlier, next year." Corliss Chiang, the sales manager for government advertising at CBS Radio wanted to keep the "tax check-off" ads on her stations. The account brought in little money, but the network benefitted from the halo effect—good will through association with a worthy cause.

When Kat hung up, the office receptionist stood at her doorway. "Kat, these gentlemen are here to see you."

Astonished, Kat stood. "Jamie! What are you doing here?"

"Oh, we just happened to be in the neighborhood." He smiled broadly, stepped into the office, and hugged her.

"This is my friend, Bill Bleuchel." Jamie gestured toward the bearded man with sandy-blond hair.

Bill was a nice-looking guy, a little taller than Jamie, and appeared closer to Kat's age. Both men's clothing was even more casual than hers. In worn-out blue jeans, sneakers, a plaid flannel shirt, and wind-blown hair, Jamie didn't look like a leading man. *He must be traveling incognito.*

Molly McKenna appeared at Kat's door and started to say something before she saw Jamie and Bill. Her eyes widened, and it was obvious she recognized Jamie, yet she maintained her friendly-but-businesslike composure. "Oh, I'm sorry, I didn't realize you had company."

Kat introduced the men to Molly, who acted nonchalant. "You get the most interesting visitors."

The truth was, she rarely had any visitors other than colleagues. Molly had once told Kat her life was "all work and no play," and she needed more play in her life—especially with a nice, single man. When Molly had offered to introduce her to eligible bachelors, Kat made it clear she didn't want to be set up. She was fed up with men... with falling in love, then winding up alone.

But she later confessed that she wished one of her boyfriends had wanted to marry her. "It would be nice to have someone you love to share life's ups and downs, the house and yard chores, vacations, and grow old together... and to open pickle jars."

Kat missed the positive, energized feeling of being in love, but couldn't stand the emotional pain when the men left her for someone prettier, thinner, or younger. She had stopped allowing men to use her as a temporary girlfriend, and bitterly accepted rejection and her solo life.

Bill offered Molly the guest chair, but she declined. "No, thank you. I can't stay. Jamie, are you involved with wildlife?"

He appeared surprised by the question. "Well... I support protecting wildlife and treating animals humanely. And I play a game warden in my next film; does that count?" Bill added, "He shoots elephant poachers in it. That's pretty wild."

"We just stopped by to see Kat," Jamie said. "I hope that's all right."

"Of course it's all right," Molly exclaimed. "She's not a prisoner here. In fact," she looked pointedly at Kat, "she needs to take a lunch break."

The hint embarrassed Kat, but she kept her mouth shut for once.

Another woman's voice called to Molly from the outer office and she turned away for a moment. A tall, attractive, fortyish woman joined her at the door. With a sly grin, Molly stepped aside and said, "Kat, introduce your friends to Susan."

"This is our Deputy Director of Public Affairs," Kat said. "Molly and my supervisor, Ron, work for her."

Susan was wide-eyed. "What on earth brings you here?"

"We came to see Kat," Jamie replied again.

As Jamie, Bill, and Kat left through the back door, she asked, "What do you guys want for lunch? There are all kinds of food within walking distance, or we can drive somewhere."

Jamie replied, "I'll eat anything. You guys choose."

Bill shrugged his shoulders and looked at Kat.

"Okay," she said, "my favorite is Paesano's. We'd have to drive, but it's not far and all their food is great. The pizzas are to die for."

"Sounds good," Bill replied. "Does it attract the kind of people who'll leave 'Nigel Stone' here alone? It's no fun when people interrupt your lunch to ask for autographs, or if he's that guy in some movie."

"Oh, please..." Jamie looked up at the sky.

Kat tried to guess how many people there at 1:30 p.m. on a Tuesday were likely to recognize Jamie, and whether they would respect an actor's right to eat lunch in peace. Society had changed since her days in Hollywood. Before an enormous wave of migrants from other states and countries moved there, almost forty years earlier, people in L.A. were accustomed to seeing famous performers in public places, and most had enough class to leave them alone. Anyone who interrupted an entertainer in a restaurant was considered horribly uncool, and might be escorted out by the staff. Back then, people had at least *some* respect for other people's privacy—even celebrities.

"I'm sure you have fans here," Kat said. "But Paesano's attracts working professionals. I'd like to think they're considerate enough to leave you alone."

"Well," Jamie said, shifting his weight, "let's go there. It'll probably be fine. If not, we can find a drive-through and eat in the car."

"Who said you could eat in my car?" Bill asked. "I just had it cleaned." He had to be joking. The SUV was littered with evidence that he'd been dining-behind-the-wheel all the way from L.A.

"We can take mine," Kat offered.

"Nah, let's take the Explorer," Bill said. He had packed it for two, so moved some gear to make room for Kat. "Unless you want to sit on Jamie's lap," he teased.

Jamie grinned and lifted his eyebrows. "That'd be fun."

Kat laughed. "If a cop saw us, you'd get a ticket. Darn traffic laws have taken all the fun out of riding around in cars with boys."

En route to the restaurant, Kat said, "You haven't told me why you're in Sacramento."

"Bill needs to find suitable locations for a film shoot at Lake Tahoe," Jamie explained. "He called, right when I was thinking it might be nice to get out of town. London's getting cold, and I needed a break before the heavy promotion starts here for *First Impressions.*"

Bill added, "I convinced Jamie to come with me, and we're on our way."

"We were getting hungry and I remembered you lived here, so we thought we'd stop and see if you were around," Jamie said, sounding blasé about it.

It would never occur to Kat that they stopped for anything other than lunch. But she wondered how he happened to bring her business card. Or was she in his phone?

"Well, you sure surprised me, and I'm glad you did," she said. "But you won't get warm at Tahoe in October... unless you snuggle up to a fireplace or... something."

In mid-town Sacramento, Paesano's stood among other restaurants, small businesses and art galleries in well-preserved Gold Rush-era Victorian homes. Bill parked the forest-green SUV around the corner from the restaurant.

"You think our stuff will be safe here?" he asked Kat.

"Yeah. It's covered, your windows are tinted, and people would notice anyone who tried to break into a vehicle here. I think it's as safe as any other public place. And safer than valet parking. God only knows where those guys take cars, or how they drive them once they're out of sight."

The young man who welcomed the trio in Paesano's greeted Kat by name, and she asked for a table in the back. Well past lunch hour, the small restaurant was only half-full. The old brick walls featured works by local artists, and a TV monitor behind the bar carried a sports talk show with video clips of American football.

"Something smells good," Bill declared. "I think we made the right choice."

Jamie agreed. "Oh, hey, I saw you in the news a couple weeks ago, talking about that guy who shot a mountain goat."

"Bighorn sheep," Kat corrected. "You're kidding. That story aired in Britain?"

"I saw that, too," Bill said. "Is the scumbag in jail?"

"No. No one ever goes to jail for wildlife crimes. Most of them get a slap on the wrist, if a D.A. even prosecutes them. But thanks to all the publicity, this guy might get the maximum fine, if he's convicted."

Looking at the menu, Jamie asked Kat, "What do you recommend?"

"My favorite is the Greek pizza, but they're all good. Serious carnivores like the Sicilian. It has enough meat to put you into cardiac arrest."

A server had just walked up. "Wait a minute," he pleaded with a smile. "No one has ever left here in an ambulance."

"I'm kidding." Kat smiled at him, then turned back to her companions. "If you don't want pizza, everything's good."

All three wanted to give in to whatever pizza the others wanted. "Remember," Kat said, "I can get my favorites any time. You guys can't, so you choose." The men wanted meat, without the heart attack: a large combination.

"Are you going to South Shore?" she asked Bill.

"I have locations to see all around the Lake, but our cabin's in Tahoe City."

"Rough duty," she said. "The weather's been nice up there. Bad for skiing and water, but good for driving. You looking for exteriors?"

"Yeah."

"Are you guys 'bear aware'?" Kat asked, knowing that people in bear habitat could be surprised by an ursine raid at any time. CDW did a lot of public outreach, and people who lived in the mountains knew to use bear-proof garbage cans and make their homes less attractive to wildlife. But tourists renting cabins often invited trouble by leaving food or garbage out where bears could smell it. Kat didn't know about Bill, but she doubted Jamie had ever faced a 300-pound bear raiding his 'fridge.

"What do you mean, bear aware?" Bill smiled as though he expected a punchline.

Jamie added, "And how are you spelling that?" with a twinkle in his eyes.

Kat's face warmed. *Oh god, he's cute.* "That's our program to help people avoid conflicts with them. California black bears don't all hibernate through the winter, and damage from wildfires and the drought forces animals to travel farther than usual to forage. When they learn that people have food, they'll break into buildings and cars to get it. They can easily rip the doors off a house and refrigerator, and make one hell of a mess."

Jamie winced. "What do people do when that happens? Should we be armed, or should we call you?"

"If you're armed, you'd better have something big," Kat said.

Bill interrupted, "I've got something big, but I'm not offering it to any bear."

Jamie and Kat both cracked up, and if any shred of formality had existed among them, it disappeared.

"Bears are big, muscular eating machines with an incredible sense of smell," she continued. "They can detect food and drinks from miles away. They're also attracted by cologne, after-shave, deodorant, pet food... When I lived there, I had to stop using my favorite suntan lotion because someone told me the coconut scent would attract bears."

"You lived at Lake Tahoe?" Jamie asked as if she'd said Buckingham Palace.

"Briefly."

Bill asked, "Where?"

"Incline Village."

"Whoa... are you rich?" he asked.

"No, I programmed a radio station there. A garage apartment at the general manager's house was part of my compensation. He was rich."

The pizza's arrival interrupted her. The large pizza didn't look very large, now that she wanted to impress Jamie and Bill, so she only ate one piece. Knowing these guys worked with women who starved themselves made her feel pudgy, anyway.

The pizza disappeared, the waiter brought the check, and Kat grabbed it. So did Jamie and Bill. With three hands holding the black vinyl check holder, three smiles erupted.

"Come on, guys, you're guests in my town, so it's my treat," Kat said, maintaining her grip on the check. All her life she had heard men complain about women who expected them to pay for everything. She made sure no one could ever say that about her.

Jamie gently pried her hand open while maintaining his grip on the check holder. "No. Call me old-fashioned; I'd like to treat you."

As Bill released the check holder, Kat protested. "Just because you earn the most money doesn't mean you should get stuck with the bill every time you go out with friends."

"Oh, I don't get stuck with Bill every time," Jamie quipped as he took a credit card from his wallet.

Bill pretended to be insulted. These guys were fun.

"Tell you what," Jamie said to her, "you can buy, next time."

"Didn't you say that, last time?"

Chapter 14: On to Tahoe

As they approached his Explorer, Bill exclaimed, "Hey, you were right. It's still here."

Jamie helped Kat into the back seat. She asked Bill, "Is your cabin right in Tahoe City, or will you have to search for it on some dark road in the forest?"

"It's not far from the main drag. Shouldn't be hard to find, even in the dark."

During light-hearted conversation on the way back to Kat's office, Jamie was very attentive, always turning to make eye contact with her.

As Bill pulled up to her office building, Jamie asked, "Where's that information about mountain lions and bears?"

"In the office," Kat said

"Back in a tick," Jamie said to Bill as he and Kat got out of the vehicle.

Plastic brochure and magazine holders covered the public affairs office entry wall. "Look at all this," he said. "Endangered species, invasive species, hunting, fishing, oil spills, Report Poachers and Polluters..."

Kat picked an issue of CDW's magazine, *Outdoor California*, and handed it to Jamie.

"Is the bear stuff in this?" he asked, flipping through it.

"Yes." She hoped he would notice her byline on a habitat restoration story later, as she gathered "Keep Me Wild" and "Living With Bears" brochures for him. Two of her colleagues came out of their offices and cubicles, and took a good long look at him. He appeared not to notice, except when Molly passed and said hi.

"Is she your boss?" Jamie asked.

"No, Molly is a good friend. There." She handed him the brochures. "Everything you ever wanted to know about lions, coyotes, and bears."

"Thanks. I'm glad we stopped to see you. I mean... I was glad, anyway. Even more for this." He moved toward the door.

"I'll walk you out. You might need protection." Kat grinned at him, keeping their San Francisco joke alive.

"Thanks for taking me to lunch. What a pleasant surprise."

"My pleasure. "

"You should have a good time at Tahoe. You probably won't see animals larger than raccoons. But if you do run into a bear or cougar," she added, casually, "make yourself look as large as you can, make noise, and if attacked, fight back. Don't play dead."

"Crap! Is that likely?"

"No. But I want you to know what to do... just in case. I don't imagine you'll see anything more dangerous than squirrels."

At the exit, Bill stood just inside the glass doors, reading a poster. A tall man who had a gray beard, mustache, and a long, gray ponytail came down the stairs next to them.

"Hi Brian. Jamie, Bill, this is Brian Galway," she said. "He's a friend and a manager in our info tech branch. Brian, my friends, Bill and Jamie." If Brian recognized Jamie, he didn't let on.

Outside, as Jamie stuffed the brochures into a backpack, Kat leaned across the front seat to give Bill one of her business cards. "Do you know how to get to I-80 from here?"

"Yeah. I've got GPS." The way he said it and winked at her revealed that Jamie had told him she didn't. "Where do you get traffic reports?"

"KXJZ, 90.9 FM... their signal is good, a long way up the hill." Kat put her hand out to shake with Jamie, standing at the open car door. "It's nice to see you again."

"You, too." He hugged her, then—to her surprise—kissed her on the cheek.

Her cheeks—among other things—felt hot around her broad smile. "Have fun!"

Jamie got into the now-running SUV and closed the door. "See you 'round." He grinned at her, then Bill drove out of the parking lot and they were gone.

Suddenly, Kat didn't feel like the mature, detached woman who respected the actor's talent and skills, but not his reputation. She felt the way she had thirty years earlier, when she met a singer she had liked... a silly, emotional high, like an adrenaline rush. A pleasant excitement enveloped her as she walked back into the building.

Keith, the public affairs officer whose daughter, Rachel, had a crush on Jamie, stood near the door, grinning at her. "Rachel is going to kill you," he said.

"Maybe you shouldn't tell her."

"Maybe not, but I don't know how long I can keep *that* to myself. You just got kissed by a guy who's going to be a star someday. And you know it's going to get around."

"Oh, please..." Kat's voice dripped with sarcasm. "Actors are always kissing people on the cheek. It doesn't mean a thing. And you're probably the only one standing around looking out the window."

In her office, Kat thought about Jamie. He was like most of the successful performers she had met... he didn't act as though being rich and famous made him better than anyone else. Another actor once told her it's not the performers that celebrity changes. It's the people around them who treat them differently when they become famous. He said it hurt and had ruined many friendships.

* * *

Jamie didn't say anything when he and Bill left Kat's office. His pulse raced, and he already wanted to see her again. Finally, he asked, "Well, what do you think?"

"Good pizza." Bill exclaimed with a grin. The look he got from his passenger confirmed that wasn't what Jamie meant. "She's nice. And funny. I'm surprised at how quickly we all got comfortable with each other, considering you only met her once, months ago. And not your usual type. Most women are either afraid to speak, worshipping you, or trying to get you into bed."

"Yeah, that's one of the things I like about Kat. She makes me feel like a regular guy she met and liked enough to see again, not like a 'celebrity'—or a trophy. Much nicer than being hounded by women like Mairi McMillan and Victor's office tart."

Mairi McMillan was a pretty Irish actor who seemed hell-bent on "catching" Jamie. She played an occasional, recurring role on *Nigel Stone*, and did everything she could to get close to him.

"How old is she?" Bill asked.

"Mairi?"

"Kat."

"I don't know... around my age. I saw her in San Francisco last month, as well."

"Oh, yeah? You didn't tell me about that," Bill said. "So, this was your third date. That means if you get lonely this week, you can invite her up and see if she *will* sleep with you."

Jamie gave him an *I don't think so* look, but would never admit that she had already turned down his thinly veiled invitation in London. "Not that I wouldn't like to... I'm surprised at how much I'm attracted to someone who's so different from the women I usually date. But I really like her. She's nice. Confident. She knows things and has a good sense of humor... and she's not needy. That's very attractive."

"Got anyone special at home, these days?"

"No. But before I start anything, I want to get to know her better, take it slow, and only proceed when I know that's not a façade hiding a harpy. I won't risk another gold digger or social climber. I'm tired of playing. I want a mature, mutually supportive relationship that'll last. You know... a love that grows from an honest, close friendship? Like I had at uni. Falling in love feels good at first, but falling *out* hurts."

Bill nodded. "I wonder if either of us will ever have a relationship like that, working in our crazy business. It takes really confident, secure women to handle our work schedules, travel, gossip, and—in your case—women chasing their husbands."

Jamie turned the radio on and tried to find the station Kat recommended. Neither man could remember the frequency, but he found some rock music they both liked.

Once they got beyond the subdivisions and strip malls of Sacramento and were in the foothills, the scenery improved dramatically. There, the effects of the drought were more apparent. Oddly shaped patches of wildfire-blackened land on sparsely wooded hills, and flattened strips of dry, yellow grasses where kids had slid down the slopes on cardboard boxes appeared here and there.

The temperature dropped as the elevation increased and the sun sank lower in the sky behind the travelers. Deciduous woodlands on yellow and brown hills gave way to fragrant green conifer forests on steeper terrain, and visible buildings became rare.

"This is so different to L.A.," Jamie observed. "The sky up here is so blue... so intense."

"Yeah... the smog makes it dull there. The valley is like a bowl that collects all the air pollution until a good rain knocks it down. It's usually nice there in winter and spring. In summer, the smog builds up, and the heat holds it there— like in L.A."

"It's gorgeous." Jamie imagined wildlife in the forest the freeway traversed. "What other animals live here, besides bears and mountain lions?"

Bill looked at him as though he were nuts. "You're asking *me*? I'm from Santa Monica. Ask Kat. She could *introduce* you to some of the critters out there."

Jamie imagined being introduced to a cougar wearing big sunglasses and acting jaded.

"Donner Pass is coming up," Bill said. "You hungry?" Sometimes he had a sick sense of humor.

As they drove out the east side of the 7,056-foot pass and down the grade to Truckee, Jamie wished they had gotten there before sundown. In the twilight, to his right he could barely see the wide valley, forested mountains, and granite rock beyond.

A couple miles down the grade, Bill said, "This is Truckee. It's a neat little town, but was better before developers wrecked it with subdivisions and more people moved in. We used to close the old part of town to shoot westerns. Some of the buildings go back to the Gold Rush days."

Bill took the State Route 89 exit and headed south. The winding, two-lane road followed the Truckee River, which flows from Lake Tahoe down the eastern slope of the Sierra to Reno. After passing the last business at the south end of Truckee, there were no street lights, and the SUV's headlights suddenly seemed barely adequate. Darkness hid the river and surrounding forest.

"Keep an eye out for deer. They never look before crossing a road," Bill said. "There are some cool restaurants around the lake, if they survived the recession."

At six o'clock they approached the two-lane road that went through the small town of Tahoe City and around the lake's north shore. Bill pointed to a thirty-foot-long bridge over the Truckee River on their right.

"In the summer, people lean over the sides to watch the fish. When you drive across, all you see is a row of butts. So it's called 'Fanny Bridge'."

"That name would have an entirely different connotation in Britain," Jamie observed, imagining women leaning backwards over the rail.

Bill drove into a Safeway store parking lot. "We need to pick up some provisions. There won't be anything to eat in the cabin."

The two men hurried through the large, brightly lit supermarket, discussing how often they'd want to cook, or go out and let someone else wash the dishes. Bill suggested they inspect the kitchen before stocking up on too much food.

"No point enticing the bears if we decide to eat in restaurants most of the time," he joked. Bill didn't seem to take Kat's warning seriously. He said he had been to Tahoe many times and had never seen a bear or heard anyone talk about them.

Jamie gave him a skeptical look. "If people don't have problems with bears, why would the state produce this much information about discouraging them?" He wasn't fearful, but would rather be prepared than assume Kat and her employer were fear mongers.

The word "DOC," painted on a large boulder about one half mile from the main road, identified the narrow dirt driveway that led to the small cabin. Located back in the woods, they couldn't see it from the road.

"Doc?" Jamie asked. "What does that mean?"

"They don't have street numbers here, and cabins need a way for people to identify them. A doctor owns ours."

The air's strong pine and fir fragrance tickled Jamie's nose. He couldn't see the entire cabin in the dark, but what they could see with Bill's flashlight looked pretty rustic.

The inside was more inviting once he found the light switch. The rough pine walls, exposed beams, and old-fashioned, braided area rugs scattered about the well-worn hardwood floor gave the place a homey feeling. A pine coffee table and an old, western style sofa and chair with red, black, and white plaid upholstery and flat, pine arm rests faced a small stone fireplace in one wall. Under a window sat a full bookshelf.

One end of the large room formed the kitchen. The small refrigerator was at least fifty years old, but adequate for their needs. They had purchased a loaf of sourdough bread, sandwich meats, cheeses, lettuce, tomatoes, bottled salad dressing, Sierra Nevada Pale Ale, small jars of mustard and mayo, coffee, milk, and cookies from the store's bakery.

Above the kitchen sink a window faced the forest—some compensation for whoever had to wash dishes. Bill opened cupboards and drawers to see what utensils were provided. "Looks like we've got the basics covered; there's four of everything."

"The bedrooms and bathroom are tiny," Jamie remarked.

"It's our escape from twenty-first century over-civilization, especially for you. And you've worked on film locations that make this look cushy."

"Yeah... just because we can afford five-star hotels doesn't mean we always want 'em, right? Hey, would you mind if I asked Kat to come up for a day?"

"No. Bring her up for the week, if you want."

Jamie didn't react to Bill's teasing. "What day would be best?"

"Doesn't matter to me. A weekday if you want to be alone. If I'm lucky, I won't have to work all weekend—if you want your wing-man here. It's your call."

"Okay. She works weekdays... let me think about it." Jamie yawned. "Man, after eleven hours on a plane and four in the car, I want to go for a run, but I'm exhausted and might get lost. And then there are the mountain lions and bears."

To his body, 7:30 p.m. Pacific Daylight Time felt like 2:30 a.m. British Summer Time. He fell asleep on the couch after eating only half a sandwich and drinking part of a bottle of ale.

Chapter 15: Walk On the Wild Side

Jamie had invited Kat to come to Tahoe on Sunday. That sounded fun, except for the return traffic jam. She loved Tahoe but didn't go there often, and she was warming up to Jamie.

Driving up the hill—a local euphemism for the seven-thousand-foot climb—she pondered his motives. He could get anyone to hang out with him anywhere. And there's no shortage of his kind of "pretty girls" at Tahoe.

That reminded her of another man who had once seemed to like her. The executive producer of a TV show had hired her to be a production assistant, then hit on her—frequently. As an unattractive, overweight twenty-year-old with the wardrobe of a pauper with no fashion sense, she had assumed he was kidding and laughed.

He was thirty-eight, nice looking, and successful. Such a man in Hollywood could have had anyone in a city full of beautiful women trying to get into show business. He couldn't have been attracted to Kat. Maybe someone had dared him to sleep with the ugly duckling. But she would never have had sex with her boss. Especially a married one.

On her way into the studio after four months on the job, the security guard told her she had "been canceled." The producer didn't even have the guts to fire her, himself! To him, she was just another "chick" to screw. *Bastard.*

After that, Kat had mistrusted financially well-off or extremely attractive men who seemed interested in her. Not that many had, but she wondered, had any of them been nice, honorable men she'd kept at arm's length because she couldn't believe they really liked her?

Jamie had acted like a platonic friend every time she had seen him— assuming his "nightcap" invitation in London was innocent—and hadn't hinted at anything else. So that must be how he saw her—as a new friend. Maybe he doesn't know anyone around here. Or maybe he enjoys hanging out with someone who's like a big sister—a woman he can talk with, who isn't trying to get into his pants. Not that he wasn't appealing, but considering how many women threw themselves at him... She needed to stop questioning his attention and enjoy it while it lasts.

When Lake Tahoe came into view, she took a moment to appreciate the scene. No matter how many times she went there, the natural beauty always impressed her. The angle of the morning sun made the lake a deep sapphire blue, contrasting with the green forests and granite crags on the mountains surrounding it. Nature at its best.

After finding the "DOC" boulder Jamie described, she knew she had found the right place when she recognized Bill's Explorer—now decorated with a lot more dirt.

Outside the car, Kat closed her eyes and inhaled the fresh mountain air as deeply as she could. She loved it there. Healthy environment, nice memories...

Jamie came out of the cabin as she soaked up the scenery. "What took you so long?" His expression told her he was kidding, but she checked her watch—two minutes early.

"Good morning!" she said as he hugged her, kissed her cheek, and invited her into the cabin. "Hi, Bill."

Bill sat at the kitchen table. "Hey, how was the drive? Any snow on the pass, yet?"

"No, and it's a good thing. If there had been snow, I wouldn't be here. Have you seen how little ground clearance a Prius has?"

"Hey, if we're lucky," Bill said with a devilish grin, "it'll snow today, and you'll be stuck here for the night." He grinned at Jamie, who shot him a *What the hell are you doing?* look.

That caught Kat off guard, with no witty response. She was a little embarrassed at the notion of spending the night in a small cabin with two men she barely knew, and her cheeks suddenly felt warm.

Jamie smiled apologetically. "Let's get out of here." He opened the door, gave Bill an admonishing look, and silently mouthed, stop that!

Bill called out, "I want you two home before midnight," as Jamie pulled the door closed behind them.

"Sorry about that," he said.

"He's teasing you, isn't he? Have you been having fun here?"

"Yeah, it's been nice. And you were right; this place is amazing! Come here." He took her hand and led her behind the cabin to a narrow path that went into the forest, where light filtered by the trees danced on Sierra gooseberry, manzanita, and mountain mule ears.

After hiking in silence for a few minutes, Kat asked, "Where are we going?"

"You'll see. I want to show you something."

The path climbed uphill, and she hoped it wouldn't get too steep. Jamie looked extremely fit. She was not. Good thing she wore hiking boots.

They continued up the gentle slope, from under the tree canopy to dry meadow, then woods again. Jamie didn't talk much. The only sounds were birds, insects, and the crunch of leaves and pine needles beneath their feet. Wildlife biologists had said to make noise when hiking, so you're less likely to surprise an animal an animal that might attack if it felt threatened. But if Jamie didn't want to talk, Kat didn't want to bug him with idle conversation.

In at least ten minutes of hiking, he only glanced back twice to see if she was keeping up with him. If he had thought of her as a date, he would have checked more often.

The slope steepened gradually for an easy hike until the dirt trail ended at a large granite outcropping, almost a wall.

Jamie stopped. "You might need a hand, here. Some of the steps are rather far apart."

It looked like he was about to climb up something she *didn't* want to climb. "What steps? *Where* are we going?"

"Up there." Jamie pointed to a ledge about twenty feet up the granite rocks.

Kat looked up, searching for a route to the top. Not quite a vertical rock face, but much too steep for her. "Uh, I don't think so. You go ahead; I'll wait for you."

"It's not that tough."

"Maybe not for you. You're fit. I'm not, and I have bad knees."

"Here, take my hand," he said, reaching for hers.

"No." She was serious and crossed her arms.

"Oh, come on. Where's your sense of adventure?"

"I have better sense than to pretend I'm a mountain climber."

"If you're strong enough to fight off a horde of my fans, you must be strong enough to climb this. I'll help you."

Kat closed her eyes and took a deep breath. About to stand her ground and refuse, she hesitated. She hated being a wimp. Slowly, she took his hand, thinking how much she also hated this sort of climbing. Even though neither of her knees had dislocated in many years, this was not unlike what had caused them to fail in the past.

Looking for flat spaces in the massive gray boulders and slabs, she carefully placed her boots and tested them for stability before putting much weight on them. Three of the little flat places Jamie called steps were far apart for someone her height. She would never have tried to take them if she didn't value Jamie's friendship, and if he hadn't pulled her up.

But why? What kind of friend would push you to do something that's so far beyond your abilities it could get you hurt? Hadn't she told him how she tore the ligaments, tendons, and cartilage in her knees while backpacking in these mountains? Maybe not, or he'd forgotten. Or... was he testing her? Why did she give a hoot what he thought of her? But she did care, and she couldn't back out, now that she was fifteen feet up the steep slope. Fear made her breathe hard, and her weak legs embarrassed her. Damn desk job.

"Just a couple more steps," Jamie said, trying to encourage his struggling companion. Having no idea this hike was resurrecting memories of a painful experience, he couldn't have understood why she was so nervous.

Kat had stuffed it away and nearly forgotten about the fall she had taken thirty-eight years earlier, dislocating her right knee, landing on and cracking her left kneecap, then tumbling down a hill and off a cliff.

Now she could see it all in living color on the big screen of her mind. But she persevered, one slow step at a time, holding a death grip on Jamie's hand. By the time she reached the wide ledge where he stood, she was gasping for breath. *Add asthma to my shortcomings, and he won't call me again.*

She sat on a boulder, looked away from him, wiped the perspiration from her face and took deep breaths, hoping she could compose herself and forget the fact that they would probably have to climb down the same way they came up.

Jamie sat down and put his arm around her shoulder. "Are you okay? What's the matter?"

She took a deep breath. "We were climbing like this when I wrecked my knees, and it's almost like being there, again. I'm not as strong or sure-footed as you, and I don't want to fall again."

"Oh, Kat... I'm sorry. You told me you'd injured your knees, but not how you did it. Were you rock-climbing? Around here?"

She told him, with details that made Jamie wince. "Falling and rolling off a cliff was bad enough. After my friends rescued me from the ledge I landed on and put my

107

knee joint back into the socket, we had to hike three more days to get picked up and driven to the nearest town. There were no cell phones, then."

"Two girls had to hike beside me the whole time and catch me, every time either knee gave out. Without them, I couldn't have taken ten steps without falling. My legs hurt so badly, I wished I had died and gotten it over with. And I was terrified that some doctor would want to cut my legs open to fix them. For a physically fit teenager who played sports all year, it was awful. It changed me from an athlete to a spectator."

Jamie apologized again and hugged her. "I assume you still swim, since you have a pool."

"Yeah. That, walking, and cycling are the only exercises that won't cause more knee problems. You like to swim?"

"Yeah, love to."

After a quiet moment, she asked, "Why did we have to come up here, anyway?"

"Look." He gestured toward a magnificent view—most of Lake Tahoe and the seven-to-ten thousand-foot peaks surrounding it. "Isn't that stunning?"

On the far shore, about twenty-five miles away, they could barely make out the town of South Lake Tahoe. "Magnificent." She paused. "I could drive you to places with views like this."

To turn the conversation away from her weaknesses, she said, "Hey, I hope you put sunscreen on, earlier. You're getting a little pink." *And I doubt it's from exerting yourself.*

"Yes, Bill insisted. Why are you all obsessed with sunscreen? I thought California law required you to have a tan."

"It did at one time, and I obeyed it religiously," Kat joked, "until doctors told us that getting a great tan every year caused skin cancer and premature aging. Didn't you hear about that when you were filming in Australia? I read they had a huge public education campaign to get people to use sunscreen because the skin cancer rate had skyrocketed."

"Yeah, they talked about it, but everyone still had a nice tan. The Aussies seem to subscribe to a 'die young and have a beautiful corpse' philosophy."

"Hmm. Knowing what aging and gravity do to our bodies, I'm not sure that's a bad idea."

Jamie looked incredulous. "You *are* kidding, aren't you?"

"Are *you* kidding?" she shot back. He had touched a raw nerve. "Our society has turned life into a beauty contest, and all of us who are *not* beautiful get screwed. Add gravity's pull to dry skin, and wrinkles from decades of tanning, and nobody wants you. We might as *well* drop dead."

Jamie looked surprised. "That's scary. Remind me not to get old." After a few minutes of silence, he asked, "Do you have some with you?"

Mentally kicking herself for letting her bitterness show, Kat was distracted. "What?"

"Sunscreen."

"Oh... yeah." She unzipped the navy blue waist-pack that substituted for a purse, pulled out a small tube of Coppertone and handed it to him. "This one did well in Consumer Reports' lab tests, and I like the fragrance. It doesn't trigger my asthma, and it reminds me of summer."

Jamie opened the tube and sniffed. "Yeah...this smells okay. Some of them have a nasty kind of sweet, artificial scent... like cheap perfume. Sunscreen causes asthma?"

"The chemicals used to make artificial fragrance do that to some people," she said as he squeezed a blob into his hand. Applying it to his face, he handed the tube back to her, and she did the same.

"Can you see any on me?" she asked.

He looked carefully at her face and neck. "No. What about me?"

109

She examined his face. "Just a little... right... here." She reached for his left cheek and gently massaged the white sunscreen into his skin with her thumb. He closed his eyes for a moment and looked as if he liked the feeling of her hand on his face. "There. We're good for a couple hours, now."

He leaned back against the rock wall. "If it was a little warmer, I'd take my shirt off."

"Yeah, me too." Kat wore a deadpan look, then smiled.

Jamie did a double take. "I wouldn't stop you," he shot back with a grin and a quick glance at her bust.

"Tell me about the film you shot in Africa, last summer. What's it about?"

"*The Ivory Reel*?" he asked. "Elephant poaching."

"Oh, no! That's horrible!"

"Well, poaching is horrible, but the film isn't. It's about a game warden who's sent to Garamba National Park in the Democratic Republic of Congo to train local game wardens on new law enforcement equipment and tactics to fight poachers.

It shines a spotlight on the real poachers who are slaughtering thousands of elephants every month. Did you know the money they get for the tusks goes to terrorist groups like ISIS and Al-Shabab? Everyone who buys anything made of ivory or rhino horn is supporting terrorism."

"That must have been a hard story to do. The cruelty those bastards inflict on animals is criminal," Kat added. "It hurts to even think about it. But we have to think about it, to stop it. What about the title, *The Ivory Reel*? I assume ivory refers to tusks, but what's the reel?"

"*The Ivory Reel* is a Scottish dance tune. I'm surprised you didn't know that."

"I've never heard it. Will it be in the soundtrack?"

"Yes. I don't remember how it goes, but it's lively. They'll play it under a series of shots that depict the wardens looking for poachers while the poachers watch for wardens, almost like a dance."

"When's the release?"

"Well, they've started post-production, and we'll have to do a lot of ADR and CGI—you know, additional dialogue recording and computer-generated imaging? They plan a UK release in November, next year. You'll get it after that."

"You keep doing films that are hard for me to watch," Kat complained, "but I want to see this one, anyway."

After silently taking in the view, relaxing, lost in their own thoughts for several minutes, Jamie asked, "You thirsty? I am."

"Yeah, I wish we'd brought some water." She watched him get up. "I don't suppose you know a safer way down, do you?"

Jamie took her hand to help her up. "Em... let me look." He walked along the edge of their perch—closer to it than Kat would have liked—looking down for a trail. "I don't see one. I'm sorry. But if you fall, I'll carry you back." He gave her the sort of grin brothers do when teasing their sisters about something that scares them.

She wasn't amused and didn't reply. Jamie must have sensed her fear as he tried to reassure her. "Just follow me. I'll show you where to put your feet. And if you lose your footing, I will catch you. I promise."

"Yeah? And who's going to catch you?" She'd been an idiot to follow him up there. Why did she want to impress him? He wasn't a potential boyfriend or employer, and even if he had been, nobody was worth this. Now she had no choice; she couldn't stay on this ledge forever. "Ian McKellen would have sent eagles," she muttered.

Jamie chuckled at her *Lord of the Rings* reference, pointed out the flat spaces they had used climbing up the rocks, then got on his knees and reached one foot down behind him, feeling for the first step.

He took another step down and looked up at her. She couldn't hide her apprehension. Falling and having to be carried to the cabin, then hauled off to Truckee Forest Hospital would have been humiliating. Ruining Jamie's & Bill's day and imposing on them would make it worse.

Jamie gave her an understanding smile and motioned to follow him.

Well, at least I'm not carrying a fifty-pound pack this time. She knelt on the edge of the rock and cautiously stretched her right leg down the side. Jamie took her boot and pulled it to the first step, farther down than she would have liked.

"There you go. Now, step about ten inches below and to the left of that one. I'll help you find it." His voice was reassuring, and he pushed her boot to the left until she found the narrow, flat place in the rock. Kat clung to every crevice she could hold on the way down the side of those rocks, conscious of the fact that Jamie was looking up at her backside—not her favorite feature.

When she got close enough to the ground, he put both hands on her waist to guide her down. "You made it!" He hugged her and must have felt her heart pounding as though it would burst through her sweatshirt.

"Thank you." Breathing heavily, Kat held onto him as though she could still fall. Her knees were weak. She was relieved to be on the gently sloping ground, and a little ticked off at Jamie for pushing her to do something dangerous. And at herself for doing it. But she tried not to show it as she pulled away from him to sit on a boulder.

"How are your knees?"

"Okay," she fibbed, massaging them both. They were weak and wobbly, but she wanted to hide that, and prayed they wouldn't give out now. Hiking down the trail to the sounds of squirrels and jays chattering at each other, Jamie stayed close behind her. To get her mind off the climb, Kat made idle conversation. "Have you seen any flying squirrels?"

"No. You have them, here?"

"Yeah, but I've never seen one. They can glide more than a hundred feet. I'd like to see that."

"Maybe someday you'll get lucky."

Me? Get lucky? Yeah, right... in my dreams.

Chapter 16: Three's Not Always a Crowd

As they opened the cabin door, Jamie's and Kat's voices woke Bill, who had fallen asleep on the sofa with a book on his chest. He sat up quickly, opened his book, and cleared his throat.

Jamie checked his watch. "It's lunchtime. Let's start cooking."

With eyebrows raised, Kat turned toward him. "Cooking?"

"Yeah." Bill yawned and stretched. "You think men can't cook?"

"No; I've known some guys who were good cooks."

Bill stepped in front of Kat, put his hand on her shoulder and looked her in the eyes like a father about to lecture a teenager. "Well, Miss Wildlife, we're going to grill steaks, corn on the cob, and garlic bread. What do you think of that?"

"Love it. What can I do to help?"

"Nothing," Jamie replied as he moved food from the refrigerator to the counter. "Have a seat, make yourself comfortable, and keep us company while we mess up the kitchen."

"Okay... I was going to offer to drive us to a restaurant, but this is better."

"No, thanks. Jamie told me about your driving," Bill said dryly, watching for Jamie's reaction. Bill's mischievous grin made it clear he was trying to embarrass his friend.

A guy who was usually unflappable, Jamie appeared flustered. "I told you she really knew her way around San Francisco." Then to Kat, "He's just trying to make you think

I'm a git. If we *were* going out, I'd want you to drive. I've seen enough of Bill's biscuit-arsed truck."

"Hey, that's a working truck, not one of your spoiled-TV-star limos." He winked at Kat, picked up a bag of charcoal briquettes, and went outside.

The friendship between these guys was classic—full of minor insults for each other, yet never hurtful. They obviously enjoyed each other's company, and Kat enjoyed being their audience. She felt like they had invited her into an exclusive club—a feeling she lost when she gave up broadcasting.

She missed being part of something special. Not that being a spokesperson for her state wasn't special; but work was tightly controlled, and the slightest error could end one's career.

"Your knees okay?" Jamie seemed concerned as he brought her a glass of iced tea.

"Yes... I'm sorry I'm not as athletic as you."

"I'm sorry I didn't ask you about climbing."

Bill came back inside, and as he and Jamie worked together in the kitchen, Kat couldn't help but notice the contrasts between them. Stick-figure-thin Jamie moved gracefully, like a dancer. He was clean-shaven, with auburn hair, and from some angles, his chin appeared a little weak. And those heart-stopping blue eyes...

Bill was a healthier weight for a tall man. He sported a full beard and moustache on a firm chin, and had broad shoulders, warm brown eyes, a tan, and multi-shaded-blond hair with bangs that fell onto his forehead. He looked like her image of a 1960s surfer. From his few gray hairs and laugh lines, Kat guessed he was in his fifties.

She found both men attractive, but Jamie was special. An unusually gentle kindness seemed to radiate from him. It contradicted his self-centered womanizer reputation.

"Oh, Kat," Jamie said, "we haven't seen any bears yet! Are you sure you have them here?"

"Yep. Don't feel like the Lone Ranger. I've spent time in these mountains almost every year of my life, and I've never seen one in-person, either. We've been lucky. I'll bet the cabins around here have bear-proof garbage cans."

"You'd win that bet." Bill grinned. "Ours is so good, 'Morning Bear' Jamie couldn't open it." His implication that Jamie was weak didn't sit well with the man slicing mushrooms.

"I could, soon as you showed me the trick. It's human-proof until you know how it works."

Bill continued, "One of the waitresses in town told us about some bear break-ins and said we were smart to get advice from Fish and Game."

"Wildlife," Kat politely corrected him.

"What's the difference? Wasn't it always Fish and Game?"

"Yes, but the legislature changed our name to Wildlife because we do a lot more than manage hunting and fishing. We study and protect endangered species and their habitats. We work to exclude invasive species, review timber harvest plans, and deal with pollution, too. Since we work with all the wild plants and animals in California, 'Wildlife' is more accurate than Fish and Game. All game animals are wildlife, but not all wildlife are game."

"How much did *that* cost us?"

"I don't know, but we're not wasting any existing materials. The law prohibits us from replacing anything until it would've had to be replaced, anyway. The business card I gave you has the old name. I've got a box of those that'll probably last until I retire."

Bill looked at Jamie and raised his eyebrows. "When do you expect to do that?"

"If the Tea Party people have their way, ten years after I'm dead." She didn't know when she would be able to retire with enough pension to live on, but she wasn't about to let

Jamie and Bill know she would be old enough in eleven years.

Bill went outside to put the steaks on the barbecue, while Jamie set the salad on the table. Feeling useless, Kat asked, "Can't I do anything to help? I'm not used to just sitting around, while people wait on me."

"You're not? Hasn't anyone ever cooked for you while you relaxed?"

"Not since I grew tall enough to set the table. It feels strange to do nothing while you guys do all the work."

"Well, get over that. No one should always have to work. Everyone should be waited on, sometimes. Today it's your turn." He flipped the pepper shaker and easily caught it with one hand. "Besides, after that ordeal I put you through, you need it. And maybe a pint and an hour on a psychologist's sofa."

Kat looked down, rubbing one knee. "It wasn't that bad," she said, softly, embarrassed at how frightened she had been, earlier. It didn't seem as awful in the safety of the cabin. Still, she didn't want to do anything like it again. "You were nice to want to share that magnificent view."

Jamie gave her an understanding look. Some guys would have written her off for being afraid of falling. Of course, he still might. Maybe he was only being nice now, while she was there.

* * *

Jamie couldn't help but be impressed with Kat for doing something that had caused serious injuries the last time she did it, and scared her enough to make her heart pound as hard as it did. Most of the women he knew wouldn't drive two hours to just hang out with two scruffy guys in a cabin, much less hike through the woods and do something that frightened them. Right then, he wished he and she were alone.

The tantalizing aroma of steaks sizzling on the fire came through the window, and they both acknowledged being hungry as Bill stuck his head in the door. "Steaks are almost done. You got everything ready, in here?"

Jamie nodded and Bill disappeared. A moment later, he came in, handed the plate with the steaks to Jamie, grabbed another plate and ran back out to get the corn and garlic bread. Mouth-watering aromas escaped their foil pouches.

Jamie stopped unwrapping one of them and asked Kat, who had joined him at the table, "I should have asked first... do you like garlic?"

"Are you kidding? With a name like Mancini?" She reached into the foil and took a slice of garlic bread. "My father was Italian; I have garlic in my veins."

"Oh, of course. What about your mother?"

"English and Scottish."

Bill was more interested in his steak. "Can I cook, or can I cook?"

"You can cook!" Jamie and Kat said—in unison, as if they had rehearsed it—then cracked up.

The lunch was perfect, and while no one said it, Jamie suspected they all would have liked to relax afterward. Instead, they made a healthier choice to walk to the lake and follow a bike trail on the shoreline.

They got back to the cabin after four, and the sun was setting on the mountains above Tahoe's west shore. "I'd better hit the road," Kat said. "Thank you both. I've really enjoyed spending the day with you; and lunch was delicious."

As Jamie walked her to her car, she asked, "How long will you be here?"

"We leave tomorrow, and Tuesday I fly back to L.A. to promote *First Impressions, Last Rites*. It opens here, Friday."

"Well, thank you for inviting me up. It's been fun. Except for the cliff climbing."

As she opened the door and tossed her jacket and waist pack inside, Jamie gently pulled her close, wrapped his arms around her, and gave her a full-body hug. She hugged him back, and he kissed the top of her head. "Thank you for coming." Hugging Kat felt good, and her hair smelled nice. He wanted to hold her a lot longer and ask her to spend the night, but she had already said 'no' once.

He put one finger under her chin and raised it. Feeling no resistance, he kissed her. Her lips were soft and warm, like the rest of her body pressed against his. As his attraction manifested in his lower torso, he reluctantly pulled away from her.

* * *

Jamie's kiss surprised Kat. She hadn't kissed anyone in years, and living alone, she never got enough hugs. In Jamie's arms she remembered how good it felt to be loved, even though she knew that wasn't why he hugged her. His warmth and the feeling of his strong heartbeat sent a warm sensation through her.

When he kissed her, her cheeks flushed. He was so warm, so gentle... a shiver ran down her spine and a pleasant sensation long absent from her life pulsed through her. *Oh, please don't stop; this feels wonderful.*

On the way home, she relived their parting scene in her mind. Damn... if only she were ten years younger... and brave enough to take a chance again... But this man would rip her heart out if she let him.

After that day in the mountains, Jamie started sending her email notes about his activities and asking what she was up to. Her attraction to him grew, despite logic.

A week later, he called her at work. "I'm in New York, doing non-stop promotion. What are you up to? Done any rock climbing lately?"

"Yeah... I scaled El Capitan yesterday."

Jamie laughed. "Sorry—I couldn't resist. How warm are you?"

"About ninety-eight-point-six... Oh, you mean outside? Low fifties. How's New York?"

"Cold and rainy. I'd rather be in California... with you."

"Well, come on out, and bring the rain with you; we need it. I have a guest room, and you're welcome to it, any time." She knew he'd never take her up on it.

* * *

Kat's offer took Jamie by surprise. A guest room? No woman had ever offered him her guest room. "Thanks, I'll keep that in mind," he said, even more attracted to her as she kept a protective wall between them.

When he returned to London, he thought about sending her a Christmas gift—maybe something related to animals or music. Or rock-climbing.

Chapter 17: Sea Otter Voice-Overs

It took Kat months to learn and jump through all the hoops SAG-AFTRA required to let one of their celebrity members volunteer to do unpaid voice work.

"Learning which agent represents a popular, successful actor isn't easy," she told her supervisor, Ron. "They don't exactly broadcast that information, and since agents earn commission on the work they get actors, they're not likely to be enthusiastic about a job that pays nothing. Even if a performer cared about wildlife, the agent might say no, and not even tell her we asked."

"Well, you've done what Susan wanted. Send her the information and copy me. She may have dropped the idea, by now."

Susan hadn't dropped it. She asked Kat how to contact Jamie's agent.

"Jamie Knight? Why do you want *his* agent?"

"I want to see if we can get him to do something special for us, like a warden recruitment video. Since he's been here and knows us..."

Knows you? Kat didn't want to ask Jamie and have him think she was taking advantage of their friendship. But Susan would never believe Kat if she said she couldn't get the information. She called TV production people she knew to learn Jamie's agent was Victor Harrington, at a big international agency. She searched for a Los Angeles office. *No—don't make it easy. Make Susan call London, if she wants him.*

Two weeks later, Ron came into Kat's office. "You're not going to like this."

"What?" All the things that could go wrong at work ran through Kat's mind.

"Susan got a celebrity to do pro bono voice work for us." He looked at the piles of paper, books, and folders on her desk.

"You're kidding. That was fast. Who? What project?"

Ron stared at the floor for at least five silent seconds that seemed like minutes. Finally he took a deep breath and said, "Jamie Knight. PSAs for the Sea Otter Fund."

"WHAT?" Of all the tasks her job entailed, voicing those public service announcements was Kat's favorite. She wanted to rip Susan's lungs out.

"I'm sorry. I told her how much you love to do that, but she thinks Jamie's voice will bring in more money than yours. You still have the Endangered Species Fund. At least she didn't ask him to do both of them." Ron gave her an empathetic look, but he couldn't change the situation. When Susan wanted something, it got done, no matter what anyone else thought.

Thanksgiving week, Jamie called Kat at work with an upbeat, "Hi, how are you?"

"Fine." Her tone was bitter.

"What's wrong?"

"What do you *think*?" Kat got up and closed her office door, steaming mad.

"I don't know. How could I?"

"The Sea Otter Fund PSAs? I told you how much I love doing those, and you come along and take them away from me—the best part of my job. Damn it, Jamie! Isn't it enough to be rich and famous, doing what you love for a living, and getting all the voice work you already get? Did you have to steal *my* gig, too?" She wouldn't even try to hide her resentment.

"Steal...?" Jamie asked. "Wait a minute. I didn't *steal* your gig."

"My boss says you did."

"Some woman representing your governor called my agent and begged him to ask me to do those spots. I agreed because I figured you were behind it. Geez, Kat... I thought I was doing you a favor. Don't go off on me!"

"Oh, no..." Kat squeezed her eyes shut. She had never heard him speak in anger, but she couldn't miss it now. "Ron didn't tell me *that*... I thought... and after I told you how much I love recording... what that little bit of voice work meant to me... I'm sorry."

"You should be. How could you think I would take something away from you? Or that I need to do volunteer work for your government? It's not as if I'm sitting around with nothing else to do."

"I'm sorry, Jamie. I was wrong to..." Bzzzt. *What was that?* Click. "Jamie?... Are you still there? Jamie?" The phone line was dead. Had he hung up on her? Kat set the receiver in the phone cradle and stared at it for a few minutes. Was he angry? Didn't he hear her apologize? Did he think he was too important to tolerate anyone else's ire? *He didn't say goodbye or anything; he just hung up.*

Or was it her fault? Why did she assume he would intentionally hurt her? That was stupid. It wasn't the first time she had jumped to a negative conclusion, been wrong, and later regretted it. Why couldn't she assume the people in her life always meant well? Because sometimes they hadn't. People who had smiled and pretended to be her friends had screwed her over too often. That hurt, but didn't justify the assumption that everyone might turn on her.

More than an hour after Jamie's call, the CDW director's office notified all staff that the building's phone system had failed and could take a full day to repair. Relieved to know Jamie hadn't hung up on her, Kat tried calling him on her cell phone, but—as usual—it didn't work. There was something about a coating on the windows that deflected cellular signals as well as sunshine. She had to go to a meeting so couldn't go outside to call right away. By the time she went to lunch with some colleagues, her mind was on wildlife habitat and had forgotten about Jamie until that evening, when it was too late to call London. So she phoned the next day, got his voice mail and left a message.

The following week, she received Jamie's PSA recordings from someone named Dan Francesci, at Ealing Studios in London. He included a friendly note wishing her luck raising money.

When she played them for her colleagues, Keith reminded her of his Jamie-fanatic daughter. "Rachel is still going to kill you. With Jamie Knight asking for donations, she'd file a tax return just so she could contribute, if she had any money."

Kat had to admit Jamie's delivery of her scripts was perfect. His voice had a smooth, rich timbre, he sounded sincere, and his English accent would catch listeners' ears. Now she felt even worse about yelling at him for "stealing" her voice-over glory. *If anyone gives me anything for Christmas this year, let it be the self-censoring mechanism I lack and the brains to think, before I get angry.*

She still hadn't heard from Jamie, so she called again to thank him for the PSAs, apologize, and explain why his last call had ended abruptly. Again, he didn't answer. She left another message. He must've been more shallow than she had thought, to drop her for being mad at him because of misinformation. Was he really such a diva?

Kat usually felt isolated at Thanksgiving and Christmas. Society's hype about idealized holidays with loved ones always made her feel like a loser. Aside from Barbara—who spent the holidays with her adult children—her only relatives in California were a cousin she never heard from and her mother. Lidia's dementia made her unaware of holidays, but

Kat always decorated her room, spent Christmas with her, and tried to revive her best memories.

Christmas Eve, Kat got up early to call Jamie during London's early afternoon and wish him a "Happy Christmas," as they say. After eight rings, her call went to voice mail—again. She left another message and wondered if he was ignoring her calls. Suddenly there wasn't enough oxygen. Yes, she liked him more than she had admitted to herself.

Bitterness slowly devoured the hope Kat woke up with— bitterness about not being promoted and about all the holidays she had spent alone. This year, it hurt more than usual. She had lost a new friend—and the first man she'd been physically attracted to in a decade. She would probably never hear from him again and that saddened her so much she became apathetic about things around her home—not depressed, but feeling nearly as bad.

Molly was sympathetic, but advised, "You need to stop being so defensive about what you think is your turf."

She was right. Kat's fear of losing the fun parts of her job likely arose from her years in radio and TV, where there were people who would have slit her throat to get her air shift or any job on a network show. But government work wasn't that competitive. It was time to throw out her defensive mind-set.

When she was home, Kellye and Jeremy couldn't get enough lap time and wouldn't leave Kat alone. Holding them was comforting, as she mentally kicked herself for apparently killing a nice friendship with the most interesting man she had met in many years.

Keeping busy that winter helped take her mind off Jamie some of the time. She applied for a job at State Parks that would be a promotion. She and Janet played in the quartet at Burns Suppers honoring Scottish bard Robert Burns, and the Scottish Fiddlers rehearsed for the

Sacramento Highland Games, which she and Molly worked to publicize, every January through April.

At work, Kat ramped up her campaign to publicize the two wildlife funds. For the first time, she had purchased magazine ads for them, including one in *Palm Springs Life*. It hit newsstands during a big film festival, and she hoped some Hollywood high-rollers would notice it and donate.

* * *

Kat's assumption that Jamie had taken her favorite voice-over task had caught him off-guard. That she'd hung up on him had surprised him even more. He couldn't remember the last time anyone had done that, and it was like a slap in the face.

Hurt and annoyed, he thought, *to hell with her,* and went about preparing for a month-long holiday with his parents, sister, and a widowed aunt. But after two weeks of skiing and family time, she was still on his mind, still perplexing him. This would be such a romantic place to be alone with her, and she would appreciate the awesome beauty of these mountains.

While in a village with wi-fi, he had to call her and find out why she'd hung up on him. But she didn't answer her phone. Was she so hacked-off she wouldn't take his call? No point in leaving a message, then.

In Zurich after Christmas, waiting for the flight home, Jamie checked his voice mail, hoping Kat had left a message for him. She hadn't. Neither had anyone else. Wait—he'd been away nearly a month, and no one had called? That couldn't be right. Now he had more to worry about. There should have been some calls about work, if nothing else.

He called his phone company as soon as he got home. Someone had hacked their servers on Christmas Day, and thousands of their customers' voice mail accounts had been compromised. They apologized and were shoring up their security, but all messages had been lost.

That evening Jamie called Kat. Again, he landed in "voicemail-jail." She must've been so mad she wouldn't even speak with him. A sadness he hadn't felt in a long time overtook him. How had he grown so fond of someone he had seen only a few times?

At the Palm Springs Film Festival in early January, Jamie schmoozed with Hollywood power brokers and did interviews to promote *First Impressions, Last Rites*. While waiting for his director and a co-star in the lobby of their luxury resort, he flipped through a local magazine. A full-page picture of an adorable sea otter in a blue ocean with some familiar text caught his eye—an ad for the Sea Otter Fund. *Kat didn't tell me she ran magazine ads.*

When his director arrived, Jamie showed it to him. "I voiced the radio announcements for this. The woman who runs this P.R. campaign is a friend." He wouldn't normally have gotten excited about something like that, but he was proud to be associated with the good cause the eye-catching ad promoted, regardless of whatever was happening with Kat. He bought a copy to take home.

Jamie told Bill about Kat's surprising, angry outburst, how she had hung up on him, and wouldn't take or return his calls.

"I miss her, but I guess there's no future there. Still, when I'm out with other women, I catch myself thinking about Plain-Jane Kat. What's wrong with me?"

"Nothing," Bill said. "Kat's no glamor girl, but she's attractive enough. She's nice, funny, smart, and doesn't seem to want anything from you. There are worse things women can do than chew you out for something you didn't do. You should call her again."

"I don't know... I've tried at least three times but my call always goes to voice mail. Apparently she doesn't want to talk to me. I'm afraid she's walked out of my life."

At home after the film festival, Jamie voiced a car advert and spent time with friends. He, Peter, and cinematographer Paul Andersen fantasized about having their own production company. When out on dates, he couldn't help but compare the women to Kat. They were prettier, thinner and better-dressed. They couldn't compete with her, intellectually, but none of them ever yelled at him.

One—Amanda—was a high-rolling CEO's daughter. She didn't need to work, but was a fashion designer's assistant and part-time model for fun. She was the kind of willowy, long-haired lady who looked good on Jamie's arm and knew people who might be in a position to help him add directing to his résumé, someday. Her personality was sweeter than Kat's. No wise-cracks or debates. She seldom disagreed with Jamie about anything.

That winter, Jamie made his agent and publicist happy by making Amanda his most frequent public companion. His mother continued pushing Trissy at him, in vain.

He missed Kat's wit and broad knowledge base, and her independence—when she wasn't going spare on him. *I wonder what she's doing.*

At several winter social events in London, Amanda glowed at Jamie's side, and the media gossips prattled about what a cute couple they made. They had met more than a year earlier, but hadn't dated before.

As Jamie got comfortable with her, he shared the confidential plot of a *Nigel Stone* episode he was shooting. Amanda couldn't keep it to herself. She told a gossip columnist, and even told the columnist where she got the scoop. *Nigel Stone's* producers were livid. The storylines of episodes were tightly-held secrets until they aired.

When Jamie asked Amanda about it, she became defensive. "You and your little TV show aren't nearly as important as you think. It's no big deal."

"Sorry? Keeping the stories secret builds up anticipation among viewers. It's worth hundreds of thousands of pounds in adverts, based on the size of our audience. That's important to everyone involved with the show, not only me. I trusted you, and you couldn't keep your mouth shut."

"Then you should have kept *your* mouth shut," Amanda fired back. "If you couldn't keep it secret, why should I? Besides, it's good publicity for the show. You should thank me."

"Are you daft? You've damaged my credibility! As for publicity, the BBC have professionals handling that. They don't need help from amateurs."

"Don't call me an amateur, you wanker. I know more than you do about marketing. You're just cheesed-off because I got a little publicity. It's not all about you, Knight!"

"It is, now." Jamie handed Amanda her purse and coat. "You betrayed my trust, and that's unacceptable. We're through."

He opened the door and she stormed out. "Go sod yourself, knob-head!"

Tempted to call her something, he bit his tongue. Closing the door harder than he usually did, he made sure the electric gate closed behind her as she drove away. In the kitchen, he poured himself a whisky. The bottle of Scotch in his hand reminded him of Kat. At least *she* only got mad at him on the phone. Amanda had betrayed him in public.

Chapter 18: New Beginnings?

Over dinner with Leigh and Bob Penrose—whose married life now appealed to him—Jamie searched for answers. "What *is* it with women? Right when I think I've found someone special, she does something stupid or rips into me. Why can't I meet a nice, intelligent, honorable woman who likes me for *me*—not my profession—and won't use me for money or publicity? Someone trustworthy, who has a sense of humor and common sense..."

"Because women like that aren't interested in Lotharios, no matter how cute or rich you are," Leigh replied. "They're interested in men who want to be their partners and build a life together." She gave him a look that reminded him that's why he lost *her*. "And you know who you're describing, don't you?"

Jamie silently gazed at his plate for a minute before looking at her. "Kat?"

Leigh nodded. "At least that's what you told *me* about her."

"Yeah... but she won't return my calls. And the last time we spoke, she was hacked-off and hung up on me."

"Why was she hacked-off?" Bob asked.

"Someone at her work got Victor to have me do some public service announcements that had always been *her* voice work—her favorite part of her job. They made her think I had gone after it, taken it from her. So when I rang her before we went on holiday, she gave me shit."

"And you still want to see her?" Bob looked at Jamie as if he were daft.

"Well, she apologized after I told her the truth," Jamie said. "Then she hung up on me."

"Perhaps she was embarrassed," Leigh said. "If she guards her job like a Scottish wildcat, maybe there's a reason. Why don't you ring her again?"

Bob stepped in with authoritarian certainty. "You can have any woman you want, Jamie. Why waste time on someone who isn't perfect for you already?"

"Bob, you know very well that no one is perfect for anyone," Leigh said. "If that had been my attitude, you and I never would have dated, much less married."

She turned to Jamie. "And *you*... think of all the times someone has forgiven you for doing something someone didn't like. When you talked about Kat, she sounded like the woman you just described, and you looked so happy... your fondness for her was obvious. Don't let her get away so easily. She probably misses you, too."

Jamie gave a lot of thought to what they—and Bill—said. The following week, he called her. *Her advert is a good excuse. If she goes off on me again, this'll be the last time.*

Kat seemed pleased to hear from him, but sounded reserved, almost business-like. She said she was fine, but didn't sound the same as she had before. Was she mad at him or walking on eggshells? Jamie wasn't as warm as he had been, either. It seemed they both wanted to talk, but needed to wipe the slate clean before they could try again.

"Your PSAs sound great," Kat told him. "Again, I apologize... I really *am* sorry for thinking you'd screw me over, and... and for being a bitch about it."

Jamie paused. He had never known a woman to call herself that and mean it. "It's okay," he said in a calm, comforting voice. "I understand why you were upset. But I wish you would have asked me how it came about, before assuming I would take something from you."

"I wish I had, too."

"And I wish you hadn't hung-up on me."

"What? Wait. I didn't hang-up on you. In fact, I thought *you'd* hung-up on *me* until I learned a street construction crew cut the phone cable to my building and the whole system crashed. Every phone line was dead for more than a day. I called you three times to explain, last December, and you never returned my calls. I thought you were mad at me for getting mad at you."

"No, I never got your messages," Jamie confessed. "My phone company was hacked on Christmas and they lost everyone's voice mail."

"I called twice before Christmas—"

"When I was in the Alps. That's why I called—to tell you I was going on holiday with my family to a remote village where they had no wi-fi or mobile service, and I'd be incommunicado until after Christmas."

"Oh, my god... and all this time I thought you were ticked-off at me—"

"And I thought the same of you," Jamie interrupted and laughed. "This sounds like an old Laurel and Hardy routine. Or Abbott and Costello."

"Yeah, it would be funny, if it hadn't hurt so much." Kat couldn't keep all her pain to herself. "I didn't realize how much I enjoy your company until I thought you'd never speak to me again."

"Oh, Kat... you're sweet. And now you know that's not the case." Now he wanted to see her again, even more than before.

* * *

Each February, Kat's elderly neighbor, Jo, came over to watch the Academy Awards with her. This year, Jo joined her for the British Academy of Film and Television Arts—BAFTA—film awards, two weeks before the Oscars.

They never watched the "Red Carpet arrivals," where people from shows like *Entertainment Tonight* babbled about the actors' clothing—especially the sleazy dresses that exposed way too much of women's bodies. Jo shared Kat's love of jeans and tennis shoes, and the view that high fashion was frivolous window-dressing and a waste of money. "Who cares?" Kat always asked. "The awards are about the work these people do, not a three-hour commercial for fashion designers." But this time, since she wanted to see Jamie and he might be on that part of it, she turned the TV on early.

With Kellye and Jeremy competing for her attention, she hoped Jamie would appear early and spare her the fashion nonsense. Forty-five mind-numbing minutes after it began, he still hadn't appeared, until—behind the talking heads—a young female group in the bleachers began squealing. As usual, he smiled, waved at the crowd, and put his hands together in a polite gesture. Was that thanks or Namaste?

In a tailored black tux, he looked more like James Bond than anyone since Sean Connery. A London chat show host asked him the same stupid question they ask everyone: "Who are you wearing?" Nothing about his movie or the nominations. He named an Italian designer.

After the dumb question, he turned to a red-head who hovered behind him and they left together. She looked business-like, much older than Jamie, and wasn't dressed like a nominee's date. She was probably either his publicist or manager. Jamie's moment in the spotlight only lasted a few seconds. Then the interviewer was talking to some teenager.

Jo rang the doorbell shortly before the actual show began. Kat brought out the tea and crumpets as they settled in to enjoy two hours of British humor and film clips.

"Jamie called me last week, and you won't believe all the weird events that caused each of us to think the other was ignoring and pulling away from us," she told Jo. The first commercial break gave her enough time to tell the tale of misunderstandings and get another laugh out of it.

In the BAFTA Film Awards, Jamie was nominated for Best Actor in a Supporting Role for his portrayal of a dirty cop in *First Impressions, Last Rites.* But a friend of his won the award for playing a more difficult role, and Jamie applauded enthusiastically for him.

After the show, Kat sent him a "condolences" email. His loss was a legitimate reason to make contact and—she hoped—put a bandage on the verbal cut she'd inflicted in November. She wrote several drafts. The one she intended to be funny seemed flippant; another read like one of her news releases. Finally, she wrote from her heart:

> It was nice to see you at the BAFTAs, Jamie. You looked terrific. I'm sorry you and *First Impressions* didn't win. You were gracious to cheer the people who did. You're such a skilled actor, it won't be long before you win that honor. Go knock 'em dead at the Academy!
> Best wishes,
> Kat

Thursday after the BAFTAs, Jamie surprised her by calling her at work. "You know I'll be in L.A. for the Academy Awards."

"I didn't know, but I hope you guys win, there."

"Thank you, but don't bet on it. Em... would you like some company, the week after?"

Kat froze. "Uh... depends on who the company is."

"An actor I know who would like to get away from it all and go swimming."

She smiled. "Anyone I know?"

"You met him in London last May. He's a fairly nice bloke, and he'd probably buy you an Amaretto if you'd go out with him."

Unable to play it straight, Kat cracked up. In her best desperate, 'helpless female' character voice, she gushed, "Oh, yes! Anything for Amaretto! Please give him my address."

Jamie laughed. "All right, but you'll have to give it to *me*, first."

"Got a pen?" She gave him her address, then said, "Wait a minute. You're not going to drive up here, are you?"

"Oh, no. I'll fly up and get a car at the airport. Sacramento, right?"

"Yes, but you don't need to rent a car. I can pick you up. The airport is only fifteen minutes from my office. Have you made your reservation yet?"

"No, I didn't assume you'd say yes. But now, I'll have my P.A. book the flights. You don't need to pick me up. I have to be back in London on Saturday. Can you be free from the twenty-fourth to the twenty-sixth?"

"Probably." Kat was ahead of schedule on all her projects and had months of unused vacation time. "I really wouldn't mind driving out to get you. Send me your flight information, and I'll meet you at the escalator you'll have to take to leave the airport. By the way, it's not exactly swimming weather. The pool is freezing."

"Sorry? Frozen?"

"Well, not actually frozen. But it *feels* freezing when I stick my arm in to test the chemicals. It may be fifty-five degrees... Fahrenheit."

"That's not cold. I swim in the lakes and ponds here, and they're colder than that. As long as I can warm up when I get out..."

I'll warm you up. She quickly censored her inner Mae West. "Of course. The house will be warm, and I'll make you a pot of tea."

"Can I get a hot shower to rinse off the chlorine?" he teased, as if California had completely dried up.

"Sure; the city hasn't turned the water off, yet. You can have anything you want here." She cringed. *Oh, crap. I hope that didn't sound suggestive.* If it did, he didn't let on.

He hesitated for a moment. Perhaps he wasn't sure he should depend on her for transportation. "All right, then. I'll text you my flight information. It'll be nice to see you again."

"You, too, Jamie. Hey—at the BAFTAs, a red-haired woman looked like she was sort-of... herding you. Is she your publicist?"

"Yeah, Judy. She got on-camera?"

"Briefly. Good luck with the Academy. Jo and I will be watching with our fingers crossed for you."

"Who's Joe?"

"My kitty-sitter, and a dear friend. She always watches the awards shows with me."

"Oh. Good. Well... see you on the twenty-fourth, then."

* * *

Jamie gazed out the window at the rain sparkling in the landscape lights as it drenched his garden. He would be rushed, blinded by paparazzi, emotionally exhausted, and disappointed at the Oscars. It would be nice to see Kat where she lived and enjoy two quiet days in Northern California. Lying on the sofa holding a script to memorize, he gazed into the crackling fire, twiddled the remote control and wished he had someone there to share the cozy evening.

When the phone rang, he decided he should be more specific when wishing for something. It was Mairi McMillan, an actor who occasionally appeared on *Nigel Stone.* She had been trying to get something going with Jamie ever since he'd taken her out—once—a few years earlier, and seemed oblivious to his polite refusals. He gave her credit for her determination, but wished she'd accept the fact that he wasn't interested.

"What'cha doin'?" Mairi asked. She had a lovely Irish dialect, but Jamie would rather not hear it on his private line.

"Going over the script for tomorrow."

"You want to work on our lines together... over breakfast?"

Oh, please... give it up. "No. I have a busy day scheduled. I'll see you on the set." His tone was strictly business. He had been nicer in the past, but Mairi refused to take "no" for an answer. He was still polite, but unmistakably cool.

"All right." Her disappointment was obvious. "Just thought I'd ask. See you tomorrow."

He hung up the phone, hated being rude, and cursed whoever gave Mairi his home phone number.

* * *

In a meeting with biologists at Department of Wildlife headquarters, Kat's mind kept drifting from the Science Institute to Jamie's visit.

Must clean the house thoroughly before he arrives... Should I try cooking or take him out? Where? What would he want to do besides swim? He said he wanted to get away from it all... maybe he'll want to relax where no one will take his picture or write about his love life. She was curious about that, but would never ask such personal questions.

After the meeting, she asked Ron for the three days off that Jamie would be there.

"No," Ron said, "you need to be here to push the tax donation funds."

Kat's heart stopped. "They're pushed. I've finished the contracts, sent the PSAs, and program managers are reviewing the draft news release for March. I'm ahead on everything."

"I don't know..."

"If something comes up, call me at home, and I'll handle it. I wouldn't ask, if this wasn't a special friend from out-of-state, that I hardly ever get to see."

"Well... I guess, if you'll keep your cell phone on and with you all day..."

"I will. If you need anything, call me and I'll take care of it." She didn't tell him who was coming to visit. Jamie wanted privacy, and she would make sure nobody knew where he was, those three days. Well, almost nobody.

As soon as she got back to her office, she checked to see if Molly was back. She had been out when Jamie called, and Kat was dying to tell her. She was one of the few people who, when asked, would keep even exciting news to herself.

Molly's jaw dropped. Her eyes widened. She stood up and leaned forward with her hands on her desk. "You're kidding! He's flying here, just to spend three days with you? Are you sure he doesn't have something else to do here?"

"No, but if he does, he didn't mention it."

"Where's he staying?"

"I don't know... he didn't say." She paused. "I told him once that he was welcome to my guest room if he ever wanted to get away from it all. Think I should have asked?"

"Yes! I would have. When did you offer him your guest room?"

"Last fall. I never thought he'd take me up on it."

"He probably won't," Molly declared. "He probably thinks he'll wind up in *your* bed. Not that it would be a bad thing. Geez, Kat, has it been so long you don't remember what men are like?"

Kat hadn't told anyone—even Molly—that Jamie had invited her to his place "for a drink" the year before. She didn't know whether he really meant only for a drink, but no one would ever believe she turned him down.

"Oh, please. He sleeps with models and actresses," Kat replied. "Guys like Jamie didn't give me a second look, even when I was *his* age. A cute TV star would never go for someone who looks like me. That's so unrealistic, it doesn't even happen in movies."

"Would you stop putting yourself down? You're not bad-looking. If *you* are, then so are the rest of us, and I take exception to that. Besides, guys like him spend so much time with bimbos looking for fame or a sugar daddy, maybe now he's attracted to independent women who have interesting lives. And he probably still thinks you're his age, unless you've told him."

"Why would I volunteer that?"

"You realize, if he *is* interested in a relationship with you—and if you want that—you'll have to tell him. A good one has to be based on honesty and openness, or it's doomed."

Their role reversal made Kat smile. Usually older friends counsel younger ones. But Molly had been far more successful in love than Kat had ever been.

"Fat chance." She took a deep breath. "It surprised me that he even called, after no communication for two months. I'm nothing more than a friend with a pool and a safe haven where he can escape the paparazzi and girls who act like fools around him."

Molly shook her head as Kat went back to her own office, concealing her excitement. She stared out the window at the parking lot under an overcast sky. Despite her certainty it would never happen, she wished someone she liked as much as Jamie *could* love her.

Chapter 19: And the Winner Is...

The hour and fifty minutes it took the Academy Awards show to get to Jamie's category—Best Actor in a Supporting Role—passed excruciatingly slowly. Kat was so anxious for him, she got up during every commercial break. Jeremy wanted to sit on her lap, but gave up and joined Kellye on the couch, stretching out next to Jo, who gave him the chin-rub he loved.

The fourth time Kat got up, Jo remarked, "I've never seen you this fidgety."

Kat lifted her eyebrows and shrugged.

"You're in love with him, aren't you?"

"No... I just think he's a great actor and deserves to be recognized by the American film industry. They ignore him." She was attracted to him, but not in love.

Jo gave her an "I see through you" look.

"Besides," Kat added, "a guy like Jamie wouldn't even notice someone like me, that way. Men like him all want beautiful, young, long-haired women with perfect figures."

"You look good when you want to, Kat. Stop running yourself down all the time. Isn't he coming here Tuesday? How can you think he's not attracted to you? Even rich men don't fly four hundred miles to see casual friends."

"He would. He flies to France to see car races and tennis matches. Men like him could fund the research that cures cancer with the money they waste."

When the Academy finally awarded the Best Supporting Actor, it wasn't Jamie, but he didn't appear disappointed. He exuded enthusiasm for the same friend who had won the BAFTA.

"He's such a talented actor," Kat said, "who knows what he really feels?"

How did Jamie feel about her? Did he think of her as a friend, or what? Would she have to work her way through a crowd to get to him at the airport? Now that he'd been nominated for an Academy Award, more Americans knew who he was. Took them long enough.

* * *

Jamie got more attention in L.A. than he used to, but not enough to interfere with normal life. Since paparazzi stalk actors at LAX, Bill convinced him to fly from Burbank. Still, in the airports and on the plane, several people who had seen the Oscars recognized him. Some said hello, and two asked him to pose with them for pictures. One asked why he was going to Sacramento. "Visiting friends."

As he stepped onto the escalator at Sacramento International, he scanned the lower level for Kat and relaxed when he spotted her. Was she was as attracted to him as he was to her? He gave her a discreet wave when their eyes met. Her broad smile and sparkling eyes erased any doubt he had about this trip and fueled his desire to hold her. People watched as he gave her a big hug and a kiss. With only a carry-on bag, they left the terminal quickly.

"How was your flight?" Kat asked as they walked to the parking lot.

"Short and sweet. I only got to doze off for a few minutes. Have you ever noticed that Southwest Airlines' seats are larger than United's?"

"Yes, and it fries me that they all keep jamming the rows closer together."

"Next time you come to Britain, you should fly B.A."

"British Airways?"

"Their seats are the best. But I may be biased. I do their adverts."

"I'll bet you fly first class, too. Those seats are comfortable."

Jamie looked down at the pavement. He was a little embarrassed about the luxuries he could afford that most people would never experience. That wouldn't stop him from enjoying them, but he knew Kat, Bill, and other people worked as hard and deserved those comforts as much as he did.

Merging with freeway traffic, she asked, "Have you had lunch?"

"No, we had a large, late breakfast. But if you haven't—"

"No, I'm not hungry." She paused and glanced at him. "You staying at Bill's?"

"Yeah... he said to say hi. He has plenty of room and we always have a good time."

"Do you want to check into your hotel or go straight to the pool?"

"Oh, let's go straight to the pool." Jamie wanted to see Kat's house. People's homes and the way they treat their guests tell you a lot about them, sometimes in ways they don't intend.

He shook his head at the width and openness of the streets and large yards as they drove to Kat's neighborhood. It wasn't the first American suburb he had seen, but the contrast with the world's older cities compelled him to say something.

"I can't believe how much space everyone has here. In most cities, ten times as many people live in the space taken by each of these homes."

"And they're miserable," she replied, "forced to hear other people's arguments, TVs, stereos, and crying babies... smell each other's cooking or cigarette smoke, hope none of their neighbors is dumb enough to smoke in bed, fall asleep, and start a fire... I'd hate living like that... like a bee in a hive. People wouldn't have to live that densely if they hadn't overpopulated their cities."

145

"You're spoiled."

"Maybe. I know how lucky I am to have been born here. But I've lived in apartments, and it sucks. I'll probably have to again, when I'm too old and decrepit to take care of my place. Until then, I cherish my quiet neighborhood and the privacy of my own home and a fenced yard."

"I know what you mean about privacy."

"I'll bet. Doesn't it bug you to be photographed and followed everywhere you go? And to have people who don't even know you speculate about your personal life and write rude things in newspapers and on the web?"

"I hate it. But it's the price of success these days. In fact, it's the only reason I date most of the women I do—to get that publicity."

He watched Kat for a reaction, but got none. "You have to stay in the public eye to get ahead in show business. Unfortunately, gossip and unflattering pictures sell. If the public would stop buying the papers and watching the shows and websites that pay for that rubbish..." He paused. "You've picked up magazines because of scandalous headlines or pictures, haven't you?"

"Nope."

"Oh, come on."

"No. Sometimes I look at the covers of magazines while I wait in the grocery check-out line. But the ones with slanderous headlines and unflattering pictures of people who usually look good turn me off. I'll admit, it's nice to know some women who look perfect on TV actually look like normal people before professional hair and make-up artists transform them. But the tabloids and magazines don't do that to make people like me think we're not ugly. They do it to hurt people, and that's wrong."

What? "It's nice of you to care about people you don't know. Most people envy their good fortune. But Kat... you're not ugly. And I hope you don't think you are."

She said nothing as she reached up to press the garage door control on the visor. Jamie kept looking at her, waiting for a response. She kept her eyes on the road and bit her lip. Did she wish she hadn't revealed her low opinion of her own appearance?

"Here we are," she said. They pulled into the garage of a modest, one-story house behind a half-dead lawn. "Sorry about the yard. It looked better before the drought. I'm going to replace the lawn with drought-tolerant native plants and trees, when we can water again."

They entered the house through a door from the garage into the kitchen—if you could call it a kitchen. It was little more than a passageway between the garage and the living room. Both cats were waiting there, a loud, demanding meow coming from the small tortoiseshell-and-white. The large gray tabby silently backed away when he saw Jamie. "Hello, babies," Kat said.

"These must be your 'fur children'," Jamie said.

"Yep." She reached down to pet each cat. "Meet Kellye and Jeremy. Kitties, this is Jamie." The cats were wary of him, and focused on Kat, likely hoping she had treats. Getting none, they retreated to vantage points on the sofa.

When Jamie didn't pet either of them, as a cat lover would, Kat asked, "Do you like cats? I hope you're not allergic to them."

"Cats are okay, but my family always had dogs."

"Oh. Too bad. Well, if Kellye gets too friendly and bothers you, feel free to gently push her away. She'll get over it. Jeremy is so shy, you'll be lucky if he even gets near you."

Jamie looked around the small but airy living room and dining area with a vaulted ceiling, as Kat opened drapes on the three windows. Her love of Hawaii, marine life, and animals showed in the large prints of tropical beach scenes, humpback whales, and orcas. The furnishings didn't all match, but nothing clashed. They were slightly worn and didn't all look the same age, probably purchased one or two at a time. A wide sliding-glass door revealed the swimming pool surrounded by a tropical-looking landscape. A blue and white-striped surfboard mounted on the wall above a window caught his attention.

"Where do you surf in Sacramento?"

"On the 'Net. The board is just art, now. Let's put your stuff in the guest room. You can change in there if you decide to swim."

"IF?" he asked, as though swimming was the only reason he came here. He followed her down the hall, past a bedroom, a bathroom, and a small room full of plastic storage totes, boxes, and musical instruments. At the end of the hall they entered a small, pale green home office—crowded by a desk, bookcase, computer hutch, and an old newsroom file cabinet, covered in political and radio station bumper stickers from the past four decades. A large window faced the street. A futon and some space in the closet were the only evidence it also served as a guest room.

Jamie decided to peruse the books later. As he followed Kat back to the living room, he saw an electronic keyboard in the apparent storage room. "Do you play piano, too?"

She pulled the messy room's door shut. "Yes, but not very well, anymore. I'm not good at anything but rhythm guitar, now." After a moment she added, "And not everyone thinks I'm good at that." She gave Jamie a look that said, *we both know I'm talking about you.*

"You're never going to let me forget that, are you?"

* * *

Kat just smiled as they walked back to the living room. "There's the 'loo,' and my room. So... what would you like to do? Swim? Take the five-cent tour of the backyard? Go somewhere? Would you like something to drink?"

"Water, please; then let's see the garden." After taking a long drink, he looked around and said, "You live here by yourself? Don't you get lonely?"

"No. Well, occasionally... Valentine's Day and Christmas, when advertisers try to make people feel like losers if we don't have lovers or families. Then I feel left out. Businesses use those images to goad us into putting more of *our* money into *their* pockets.

She paused then added, "Not that I've ever said 'no' to a box of dark chocolates... Come on outside." She opened the glass slider to the large backyard and wondered if Jamie didn't live alone.

"Nice pool. How big is it?"

She grinned. *Men's obsession with size...* "Big enough to satisfy *me*."

Jamie raised one eyebrow.

"Twenty by forty feet," she added.

A fragrant star jasmine encircled a wooden post that supported an old, faded arbor. "That doesn't normally flower until April, but this winter has been so warm and dry, everything bloomed early; even the daffodils." As they strolled around the yard, Kat identified plants: "Chinese pistache, agapanthus, fatsia japonica..."

"Brilliant. Did you plant all of this?"

"Most of it. I paid someone else to install the lawn and flagstone."

"Well done," Jamie said. "So... let's swim."

"*You're* swimming. I'm on lifeguard duty. I started the solar heat system as soon as I knew you were coming, but the water is still only sixty-two. The panels need two weeks of hot days to heat all that water to seventy, and that never happens in February."

Jamie knelt next to the sparkling pool and reached into the water. "That's not too cold."

"It is for me." She turned back toward the house. "But you're welcome to it. I'll get you a towel and sunscreen while you change." She slid the door to the living room open and motioned for him to go in.

"I don't need sunscreen." He set his empty glass on the dining table.

Kat refilled his glass, got one for herself, and took them—and a beach towel, straw hat, and a bottle of SPF-35—out to the patio table. Jamie came out in his swim trunks. *Good lord, he's thin!* But he had well-defined muscles, not an emaciated appearance.

"I feel strange, swimming in your pool, when you're not," he said. "Come join me."

"Not until the water's in the seventies. Besides, someone has to lifeguard," she joked to make sure he knew she was kidding. She sat down at the round glass table she had scrubbed that morning, as Jamie started down the steps into the pool, then turned around and stepped back out. "Colder than you expected?" she asked with a "told you so" smile.

He grinned at her without saying a word as he walked to the deep end and dove in. Kat shuddered at the thought of diving into that cold water. Jamie performed a powerful freestyle stroke to the shallow end, did a kick-turn, and swam back to the deep end. After four more laps, he stopped adjacent to the table and his host.

If he had swum in England's icy lakes and ponds all his life, the sixty-two-degree water on a sunny, sixty-four degree day in northern California must have felt fine. So, of course, he had to tease her. "This isn't cold. What a softie!"

"Softie?"

"Em... wimp?"

"Yep, that's me," Kat said. She wished she had more tolerance to cold, but that was also a good excuse to remain fully clothed, and not reveal her less-than-perfect figure.

"You really think you could pull me out if I was drowning?" he asked.

"Yeah, I used to be a lifeguard and water safety instructor." She wasn't sure she still had all the old skills, but knowing she wouldn't need them, she wasn't about to admit it to Jamie.

"You did? Where? When?"

"At my high school, the Mount Diablo YMCA, and a summer camp in Malibu."

"No kidding? Well, I feel *much* safer, now." Jamie grinned and splashed water at her. It fell short of his target. He went back to his laps and executed every stroke and kick perfectly.

He had a swimmer's muscular shoulders, which Kat had always found attractive. And nice legs! Why didn't swimming laps do anything for her legs? *Oh, right... I don't run, play sports, and have a personal trainer.*

Kat could hardly believe this popular actor was at her house, in her pool. She hoped it meant their friendship was back on stable ground. The fact that he'd flown four hundred miles to spend two days with her should have been convincing enough. But she learned years ago not to make assumptions about where she ranked in anyone's life—especially someone with money to burn.

Jamie switched from the difficult butterfly stroke to skimming on his back. "You sure you won't join me? The water's not that cold."

"It's too cold for me. I walked down two steps, yesterday, and back out of there, fast. I don't need bath water, but it's got to be at least seventy, or it brings up bad memories of forced winter swimming in high school. Come back this summer, and I'll race you."

"You're on." He stepped out of the pool. "Did I tell you I got a role in that film Bill was scouting for at Lake Tahoe? I'll be there, this June and July. If I have a couple days off during the shoot..." He pointed at her with a look that implied a duel was coming. "You'd better start practicing." He approached the diving board. "How deep is this?"

"Eight and a half feet. It's safe; the board doesn't have much spring."

Jamie bounced on the end of the board to get the feel of it. "No, it doesn't. That's all right, as long as you're not trying to do double flips." From the back end of the board, he took three long steps, sprang up, out, and into the water.

When he surfaced, Kat asked, "Were you on the swimming or diving team at school?"

"Both. You?" Jamie climbed out of the deep end and went back to the diving board.

"Swimming. I tried out for diving... wasn't good enough. But that's okay. Gave me time to practice guitar and drums."

"You play drums, too?" He stepped up onto the board.

"Used to... haven't played in years. Sometimes I think about cleaning out the music-junk room, and putting a used set in there. It would be fun to play again."

Jamie took another dive, this time going into the water straighter, with less splash. Kat judged it a seven and wished she could be that physically fit. But that would take knee surgery and more exercise than she cared for. And she'd have to give up Tillamook Mudslide ice cream.

Jamie hoisted himself out of the pool—displaying well-defined arm muscles—and came over to the table where she sat. He grinned and shook his head like a wet dog, giving her an uninvited shower. The ends of his hair curled all over.

"That was nice. And there's no chlorine smell." His expression changed to concern. "You do use chlorine, don't you?"

"Of course. You won't smell a properly chlorinated pool unless there's ammonia or a lot of organic matter in it. Then you smell the chloramines created when chlorine breaks down organics. That's what people really smell when they think they smell chlorine."

"Really? I've never heard that." Jamie sat down, looking skeptical. "Everyone always refers to that odor as chlorine. Do you handle the chemicals yourself, or does a cute pool boy come and take care of you? I mean... them." Flashing a devilish grin, he reached over and squeezed Kat's arm.

As he touched her, a tingling sensation in her cheeks moved back to her ears and slid down her spine. She had to stifle a giggle. *Mustn't... let... attraction... show!*

"Yeah, right... in my dreams. No, I do everything I can, myself."

"What about the drought? Does anyone give you shit for using all that water?"

"No, and if they did, they'd be mistaken. Once it's set up, a pool uses less water than a lawn the same size would."

"That's surprising. It's a nice one."

"Thanks. I never have to mow it."

They lost track of time while talking, until the Delta breeze picked up and the sun began to slip behind a neighboring house. Indoors, Kellye jumped off the recliner to greet them. She was more interested in Jamie than Jeremy was. He monitored the new human from his perch on the back of the sofa, then followed Kat into the kitchen.

"You hungry yet?" she asked. "I want to take you to a place on the river for dinner, after I feed the cats."

A few minutes later, Kat stood at her kitchen sink. She couldn't believe this charming, attractive man she liked was in her shower. He would never be anything more than a friend, but damn... if she could ever trust a man again— wouldn't it be nice...

Chapter 20: Oh, What a Knight

Jamie laughed as Kat drove toward an isolated sign on the side of a narrow levee road next to the Sacramento River. "The Virgin Sturgeon? What is *that*?"

"That's where I'm taking you for dinner." She steered the car onto the dirt shoulder where four other cars were parked near leafless trees. Looking all around, he couldn't see a building until they walked across the road. There, below the levee, on the water: a floating restaurant that had a deck for outdoor dining and a dock where small boats could tie up.

"Normally, you can see it from the road," she said. "See how low the water is? Drought." That made the wooden gangway to the entrance precariously steep. Jamie took Kat's hand as they carefully made their way down to water level. A hostess took them to a table where they had a view of the river and the far bank, still in its natural riparian state, with a massive oak tree on the levee.

"Would you like to order drinks?" she asked.

Kat said, "A hot tea, please?"

The server nodded. "And for you, sir?"

"I'll have the same."

"Wouldn't you rather have wine or beer?" Kat asked. "Don't skip it just because I'm not drinking."

"I'm not. I don't drink all the time, either. I ordered wine that night at the Club because I was wired and wanted to wind down. And I assumed you'd order a drink and didn't want you to feel uncomfortable if I didn't." He noticed the gold dolphin necklace she wore again. "You know, I've never seen you wear any other necklace. "

"Oh, I have a whale tail and a few others, but this is my favorite. Don't you like it?"

"Yeah, I didn't mean it that way. Most of the women I know have so much jewelry you hardly ever see the same piece twice."

"Hmm... I've never been into that kind of flash. I'd rather be known for substance."

"Really? Me too," he said. "I have to do a lot of 'window dressing' to please Hollywood, but I'd rather donate that money to a reputable research institute or an organization that helps underprivileged kids stay out of trouble."

Over a fresh wild trout dinner, Jamie told her about behind-the-scenes activities at the Academy Awards. "Some woman—an actor I've never met, working as a seat-filler— kept turning up everywhere I went, except my seat. She appeared in the lobby, the aisle, the hall, backstage, even by the loo, er... toilets. It seemed like she was stalking me."

"Really? What made you think she's an actor?"

"A local told me. You don't expect people in the business to do that. She wasn't doing anything in those places... just loitering. And she always made eye contact with me and smiled the way they do when they're trying to start something with you. Know what I mean?"

"As if she'd like to get to know you... really well?"

"Exactly. I see that more often than I'd like. The coy way she said, 'Oh, hi,'" he mimicked a young woman's voice, "as if she was surprised to see me each time, made me suspicious."

"How'd you handle it?"

"The last time I saw her, I gave her a contemptuous look to show that I knew what she was up to, turned around and went the other way. I was a bit cross by then. She must have gotten the message, because I didn't see her again."

The restaurant was quiet, and no one seemed to recognize Jamie, which pleased him, and Kat, too. Again, she tried to pay, and he wouldn't let her.

"But you're *my guest* here," she protested.

"Save it for your drum set." He took the bill holder from her and held her hand.

"Thank you, Jamie." She paused a moment, looking at and thinking how nice his hand felt wrapped around hers. "What would you like to do this evening?"

Jamie wanted to turn up the heat but he played it straight for the moment. "I don't know. What do you normally do on an evening like this?"

"Work on publicity for the Scottish Games, or rehearse... maybe read, or watch TV or a movie. But not when I have company."

"Want to go home and watch a movie? You have some that I haven't seen."

Walking up the steep gangway as they left the restaurant, Jamie held Kat's hand. "Hmm... this seems familiar."

She chuckled. "Yes... reminds me of a day last fall when a guy tried to cripple me."

As they crossed the road, the clear winter sky revealed few stars. Jamie put his arm around her to keep her warm as they walked to her car.

On the way back to her house, he quietly looked out the window. The city's lights danced on the river's dark water. California's Capitol building was brightly lit and an office building on Capitol Mall had an eerie green glow.

* * *

At home, Jamie teased her about her nineteen-year-old analog TV set.

"I know... I'd like a big, LED, hi-def, flat-panel TV, but they're still too expensive to suit me. And I'd have to buy a new stand, dismantle the old entertainment center and move it, then re-wire all the components to run the audio through the system. So as long as this set works..."

157

Jamie shook his head as she added, "Besides, one key to happiness is to be content with what you have, and not let Big Business make you think you always have to have the newest, biggest, or best of everything. Once we've met our basic needs and can live in reasonable comfort, the rest is want, not need."

"This is unreal. That's my philosophy, too. Hardly anyone else ever says that."

They watched The Beatles' first movie and then *Mamma Mia!*—both light, musical comedy romps. Watching the screaming Beatles fans in *A Hard Day's Night,* Kat teased him about some of his squealing young fans.

"Makes me feel a bit pervy when they're young enough to be my children."

"I can't believe you've been so focused on classic theater and serious, dramatic films, you haven't seen either of these," she said.

"I can't believe *you* know all the lyrics to the songs in both of them."

Sitting next to Jamie on the sofa, Kat had Kellye on her lap, and Jeremy curled up on the other side of her. Mid-way through *Mamma Mia!,* Jamie put his arm around her. She looked up at him, smiled, and leaned against him, ever so comfortably.

He smiled back, squeezed her shoulder, and kissed the top of her head.

It had been a long time, but Kat recognized each little move toward greater intimacy, and listened to the debate between her defensive brain and her patched-up, lonely heart.

Where's he going with this? What if he wants to...?

Don't. That always ruins friendships. Besides, you're not into casual sex.

But it's Jamie Knight!

That shouldn't make any difference.

But it does. And I really like him...

Are you nuts? He's a player who's slept with every actress and model in London. He couldn't possibly love you, so if that's what he has in mind, he just wants to get laid.
So what? Apparently, so did all my ex-boyfriends.
Yeah, but you thought you loved them. You swore you wouldn't let that happen again.

With their bare feet on the coffee table, Jamie tried to grab her feet with his toes. Kat's feet evaded and grabbed his. All that movement was too much for Kellye and Jeremy, who both got up and left for seating that didn't move. When they stopped laughing, Jamie pulled Kat close to him again and kissed her cheek.

She leaned against his warm body and laid her head on his shoulder. His touch stirred her senses. *Oh, this feels so nice. Why am I afraid? Jamie's a different generation from all the guys who led me on; maybe he has a different ethic.*
Not likely. You know his reputation.
But he's a playboy with pretty, young women, not women like me. Should I give him a chance?
No. Don't risk another broken heart.
But it's been so long... and I want him.
Then make sure he wears a condom. After all the women he's slept with...

While the closing credits rolled over ABBA's *Thank You For the Music*, Jamie leaned over and kissed Kat's cheek. Then her mouth. A proper kiss. Her face flushed with heat. He pulled her body against his and kissed her again while gently caressing her back and shoulders for several minutes. Her spine tingled and she could hardly believe it—nor the long dormant feelings he awoke in her.

She put her left hand on his thigh, and his body responded, even as she moved her right hand to his back. When they came up for air, he brushed his hand across her forehead, moving her hair to one side while looking lovingly into her eyes. He must have known what a turn-on that was. He kissed her again and moved his hand from her shoulder down her side to squeeze her thigh, then gently up her torso to cup one breast in his palm.

With her right arm around Jamie's back, Kat moved her left hand up his thigh to his side, touching his arm and chest, then stopping at his right shoulder.

She'd had no desire to make love in years—until now. She had been raised to believe women weren't supposed to initiate physical intimacy, but social rules had changed, and Jamie was a decade younger... The analytical part of her brain said *Don't do it,* while the emotional part said *Go for it. ASK him.* The next time Jamie pulled back and gazed into her eyes, she struggled to ask, "Would... Would you like to... um... spend the night... here?"

"In the guest room?" He teased with a knowing look.

"Did you bring protection?"

"Em... no. Don't you have any?"

Her shoulders slumped. "No. I haven't slept with anyone in... well... ages. It never occurred to me that you'd want to... with me."

"It didn't? Oh, right. You think you're not pretty, so—"

"Come on, Jamie. Every picture I see, you have a gorgeous young lady, not anyone your own age, or who looks or dresses the way I do. And while you really turn me on, if you've slept with half as many women as your publicity suggests—"

"You think I'm an S.T.D. carrier?" He had read her mind.

"How about a walking petri dish?"

Jamie laughed, then spoke softly. "That's just P.R., Kat. I want to make the A-List, and to do that, you have to stay in the entertainment news. And except for a few big events, they only cover actors they can gossip about." He kissed her again, then stood, lifting her up with him, wrapped his arms around her, kissed her again, and squeezed her backside.

Kat couldn't miss the bulge in his pants and suspected that he hoped she wouldn't hold out for a condom. But even

Jamie Knight wasn't worth a case of syphilis. But if she said no tonight, would he come back tomorrow? Or ever? "Your reason for sleeping around doesn't change—"

"Isn't there an all-night chemist around here?"

"Drug store? No. I don't know of any that are open this late."

"Okay," he said. "Tonight we can only hold each other. I'll buy condoms tomorrow."

Kat hesitated. She lifted his left hand and kissed it. "I don't know... I'd like that. But I don't trust either of us to not give in to what we both want. Do you?" She bit her lower lip, concerned about how he would react.

He looked disappointed and sighed as he caressed her cheek with the back of his fingers. "I think we can. But if you don't, I'll take the guest room tonight. Or go to a hotel."

That made Kat feel like a heel for not trusting him. She pressed her forehead against his chest. Knowing what someone had told her about the painful injections administered for—was it syphilis or gonorrhea?—gave her the strength to say, "I'm sorry. Thank you for understanding."

She turned off the TV and light, took Jamie's hand and led him down the hall. "The main bathroom is all yours." At the door to the guest room, she kissed him and said, "You're a good man, Jamie Knight. Sleep well." One last hug and a long kiss, and she walked away, fighting the urge to turn around and pull him into her bedroom.

More than an hour later, with Kellye and Jeremy at her sides, Kat still hadn't fallen asleep. She felt bad about making Jamie sleep in the guest room. Would she regret that? The two sides of her brain argued about her relationship with him—again.

When she was about to give up and try reading a book, her bedroom door creaked and opened slightly. Both cats stood abruptly as an outside light that came in through the bathroom window created Jamie's silhouette outside the door.

"Kat?" He spoke so softly, he wouldn't have wakened her if she'd been asleep.

"Hi, Jamie. Having trouble sleeping?"

"Yeah." He paused. "I can't stop thinking about you."

"Me, too. About you." She paused, but Jamie didn't speak. "Can I trust you—"

"Yes. I can wait. I just want to hold you."

"Okay, come on."

In the faint light coming through the windows, Jamie found his way to the far side of the queen-sized bed. The cats left as he got in and reached for her, leaned over and kissed her, missing her mouth at first. She rolled against him and put one arm around his warm torso. He, in boxer shorts and she in pajamas, fell asleep that way.

It wasn't until after Jamie spent the night with her that Kat recalled Barbara saying, in London, that she still talked in her sleep. She always had—and not the mumbling way most people do. She spoke in complete sentences, loud and clear, as if doing a radio show. *Oh, man, I hope I don't do that while he's here.*

After a leisurely breakfast, Kat took Jamie to the Crocker Art Museum, then to Old Sacramento, a historic, commercial neighborhood on the Sacramento River. Originally built during the Gold Rush, the city had restored the neighborhood in its original style, which was now popular with both tourists and locals.

Most of the time they strolled the 19th century boardwalks, he either had his arm around her or held her hand. Eating lunch on a sunny deck over the river, they talked about their lives, work, and environmental crises like the drought and rapid climate change. Two people recognized him and asked if he was "that guy" in a movie. He graciously posed for pictures and signed autographs. The drive home included a stop at a drugstore.

That evening, while Jamie checked email, Kat made capellini marinara. He said he liked it. Knowing herself to be a lousy cook, she hoped he wasn't merely saying that to be nice. And what a guy! The Olivier Award-winner helped her clear the table and load the dishwasher. She couldn't believe how completely at ease he seemed at her house... as though he lived there.

Kat was so comfortable with Jamie, she could have fallen asleep leaning against him. As the *Quartet* credits rolled on the TV, he leaned over, kissed her, and pulled her close to him. His soft lips and warm embrace always sent her temperature soaring. When he stopped, she turned the TV off and stood up, gently pulling him up with her. He took her in his arms and kissed her again.

Kat ran her hand down his back, from his shoulder blades to his muscular backside. When he stopped kissing her, they held each other in a full-body hug for a few moments, until she took his hand and led him into her dark bedroom, thinking, *I can't believe this...*

The pack of condoms lay on the nightstand, one already out. Jamie pulled her sweater off and they slowly unbuttoned and removed each other's shirts. He unhooked her bra, slid it off, and she shivered as he pulled her close to him. Her breasts pressed against his bare torso. His strong, warm hands were soft and gentle. She liked the smooth feeling of his nearly hairless chest against her face and couldn't help but feel the erection he pressed against her.

"Jamie, I..." she took a deep breath. "I haven't done this in a long time," she confessed, as he unzipped her jeans, slid them down her legs, and she stepped out of them. She wasn't exaggerating. It had been nearly a decade since she had slept with her last boyfriend. And she had never wanted to sleep with anyone as much as she did now.

Jamie's hands slid up the sides of Kat's legs and he kissed her abdomen, breasts, her neck, and finally her mouth. She fumbled with the button atop his jeans and pushed them down off his narrow hips. He stepped out of them gracefully, never taking his hands off her.

"I find that hard to believe," he whispered as they moved onto the bed. "But don't worry. I'll take care of you."

And he did. Jamie not only knew the importance of foreplay, he enjoyed it. He knew exactly what to do. Kat had never known such a sweet lover. *He makes love the way a man who truly loves someone would.* And she did everything she could to make him glad he had stayed. He held her in his arms, occasionally kissing her cheek and forehead, until she fell asleep with her arms around him.

During the night, she awoke with lyrics from an old Bob Seger song—*We've Got Tonight*—playing in her mind. But they weren't all apropos. The old "live for today, forget tomorrow' philosophy was dangerous. If you didn't consider the consequences of your actions, didn't plan for your own future, and let the cards fall where they may, you could really screw up your life.

The next day, the hopelessness of Seger's lyrics struck her. Surely *Jamie* was never lonely, and his plans didn't include her. But now she had that night, and she would never forget it.

When she awoke, she was lying on her side with his body spooning her back, his arm draped over her and his hand on her chest. The cats were by her feet. She closed her eyes and drifted back to sleep until Jamie's soft lips and warm breath touched her cheek. She rolled onto her back and looked into the angelic blue eyes gazing into hers.

"Good morning," she purred, thinking, *I must look awful, but at least my morning voice is Lauren Bacall deep.*

"Good morning." His rich baritone was deeper than usual, too, and remarkably soothing. He kissed her. "Did you sleep well?"

"Oh, yeah." She slid her hand up his arm to his shoulder and caressed his cheek. "How could I not sleep well with you wrapped around me? Did you?"

"Very well." Jamie kissed her. "Do you want to wrap yourself around me, again?"

Kat smiled. *Where are those condoms? Ah, the other nightstand.* She gently rolled him onto his back, reached over him, and took one. "Did you hear, the Burger King got Wendy pregnant? He forgot to wrap his Whopper."

Jamie's expression suggested he wasn't very familiar with those American fast-food franchises—even though they were in the UK—and the joke bombed. She felt stupid, but "wrapped his whopper," and as he lifted himself over her, she reached down and helped him find his way.

Something about Jamie made Kat less inhibited than she had been in the past. Perhaps knowing she would never be his girlfriend, she felt no pressure to earn that status.

He was so attentive, loving, and emotionally present, if she had been more naïve, she might have thought he actually cared for her. She hoped it was more to him than just another "shag." She could only hope, because he didn't reveal his feelings. His eyes said, "I love you," but she knew better than to believe that.

Pleased to have lost weight, she was all too aware of gravity's effects on her body. Losing weight in her late forties had reduced her 38-DD bust to 34, and left her breasts sagging more than they should at her age. She was terribly self-conscious about them. Jamie must have noticed, but whatever he thought, it didn't send him running out the door.

To mask her embarrassment she joked, "In my twenties I had what men called a 'great rack.' But I've gained and lost weight since then. Losing weight was good, but... well... the bigger they are, the farther they fall."

Jamie chuckled and kissed each breast, then put his arms around her and kissed her again.

"You look fine to me." Maybe he liked her enough for other qualities that slightly saggy boobs didn't turn him off.

She experienced a twinge of guilt for not telling him her age, but she enjoyed his company and didn't want to do or say anything that might cause him to disappear. He certainly would, when he learned she had ten years on him.

At the airport, Kat would have given anything to sit with Jamie at the gate until he boarded his plane. But the restrictions forced on travelers after 9-11 made them part at the security checkpoint. He held her hand or had his arm around her, constantly, while she waited in line with him as long as the rules allowed.

After a long hug, Jamie asked, "I don't suppose you're coming to London anytime soon, are you?"

"I wish. I'll have to find another contest to enter."

More than a few people watched as Jamie gave Kat a passionate goodbye kiss, before he went through security to fly back to L.A. From there, he would return to London and she wouldn't see him again until summer—if then.

She left the airport feeling very much alone again. She reviewed the two days and nights with Jamie, knowing the best she could hope for was a lasting friendship. At least now she was a very *good* friend.

"I knew it," Molly declared, flashing a victorious smile the next day. "I knew he wouldn't spend the night in a hotel *or* your guest room." Kat had considered not telling her she had slept with Jamie, but she couldn't lie. She didn't reveal details and swore Molly to secrecy.

"I know it won't last," Kat said, "and I don't want to be the subject of gossip around the department when he stops calling."

"Maybe he won't stop."

"You optimist. Of course, he will. They all stop. Six months to a few years is all I ever get—and that's with average guys."

"You must be something special to him. He must know women in L.A. who would love to spend two days and nights with him. But he flew up here, to be with you."

Kat shook her head. "Do I dare let myself think...?" They walked in silence for a few minutes, then she concluded, "No. I'm just a friend with benefits. And a pool."

Back in the office, Molly called her over to her computer. "Did you see this?" She pointed out a photo on Instagram of Jamie and Kat holding hands in Old Sacramento, and another shot of him standing beside a young woman who had recognized him there.

Jamie phoned and emailed more frequently after those days at Kat's, and the conversations were more personal than they had been previously. The week after he left, she received a box of Lauden dark chocolates and a note: "Hoping you'll never say 'no.' Thank you for the lovely mini-holiday. Yours, Jamie."

Well, I guess he doesn't care about my weight. Their nights together made Kat more self-conscious than ever about her figure, so she kept exercising, and even did some research on cosmetic surgery. Unfortunately, what she *might* do, she couldn't afford—and no one offered a painless "boob-lift" that wouldn't leave scars.

In March Kat's friend, CDW photographer Roni Jorgensen flipped the pages of a Hollywood gossip magazine in the office break room while Kat washed her coffee cup. Someone had left it open to a page with four photos of Jamie—each with a different pretty young lady and the headline, **Which Lover Tops Jamie Knight's List?**

"I suppose you saw this," Roni said.

"Couldn't miss it. Wonder who put it there to remind me I'm nothing special to him." Kat loved the fact that Jamie had come to see her, stayed at her house, and made love to her. But because of who he was and who she was, she knew that—to him—it was just sex.

"But it was great sex and it felt like love. I'll always enjoy the memory," she later told Molly. "There's no way I'll ever be his girlfriend. And if he's the skirt-chaser they say he is, he may never call again, now that he's scored."

Chapter 21: Moonshadows

Jamie was busy shooting *Nigel Stone* and a car commercial. His agent had asked him to take out some young actresses the agency had recently signed, so they could meet show business people and "be seen with a big star." Victor only called him that to make it hard for him to say no, but he wanted to help young actors, as others had helped him. As usual, London's entertainment media declared each one "Jamie Knight's latest flame."

"I hope Kat doesn't see that," he told Leigh and Bob over dinner at his house.

"Have you told her how you feel?" Leigh asked. She and Bob were the only people Jamie had told that his affection for the American was growing into love.

"No," he said. "I want to. I'm not seeing anyone else on proper dates. But I want to spend more time with her, to be sure before I take that step." Jamie looked away, then back at Bob, then Leigh. "Saying 'I love you' is a step toward commitment, isn't it?"

"Good idea," Bob said. "Don't say it until you're certain you want to get serious."

"But if you wait too long," Leigh added, "she may think you're only there to shag her, and that doesn't sit well with most women over thirty-five. Especially independent women who don't need a sugar daddy and aren't into casual sex."

* * *

Kat's affection for Jamie grew daily, despite her attempts to subdue it, and she looked forward to his phone calls, emails, and text messages. It felt a little like being in college, waiting for a guy to call, although he contacted her more often than those boys had. By late March, his PSAs for the Sea Otter Fund were getting a lot of attention—a good excuse to send him a no-risk email.

"Your PSAs are airing all over California. Even stations that rarely ran mine are airing yours in unsold commercial avails. And more people donated more money in January & February than they have in recent years. I'm sure that's because of your velvet voice. Thank you for doing them. (Apologies, again.)

I'm glad you came here last month. The time we spent together was wonderful. I hope that won't be the last time. You're always welcome. Take care."

Jamie replied: "Well done, Kat! I enjoyed our time together, as well. I miss you and WILL be back. You're a special lady, and I'm glad you're in my life now. How's the PR going for the Highland games? I have to be in LA on 13-14 April. Can you come see me? I'll provide transportation, of course."

Kat: "I wish I could, but that week is the final push for the tax donation funds. Ron complains if I even take an hour for lunch, now. The Scottish fiddlers rehearse on the 14th, then Earth Day... I can't go anywhere in April, but thanks for asking. I'd love to see you."

Jamie: "Sorry you can't come to L.A., but I understand. We're shooting *Nigel* the next few weeks on an insane schedule. When it gets overwhelming, I'll think of relaxing with you by your pool. Are you swimming, yet? By the way, when is your birthday? I miss you. Hugs, JK"

Kat liked the "hugs" sign-off. He probably wanted to know her birthday to search the web for her age—as she had for his.

April email from Jamie: "We finish *Nigel* next week, then I start memorizing lines for Pine Lake Summer. Shooting interiors in L.A. next month, then on to Lake Tahoe in June. I want you to come up while I'm there. Are you practicing for our race?"

Kat: "Glad you survived your crazy schedule. Of course, I'm swimming laps for speed. I'd love to see you at Tahoe. Tell me when, where, and I'm there. Your personal lifeguard..."

May email from Jamie: "How did things go at the Highland Games? Wish I could hear your group. Whenever I see anything Scottish now, I think of you.
I met a friend of yours here, in L.A. Karen Treanor is consulting on fire scenes, and she told me all about you. (Oh, my!) Can you come down on 16-17 May? Looks like I'll have that weekend off. Let me know and I'll make arrangements. Big hugs... ♥"

Kat: "Karen's a dear friend and she told me about YOU, Don Juan. ☺ The Games went well. I'd love to spend that weekend with you. Are you ready for the great race? Looking forward to seeing you again. Hugs..."

In the past, the Sea Otter Fund donations reached the minimum amount required sometime between July and October. This year, it hit the goal in April. That made Kat a rock star at work and among sea otter advocates, who were now Jamie Knight fans for his help.

During her flight to Los Angeles, Kat felt uncomfortable about not paying her own way. On the other hand, she couldn't afford to fly wherever, whenever. Jamie has more money than anyone needs. *If he wants me there, why do I feel guilty?*

"You have this entire suite to yourself?" Kat asked Jamie at the Beverly Hilton. "Two families could live in this."

"I know. It's not what I asked for, but it's where they put me, and I'm not complaining. Take your shoes off and feel the carpet on your bare feet." He was already barefoot, wearing jeans and a sky-blue T-shirt. As she set her Nikes neatly against a wall, he added, "It's only for the weekend, so we may as well enjoy it."

"Where are you staying the rest of the time?"

"At Bill's. He said you were welcome there, but I didn't know whether you'd be comfortable with that." He pulled her close and whispered, "Besides, I want you all to myself, and a lot of privacy."

Kat felt "wood" pressing against her and knew what else he wanted. "Wait," she said, pushing herself away and feigning disappointment. "You mean you're not taking me to Disneyland?"

"I am—to Fantasyland. Tell me your fantasy, and it's yours." He pulled her close again.

Kat felt awfully warm, all of a sudden. "Oh, no. I could never do that."

"Why not? Kat, you're turning red. Are you embarrassed?"

She turned her face to the side, against his chest, now embarrassed about being embarrassed. How stupid. At her age, she shouldn't be embarrassed about sex. Or to ask for what she'd like. But she was.

Jamie persisted, running his fingers through her hair, then lifting her chin for a kiss. "Oh, come on; tell me. What have you always wanted a man to do to... *for* you?"

Kat paused and looked at the floor, unable to make eye contact. Breathing deeply, she struggled to think of something that wouldn't embarrass her. "I can't."

"What are you afraid of? It'll be fun for me, too, you know."

Oh no... wait—if I ask for the impossible, will he let me off the hook? "Okay... A knight in shining armor to take me away, make passionate love to me, and never leave." That was as close to her dearest wish as she could say aloud. She expected him to tap dance around that, even though she couldn't utter the words, "ask me to marry him." The implication in "never leave" was dangerous enough. Instead, he surprised her.

"You've got it!" Jamie picked her up as though she weighed nothing, carried her into the bedroom, set her on the enormous bed, and hovered over her as he kissed her and smiled. "I *am* your knight, you know."

Kat's broad smile spoke volumes. "You're the sweetest knight—and the best lover—I've ever known."

"You're damned good yourself." He unbuckled her belt and unbuttoned her shirt as she worked on his. She couldn't wait to feel his soft skin against hers.

After pulling her jeans off, then his own, he pulled his T-shirt over his head. His chest and arms were more muscular than they had been at her house. She sat up to kiss him and touch his chest. He shuddered and gently guided her back onto her back and kneeled above her, kissing her everywhere, eliciting giggles when he tickled her. They fell asleep in each other's arms until his mobile rang.

"No. I told you, I'm not dealing with those people— especially Angela, after that stunt she pulled at the Oscars." He paused to listen.

"Yes, I can. They're not the only game in town. I'll talk with the others next week, but not them." He looked at Kat and winked, then said, "Okay. And listen, I'm not available for anything this weekend. No, I'm spending it with someone special, and if anyone wants me, they'll have to wait. Monday evening. All right. Thanks." He hung up. "That was Judy, my publicist."

"You're passing up an opportunity to publicize something because I'm here?"

"Well, if anyone wants me this weekend, I am." He paused, touched Kat's cheek with the back of his fingers, then wrapped his arms around her. "This weekend is for you and me. No work for either of us. All right?"

* * *

In a sexy, rented Jaguar, Jamie drove Kat to Malibu for dinner. Bill had told him about a nice steakhouse on the Pacific Coast Highway that had an unobstructed view of the ocean.

"This looks familiar," Kat said, looking around as they walked up to a small, wood-shingled building. There were no windows or signs facing the road—only a boardwalk that led to a side door. As the entry came into view she exclaimed, "Moonshadows? Oh, my god! I heard it had closed."

"You've been here?"

"Not since I lived here, ages ago. This was my favorite restaurant, but I couldn't afford it, then. Jamie... How did you know?" Kat hugged him.

"I didn't. Unless you thought about it, and we're telepathic," he joked.

Their timing was perfect. The sun appeared barely above the Pacific horizon when the hostess seated them at a table next to a tall window that ran the length of the building. When the waiter brought menus, Kat's didn't have prices on it. She looked irritated, as if insulted.

Jamie recognized that look. "Order whatever you want, Kat. I know you're price-conscious and considerate. But there's no reason not to order your favorite. In fact, I'll be insulted if you order something inexpensive. Do you understand?"

"Yes... but—"

"No. I mean it!" His displeasure was audible. "Don't be miserly with yourself when I'm buying. If you are, I'll tell the server to bring you steak and lobster. I know you like that... in fact, that's what you're getting." He softened his expression but clearly, Kat wasn't happy. He took her hand. "What's wrong?"

"You're chewing me out as though I've done something wrong. It's not wrong for me to not take advantage of you."

He spoke more quietly now. "I didn't mean to make you feel bad. But it's not wrong for me to spend money on you, either. And... well, it makes me cross when you act as if I'm on a tight budget. I make more than anyone who hasn't cured cancer deserves, and I want to share my good fortune with you. You know why?"

"Because you're kind and generous. And I appreciate it. I just don't want you to think—"

"I don't! Would you please believe me? I know you're not a user and you'd never take advantage of anyone. Could we move on? It makes me feel good to do things for people I care about; and I care about you. Would you please let me?"

"Okay." Kat looked down. "I'm sorry."

For a few minutes of uncomfortable silence, they both looked at the ocean view until the waiter came to take their order.

Over perfectly grilled steak and Australian lobster tails, they talked about Jamie's crazy days shooting the last episode of the *Nigel Stone* series, the film he had started work on, other people on the shoot, Kat's work, the Scottish Games, and how California's extreme drought made wildfire season longer and more deadly than ever.

Walking out to the car, Kat looked into the night sky. "Now, the smog that gave us that coral sunset blocks the stars." She paused, then added, "But who needs the cosmos when I've got my favorite star beside me?"

Jamie pulled her closer. "You're *my* star, tonight."

* * *

Paparazzi were prowling around the Beverly Hilton when Jamie and Kat arrived. "Hold my hand and walk in, quickly," he told her. "I suggest you act as if they're not there. Just look natural and don't hide your face. That makes people appear to have something to hide, and we don't."

Kat's chest felt tight. She took a deep breath and exhaled slowly. "You don't mind being photographed with someone who doesn't look like an actress?"

"Actor; it's gender neutral. No, and you look lovely." He kissed her hand. "I'm happy to be seen with you; you're real... a normal, respectable woman."

Kat counted three paparazzi, but their cameras' rapid-fire flashes blinded her, as if there were a dozen.

"Damn, Jamie... if you hadn't pulled me along, I couldn't have found the door. How could you see your way inside?"

"Practice. I'm sorry about that. It's a fact of life for me. You won't stop going out with me because of that, will you?"

She squeezed his hand. "I'll only stop going out with you if you stop inviting me." That was inevitable... someday.

Jamie's suite had an enormous flat-panel TV with hundreds of channels and networks, but Kat wanted to see nothing more than the man sitting next to her on the luxurious sofa. Jamie wasn't interested in TV either, so she turned it off and leaned into him, resting her head on his chest.

Jamie kissed the top of her head and squeezed her. "I can't believe how comfortable I feel with you. From the first time we sat and talked at the club, it's been as if we've known each other for years. Know what I mean?"

"Yeah. I didn't feel it until San Francisco. In London, I was too conscious of your status, and the fact that I was merely a tourist. It never occurred to me that I'd see you again."

"No, me neither. But you kept sneaking into my head. Now you're there more than you know." He squeezed her, then pulled his body away. He wore a serious expression when he took both of her hands and looked into her eyes as though he'd found her soul. "Kat... I love you."

Her mind and face both went blank. She had been sure no man would ever say that again, least of all anyone as special as Jamie. Her mouth opened slightly, but she had no words.

"Kat?"

"Uh-huh?"

"I love you. I've been afraid to say it because some women think it's practically a proposal. But you're not like most women. That's one of the things I love about you. You know I'm just honestly sharing my feelings."

Stunned, Kat didn't respond. *Oh... my... god!* Her heart wanted to sing, 'I love you too,' but her head ordered caution. Could this be some kind of set-up? A George Clooney prank with a hidden camera somewhere? Or was there a bet pending to see if she was gullible enough to think a younger, good-looking, popular actor could fall for her? After being rejected by every man she'd ever loved, how could Jamie Knight love her?

Smiling, obviously waiting for a response, Jamie placed a finger beneath her chin and pushed her mouth closed. She must have looked stupid, just sitting there, staring at him with a blank look. She smiled, looked down, then back at him.

"Jamie, that's... I... I'm shocked."

"Well, that's a first. No one's ever said she was shocked that I loved her."

"You... you say, 'I love you' to a lot of women?" That put a damper on the thrill.

"No, but at our age, you can't think you're the first."

"No. And I never imagined you could love *me*. I'm hardly a movie star magnet."

"I'm not a movie star—yet. And this isn't an actor talking; it's me, a real man who loves you. You underestimate yourself, Kat. And men. We're not all infatuated with live mannequins who only care about what everyone else thinks of their appearance. You're real. You care about other people, animals, the environment, and what's going on in the world. You're interesting. I can talk with you about anything. And my job doesn't control my heart. You understand the world I work in and you care about what I'm doing and how my day went. Not everyone bothers to ask, but you do, and mean it. That means a lot to me."

Kat had suppressed her growing affection for Jamie, trying to keep herself from foolishly falling for an unattainable man. At that moment, she couldn't deny that she loved him, too. Did he want her to say it? She wanted to, but this surprising relationship couldn't possibly last, and when she had said 'I love you' in the past, sometimes that was the beginning of the end. She didn't want this one to end. Not yet.

She leaned forward and kissed him. "You can't imagine how good that makes me feel, Jamie." After a hug, she took his hand, stood up, and pulled him toward the bedroom.

Jamie reached for the remote. "Aw, come on... there must be something good on telly..."

Kat turned around and tried to pick him up and carry him. She lifted him a few inches off the sofa, then dropped him, laughing. For that, he tickled her and chased her into the bedroom, grabbing her around the waist. She doubled over, still laughing, as Jamie picked her up awkwardly, and they both fell onto the bed. He kissed her passionately, and she pressed her hand between his thighs. In seconds a firm handle materialized that would open his heart even further. That night would be even better than the afternoon, and hearing Jamie say he loved her made Kat happier than she had been in a long time, despite the warning flags her mind waved at her.

* * *

While they had played in L.A., smartphone photos taken of Jamie and Kat at Moonshadows and the hotel had been shared on social media. London's salacious tabloids copied them, and professional shots from outside the hotel were sold to the highest bidders. "Jamie Knight and his California Girl" were in the next day's British entertainment news. Negative comments on the tabloids' websites outnumbered the positive. One called his date ugly, another frumpy. One even wrote that Kat was "probably a hooker. Poor Jamie."

Jamie's agent and publicist saw them and questioned him about his date when he returned to London.

"Are you frickin' kidding me?" Jamie was livid. "That's bollocks, probably written by delusional teenagers who are dumb enough to think that, if not for Kat, *they* could be my girlfriend. And, yes, *she is* my girlfriend—someone I can admire and respect as well as love."

Victor held up a page with an unflattering photo in *The Globe*. "If this is her, your job prospects are limited, Jamie. There's a *reason* we want you seen with beautiful, fashionable women."

"Oh, for chrissake, Victor, I'm forty-four years old! Hollywood can't expect me to keep pretending I'm a young stud muffin, breaking into the business. I'm through with the Casanova act, *through* spending my evenings with people who don't know or care about anything other than themselves, *through* pretending to be a heartless git who uses women just because I can. You don't need to be attracted to Kat. In fact, I'd prefer you weren't. I pay you to get me suitable roles, not to run my personal life!"

* * *

Some of Kat's friends saw the tabloid photos and emailed her links to them. The rude comments hurt, but she wouldn't tell anyone that.

"Molly, I don't know what to do," Kat confessed. "Could the tabloid crap be the reason I didn't get the State Parks job? And Jamie... he says he loves me, but I can't believe it. It'd be too good to be true. And even if he does, now, it won't last."

"Why? Stop thinking you're not good enough for him. You're as good a person as anyone else, and if he says he loves you, believe it. Stop fighting your feelings. You love him, too."

"Oh, god... of course I do. But men never stay with me, Molly, and I wasn't being insulted in the media, then. Jamie is so special..."

"Exceptional?"

"Yes."

"Then maybe he'll be the exception to the rule. You'll never know if you don't open your heart and let him in. You'll never enjoy love until you surrender to it—and all its possibilities."

Kat wanted to do that, but the certainty that Jamie would eventually dump her kept the wall up around her heart. At the same time, she hated the prospect of spending the rest of her life alone. Torn, she kept telling herself, *I can't be in love with him. I can't take him seriously. I can only like him a lot, and enjoy whatever we are to each other, as long as it lasts.*

But her heart knew better. Resistance was futile.

Chapter 22: Pine Lake Summer

In June, Jamie began shooting *Pine Lake Summer* at Lake Tahoe. "The script is exciting, if somewhat predictable," he told Kat on the phone. "I play a camp director who has to get all the campers and staff out safely when a wildfire rushes up the mountain and blocks the one access road. The only cell tower gets burnt, and they don't have a satellite phone, so they can't call for outside help. He's a cliché hero working against all odds."

"Sounds exciting," she said. "Is it easier to play a cliché than something else?"

"In a way, but harder to make believable. While they try to escape the fire, he keeps the kids from knowing how much danger they're in, calms the ones who are panicking, and coaches the twenty-year-old counselors to hide their own fear and do the right things."

"Do you make them climb nearly vertical rocks?" Kat asked dryly.

"Of course." He laughed. "And there are some good sub-plots: firefighters trying to get to the camp, pro- and anti-logging groups fighting in the news over whose practices caused the firestorm, a drone-flying tosser interfering with planes that drop retardant, and reporters tripping over each other to get the latest details and best pictures."

The script included scenes of wildlife trying to escape the fire, and friends and family—including a fiancée for Jamie's character—worried sick. To spice it up, one of the camp counselors—who was much too young for Jamie's character—had a crush on him, while one of the young campers had a crush on her. They both got a reality check by the end of the story.

"There's a character you'll love to hate," Jamie said. "He's a grandstanding prat the governor appointed to a job he wasn't qualified for. He's ignorant, arrogant, refuses to listen to experienced employees, and makes a dire situation even worse."

"Oh, man... that's not fiction. There are real people like that—usually big campaign donors. Or their offspring. You wouldn't believe how much those people cost the government."

"I know. Your friend Karen told me about one she had to work for."

They would shoot *Pine Lake Summer* in locations Kat knew well, including a state park and the old Ponderosa Ranch. They shot interior scenes, like the CalFire command post and scenes that required the use of actual flames, on a sound stage in Hollywood.

The producers would edit green screen technology into real wildfire footage to simulate a burning forest for the actors to escape. That's where Karen Treanor was consulting. After twenty-six years as a firefighter and senior public affairs officer, she could help ensure their firefighting scenes were realistic.

Jamie called Kat again, his first night at Tahoe. "What are you doing next weekend?"

"Oh, I thought I'd take my private jet to Hawaii, but that gets boring..."

"You smart-ass," Jamie laughed.

"Of course."

"Want to come to Tahoe? When we finish Friday's scenes, I'm off until Monday."

"I'd love to. Where are you staying?"

"Some dump called the Rubicon."

"Oh, you poor baby!" Her voice dripped with sarcasm. "I'll bring you a can of Raid and a care package."

The Rubicon was an expensive resort that had a five-star restaurant and well-appointed rooms nestled in the forest. Kat had stayed there once for a conference and had wanted to go back, but didn't like paying a lot for a room she wouldn't spend much time in.

Jamie laughed, "Okay. I won't know for certain when I'll be free until Friday afternoon or evening, but plan on coming up Saturday morning."

"What time?"

"Em... that'll depend on how late we shoot on Friday. Can I call you then?"

"Sure. Shall I pack ace bandages, or can we skip the mountain climbing?"

"I promise you won't need bandages. What do you think of canoeing?"

"That sounds fun. I know where we can rent one."

"Good. I'll call you, Friday. Love you!"

"Thanks, Jamie, you, too." Kat hung up, grinning like a teenager in love. *Stop that. You cannot fall in love with this guy!*

Janet reinforced that edict at a fiddling rehearsal when Kat told her about her weekend plans. "That sounds cool, but how long can you resist a nice, sexy, affectionate guy who's way out of your league, and too young for you?"

At the entrance to Rubicon Resort, Kat faced a security checkpoint worthy of a wartime military operation. When she gave the guard her driver's license and told him Jamie Knight was expecting her, he glared at her as though she were a fifteen-year-old groupie trying to get backstage at a rock concert.

Insulted at first, she remembered that young women and girls followed Jamie around London and New York. And he wasn't the only popular actor here. That made her glad the grounds were closed and well-guarded.

183

After checking a clipboard, the guard returned her license and signaled another man, who moved a barrier from the road. "Go on," he ordered.

Why does he act like that? Who—or what—does he think I am?

The clean mountain air and conifer forest scent made her feel healthy and adventurous, like the young outdoorswoman she once was. Jamie had given her directions to his room, but he didn't answer the door when she arrived. She waited a minute and knocked again. Still no answer. She adjusted her waist-pack as her stomach growled.

"Hello," a woman's voice called from down the hall. "Are you Kat?"

Startled, Kat turned to see a short woman with long black hair coming toward her. "Yes?" *Uh-oh... what's happened?*

"Hi, I'm Melinda. Jamie sent me to get you. He had to re-do one of yesterday's scenes. Want to come with me?"

Melinda led the way out the back side of the building, across a narrow asphalt road lined with trailers and equipment trucks, and downhill to a tennis court surrounded by towering trees and bright lights on tall metal stands.

She stopped thirty feet behind the film crew, turned, and held her index finger vertically against her lips. It wasn't necessary. Kat knew everyone must stop moving and remain silent when cameras were rolling. Half a dozen crew members stood like statues near the tennis court, where Jamie helped a boy work on his swing. One of the crew held a boom mic— a microphone on the end of a fifteen-foot pole—over the actors' heads.

As Jamie said, "Okay, let's try it again," a man off-camera on the other side of the net gently hit a ball to the boy, who swung and hit it back. The ball came back, and the boy hit it again. Two more volleys crossed the net before the ball didn't come back. The boy jumped up and down, cheering. Jamie beamed, gave him a high-five, and said,

"Well done!" He put his hand on the boy's shoulder and they stood still, smiling at each other for several seconds.

"Cut!" a man's voice shouted from next to the camera. "Okay, let's see if we got it." The crew began moving while the actors remained in place until the director said, "It's good!"

Jamie spoke briefly with him and then with the boy, whom he gave a pat on the back and a fist-bump as everyone else moved equipment. Jamie headed up the slope toward Kat and Melinda, looking handsome with his hair longer and shaggier than he usually wore it. Kat reminded herself not to say that, since, in England, "shag" was an impolite sexual verb.

When Jamie spotted her, his face lit up and he picked up his pace. He thanked Melinda and gave Kat a long hug. "I'm glad to see you." Then he kissed her. She hadn't expected that, in front of his colleagues.

He took her hand and led her back up the hill to his room. "Sorry about this," he apologized, as though he had inconvenienced her.

"Why? I love watching film production, and I've never seen you work before. It's an unexpected treat."

Jamie looked great in jeans, hiking boots, and a sky-blue T-shirt that said, "Camp Wildwood" on the back and "Director" on the left chest. Dressed like that—and all muscular, with his hair falling onto his ample forehead—he seemed almost rugged.

"I don't suppose anyone's ever told you that blue is the perfect color for you," she said. With those eyes, he must have heard it all his life. They were like pools she wanted to dive into.

"No! Really?" Jamie grinned. "Do you ever wish you could work in TV or film again?"

"Mmm... Sometimes. I'd love to do more voice work. But production? Maybe if I could write or associate produce. I wouldn't want to start over at the bottom of the food chain."

As they entered his "room," Kat's jaw dropped. "Geez, Jamie, you didn't tell me you were roughing-it." He had a luxurious townhouse with a fireplace and hot tub. The living area and private deck had a lovely view straight into the forest. You'd have to peer straight down over the edge of the deck to see anything man-made. "This is six times the size of the room I had here."

"Well," He pulled her close and wrapped his arms around her. "Now you can stay in this one, and you don't have to organize a conference for it." He kissed her, and she melted in his arms.

Jamie appealed to her in every possible way. He was intellectual, kind, and gentle. He had integrity and a dry sense of humor. Not everyone considered him handsome, but Kat did. His compassion for people suffering from debilitating diseases and his willingness to speak up for them—as well as donate staggering amounts of money to organizations that assist them—were all very attractive.

When he touched her, even casually, a warm sensation she hadn't felt in ages rushed through her body. When his touch was *not* casual, she tingled all over and wanted him more than any man she had ever known. Could that be the "transference of positive energy" that people who are into metaphysics talk about?

He pulled away and headed for the bathroom. "Let me get this make-up off. Where is the place with canoes?"

It took Kat a moment to clear the fog—or steam—that had filled her head. "Uh... canoes... oh... Meeks Bay. You still want to do that?"

"Yeah, don't you? We can get some lunch on the way. Let me put on my own shirt." Jamie came back to the living room and pulled the movie-camp T-shirt off. His arms and chest were even more muscular than they had been in L.A. He was buff.

"Whoa, dude!" She laughed and squeezed his bicep. "You been lifting weights for this role?"

"Oh, you noticed." He looked pleased and stood straighter. "No one else has."

"Good. I mean... um... I meant, uh..." she stammered.

"I know what you mean."

"No, really... I... I didn't mean... I just... um..." She shook her head, embarrassed and searching for the right words. "I just meant... Oh, hell... I don't know what I meant. But you look like a stud-muffin. Not that you didn't look good before! Oh, crap..." She covered her face with both hands and shook her head for putting her foot in her mouth.

By this time, Jamie was laughing at her attempt to backtrack. He pulled her hands away from her face and kissed one.

"You're cute when you're embarrassed. Thanks for noticing. It took a lot of work." He flexed a bicep. "And no, I haven't taken my clothes off with anyone here." He kissed her forehead and went into the bedroom to put on a pair of denim cut-offs, a T-shirt, and trainers.

Glad to hear his assurances, but feeling stupid, Kat flopped onto the sofa and put her head in her hands. Why couldn't she censor herself when she thought things that might be inappropriate?

The security guard who had glared at Kat on her way in was gracious toward Jamie as they left the resort's perimeter. As she drove south, Jamie said, "Oh, you're not going to believe this. Remember that actor who was stalking me at the Academy Awards?"

"Yeah."

"She's here."

"What? Is she stalking you again?"

"No, she's playing a young camp counselor who has a crush on my character. Her name is Rosanne Kaminsky."

"Oh, no!"

"It's all right. Her character is much too young for mine, and he's engaged. He rebuffs her several times and finally tells her to bugger off. I won't be acting when I do that." Kat looked pleased as Jamie continued. "May I ask a favor?"

"Of course."

"When we're around the cast and crew," he said, "especially when Rosanne can see us, I want them to know you're my girlfriend. Would you mind?"

Hard as she tried, Kat couldn't make her face muscles suppress a smile. "Why would I mind that?"

Out on the lake, Jamie marveled at the clarity of Tahoe's water. "How deep is this?"

"More than sixteen hundred feet."

In the back of the canoe, he leaned over the side to get a better look. "How far down do you think we can see?" The canoe tipped far to starboard, and he was about to swamp it.

"Whoa!" Kat said, forcefully, as she leaned hard to the port side. "I do *not* want to swim in this forty-degree water, thank you. There's only about seventy feet of visibility, now. It used to be more than a hundred, but pollution from development has reduced the clarity."

"Then why do they keep building things?"

"Because the developers don't care. They buy politicians' favor with campaign donations. When those politicians get the power, they change zoning laws and weaken environmental protections. Then their big donors can do whatever they want, make more money at the ecosystem's expense, and keep funding the politicians' campaigns."

"Geez..." Jamie had hit an environmental nerve.

"It's greedy business and profit versus a healthy environment... a never-ending battle between those who would destroy everything nature created here, to make money building more subdivisions and strip malls, and people who want to preserve the health and beauty of the lake."

"Wait. If new construction harms the lake, wouldn't some visitors stop coming here, and wouldn't that hurt local businesses?"

"Of course. And it's deadly for wildlife. But powerful outsiders only care about their own short-term profit."

"Well, then," Jamie said, "take THAT!" With his paddle, he splashed a wave of ice-cold water onto her.

"Aaaaah! You varmint!" She smacked the water with her paddle, sending a sheet of water back at him, rocking the canoe. Now they were both soaking wet.

Jamie probably hadn't expected an immediate counter-attack. Surprised and laughing, he said, "Varmint?" and slapped another wave of cold water at her. "*Varmint*, you say?"

The water hit its target. They kept the water fight going—and the canoe rocking—until she put her head down and waved a two-fingered peace sign. "Stop! I surrender! Damn, that's cold! And there's a lot of water in the canoe. We have nothing but our hands to bail it out."

"Really? You surrender?"

"Yes. I surrender! I don't have a white flag. What do you want?"

"Hmm... let me think. You call this cold? What a softie! You wouldn't last five minutes in the ponds near my house."

"I wouldn't swim in a pond, thank you. God only knows what else is in there." She wrung water out of the lower part of her T-shirt. "I swam and water-skied here as a kid, but it didn't seem this cold, then."

Kat was glad she had worn a loose-fitting, turquoise, heavyweight cotton shirt. She didn't want to resemble a wet-T-shirt contestant when they paddled back to the beach.

Intensifying her exercise routine had paid off, too. Canoeing took more upper body strength than her usual activities, and she didn't want Jamie to think she couldn't pull her weight in the boat. But after two hours of paddling, her arms were tired, and she was a little short of breath.

When they returned the rented canoe, a few people watched them. Did they recognize Jamie, even with long hair, a straw hat, and sunglasses? Kat handed him a tube of sunscreen. "Your face is pink."

He gave her a sexy smile, took her hand, and led her to a picnic bench, straddled it, and guided her to do the same, facing him. "You put it on me." With the combined length of their thighs separating them, they both had to lean forward for Kat to reach his face.

Jamie lifted her knees up over his thighs and pulled her close enough to earn an R-rating. With her legs wrapped around his hips, it looked—and felt—rather intimate. He closed his eyes as she gently applied the white cream that smelled like summer to his face and neck. If he'd been a cat he would have purred. She kissed him and handed him her sunscreen lip balm.

"Your nose is pink," he said as he dabbed a little sunscreen on it. "You're such a fanatic about this." Some people were watching them as they rubbed the Coppertone on each other's arms and legs, so he kissed her before she could reply.

"With you I am. I don't want you to get skin cancer, or your director to hate me for letting you get sunburned." She scanned the area. "Want to see some of the shoreline?"

"Sure." Jamie followed her on a path through tall, dense brush that wrapped around the beach. A western sagebrush lizard scurried across the path to the safety of a manzanita bush.

The brush gradually opened to a clearing with an outcropping of large boulders at the water's edge. Kat climbed onto the rocks and checked to make sure Jamie was still right behind her, and no one had followed him. They were alone. At the highest point—about five feet above the sand—she stood and admired the postcard view of the lake and the eastern shore, two miles away. Jamie put his arm around her shoulder. Most of their clothing was still damp.

"Shall we sit here and dry off?" he asked.

"Okay." She scanned the rocks and climbed over to a spot where they could sit on one boulder and lean back on another. Jamie took in the scene for a moment, then sat down next to her.

"Nice view. Did you know this was here?"

"No, but there are so many rocky places like this around the lake, I hoped we'd see one. They're good places to sit and enjoy the scenery... clean air... bird song..." The noisy motor of an approaching ski boat interrupted her.

"I hear it," Jamie said. "What species is that?"

She held her hand to her ear. "Sounds like a white-bellied SeaRay." She hoped Jamie knew SeaRay was a boat manufacturer.

He grabbed her and tickled her sides, causing her to curl up and fall into his lap, laughing and begging him to stop. He stopped, leaned over, and kissed her cheek. Then he helped her sit upright, and when she turned toward him, he kissed her properly.

Oh god, I love this!

Jamie ran his fingers through Kat's soft, baby-fine hair. "Your hair is lighter. And there's more red in it."

"Yeah, it does that in the summer. My mother has auburn hair. The chlorine and sun bring it out in mine. In winter it's darker, more like my father's." She assessed Jamie. "And yours... I know it gets changed for the roles you play, but what is your natural hair color?"

"This. Auburn."

"I like it."

"Thanks." He scanned the far side of the lake and nodded toward the mountains. "Tell me again... where did you live when you were here?"

Kat pointed northeast across the lake. "Incline Village, on the Nevada side."

"Oh, yeah... Bill and I had lunch there. Nice little place. Were you a deejay there?"

191

"Yes, and Program and Promotions Director. But I started as News Director."

"Those sound like good jobs. Why didn't you stay?"

"It didn't pay well. And after a while, I missed my friends and family, and the bands I used to sing with. I was driving down to the Bay Area every other weekend."

"You were a singer? You never told me that."

"Well, I wasn't successful. My general manager said we had budget problems. I would have to lay-off one of the jocks, and the rest of us would have do six-hour air shifts. My staff were all here because they loved Tahoe and would do any kind of work to stay. I would have been just as happy working in San Francisco or L.A., and because I had more experience than anyone else, was sure I'd land another job pretty easily. So rather than put one of them out of work, I laid *myself* off and moved back to the Bay Area."

"Are you having a laugh?" Jamie appeared incredulous. "You sacked *yourself* rather than one of your employees? Why?"

She shrugged her shoulders. "It seemed like the most logical and honorable thing to do."

"I've never heard of anyone doing that. How'd it work out?"

"Better for them than for me. I was too focused on programming the station to notice the job market was tighter than a frog's ass. I couldn't get another full-time gig in any city I wanted to live in. So one more time, I tried to get a recording contract. No luck."

They sat silently, watching a golden eagle scoop a fish from the lake in its talons. Jamie put his arm around Kat and pulled her closer. "People who care that much about fairness and doing the right thing should run corporations—and countries." She rested her head on his chest, and he sighed. "It's nice to relax in this breathtaking place with someone I love and no pressure for a couple of days."

They sat quietly enjoying the sun's warmth for several minutes before she asked, "Have you been to Emerald Bay?"

"Bill pointed to it as we drove past, last autumn. Is it nearby?"

"About two miles south. Want to see it?"

Jamie checked his watch. "Okay."

"Got a date?"

"I hope so." He kissed her temple.

At a vista point on the road, Jamie stood behind Kat, holding her against his body. Steep, green-forested mountains rose around three sides of elongated Emerald Bay and cast shadows on a small island, as the warm afternoon sun slipped behind them. Without speaking, the couple simply enjoyed the view. After some time he said, "Let's go home."

Back in his townhouse, Jamie asked, "Are you hungry?"

"Not terribly. Are you?"

"Not terribly." With a sly look, Jamie came over and took her face in his hands and kissed her deeply. She put her arms around him as a warm sensation ran from the back of her neck, down her spine, and through her entire body.

Kat was so turned-on by Jamie's touch she could hardly stand it. She loved the feeling of his strong, muscular arms holding her close. He pulled his shirt off, then hers. While kissing her, he unhooked her bra with one hand and danced her over to the sofa, then dropped to one knee, kissed her stomach, unzipped her shorts, and pulled them down to her ankles and off. His hands slid up her legs, and he kissed them, then her abdomen and breasts.

When he stood, she slowly unzipped his denim cut-offs and pushed them down to his ankles. He kicked them off, kissed her as she leaned back on the sofa, and hovered as though he was going to do push-ups over her body while kissing her.

In her younger days, she had been shy about taking hold of a man, usually waiting for him to put her hand where he wanted it. But it would have been stupid to pretend she didn't know what to do, now. With Jamie, she didn't hesitate. She was older, wiser, and knew what he wanted. He was rock-solid, exceptionally skilled, and after a few minutes, she let her mind think she was in love.

* * *

They talked and made love all evening, finally collapsing in each other's arms, tired and out of breath. As they lay there, holding each other comfortably, Jamie thought about the times they had spent together, Kat's attitudes toward life's ups and downs, her empathy for others, and their similar philosophies on important issues. He really did love this woman. *She is the one I've wanted in my life... but an American? I never expected that.*

Chapter 23: Bears, At Last!

Sunday morning, Jamie held Kat's hand as they strolled into the resort's brightly lit restaurant. "Do you see Rosanne?" Kat asked discreetly.

Jamie scanned the room. "Em... No." Still, he kissed her hand and clenched it, as though he feared someone might try to pull them apart.

They joined four of the production crew at a large table. Jamie introduced Kat to everyone and thoughtfully used their names in the conversation to help her remember them. The men focused on the scenes they'd shoot that day, but the women were more interested in Jamie and his "girlfriend."

Kat let him answer their personal questions and kept her responses short. He deflected those so deftly, he had obviously done it often.

The script supervisor asked Jamie, "Have the paparazzi found you, yet? "

"Not that I know of. My PA will tell me if he sees anything."

"You know you're only safe while you're on the grounds, here," Glen, an older, wiry, leather-skinned grip, reminded him. "Once you leave the security perimeter, you're fair game." He winked at Kat.

What was that supposed to mean?

"Yes," Jamie sighed. "We got some curious looks yesterday, but no one said anything. Either the people are cool or no one here knows me."

"You've just been lucky," Jenna, who looked about twenty-five, said.

"Well, I'm not going to hide here, especially when I've got my girlfriend from the Ministry of Wildlife with me." Jamie smiled and gave Kat a one-armed hug. Turning to her, he said, "By the way, I still haven't seen a bear!"

Glen responded before Kat could.

"You probably won't unless you're near open trash dumpsters. They're all bear-proof, here, and there's no trash on the grounds. They must have people picking up after litterbugs."

"So, what are you doing today?" Jenna asked Jamie. The way the hair and make-up assistant asked gave Kat the feeling it wasn't a rhetorical question. If anyone might tell the entertainment media what Jamie's doing and where, Jenna could be the one.

Jamie dodged the question. "We haven't decided. Maybe go to Reno or Virginia City... playing it by ear." He put his hand on Kat's back and asked, "Shall we?"

"It's nice to meet all of you," Kat said. "I hope your shoot goes smoothly."

Jamie held her hand all the way to his room. "Sorry about the 'Twenty Questions' in there."

"That's okay. They only asked about me because they're interested in you. I'm glad you spoke up. I don't know how much you want others to know about your personal life."

"Thanks. I'm not secretive, but I don't care to share everything with everyone. I hope you don't mind me saying you're my girlfriend."

Kat beamed. "Not at all. I just hope they don't think 'girlfriend' is a euphemism for a one-night-stand... or a hooker."

Jamie stopped with a shocked expression that made Kat regret adding "or a hooker."

"They'd better *not* think I'd pick up a hooker!" Then he started laughing uncontrollably.

"What?"

"You! I can't imagine anyone taking *you* for a prostitute! You're so... so..." He shook his head, laughing at her.

His laughter made Kat laugh, too. "What?"

"So... wholesome and... girl-next-door natural-looking, you couldn't even *play* one! There's not enough makeup and hair spray in all of California to make you look like a hooker!"

Jamie was still laughing when they entered his townhouse. It was an unlikely notion. She was old-fashioned enough to care about what others thought of her—and of this man she had grown to love, despite her best efforts not to. If only she were a few years younger and able to believe...

While Jamie was in the bathroom, Kat phoned the state wildlife rehabilitation facility near South Lake Tahoe to see if anyone she knew was working that day. "I'm on the north shore, visiting a special friend I'd like to bring down there. Do you have any guests?" She was in luck. They had two raptors and three bear cubs.

When Jamie came out, Kat said, "I have a surprise for you."

Jamie came over and put his arms around her. "Oh, yeah?" He kissed her. "Tell me."

"If I tell you, it won't be a surprise. We need to drive to it. Are you ready?"

"Em... do I need to take anything? Bear spray?"

"No." She straightened her shoulders and stood as tall and strong-looking as she could. "Remember? I'll protect you."

On the way to Kat's car, they ran into a production manager who told Jamie his scene, Monday, may be delayed. In the car Jamie said, "Is tomorrow your Monday off? If they change my call time, would you like to stay another night?"

Kat gave him a broad smile and nodded.

* * *

They drove south along the west shore, taking in the scenery. Jamie wondered how Kat felt about him and about telling her he loved her. Had he said it too soon? Maybe he should've waited until *she'd* said it. Women usually said it first. But she wasn't like most women. What if she was unattached because she *wanted* to be? He listened for an opportunity to learn her attitude toward long-term relationships and maybe even marriage.

Kat pointed out landmarks like Bliss State Park and Camp Richardson. "Did Bill bring you to the south shore, last fall?"

"Yeah. We went into a casino and nearly choked to death. You really know you've left California when you walk into one of those!"

"Yeah, it's hard to believe we all used to put up with smoke everywhere. I was glad Britain banned smoking in restaurants and pubs before I went there. Now I hope Australia and New Zealand will do the same."

"I heard they did. Have you been there?"

"No, but I'd like to go, someday."

"Maybe I'll take you there."

Kat smiled, but her eyes said she didn't take him seriously. Jamie could almost hear her thinking, *Yeah, right! In my dreams.* She turned off the main highway and drove through a neighborhood of rustic forest homes, then onto a gravel drive. A large, wooden Wildlife Care Center sign featured the California Department of Wildlife logo.

"Hey," he said, "Are you taking me to work?" Kat just grinned, so he reached over and squeezed her waist. She laughed and grabbed his wrist as she parked under a lodgepole pine. When she turned toward him, he kissed her quickly, and felt quite pleased with himself. She leaned over for another, longer one.

It smelled like dog food in the two-story redwood building's front office where a pretty young woman worked at a computer behind the public service counter. She glanced up and said hi to Kat. Then her eyes widened and her jaw dropped.

"Hi, Tina! I'd like you to meet Jamie. Jamie, this is Tina; she takes care of the animals here."

Jamie reached out to shake her hand. "Pleasure to meet you."

"Oh, my gawd," Tina said as she shook his hand. "Same here. When Kat said she was bringing a special friend, I figured it was a guy, but I never guessed it'd be Nigel Stone!"

Jamie looked at Kat. How many guys had she taken there?

"Jamie's shooting a film here, so I thought I'd show him the rehab center. He doesn't believe we have bears!"

"Oh, we got bears, all right," Tina confirmed. "A new cub came in, last week. His mother got hit by a car and didn't make it. Want to see him? We have to stay out of his sight so he won't get habituated and we can release him when he's old enough to make it on his own."

"Habituated?" Jamie asked as they passed through the office and out a side door.

"Accustomed to humans," Kat replied. "Wild animals that get used to people lose their fear of us. In places like this, they learn to associate us with easy meals. If we release them after that, they always find their way back to where people are and raid garbage cans, campsites, and break into homes and vehicles to get food."

"They become nuisance bears, then public safety bears," Tina added, "and they end up being euthanized, because you can't train them to stay away from people."

"Really?" Jamie was shocked. "You kill them for raiding rubbish bins?"

"Well," Tina said, "They have to do more damage than that."

"They progress from dumpster-diving to breaking into buildings, cars, and trashing campsites," Kat said. "Then public safety is at risk. A bear may just want a meal, but if it thinks you're the reason it can't find one, *you* might be on the menu."

"And if it's a sow with cubs, you can kiss your ass goodbye," Tina added, laughing.

By then they had reached the bear barn, a wood structure the size of a two-car garage. A one-way window prevented the cubs inside from seeing the people outside. Jamie cupped his hands around his eyes and peered into the building. "Oh, wow... Are those grizzlies?"

"No," Tina and Kat answered in unison. Kat deferred to Tina. "California hasn't had grizzlies since the 1920s—except on our flag. Our native species is the black bear."

"None of these are black," Jamie observed.

"That's the species name, not a description," Kat said. "Their coat colors range from black to cinnamon to almost blond."

"Are the dark ones envious of the blondes?" Jamie grinned.

Kat smiled and squeezed his hand as Tina groaned and continued. "These little guys were all born this spring, then got orphaned or injured."

Jamie peered through the window again. "Are those bandages on one bear's paws? What happened to him?"

"She got burned in a wildfire," Tina said. "We get one or two burn victims almost every year. Injured animals don't last long, even if their injuries aren't fatal. They become easy prey for predators, and if they can't forage, they starve."

Jamie stepped back from the window, taking in all the information being thrown at him. He turned to Kat. "You weren't kidding us, were you?"

"Nope. You and Bill weren't likely to run into bears, but I wanted you to know what to do if you did."

Tina grinned and poked Kat's arm. "She just didn't want to be the P.I.O. who'd get drawn and quartered by your fans, after telling *Inside Show Biz* a bear ate Jamie Knight!"

Kat and Jamie chuckled, then he asked, "What's a P.I.O.?"

"Public Information Officer," Kat said. "Generic term for someone who provides government information to the news media." Turning to Tina, she asked, "Who's in the aviary?"

"A golden eagle with a broken wing and a great horned owl that ate a rodent that ate anticoagulant rodenticide."

"This is brilliant." Jamie looked around the compound as they approached a large aviary. "Do people bring animals here?"

"Sometimes, small animals," Tina replied. "Usually they call the department and one of our wardens or biologists goes out. Or one of the local rescue groups' trained volunteers with the right equipment capture an injured animal and bring it in. We don't want the public trying to catch wildlife. They can get hurt, the animal can get hurt, or it will run or fly off, if it can. Then we have to search, and usually can't find it, so it suffers longer than it has to."

"I guess we don't have to hide from the birds," Jamie observed as they approached the wire-enclosed aviary.

"Not these, but we would, with chicks," Tina said.

"Can you teach Jamie how to hide from chicks?" Kat teased, gently pinching his side.

Grinning, Jamie grabbed her waist and pulled her close in front of him. "Come here... I'll hide behind you." Then he kissed the top of her head. He loved her quick wit and puns.

Tina giggled at their playfulness. "We won't release these birds unless they recover completely. The owl is really sick."

"Poor thing," Kat said. "Where's Bruce?"

"He had to run some errands. Should be back any time, now."

"Bruce Livingstone is one of the wildlife vets who works in this center," Kat told Jamie. She looked hopeful as she turned to Tina. "Got any kitties?"

"No, no kitties."

"Kitties?" Jamie asked.

"Mountain lions or bobcats," Kat said. "You know I'm partial to cats."

Jamie looked at her as if she was insane. "You like mountain lions? Are you daft?"

"I like all kinds of cats."

"You wouldn't want a puma curled up on your bed, though," Tina interjected.

"Uh... No. But a tiger..." Kat pumped her eyebrows and gave Jamie a sexy *I'm talking about you* smile and squeezed his hand.

He grinned and turned to the aviary. "How did the eagle break its wing?"

"Probably hit by a vehicle," Tina replied. "We're not sure, but someone reported it, standing by the highway. When they get focused on a meal, like a squirrel running across a road, they don't notice anything else, and they'll fly right into a truck."

"Poor thing," Kat lamented—again.

Jamie didn't have quite as much empathy for animals, but found hers endearing.

Walking back to the office Tina asked him, "What movie are you making here?"

"A drama about a wildfire threatening a kids' summer camp," he said. "The working title is *Pine Lake Summer*. Kat can tell you the release date when we know it."

"Is she your publicist here?" Tina asked Jamie, then turned to Kat. "You moonlighting?"

"No, but you know I like to promote things I believe in. And I believe in Jamie."

Jamie smiled, put his arm around her, and pulled her close to him. "You *could* be my California publicist, couldn't you?" He hugged her.

Tina asked, "What are you guys doing, today?"

"We haven't decided," Kat said. "Where do you like to go for lunch here?"

"I usually bring a sandwich from home, but I like Freshie's on Highway 50. It's kind of Hawaiian.

Jamie asked, "Would you like to join us?"

"Are you kidding? I'd love to! But I can't go anywhere until Bruce gets back. Thanks for asking, though. Maybe next time?"

"Okay," Jamie said. "Next time."

Driving back to the resort after lunch—and two requests for autographs and photos—the couple stopped at Emerald Bay State Park. This time they took the steep, one-mile hike down to Vikingsholm, a "summer home" built in 1929, modeled on an eleventh century Norse castle. Jamie had to promise Kat he would carry her back up, if necessary.

"This is a summer home? For whom? Odin?" Kat had expected many more people there on a Sunday afternoon in June, as she and Jamie strolled around, holding hands most of the time.

"This would make a brilliant historical film set. Wouldn't you love to have a home like this, with this amazing scenery?" he asked.

"Mmm... maybe... if someone else cleaned it, paid the winter heating bill, and we had four-wheel-drive SUVs to get in and out of here."

We...? Could her feelings about our relationship be the same as mine?

Back at the Rubicon, Jamie got a message saying he wouldn't be needed in make-up until 2 p.m. Monday. Kat could stay another night. She pulled a box wrapped in blue and green paper from her overnight case. "Since I won't see you on your birthday..."

"Oh, Kat, that's sweet of you." He tore the package open to reveal a book of magnificent photographs by Ansel Adams, all taken in the Sierra Nevada Mountain Range. "These are extraordinary! Thank you!" Jamie kissed her and held her for a long hug. "I'll think of you every time I look at this. Has anyone ever told you what a thoughtful person you are?"

"Happy Birthday. You are, too. And you deserve much more than a book... but I don't know what you want or—"

"I want you," he said, softly as he held her.

Kat whispered, "I'm all yours."

"Good." He held her close and kissed her.

* * *

That evening Kat and Jamie joined *Pine Lake's* Director Todd Swauger, Associate Producer Carla Mendoza and Jamie's co-stars, Don Ortega and Heather Nelson, for dinner in the resort's five-star Rincon Room. Most of the conversation centered on the film and Tahoe. A question came up about the animals campers might see there. Jamie looked and nodded at Kat.

"Squirrels, chipmunks, lizards, snakes, scrub jays, and bald and golden eagles, among other things. At night they might see bats, a raccoon, skunk, or opossum; they might hear owls and coyotes, and be seen by a bobcat or mountain lion, but *they* probably wouldn't see one. The cats are secretive and usually avoid humans."

"Rattlesnakes?" Don asked.

"Oh, yeah. And if you ever have to move a rock, lift the far side first." She demonstrated with an imaginary rock. "That way, if there's a snake under it, it has an escape route away from you. Most animals want nothing to do with us. They're most likely to attack when they're surprised or feel threatened. If you make noise when you're hiking, they'll hear you coming and most will move away from the trail."

"Are you a teacher?" Heather asked.

"No, I work for the state Department of Wildlife."

Carla asked, "Are you ever on TV?"

"Yes."

"That's why your name sounded familiar!" Carla exclaimed. "I think I've seen you on the news."

"Thanks! If you ever need a wildlife biologist, game warden, or any information, call me. Jamie has my numbers and I can either get answers or get an expert to call or come here to help you."

Jamie beamed. "Kat is my contribution to accuracy."

After dinner, he and Kat walked around the softly lit resort grounds, talking about their lives and professional goals, holding hands most of the time. Standing on a bridge over a stream, he asked her about what might have been a touchy subject.

"I can't suss out why you've never married. Did you not want to?" Kat took a deep breath. "Oh, I'm sorry if—"

"No," she interrupted, "it's okay. I just haven't thought about it in a long time. I wanted to be married. But my parents and my sister were each married three times, and I saw how divorce affected them. On top of the emotional pain, most women's standard of living drops forty to sixty percent. More, if they have kids. I saw Barbara go through that and swore I never would. I had to build a career to support myself first."

"Good thinking."

"Self-preservation. And losing my high school boyfriend hurt so much, I couldn't imagine being left by someone who'd vowed to spend his whole life with me. I decided early on that I wouldn't marry anyone until I was certain he loved and respected me as much as I did him. We'd have to have a lot of common interests and values, and he would want to be my best friend and equal partner as much as I wanted to be his. He had to *want* to spend his life with me, be monogamous, be a team... 'You and me against the world.' Know what I mean?"

Jamie nodded. "Mmm-hmm."

"But that never happened. The few boyfriends I loved and thought I'd like to spend my life with weren't the ones who wanted to marry me. I guess I set the bar too high. But after living with parents who fought and yelled at each other all the time, I figured living alone would be better than that."

Thinking about it made her sad. She would have loved to have shared her life with someone like Jamie. He was a rare bird. She would have glorious memories of these days and nights with him, but... at nearly fifty-five, she would surely spend the rest of her life alone.

Jamie appeared pensive, and after a few minutes of silence, said, "I don't think you set the bar too high. I think you were wise for your age. The only divorce in my family was Christy's, but I'm single for some of the same reasons. The match has to be right for both people, or it won't work for both. Divorce isn't the end of the world, but it's too painful and expensive to not try to prevent it."

Kat liked hearing that he believed some of the same things she did about such an important subject. "Well, if I screwed myself out of a better life, at least I'm in good company." *Until you meet the lady you want to marry.*

When they made love that night, she had more passion for Jamie than ever before. She didn't know he felt the same until he said, "I wish you could stay longer. Do you know how much I love being with you? And not only in bed."

"I wish I could, too, Jamie." She kissed him and without thinking, said, "I love you. The times we've spent together this past year have been fantastic." For once, she felt loved and wanted, even if only temporarily.

Jamie squeezed her. "I love you, too, Kat."

* * *

Monday morning, Jamie awoke to the sound of a bird outside the townhouse. He felt almost weightless, his heart bursting with joy to know Kat loved him. A text from Danny, in London, flattened it. "Photo of you and some girl in the Sun. You look good. She doesn't."

While Kat was in the shower, Jamie went online to see. It showed the two of them at Freshie's. Neither was prepared for a photo shoot. Kat was chewing food, which made anyone look odd; and her wind-blown hair didn't help her appearance. Strange... she had looked fine to him. The caption said, "British actor Jamie Knight, spotted in a Lake Tahoe restaurant."

Knowing it would bother her, he didn't tell Kat about it. She'd have to get used to it if their relationship went where he wanted it to go. But not that morning. That morning was too nice. Last night had been too nice. He wanted her to drive home with that memory, not this photo.

Others working on *Pine Lake Summer* saw the picture, too. The following afternoon, some electricians were reading a tabloid near the set, and one of them asked Jamie, "Why would a star like you want to be seen with a dog like her?"

Jamie's pleasant expression turned foul as he went off on the unsuspecting man. "She is not a dog! She's a normal woman, not some Photoshopped fantasy. Intellectually, she could run circles around you. I care about what's in a person's heart and mind. And you're no Bradley Cooper, yourself!"

Chapter 24: Summer in the City

Two weeks later—June 30—Kat called to wish Jamie a happy birthday, and he had a surprise for her. "I'll have four days off, this week. Todd and Laura think the crowds coming for Independence Day weekend will interfere with us, so they're going out to shoot wilderness footage. Want some company?"

"Does a bear sleep in the woods?" she asked.

Early Friday morning, Jamie crouched under a blanket on the floor of an SUV as it left Rubicon Resort. If any paparazzi were watching the film site, he didn't want them following him. He made his driver swear on his life that he would never tell anyone where he had taken him.

"How are things at Camp Wildfire?" Kat played with his film's setting.

"Good." Jamie hugged and kissed her. "We're on schedule, within budget, and Todd and Laura mean to keep it that way."

"Isn't that unusual?"

"Very. I like this team. They think ahead and anticipate problems. And Todd doesn't let the studio bully him into a schedule that's impossible to keep."

"Has Rosanne tried to get into your sleeping bag?"

Jamie recognized Kat's insecurity. He put his arms around her. "No. And she'd better not." He kissed her again. "You're the only one I want in my sleeping bag, anymore."

He sat down on the sofa and gazed at the pool. He was in no hurry to go swimming, even though it was already ninety-six degrees Fahrenheit. Kat's house was as clean as an operating room, again. She probably wouldn't pay a housekeeper and must have scrubbed every inch of the place to impress him. No one but the Queen lives with no dust. *Or cat hair,* he thought as Kellye jumped onto the sofa and for the first time, allowed Jamie to pet her.

Kat squeezed his other hand. "Have you done any interviews at Tahoe?"

"No."

"If you do, would you tell me?" she asked. "I don't want to waste my time watching gossipy shows unless you're going to be on."

"Do you ever watch *Inside Show Biz?*"

"Not unless I hear they're covering someone or something I care about. I'm not into sleaze and scandal-mongering."

"Glad to hear it. One host, Angela Shearing, keeps asking to interview me, but I want nothing to do with her."

"Why not? Is she the one you told Judy you wouldn't see, in May?"

"Yes. When she interviewed me at the Academy Awards, she had a sketty friend with her, who acted like a teenaged groupie. I kept my distance and left her set as soon as I could."

"So you're leery of her, now?"

"Very. I don't respect people who do things like that. It's unprofessional."

After nearly an hour of conversation about the entertainment industry, work, and the unfairness of having to pay for TV channels you'll never watch, the doorbell rang.

"Hi, need your signature," a delivery man said. A cardboard box beside him was big enough to hold a small mattress.

"Are you sure you have the right address? I'm not expecting anything."

The man showed her the label, and sure enough, it was addressed to Kat. He gave her a sealed envelope with her name hand-written on it. Inside was a *Star Trek* birthday card: "Welcome to the 21st century! Love, Jamie."

Kat looked mystified as she turned to him, and he got up from the sofa, grinning from ear to ear. "Jamie?"

"Let's bring it inside," he said. The men carried the heavy box into the living room while Kat signed an electronic receipt.

"What *is* this?" she asked. The box had no printing to suggest its contents.

"Open it!" Jamie grinned as the delivery man returned to his truck.

It took a screwdriver to pry the big staples out and open one end of the box. Inside the packing material was another box: "65-inch, 1080, HDTV."

"Oh, my god! Jamie! Are you kidding?"

"Happy birthday! I know it's early, but I wanted to be here when it arrived, and I don't want to watch films on that Model-T of yours."

Kat seemed to enjoy giving, but was visibly uncomfortable receiving gifts. Especially expensive ones— even from Jamie, who could easily afford them. Blushing, she seemed embarrassed, repeating, "Oh my god, I can't believe this," and "Thank you!"

Jamie wrapped his arms around the overwhelmed lady and held her close. The delivery man came back and in less than an hour they had set-up and rewired the new audio-video system.

"All right!" Jamie said. "Now we can hit the pool!"

"So *that's* why you didn't head straight out there!" Kat took both of his hands in hers. "Jamie, you are too generous. I don't deserve this."

"Yes you do."

"No... really... I'm... what do you say? Gob-smacked? I can't thank you enough!"

He hugged her again. "You're welcome! I'm glad I could make you happy so easily. I couldn't let you watch the next

Nigel series on..." He gave a disapproving look to the boxy, black dinosaur of a TV that sat on the floor. "You can't even see the entire picture on that thing!"

* * *

He was right. She had considered a high-definition TV for several years, but the prices were too high for a non-essential item. She had never imagined somebody might give her one.

"Okay, now you're going to earn that." Jamie took his overnight case to the guest room, saying, "The race is *on!* How many laps can you swim non-stop?"

"I've done thirty-three—a quarter mile—but I needed oxygen afterward," Kat exaggerated while getting into her swimsuit. "And I wasn't racing. Remember, I have asthma? Swimming for speed, I'm gasping after ten laps."

"Oh, right... I would hate to have to give you mouth-to-mouth resuscitation." Entering her room with a sly smile, he grabbed her waist and began tickling her.

Laughing, she squirmed and pulled away. "Hey! You're trying to get me winded before we even start. That's cheating! And you really don't need an advantage. You're so much more fit than I am, you're going to kick my ass, anyway."

"Oh, I wouldn't do that. I might *kiss* your ass, but..."

As Kat started to swat his arm, he caught her hand and kissed it." See you at the deep end!"

Standing at the pool's edge with the diving board between them, Jamie said, "Okay, how about eight laps? The Butterfly is my slowest stroke. If I do that and you do any strokes you want, does that sound fair?"

Kat knew she still didn't have a snowball's chance in hell, but who cared? She had issued the challenge to entice him to come see her again, and he had. So she pretended to believe she could actually compete. "Fair enough. Are you ready? Set? GO!"

Kat didn't hear Jamie dive in until she reached the far end of the pool, and he still easily got ahead of her in two laps. He probably could have finished while she was still on her fifth lap, but—since he wasn't the kind of guy who would humiliate a friend—he didn't.

At the end of her eighth lap, Kat held the edge of the pool deck, out of breath. "Well, I guess you'll (gasp) have to take the (gasp) TV home with you."

"Sorry?"

"I lost. I didn't earn it." Faking disappointment, she lowered her head.

Jamie moved closer and put one hand on her waist. "Well, I can think of other ways you can earn it, if you insist." He kissed her passionately and put both arms around her. After a minute, she let go of the deck to hold him and they sank, still kissing, until she needed air.

In an abysmal southern accent, she exclaimed breathlessly, "Whah, suh! Ah you suggestin' ah would compromise mah vuhtue fo' a television? Ah am insulted!"

Jamie's much better American Southern accent assured her he would never question her virtue, and he kissed her again.

* * *

That night, while Jamie and Kat were snuggling, Kellye jumped onto the bed. She trotted up and put her cold nose on Kat's face, meowed long and loud, and looked at her as if to ask, "What the hell are you doing?"

That was too much for either of them. They laughed hysterically and Kellye ran from the bed. For the rest of his stay, Jamie had a brief chat with the friendly feline each night. Kellye got the message; she let him have her place on the bed. No more cattus interruptus.

They spent most of their four days together at the house, swimming, watching movies and YouTube, talking and acting like young lovers. Jamie helped Kat put up drapes in the guest room, and made her tell him about the people and activities in one of her photo albums.

Saturday night, the Fourth of July, she took him out to a spot along the American River for a view of the fireworks show over Cal Expo. The cats got friendlier with him, and he warmed up to them, too. Kellye even sat on his lap—a sure sign of her approval.

During his last night at Kat's house, Jamie awoke, propped himself up on one elbow, and gazed at her for a moment. She looked as happy as anyone could while sleeping. He touched her cheek and whispered, "I love you, Kat." She was sound asleep, and soon he was, too, with her in his arms.

* * *

Those were the four most happy, relaxing days Kat could remember, and they passed much too quickly. She wished such days could go on forever. It was hard to say goodbye, watch the driver take Jamie away, and wonder if this love could possibly last. That evening, the normal quiet of her home rang in her ears.

At her office two weeks later, she received a large flower arrangement and a romantic birthday card, signed "Love, Jamie." Everyone in the office saw the flowers and knew who sent them. Whatever her relationship with Jamie was, it was no secret at CDW. As if that wasn't enough, he sent another bouquet with a funny card to her home. "All my love, Jamie."

"Why do you still doubt him?" Molly asked. "Men don't sign cards with 'love' if they don't mean it. And guys like Jamie must be even more cautious than most. You're more than a good friend with a pool."

"Maybe." Kat gazed at the extravagant bouquet. "It's impossible to not love someone as good and kind as Jamie. I have to kick myself, every time I feel it. I'm afraid, Molly. You know how many men have sent me flowers or said they loved me, in the past thirty years? Have you ever seen one of them? No. They all left me for someone else."

Kat joined Jamie at Tahoe once more and got to watch some filming. He and the production crew had fun with their work, especially when actors flubbed their lines. Some of the cast and crew were friendly toward her, while others treated her like an interloper when Jamie wasn't nearby. She had always been unsure of her place in the world. Should she really be there, since she wasn't working on the film? The producer and director welcomed her, and Jamie made it obvious *he* wanted her there. Was that enough to make it okay?

Rosanne Kaminsky, however, was downright hostile. Kat had been polite to her. She had no legitimate reason to be rude, but her flirting with Jamie exposed her motivation.

When Angela Shearing reported on *Inside Show Biz* that a source said Kat was a manipulative control freak who all but hissed at any woman who spoke to Jamie, his publicist, Judy, phoned him about it. He told her the report was bollocks, he knew the source, and would make it stop.

Photos of him with Kat were being taken and posted on the web, even though Jamie and the producers had asked everyone to leave them alone. Internet trolls wrote derogatory comments that made Kat sound like the nastiest bitch in all of California. Since she didn't spend time on the web during her days with Jamie, she didn't see any of it until friends sent texts.

Mortified, Kat asked, "Who would write things like that? I swear, Jamie, I've been courteous to everyone here and stayed out of the way..."

"I know you have. I think I know who's posting that shit. I'm going to tell her I know, and if she doesn't stop, I'll tell the world she's doing it and why."

Kat struggled to control her emotions, which alternated between feeling hurt and wanting to take a baseball bat to the perpetrator. Jamie held her and kissed her head. "I'm sorry, Kat. Don't blame yourself. It's because of me that someone's maligning you, and everyone else knows it's bollocks. Don't take it seriously."

"How can you *not* take it seriously? Aren't you afraid it could hurt you, too? I should leave."

"No. People who know me know I wouldn't tolerate anyone who behaved that way. And people who don't know us will learn the truth when they get to know us. The truth will always come out in the end. I love you, and I have no time for mean, jealous people."

That made Kat feel a little better, but she was insecure enough to be even more sheepish the rest of her time at Rubicon.

"I don't want you to leave," Jamie said on Monday morning. "Call your boss and ask if you can stay for my last week here."

"I don't want to leave you, either. But I don't feel welcome here when I'm not with you."

"Margaret and Todd like you, and since I'm happy to have you here, they are, too. You're nice, you know the rules at a shoot, and never get in anyone's way, so everyone but Roseanne either likes you or seems neutral. Anyone else can sod off."

Kat called Ron. When her head and shoulders dropped, and the light in her eyes disappeared, his answer was obvious. She didn't want Jamie to feel bad, but she couldn't hide her disappointment. As she put the phone down, she wished she didn't need her job to survive. After too many years with no love in her life, being with Jamie was like a feast for someone who had been starving, and she wasn't ready to leave the banquet.

"Why does Ron insist that I be there, now? There's nothing on my desk that has to be done this week." For the first time, she hated her supervisor.

"I'm sorry," Jamie said as he hugged and held her. "But I admire your work ethic. Our careers have to be our top priorities—for now."

Leaving Jamie was painful, knowing she wouldn't see him until his next trip to California. She didn't know when that would be, and it couldn't be soon enough. She was hooked.

He expressed similar feelings as they stood by her car. "I wish our time here could go on much longer, or I could take you home with me. But I have to memorize and rehearse a play that opens in a month. I'll be back in September, long enough for the Emmy Awards. May I come see you, the day and night after?"

"Of course! Consider my house your Northern California home. Just tell me when you're coming, and I'll request time off and stock the 'fridge with things you like." They hugged, and she added, "I love you, Jamie. You can't imagine how much I'm going to miss you."

"I'll miss you, too," he said. "I love you. I'll call you tomorrow night."

He kissed her so long, she hoped he would invite her back to his room, but she knew he wanted her to get home safely before it got too late. As she drove away, in her rear-view mirror, Kat saw Rosanne slither from the building entry toward Jamie, and her heart sank further. Her old nemeses—jealousy and fear of losing the man she loves—returned. *I hope he does tell her off.* Jamie called and emailed less often after that. He was busy, but Kat feared Rosanne might have caught his eye—or other parts.

* * *

In fact, Jamie had no use for Rosanne and felt better after telling her he knew she was posting hateful things about Kat online, and she'd better stop. He also told her—both personally and in character—to stay away from him.

The day after he got back to London, Jamie began rehearsing for a major theatrical production of Shakespeare's *Much Ado About Nothing*. He thought about Kat and wished he didn't miss her so much. Memorizing lines and action was hard enough without being distracted, wanting someone he loved who was five-thousand miles away.

Certain of his feelings, he told friends, "Kat is the woman I thought I'd never find. I simply needed to look at the valuable gift inside a plain wrapper, instead of flashy packaging that disguised lesser contents."

"Are you thinking of... you know... proposing?" Peter asked.

"Yes. But I want to bring her to London and introduce her to my parents, friends, and my lifestyle before I do that. She'll need new friends here, to make this her home."

Chapter 25: After The Emmys

Nominated for Outstanding Actor in a Miniseries or Movie—*Nigel Stone*—Jamie returned to Hollywood for the Emmy Awards in September. Kat wondered whether the pretty woman sitting next to him was his date, a colleague, or a seat-filler. Whomever she was, Jamie had left Kat out of another important event. You don't do that to someone you love. But he was coming to see her after the Emmys. So, *what was* she, to him? She wanted to ask, but was afraid he'd think she was possessive.

Picking him up at the airport was a little harder this time, as more people recognized and wanted to talk with him. Two young women even followed them halfway to Kat's car.

"You looked gorgeous at the Emmys," she said, hoping he would tell her who sat with him. "I'm sorry you didn't win."

Jamie never mentioned the woman who sat next to him all evening. He put his overnight case in Kat's bedroom and joined her in the kitchen. Disappointed, she turned chicken parts marinating in a glass dish when he came up behind her, put his arms around her and kissed her neck. She gasped as her skin tingled. "If you're trying to distract me, it's working."

"Good," he said and nuzzled her neck.

She ignored the tease, covered the chicken, and pulled away from him to put it back in the refrigerator. "Want to go for a walk before it gets too hot?"

In the shade of old Valley Oak trees on the levee above the American River, she asked Jamie about his rehearsals in

London and the Emmys. "Who was that, sitting next to you all night?"

"Some new client at my agency. What are you working on, these days?"

Typical man: change the subject. "Watch Out for Wildlife Week, Sea Otter Awareness Week, and next winter's ad campaigns for the tax donation funds."

Kat's enthusiasm for the research and conservation work those funds supported had always been obvious when she talked about it. Her voice became animated, her face lit up, she walked faster, and talked with her hands more.

"Have you ever done TV spots for them?" he asked.

"No, we can't afford air time or talent, and most stations don't air PSAs anymore."

"You could run them on your website and YouTube, then link to social media. Would stations be more likely to air them if someone famous did them?"

"Maybe, but I don't have enough money to even pay scale."

"Well, if you ever want to try it, I'll do it, and waive my fees again... if you want."

Kat stopped walking; she couldn't believe it. That would be worth big bucks... and they'd get to work together!

"Are you serious? That's incredibly generous, Jamie." She paused, then her enthusiasm faded. She had never directed a TV commercial or talent of Jamie's caliber. "But that would put me in the position of directing you." Surely he wouldn't go for that.

He grinned. "I'll take you in any position, Kat. So, you're a director, too? Wait a minute. Didn't you tell me you tried directing and didn't like it?"

"Yes, but I have to do everything for these campaigns. I research stations' ratings, issue a request for bids, buy the air time, and manage the contracts. I write, produce, edit, and voice the PSAs, and send them to all the stations that might air them. If someone else voices them, I direct. This is a government program, not a New York ad campaign."

Jamie looked pensive as they walked in the shade of an enormous oak. "So you're a one-woman ad agency and production company."

"Well... two women. Our administrative officer does the paperwork—but yes, on a shoestring budget. I call us Wildlife Productions." They walked in silence for a few moments, Kat's earlier excitement doused like an unwanted campfire. "I don't suppose you'd want to do it, under those conditions. But thanks for offering."

Jamie stopped walking and grabbed Kat's elbow. "Wait a minute. You think I'd back out, just because the director isn't a member of the Guild? Of course, I want to do it! How could you think I'd be such a git? Don't you know me better than that?"

Breaking eye contact, she stared at the ground between their feet. "I'm sorry. Jamie, I don't know what to think."

"Well, stop thinking you're not worthy, or that I don't respect you. You're a successful, talented, smart woman. If you weren't, I wouldn't be here. When would you want to shoot it?"

She cleared her throat. "I'll have to develop a concept, write a script, get it approved and schedule one of our videographers. Of course, it would have to be when you're here and can spend all day doing it."

Jamie raised his eyebrows and gave her his best "dirty old man" voice. "Honey, any time you want to spend all day doing it..." He pulled her close to him.

Kat snickered and put her arm around his waist. "I hope it wouldn't take all day to shoot a sixty-second PSA, but it wouldn't surprise me, given the way production goes. What do you think?"

"Well, you know that pre-production planning takes more time than the actual shoot. If you plan it well and have everything we need, one day should be more than enough.

Then we'd have time to do something fun, afterward. But if you don't..."

"I will! I won't waste a minute of your time." The whole idea intimidated her, but she couldn't pass up an opportunity to work with Jamie and make the PSA benefit him, as well as wildlife.

"I'll be back in L.A. this December. Can you go there to shoot it?"

"Yes. Ron's approved my travel to anywhere in the state to record a celebrity voice. But I don't have the skill to shoot a good video. I'll have to ask him to approve travel for one of our photographers... and we'll have to rent a studio, unless we shoot in a public place, like one of our ecological reserves... or Griffith Park. But that wouldn't work for the sea otter part. And most outdoor shoots have such lousy sound, we'd have to do A.D.R. afterward, which means paying for studio time. And I won't ask you to spend any more time than you've already offered... Oh, hell! The Department won't spend money on a studio *or* A.D.R. Between the bureaucracy and the budget, it's impossible."

They walked in silence for a few moments. Kat walked more slowly, staring at the ground. She never could hide her feelings.

"Well, don't give up the idea," Jamie said and took her hand. "Let me see if I can come up with something. I have friends in L.A., and Bill knows everyone in the business there. We may pull this off, despite all your government limitations."

Kat sighed and squeezed his hand. "Anyone ever told you what a good guy you are?"

"I try to be." Jamie put his arm around her. "You are, too, Kat, with a worthy cause. We're a good team."

That was music to her ears, even though she was still afraid to believe it would last.

Since Jamie's last visit, Kat had practiced cooking on the backyard grill, with Jo coaching her. The moment of truth would be this night when she grilled chicken and veggies for dinner. It turned out well, and they spent the warm evening in her backyard, playing in the pool, talking, and trying to identify stars and constellations... at least the few they could see through Sacramento's air and light pollution. She was happier and more comfortable with him than she could remember being with any man. The evening was lovely until mosquitoes defied the citronella candles and launched an attack.

Escaping to safety indoors, they checked each other for mosquito bites, and one thing led to another. For one more night, Kat forgot her self-doubt, and Jamie seemed to forget that opening night was a mere three days away. After years of insomnia, she slept like a rock with Jamie beside her.

Over breakfast the next morning, he took her hand and said, "You make me feel so comfortable here, I wish I didn't have to leave. I want you to come to London after *Much Ado* closes. Can you take a holiday, the last two weeks of October?"

"Seriously?" She sat up straighter as she felt something swelling in her chest. "I'd love to. I still have enough vacation time."

"Good. Call me as soon as you know; then I'll book your travel. I want you at my house."

"Jamie, that's incredibly generous!" The couple-thousand pounds it cost to fly from San Francisco to London wasn't a lot of money to people in his income bracket, but to her... *Oh, please let this mean our relationship is more than I can let myself believe!*

The morning after Jamie left, Kat was dying to tell Molly, but she wasn't in her office. If she didn't tell someone, she'd burst, but Molly was the only friend at work she could confide in. She tried to write a story for the department's magazine, but couldn't concentrate to save her life. Finally, a little after ten, she heard Molly's voice and headed for her office. Isabel Lorenzo—a young assistant public affairs officer who coveted Kat's job—was already there; she'd have to wait. When Isabel finally left, Kat slipped into the office and closed the door.

At first, Molly looked concerned, probably because Kat never closed the office door. But Molly couldn't miss the excitement in her face. "What?"

"You're not going to believe this." She was so excited she could hardly say it. "Jamie has invited me to London."

Molly's jaw dropped. "No! Are you sure you didn't dream that?"

"I know, 'in my dreams,' right? He asked me yesterday."

"For how long?"

"Two weeks. I know that's not long, but... two weeks with Jamie, at his house? I can't believe it. I figured I was just a friend with benefits—maybe one of several. Now I don't know what to think."

Molly laughed. "Oh, please. We know you're more than just a friend. When do you go?"

"In three weeks. You think Ron will let me have the time off? Not that it matters. I'm going, even if I have to call in, dead." Her smile stretched from ear to ear and she wanted to talk more, but Molly had deadlines to meet that day. Her workload was a nightmare.

"So, is this a secret?"

Kat shared little about her personal life with people in the office. She had nothing to hide. She merely valued her privacy. Molly said that was strange for someone who used to joke about everything in her life for thousands of radio listeners she didn't know at all.

"I think so. What do you think?"

"Well, everyone knows you have a relationship with him. He voiced your PSAs, and some of us saw him kiss you last year. The flowers he sent... and of course, Tina Steinberg has told half the department you're practically engaged."

Kat laughed. "Oh, Molly, do you think...? I'm afraid to even *dream that* could happen!"

"For Pete's sake, the man flies here to see you, says he loves you, buys you a TV, and now he's flying you to England, to be with him! Don't be such a pessimist. Still, you may want to keep it quiet until you get Ron's okay and airline tickets in hand."

"That's a good idea. Oh, man... how can I go write about putting bands on birds' legs, now?"

Molly smiled in her knowing way and softly said, "I'm thrilled for you."

Kat recognized her polite cue to leave. She went back to her office and realized she had forgotten to tell Molly about Jamie's offer to act in video PSAs. She tried to write about dove-banding, but she couldn't focus on it. *I will make this article a good one... but maybe not today.*

Instead, she started writing Jamie's contract and another letter to SAG-AFTRA. She couldn't believe he had offered to do them with no compensation, just because he liked her. Donations would double when people saw Jamie asking for them!

Chapter 26: To Jamie's London

Jamie had told Kat someone would meet her at the gate when she arrived at London-Heathrow, and take her to a secure part of the airport where celebrities could arrive and depart without being mobbed by paparazzi and fans. It sounded like the private clubs airlines offered their best customers, with its own security and customs staff.

But on the day, no one was waiting for her. She watched the other 344 passengers and crew disembark her plane until she stood alone at the gate, worrying. Jamie had forgotten her. The insignificance she'd felt as a girl, when her mother forgot to pick her up from after-school sports rushed through her. One of her psychology professors had called it an "abandonment issue." Kat's parents had never abandoned her, so several lesser incidents must have convinced her she was easily forgotten.

After waiting another fifteen minutes, she asked an airline employee's advice. He phoned "the star gate" and learned that an escort was on her way. Star Gate? Was that the airport's name for it, or the staff's private joke? Relieved, she took a deep breath.

At last, her escort arrived and led the way through secured doors and down two flights of steel stairs. A cheery young woman, she asked, "Are you meeting someone special?"

"Yes. But I think someone else is picking me up."

After a quick pass through customs, they arrived at the 'star gate,' and Jamie was there, chatting with a man. "Oh my god, he's here!" Kat thanked the escort and headed toward him.

He turned, and with open arms and a big, warm smile said, "You made it!" He gave her a bear hug and a kiss, took her carry-on bag, and introduced her to the theatre producer he had been talking with.

"I didn't expect to see you here," she said, with Jamie's arm around her as they walked toward a service counter.

"Why? Did you think I'd send a stranger to pick you up? That would have been cheeky. You've been through customs, haven't you?"

"Yes. I just need to get my suitcase."

"Suitcase? Only one? You travel light! They should have it here." He led her to a service counter. "What colour is it?"

"Bright blue, like this." She tapped the overnight bag he carried. That Jamie had kissed her in front of all those people gave her confidence and hope that perhaps he really did love her. She had dated too many men who were affectionate when alone with her, or with *her* friends, but acted like platonic pals in public and around *their* friends.

Jamie took her big blue suitcase from an attendant and they walked out to a larger hallway. "Here, let me take this," Kat said, pulling the carry-on bag off his shoulder.

As he led her through an unmarked door, they entered an underground car park full of expensive vehicles, including his sleek, black sports car.

"So is this how Aston Martin pays you for voicing their commercials? Not bad."

Jamie laughed. "No, but they've paid me enough, and gave me an extraordinary deal." He put her luggage in the boot and walked toward the passenger door. Kat headed for the other one, then stopped. *Oh, right...* Jamie grinned at her while holding the door on the left side of the car open.

She shook her head, a little embarrassed—in part for forgetting about the automotive differences in Britain, and in part, because she was unaccustomed to having someone open every door for her. Not that her male friends at home weren't gentlemen. It was just that she had acted like "one of the boys" for so long, she never expected or waited for anyone to perform such old-fashioned courtesies.

She sank into the luxury of the car's buttery-soft leather seats that warmed quickly. The instrument panel looked like it belonged in a small airplane. When Kat had bought her Prius, its dash panel seemed pretty cool, but this was James Bond cool.

"This doesn't have a passenger ejection seat, does it?" Jamie appeared pleased by the *007* reference. "No. But the traffic into town is so bad right now, you might want to eject. I thought I'd take you somewhere else, first. Okay?"

"Sure... whatever you want to do... I'm just glad to *be* here."

"I'm glad you're here, too." He leaned over and kissed her.

Kat was tired but excited to be in London, the guest of this sweet man. She was still a little uncomfortable about not paying her own way—and she had a feeling Jamie would give her more opportunities to work on that flaw in the next two weeks.

They drove west on the M3 motorway into green countryside, catching up on each other's activities. Jamie told stories about the Shakespeare production he'd done, while Kat enjoyed the scenery. Nearly two hours after leaving the airport, a circle of familiar, ancient monoliths rose on the horizon. "Stonehenge?" She was wide awake now. "I've always wanted to see that! How did you know?"

"You mentioned it on our first date, when you asked me about places to visit here. I think you also said you want to see the Callanish standing stones in Scotland, but that's a holiday trip. We can take the train up there, sometime. Stonehenge is so close, I thought it'd be a good way to start your visit and avoid the morning traffic before going home."

Few people were at the historic site that early on a weekday morning. The air was fresh, cold, and smelled different from any place at home. Kat inhaled slowly, wanting to remember everything about it as they walked around the site. Documentaries she had seen about the stones barely conveyed their immense size.

"This is incredible. It's one thing to read about a stone monolith that weighs thirty tons. But to actually see one sticking out of the ground is something else." While Kat wasn't into metaphysical philosophy any more, there was something oddly spiritual or other-worldly about the place.

"Amazing, isn't it? They started building this at least five thousand years ago, and it's evolved in phases." Jamie took her hand as they walked. "Some people believe it was a temple. Others think it's an astrological device. On the summer solstice, if you stand in the center of it and watch the heel stone over there, the sun rises straight up from it. They can track the moon with it, too."

"I wonder if anyone will ever figure out why they built this."

"They think they know *how*. But *why*? Who knows? I don't believe the theory that it's a calendar, or was built only for the sun to cast a beam of light onto a particular spot on the summer and winter solstices. It took too much work to be for that alone."

After walking a few minutes in silence, Kat asked, "Do you suppose—if we don't make the planet uninhabitable—hundreds of years from now, people will wonder why we built some of our structures? Like the Eiffel Tower... or that giant arch in St. Louis?"

"Well, if they dig up a McDonald's nearby..."

She laughed. "Petrified hamburgers!"

Inside the visitor centre, they admired the enlightening presentations of prehistoric artifacts. Kat took Jamie's hand and said, "We're in a museum, again."

"Yes. We met in a museum... had our second date in a museum... Let's make it our tradition. At least once a year we go to a different museum, okay? If we do it the rest of our lives, we still won't see them all."

As she reached around Jamie's back and pulled him close to her, Kat's heart raced, as if shot with adrenaline. Her smile was broad enough to stretch her cheeks.

On the way back to London Jamie turned off the M3. "I need your advice while you're here."

"Really? About what?"

"Guitars."

"Oh, man... I'm no expert. I only know what I've played and like. What do you need?"

"If you were going to buy a new guitar, what kind would you want?"

"Depends on what I wanted it for. For Scottish fiddle & pipe tunes, folk, and old pop songs—I love Martins, but they're awfully expensive. My Martin 12-string has the richest sound. If I were buying an electric, and could afford it, I'd buy an old Fender Stratocaster, from the 1960s. I have a cheap copy of one. Why? Do you play?"

"No, but I'd like to try it. Would you maybe teach me?" He asked so tentatively you'd think he was asking for the moon.

"Of course. I'd love to."

In Guildford, Jamie pulled into the car park at Reilly's Music, a store the size of a large supermarket. Acoustic guitars covered every wall of the front section of the store. Another section featured electric guitars, and beyond that, all kinds of other instruments. Kat's eyes widened, and she slowly gasped, "Oh, Jamie... Do you know what you've done?"

"Hmm?"

"You've brought a junkie into the dealer's warehouse!"

Jamie put his arm around her, pulled her close to him and whispered in her ear, "Good." He kissed her cheek, gently pushed her forward and watched as she wandered the aisles, admiring every instrument, the way he would the prototype cars at an auto show.

Inspecting Gibsons, Taylors, Yamahas, Takamines, Fenders and makers she had never heard of, Kat carefully lifted a £1500 Martin off the wall mount and gently touched the light golden top and rosewood side. The wood scent tickled her nose as she tucked the body under her right arm and played an F major 7th chord.

"That sounds nice," Jamie said.

After trying three guitars, she handed a mahogany Fender Newporter to him. "Try this one." She showed him the three strings to press with his long, slender fingers to make a G chord. He strummed all six, making a dull, muddled sound.

"You need to press the strings harder, slightly above the frets, and don't let your fingers touch any other strings." He pressed harder, strummed again, and it sounded better. "There you go."

"Ow! That hurts." He checked his left fingertips for damage. "How can you do that for an entire hour?"

"You have to build up callouses on your fingertips." She held her left hand out to him, palm up. He took her hand in his and rubbed a finger across her smooth, hard fingertips.

Jamie handed the guitar back to Kat, wrinkling his forehead.

A man wearing jeans and a Reilly's Music T-shirt came in. "Hi. I'm Adam. Looking for anything in particular?"

"I'm thinking about buying a guitar. My girlfriend's going to teach me."

As Jamie spoke, Adam's expression and posture changed slightly, enough for his new customers to see that he recognized the actor. But he didn't say anything about it. "What kind of music do you want to play?"

"Something easy, to start out," Jamie said and looked to Kat.

"Rhythm guitar for some easy folk, rock and pop tunes," she said.

As she expected, Adam led them to the most expensive guitars in the store, secluded in a small, locked room. She let him pitch a £5,000 instrument, then said, "These are beautiful, but for someone who's just going to try it, it would be wise to start with a mid-range instrument. Good quality, but I wouldn't spend a fortune on something that might end up in the case most of the time."

Now, £5,000 wasn't a fortune to an actor who earned half-a-million pounds for one film, but Jamie once mentioned that—despite his income—he didn't believe in wasting money. Kat led them back to the main showroom and took the Martin she had played earlier from the wall. "The best way to choose a guitar is to try them until you find one that sounds good to *your* ear and has a neck and body that feel good to you."

"*Your* neck and body feel good to me." He grinned and squeezed her waist.

Kat deadpanned, "Good. Try the guitar. You can play *me, later.*"

Jamie snickered and put his fingers on the strings to make a G-chord again, and strummed, as Kat gave him an encouraging nod. It sounded muddy. He pressed harder, strummed again, and it sounded better. She turned and picked out a Taylor for him to try.

"You want to learn on an instrument you can play comfortably."

"Okay. Which one would you buy?"

"If I were going to replace my Blueridge, I'd want a Martin. I've always liked their rich, mellow sound."

Jamie tried two Taylors, a Gibson, and an Ovation, then went back to the Martin. "My fingers are about to bleed," he told Adam, "but this one is comfortable to hold, and it sounded lovely when Kat played it. Do they make softer strings?"

Adam recommended light-gauge strings and offered to put them on it.

Jamie checked his watch. "How long does that take?"

"About ten minutes," Adam said. "We can do it while you pick accessories."

Jamie turned to Kat. "What do you think? Do you like this one?"

"I love it. But you're the one who's going to play it, so choose the one *you* like best."

"Okay, we'll take it." Jamie beamed at her. "Now, what else do you—I—need?"

"A solid case to protect it—"

"We have the Martin case for that," Adam said.

Kat nodded. "...a strap, an electronic tuner, some picks, and a book with diagrams of all the chords, then you can learn them on your own. And you might want a songbook."

"All right, let's do it." With sparkling eyes, an excited Jamie picked her up and spun around.

Adam took the guitar to a back room while Jamie selected a Baroque-designed strap and flipped through songbooks.

"You'll need a stand," Kat added. "They're not expensive."

"Kat?" Jamie gave her a look to remind her he didn't live on her salary.

She got it and gave her cheek a stage slap. "Sorry." She chose a tuner, a sturdy stand, and the same *Mel Bay Encyclopedia of Guitar Chords* she used.

Jamie peered at a tray full of guitar picks in the display case. "You use a pick, don't you?"

"Usually." She thumbed through a Beatles fake book. "Get a few in each size and try them to see which ones you like."

Adam placed the pick tray on the counter. "These are the most flexible; the medium-firm ones are in the middle, and the stiffest ones are on your left."

"Kat?" Jamie looked toward her.

"I like the stiff ones," she replied, without looking up from the music book.

Jamie stepped to her side and whispered, "I know you do. But what about guitar picks?"

Kat swatted his arm and snickered, "You're bad," hoping Adam hadn't heard that. Jamie grinned, kissed her on the cheek, took a copy of the Beatles songbook, and went back to the picks.

By the time Adam bagged the small items and rang up the purchase, a young man who had re-strung the guitar brought it out and placed it in the case. "That's a nice guitar," he said, then recognized Jamie. "Hey, aren't you the crooked D.I. in the *Last Rites* film?"

"Yes."

The young man beamed. "That was blinding!"

As he drove back onto the road that led to the M3, Jamie looked like a little kid who had just gotten his first bicycle.

"I'm glad you want to play guitar," Kat said. "So you're going to be a rock star, too! Is there anything you *can't* do?"

"Of course. I can't play guitar... yet." He smiled as he accelerated onto the motorway and took her hand.

The next two weeks were going to be unforgettable.

Chapter 27: Warm October at Jamie's

Celebrities had a harder time keeping their private lives private than in the past, but Kat couldn't believe the things fans had done to get near Jamie. Some had even gone to his previous home and peered through his windows. The local attention that followed *Nigel Stone's* success had prompted him to move into a gated community with twenty-four-hour security. An electric gate closed behind them as he drove up a small hill to his four-car garage.

"Want the six-pence tour?" Jamie asked.

More like six-million pence. To Kat, the three-story house seemed enormous. It had a reception hall, drawing room—"living room" in the States—family and formal dining rooms, and six bedrooms—each with its own bathroom. Large stone fireplaces were focal points in the drawing and family rooms. Old paintings of the English countryside and natural scenery from throughout the British Isles reflected Jamie's appreciation of nature and tradition.

White walls with large oak-framed windows gave the entire house a light and airy atmosphere. And it was as spotless and clutter-free as the homes featured in magazines.

An oval table that could seat twelve filled the center of the long dining room. Real oak cabinets and drawers lined a spacious kitchen that had every appliance you could want, a big center island with storage inside, and a view of the back garden.

"If Barbara had a kitchen like this, she would think she had died and gone to heaven," Kat declared.

"Do you think she'd cook for us if we had her over?"

"Oh, yeah... in a heartbeat. Wait... What do you mean 'we'?"

"You and me," Jamie said, tilting his head to one side. "What do you think?"

"I like the sound of that." Kat's heart skipped a beat.

He took her hand and led her into his screening room, furnished with comfortable brown chairs, loveseats, and sofas. Framed posters of classic British films, the iconic masks of comedy and drama, and bright, jewel-tone throw pillows gave the room color and atmosphere.

"I've dreamed of having a home theatre like this ever since I saw one in Beverly Hills, when I was eighteen," Kat confessed. "What's the last thing you saw in here?"

"Some raw footage from *The Ivory Reel*."

"Are you happy with it?"

"Oh, I can always find things I wish I had done better. But it's shaping up. Since you're into wildlife, you should enjoy it."

"Mmm... I don't know, Jamie... I want to see all your films, but I can't stand to see animals being abused or killed, even though the animal actors are allegedly not being hurt."

"They're not."

"Knowing elephants really *are* being hacked to death with machetes infuriates me and breaks my heart." One of her hands held the whale fluke on her necklace as the other made a fist. "I hate crying in a theater, in front of people."

"Really? You have that much empathy?"

"Sometimes more than I'd like. It's embarrassing to fall apart over fictional characters and situations, but when the actors and sets are convincing, and the music is right, I get all wrapped up in a story. That's one reason I don't go to movies as often as I'd like to. That, the high price of tickets, and inconsiderate jerks who use their phones during the film."

"You shouldn't let *that* stop you! Theaters are dark enough; no one can see your tears."

"My date—or friends will, and it's embarrassing."

"Kat, that's the response we *want*!" He put his hands on her shoulders and bent his knees to meet her eye level. "Actors strive to play parts well enough to make the audience cry, cringe, laugh, or feel angry or frightened. We love people like you, who sense the emotions we're projecting. You shouldn't be embarrassed to have feelings and empathy for others." He hugged her. "And who are you dating? I thought you loved *me*."

"Only you, now."

"Good." Jamie took her hand and led her out to an enormous backyard that looked mostly natural, but had a few formal garden features. The deciduous trees had lost most of their leaves, but mature evergreen hedges and trees hid everything outside the property, creating a sense of isolation. As they walked around, Jamie pointed out his favorite spots. "The property is slightly over two acres. I like my space, too. Would you be comfortable living in a place like this?"

"As long as you were with me." Jamie's house and yard were so much like the ones Kat had fantasized about having—when she was young and naïve enough to think she might someday be this successful—it was almost creepy. Had some deity she didn't believe in stored those dreams and arranged for her to meet a man who shared her idea of the perfect home? Yeah... just to tease her. But was Jamie suggesting...? *No. Don't even think it.*

Back in the house, he showed her the bright cobalt blue-tiled steam room, large enough for six adults. But he saved his favorite room for last.

"Are you kidding me?" she exclaimed. "Why didn't you *tell* me you had an indoor pool? All this time I've been feeling sorry for you, thinking you were swimming in cold, nasty ponds full of bugs, algae and duck guano!"

"Occasionally, I do... but I knew I'd bring you here someday, and I wanted to surprise you. You're not mad at me, are you?"

"Of course not. Just surprised. And how long have you 'known' you'd bring me here?"

Jamie ignored the question. "That's good." He grabbed her around the waist and, smiling, pulled her toward the pool. "Because if you were mad, I'd have to throw you in!"

"No!" Kat struggled, pretending to be afraid. Then it occurred to her that he might actually do it. "No—Jamie, please... I don't want to be cold and wet!" Her laughter gave her away. He put his arms around her and kissed her.

Softly, he said, "I turned the heat up for you. It's twenty-six degrees—eighty, to you."

"But you didn't tell me to bring a swimsuit."

Jamie brushed her ear with his lips and whispered, "You won't need one." His warm breath on her ear sent an oh-so-pleasant jolt through her entire body.

"Oh, no way!" Kat was very modest; she would never go skinny-dipping. Yet the idea excited her almost as much as it unnerved her. *Gotta buy a swimsuit, ASAP.*

"Let's get you unpacked." Taking her suitcase and carry-on bag upstairs to the master bedroom, he opened the door to a huge walk-in closet. "This section's for you." He motioned toward nearly a third of the hangers and drawers that filled the cavernous space.

"Good lord. This closet's as big as my office." Her clothing took up little of the space he offered. Was he saving it for someone?

"Okay," Jamie said, "how about a guitar lesson?"

"I'd love one! Would you teach me some British hits?"

"Sorry? *You're* going to teach *me*." Laughing while trying to grab and tickle her, Jamie chased her down the stairs to the family room where they had left his new guitar and accessories. Kat picked up the guitar stand and held it up in front of her, imitating the "lion tamer" on antique circus posters.

Jamie dropped to his knees in front of the guitar case and opened it, grinning like a little boy at Christmas. How did a guy from a well-to-do, artistic family never own a guitar? His first strum produced an unpleasant combination of notes, and he gave her a pathetic look.

"It's just gone out of tune," she said. "New strings always stretch. You may need to tune it every day, for a week or so. Once they're stable, it'll stay in tune a long time, unless it's exposed to extreme heat or cold."

"Really?" He seemed surprised. "What happens if it gets too hot or cold?"

"If you're not talking about extremes, it'll only need to be tuned more often. Extreme temperatures are bad for the wood. This is a fine instrument, Jamie. If you take good care of it, it will appreciate in value."

"Maybe I should buy more of them," he joked, as Kat attached the strap and handed it to him.

Jamie put the strap over his head and shoulders awkwardly and tried to get comfortable after she adjusted it. "Why don't you sit on the ottoman, and I'll show you how to tune it." On the coffee table in front of him, she opened the encyclopedia of chords to the page that had a diagram of the neck, head, and strings.

"Clip the tuner to the top of the head, like this, and press this button to turn it on."

"That's almost as easy as turning *you* on."

Kat kissed his ear as the little square screen on the black plastic turned green. "No one's ever turned me on like you do. Now, take a pick, and gently pluck your low E—the wire-wound string closest to your face."

Jamie pressed the string and let go. The indicator on the screen barely moved. Standing behind him, Kat turned the tuning key, then had him do it, while plucking the string until the meter pointed to zero.

She coached him through each string, then—because each one stretched in the short time it took to tune the others—he tuned them again. When they all stayed tuned, she showed him a simple strumming rhythm and how to make a C chord.

"Damn!" Jamie examined the dents in his pink fingertips. How do you get past the painful part?"

Kat took them in her hand and kissed them. "I'm sorry it hurts. Play a little every day, until it hurts, then play a little more. Stop when it's too painful, then come back and do it again several hours later, or the next day. Play a little bit longer each day, and eventually you'll build up callouses that'll let you play for hours."

He clumsily took the guitar off and handed it to Kat. "Here, you play something."

Kat had been playing for so long, she put the guitar on like a jacket and wore it. All she could think of were love songs. She took a chance and sang a favorite old John Denver tune, "For Bobbie." The lyrics promised romantic scenes like walking in the rain together—a metaphor for helping each other through life's trials—hand-in-hand, loving him more than anyone else could.

"I hope you mean that," Jamie whispered, "because that's how I feel about you."

Danny—Jamie's cousin and personal assistant—interrupted their sweet musical moment, walking in carrying a handful of mail. Jamie took the mail, introduced Danny to Kat, and told him he would text him if he needed help there in the next two weeks.

The look Danny gave her made her wonder if she was just the latest in a parade of women Jamie brought home for a few days of "playing house."

That evening, jet lag overtook her and she fell asleep on the sofa with Jamie's arm around her. When he woke her and took her to bed, he held her in his arms and said, "I'm so glad you're here, Kat. I want you here, with me, forever."

Oh... My... God! Shocked, her mind went blank. Instantly, the entire world seemed lighter, brighter. She stopped fighting her feelings. Could that space in the closet be hers for more than two weeks? It seemed too good to be true. But Kat had never been happier than she was that night.

She kissed his neck and said, "Jamie, those are the sweetest words... I've been afraid to think you could want me... There's no place in the world I'd rather be than with you... forever." She pressed her cheek against his chest. *Oh, please... this time, let it be!*

* * *

Jamie relaxed. Why hadn't he told her sooner? Now that he had, and knew she felt the same, a warm, peaceful feeling came over him. He had been running on a treadmill, going nowhere; and now that he had stepped off it, he was right where he wanted to be. Now he could relax. He imagined sharing those rainy nights by the fire with Kat—someone he loved, who loved him, and wanted to be there with him as much as he wanted her, with no ulterior motives.

* * *

That week seemed like a dream to Kat. Jamie took her to the Natural History Museum in South Kensington, and out to the countryside for a leisurely hike and a picnic.

"It's beautiful here," she said, "as if we've stepped into a Jane Austen novel."

"May I be your Mister Darcy?"

"Is there a pond around here?"

Another day, they had lunch with Jamie's friend, Leigh, who welcomed Kat to London. "Jamie told me how you two met. And neither of you thought you'd ever see the other again?"

"No," Kat said. "His invitation surprised me that evening, and we had a good time, just talking. When he called me, two months later, I thought he was one of my friends, impersonating him!"

Jamie laughed. "I had to tell her about our first date to convince her it was me!"

He seemed completely relaxed with Kat. The way they looked at, touched, and kidded each other, anyone could have seen they were in love.

"Sometime when Jamie has to work and I don't, I'll take you to some places he might not think of. And you'll both have to pop over for dinner with Bob and I."

"Thank you, Leigh... I'd like that."

"You'll have to wait until her next trip," Jamie said as he pulled her close to him, "because I have plans for every minute she's here, this time."

One evening they went to the cinema, and he had his arm around her the whole time. She felt like a teenager on her dream date.

She taught him another guitar chord each day, and he worked on switching between them, until his fingers hurt too much. "You're on your way, if you stick with it," she said.

She never would have guessed that someone ten years younger could make her feel so safe, so secure, so... loved. She hoped Jamie felt as safe and content with her as she did with him.

He was the sort of man she had always longed for, but never expected to know. He was passionate in a kind, gentle way, and loving on an emotional level that convinced Kat he really did love her. To her, that made all the difference in the world. She wanted to lie in his arms forever, and now believed it might be possible.

Chapter 28: Forget Props. Call Wardrobe!

Kat never dressed up at home. At least, not what most people consider dressing up. But now her lifelong battle with The Fashion Police was biting her on the butt. She hated dresses and only owned one. She had lived in Levi's and tennis shoes since leaving high school.

Once it had been a statement—a way of standing up to authority figures who insisted that women dress a certain way, no matter what they were doing or how inappropriate, expensive, or uncomfortable the clothing was. She took pride in refusing to cater to their demands and liked to say, "I'm not working to support the fashion and dry-cleaning industries!" Now she wanted to look like she belonged with Jamie and make a good impression on the people in his life.

None of her clothes were suitable for the fancy places Jamie wanted to take her. One morning, while she tried to decide what to wear, he came up behind her in the closet, put his arms around her, and kissed her neck.

"Are you thinking you'll look out-of-place here, in your California wardrobe?"

"Yes." Her voice reflected resignation and irritation with herself. If she wanted to change her life, she would have to change her ways. "I've always valued comfort over style. It didn't matter before, but now... I'm sorry, Jamie. I hate being uncomfortable, have no fashion sense, and now it's embarrassing."

"Don't let it bother you. Fashion doesn't always make sense. I didn't tell you every place I wanted to take you, so you couldn't have known what to bring. Let's go shopping.

We'll find clothes you like that'll be both comfortable and suitable."

Jamie had impeccable taste and had modeled for top designers. He dressed perfectly for every occasion. "I know where to take you. You belong with me, whatever you wear, and if you want to look the part, you will."

In a fancy shop Kat never would have entered on her own, he helped her put pieces together that featured the blues she loved, and he chose one bright red dress that brought out the color in her face. Fortunately, she liked most of them. The four outfits they both liked best were awfully expensive, but she was willing to break the bank to look right.

When she pulled out her Visa card to pay for them, Jamie pushed her hand back into her purse. "This is on me, love."

Kat had expected that. "No, Jamie. You're not responsible for—"

He interrupted her objection with a kiss. "Yes, I am. It's my fault you need anything other than what you brought."

"No. I appreciate your generosity, but I will pay for my own clothes."

The store clerk helping them looked dumbfounded as she watched this woman, who clearly wasn't posh, objecting to an affluent man's attempt to buy her clothing.

"Not under these circumstances." He took her Visa card and dropped it into her purse, which he then zipped shut. "I *want* to buy these for you. I love you. You can buy lunch."

Kat struggled inside to accept the generosity she didn't think she deserved. "Thank you, but this isn't right. You're too generous, Jamie. I appreciate it all—the clothes, your advice, and your kindness. But..." She could feel tears welling up and began blinking madly to resorb them before he noticed.

"You're welcome." He hugged her. "Picking out clothes for you is recreation, to me. I feel like an artist, adding a complementary frame to a painting I like. You know you're the first woman who ever let me choose outfits for her? I'm having fun."

Some people might have taken that as an insult, implying they needed help to look good. Not Kat. She did need help, and Jamie's smile and frequent hugs told her that what he said came from love.

Shoes were a unique challenge. She had never been able to walk in high heels and hadn't owned her only pair since she was thirty. She had worn cowboy boots with 1½-inch heels in the 1980s. But those were thick and supportive, unlike most women's shoes.

"Nature didn't build us to walk around on our toes," she said, "and high-heeled shoes aren't even designed for a human foot! Look at the footprint they make. Do you know anyone whose bare feet leave prints shaped like that?"

"No, you're right," he conceded.

"I sprained both ankles too many times when I played sports in school and the ligaments are weak. Even low pumps make my ankles bend sideways, and I fall. And my heels are so narrow, they slip out of dress shoes every time I take a step—even with heel pads in them."

She agreed to try wearing a pair of 1½-inch pumps that were supposed to be comfortable. They weren't comfortable to her, but she wouldn't complain. Jamie was doing so much for her, she would work at keeping her ankles straight and endure the shoes for him, when it really mattered. *My twenty-eight-year-old self would kick my ass for capitulating like this. But where did fighting social norms get HER?*

Kat was especially glad Jamie chose the dress she wore when she met his parents and sister for dinner at a high-end restaurant, even though it exposed her legs to the cold air. Under the table she slipped the cruel shoes off her feet.

Immediately, she could see where he got his good looks. Tall, handsome Reginald Knight had a full head of mostly white hair and an athletic build. Jamie's mum, Edith Davison, was heavier than when she'd played a Bond Girl in the 1960s, but she was still pretty, with her light auburn hair softly curled to land on her shoulders. They both had deeply blue eyes like Jamie's. His short, blonde, much-older sister—Christy—was attractive too.

Light, friendly conversation lasted about half an hour before Edith and Christy shifted gears. At times Kat thought they were challenging her. Still, she answered every question with a smile—or at least a neutral expression and vocal tone. She refused to let anything agitate her that night. She had to make a good first impression. Jamie, on the other hand, didn't hesitate to intervene when the questions seemed impertinent.

"Jamie says you're a musician," Christy said. "What kind of music do you play?"

"Folk, rock 'n roll oldies, traditional Scottish... Are you into music?"

"I like sixties rock," fifty-nine-year-old Christy said. "Who's your favorite?"

"The Beatles. "

"I like the Stones and the Who. Who else?"

Jamie looked as though he suspected his sister was digging for something, but Kat kept answering the questions and tossing them back to Christy. "The Association, Linda Ronstadt, Neil Diamond, Peter, Paul & Mary, and most of the artists we call the British Invasion."

"Oh? Such as...?"

"The Dave Clark Five, Petula Clark, Herman's Hermits, Chad and Jeremy, Dusty Springfield, Peter and Gordon..."

After some artists' names, Edith interjected, "Oh, I liked them."

Finally, Christy asked, "What about the Buckinghams?"

"They were good, but they were Americans. They gave themselves an English-sounding name because British bands were hot—and it worked! A lot of Americans believed they were from England, so they rode the wave."

Christy's eyes narrowed. "You know an awful lot about the sixties for someone Jamie's age." Her tone suggested she believed Kat to be much older than Jamie.

"Kat used to be a disc jockey," Jamie stated in a tone that told his sister to back off. "She *played* the oldies. She *had* to know about all those artists and their music."

"And my older sister played them all the time, when I was little," Kat added. She hoped Christy would drop it and was relieved when Reggie spoke up. Judge Knight had been sitting back, listening as the women cross-examined his son's new girlfriend. The conversation lightened up once he joined it.

"Where were you a deejay?" Reggie asked.

"San Francisco, Los Angeles, Anchorage..."

"Alaska? How was that?"

"Beautiful, cold and expensive. I only spent a year there. Then I moved to Ottawa, where the humidity made it feel even colder than Alaska."

"And now you work for the government of California? Why did you leave radio?"

"I loved the work, but not the lack of job security. And it paid poorly. I gave it sixteen years, then got 'a real job' and made my parents happy."

"It's nice that you could spend that many years doing something you enjoyed. Too many people don't even try to follow their dreams, and spend the rest of their lives wondering whether they could have succeeded, doing what they loved." He gave a knowing look to Christy, who frowned at her plate.

Kat nodded. "I was lucky. I had some good times and experiences money can't buy."

"Working for the government can't pay very well," Edith declared.

"Public employees don't get rich, but I earn enough to support myself comfortably. I can't run out and buy everything I'd like to have, but I have everything I need and enough to save for retirement, donate to charity, and support my mother. Most people don't need nearly as much stuff as we think we do."

Jamie appeared pleased, and Kat hoped that was the end of his sister's interrogation. He was demonstrably affectionate, holding or touching her most of the evening, making it clear to his family—and anyone else who might look—that she was his girlfriend.

Knowing how protective mothers and sisters could be, Kat did not hang onto him. She didn't want to appear "clingy." If *her* brother were rich, famous, and single, she'd probably suspect every woman *he* dated of being a gold digger until proven otherwise. Given Jamie's generous nature, people must have taken advantage of him.

Back at Jamie's house, Kat couldn't wait to get the "iron maidens" off her aching feet. And she needed some reassurance from him. She had been on trial and now worried about his family's verdict. As he perused the mail, she came up behind him and put her arms around his waist.

Putting one hand on her forearm, he said, "Hi," and kept reading an invitation to a charity fundraiser.

Kat leaned the side of her head and the rest of her body against him, clasping him. The fact that he didn't react made her wonder... *Did I say something at dinner that I shouldn't have? Was my tone ever...?*

She mentally reviewed the evening and couldn't think of anything that might have displeased Jamie or offended anyone. But she needed him to hold her, to draw out the hostility she had absorbed from Christy. He kept reading the mail. She gently slid one hand down the front of his trousers.

Softly, he said, "If you're trying to distract me, it's working." He set the letter down, turned around, and hugged her tightly. She said nothing. He must have sensed what was bothering her.

"You were brilliant tonight. Don't let Christy make you feel unwelcome. She was fifteen when I was born, and with Mum's career going strong, she raised me as much as Mum did. She's protective, but doesn't want *me* to think she cares at all. When she gets to know you, she'll understand why I love you so much."

"I hope you're right." They stood holding each other a few moments. Then, taking Jamie's hand, Kat led him upstairs to the bedroom and slowly unbuttoned his shirt. She pulled it off as she kissed him, then unzipped his trousers, gradually removing all his clothes. His body language told her he liked the role reversal. This time, she took the initiative and led *him* into physical and emotional bliss.

Scottish folksinger Jim Malcolm had once told her, "Women who think the way to a man's heart is through his stomach are aiming too high." That night, Kat lowered her aim and hit the bullseye. She awoke the next morning to see him propped up on one elbow, smiling at her. She sensed that Jamie's heart was hers and prayed it would remain so, always.

Chapter 29: Now You're Cooking

Jamie enjoyed cooking, as long as he didn't need to impress anyone. He called it "playing in the kitchen." One afternoon they tried to replicate the "bridies" Kat remembered from McLaren's Bakery in Forfar, Scotland. The savory meat and onion baked inside a pastry crust tasted delicious but looked like a Cornish pasty someone had sat on.

They spent a lot of their time just talking and growing closer every day. When they shared events from their childhood or early adult years, both were surprised at how often the other would say, "Really? Me, too!"

Despite growing up in very different circumstances, both had felt inadequate, desperately wanted their parents' approval, and seldom thought they had it. Both had been accidents, with parents who were older than their friends' parents, and who worked constantly.

Each of them, at times, felt unloved, unwanted, and sure to fail in life. Conversely, both had sometimes felt like they were on top of the world and could accomplish anything.

"Maybe everyone feels like a winner sometimes and a loser at other times," Jamie speculated. "Maybe there's nothing unique about it."

Often when they went out, people took Jamie's picture and paparazzi shots showed up in the tabloids. Obviously, Kat had never experienced anything like that. "How can you stand having people watching and photographing your every move?"

He shook his head. "I don't know anyone who likes it, but it's the price of fame. You try to ignore it. I'm afraid I brought it on myself, thinking it would make Hollywood pay attention to me. These days, it's nearly impossible to enjoy success in show business without being followed. Some people manage, though. I don't see Emma Thompson or Tom Hanks being libeled, or their pictures with salacious captions in the press. I'd like to learn how they avoid all that negative attention before—*and if*—I ever reach their level."

"*If?* Sweetheart, you're on your way. Talk with them, soon, before people who love to tear others down make your life miserable. The vultures are already circling. I never thought I'd be one of their targets, but they clearly think you deserve someone better than me."

"Well, they're wrong!" Jamie squeezed her hand. "They don't know you."

At least one photo of them appeared in a British tabloid every few days during Kat's visit. Jamie could tell the captions, like "Jamie Knight and his unattractive companion..."—and worse—upset her, although she tried to hide it. People had always seen him with beautiful women, and she knew she wasn't as pretty as they were. One tabloid even called her a scud—British slang for someone who looks okay from a distance, but not up-close. Another referred to her as "the ugly American," playing on the 1951 book.

"That one *really* hurts," she said, "because the book's title referred to ugly *behavior*. I've always made a point of respecting the cultures and people of the places I've visited, and not being anything like that arrogant character."

"They're wrong, Kat. Don't take it personally. They're always writing negative shit about people." He paused and hugged her. "Sod 'em. I love you, you're beautiful, and we both know what they say is bollocks."

Jamie hadn't been able to postpone a few business errands, including a commercial voice-over that week. Since he wanted Kat to see his working part of London and wanted his business associates to meet her, he took her with him. She seemed to enjoy it, especially talking shop with audio engineer Dan Francesci, who had recorded the PSAs Jamie voiced for the Sea Otter Fund the previous winter.

Nigel Stone producer Neil Tennison did a double-take when Jamie brought the sweepstakes winner he had met at the museum, a year and a half earlier, to his office and introduced her as his girlfriend.

Jamie's agent, Victor Harrington, called. "He's working on something big for me," Jamie told Kat, "a leading-man role that could be my ticket to stardom, if I can get it."

"What is it?" Kat asked.

"That's all Victor would tell me, but he's really excited about it. And he doesn't get excited about much, so now I'm excited about it. "

* * *

Two nights before she left London, Jamie took Kat to a pub where his friend, Allan MacKenzie's quartet played. "These guys know enough music to play 'stump the band,' and dare patrons to name a tune they can't play. I think they know every song that's been popular here or in the States at any time in the past fifty years."

"That's amazing," she said. "They must all play by ear."

When the band took a break, Allan joined Jamie and Kat in their booth for a pint. The older man had pink cheeks and a full brown and gray beard and moustache. She asked him about his custom-made guitar, which led to conversation about instruments, and Jamie told him she played.

Back on stage, Allan did his usual post-break patter, and as Kat whispered in Jamie's ear, she was startled to hear her own name from the stage.

"Come on up, lass, don't be shy," Allan said on-mic.

"What...?" she asked Jamie.

"Go on," Jamie said, grinning, pushing her toward the edge of the seat they shared.

"No, please." She grabbed both of his forearms. "I don't want to be on stage. I want to be here, with you. Jamie, we have so little time left..."

But Jamie insisted. "We're not leaving until I hear you play with them. Do I have to carry you to the stage?" He kissed her, then pushed her out of the booth, grinning like a little brother who'd just put a frog in his sister's lunch bag.

Suspecting that Jamie may have told Allan she was a talented musician, Kat told him, "I'm not in your league, musically." It didn't matter. The band played every tune in the same keys as Kat's groups in California did, so she played well and had fun, despite her protest. She was a better musician than she would admit, and Jamie beamed with pride.

Later, he admitted he had previously asked Allan to invite Kat to sit-in with the band, and had given Allan the tune set list from the Sacramento Scottish Fiddlers' website, so he'd know her repertoire.

Sitting in the booth with Kat next to him on the outside, Jamie had gone unnoticed until he pushed her out to play. Then, some people recognized her date. While trying to play well with a band she didn't know, she watched women go to the booth to chat with him and ask for autographs and photos. That old fear of fading into the background crept into her psyche and took some of the fun out of making music.

Enthusiastic applause followed her set. "You were amazing," Jamie said. "Let's see the papers write about *that*!"

Driving home, Jamie smiled continuously, like a kid hiding a fun secret. As they stepped inside the house, he slipped Kat's coat off, took her hand, and led her to the candle-lit drawing room, where the fireplace was aglow.

"Who lit a fire while we were gone?" she asked. "Is someone else here?" She hoped not.

"Faeries," Jamie grinned. Reflections of flames danced on two empty champagne flutes on the coffee table, creating a romantic atmosphere as he guided her to the sofa. Tired, Kat yawned, wrapped her arms around his waist, laid her head on his chest, and snuggled in to absorb his body heat. "They're good decorators." She closed her eyes and inhaled Jamie's barely detectable scent, wanting to take the memory home with her.

Sitting together silently, listening to the occasional pops and crackles of the fire was so relaxing, one could have easily fallen asleep. In fact, *one* nearly *did.*

"You still love me?" Jamie asked softly, brushing his finger around the curves of her ear.

"More than you can imagine." His touch sent a sensual vibration through her body, but her eyes remained closed.

"Are you happy here?"

"Mmm-Hmm. Very." Only half-awake, she could barely project her voice.

"Want to stay?" He kissed the top of her head, still on his chest.

"Mmm-Hmm." ...*and sleep.*

"Then marry me."

"Okay." *You tease.* Sinking into sleep, Kat didn't move until he squirmed, then lifted her left hand from his stomach. She opened her eyes to see him slip a gold and diamond ring on her third finger.

"Jamie? What...?" Sitting up, looking at her hand, then at him, then at the ring and back at him again, she couldn't believe what was happening. Her expressions of joy and shock—or maybe "shock and awe"—made him laugh.

His sparkling eyes said more than words could. He pulled her close and kissed her so passionately she imagined their bodies could merge. "Jamie, are you serious?" her voice wavered, and her face felt hot.

With his loving smile, he said, "You think I'd propose to you as a joke? Of course I'm serious. I told you I want you with me forever, and you said you'd like that, too."

"Oh, my god... yes! There's nothing in the world I'd like more than to marry you and spend the rest of our lives together."

"Good!" He kissed and hugged her tighter than ever. "You're no longer my girlfriend. You're my fiancée, and you'll be with me at all the awards, premieres, and other big events from now on. Soon, I'll be your husband, and I promise to be the best life partner you can imagine."

Talk of logistics and other practical matters could wait. Tonight, Jamie Knight and Kat Mancini were the happiest people on Earth, glowing in the certainty of the loving life they would have together.

Chapter 30: For Your Own Good

Before Kat flew home, Jamie told her how she would become show business news when the entertainment media learned of their engagement. Even though he wasn't a household name in America, he knew people from programs like *Show Biz Tonight* would start calling her, and a few paparazzi might stake out her home and office to get photos they could sell.

Kat didn't think the public would be interested in her, an ordinary state employee. "And my phones are both unlisted."

"Yes, but your office phone and address are on the state website," Jamie countered. "Believe me, those people can find anyone's private phone number, address, and email. Let me tell you what's happened to some other 'civilians' who've married well-known performers." Those stories convinced her, and they agreed to share their plans with only a few close, trustworthy friends and family until she moved in with him, in the spring. Then she would be protected by his home security and safety measures.

*　*　*

Saturday, Jamie went to the home where he had grown up, for dinner with his parents. He loved the elegant, old, brick home on nearly half an acre of well-maintained grounds, far back from the private avenue in a gated, guarded community.

Edith stood at the sink in her large kitchen, washing greens for a salad. To see her then, one would never guess she had once had the body of a Playboy bunny. She wore the kind of slacks and blouse any woman might wear at home—comfortable and not flattering on anyone. She had gathered her hair in a tortoiseshell clip at the back of her neck, and that night, this successful actress seemed content simply to be somebody's mum. Some other time, she could get costumed and made-up for a glamorous role.

Jamie asked, "Is there anything I can do to help?"

"No, thank you, I have it all under control."

He sat down at the kitchen table and said nothing. That wasn't typical. He usually headed straight to the 'fridge, talking about his latest job or what he and his friends were doing. This evening he had something on his mind.

Edith asked, "What have you been doing with yourself?"

He used to snicker at that question and say, "playing." The unspoken "with myself" always got a laugh. But it wasn't as funny now as it had been twenty years earlier. "I've been thinking about my life."

"The life of a big telly star?"

Jamie detected a hint of sarcasm in her voice that made him uncomfortable. She was far more successful than he. "You know what a double-edged sword that is. But, no... I've made a decision about my personal life."

Edith turned off the faucet and turned to her son. "Oh?"

"I'm ready for a change. I'm going to marry Kat."

Edith gave him an incredulous look. "Katerina? That American you brought here? Darling, she's as old as Christy! That would be like marrying your sister!"

Jamie had expected a less than enthusiastic response, but nothing that negative. "She is *not*. And she's nothing like Christy! They're chalk and cheese. Kat is bright, self-sufficient, and nice. *She* respects me, and would never push me around like some mug!" He did nothing to hide the pain inflicted in the past by his sister's incessant criticism.

"She treats me like her best friend, and she loves me. The *real me*—not an actor. She's kind, independent, generous, and more intelligent and well-informed than any woman I've ever loved. And I feel as safe and relaxed with her as I do with you, Dad, and my closest friends. She left only two days ago, and already I feel like a part of me is missing. I love her, and I want her with me for the rest of my life."

Edith challenged him. "Do you *know* how old she is? You want children. Does *she*? Can she have them? She may be too old! How do you know she's not after your money?"

Jamie scowled, and his jaw tightened. "Because she always tries to pay for things we're doing, she doesn't think she deserves gifts, and made it clear she doesn't need anyone to support her. And she didn't chase *me*; I pursued *her*! Yes, I know how old she is, and she's much younger than Christy. We haven't discussed kids, but... doesn't that change happen in your sixties?"

Edith ignored the menopause question. "Well, you'd better ask how she feels about children, if you're thinking of proposing marriage. You both need to know everything about each other—good and bad. And while we're on the subject, I hope you *will* marry—someone like Beatrice—and not waste time living together, like you did with Maggie."

Jamie resented having his "failed" relationship brought up—again. Maggie had been his girlfriend after Leigh married Bob. "That happens to many people. It's a learning experience. Maggie and I were too young to make the best choices, then."

"What about this age difference? Kat must be much older than you. Listen to the entertainers and world events she talks about. Have you gone on the internet to see what's there about her? What's on Facebook? How old are her friends and family?"

Feeling like he was being grilled, Jamie straightened his posture and raised his voice defensively. "Yes, I've looked, and I've met her older sister. *She* looks close to Christy's age. But so what? You're eight years older than Dad. It doesn't matter. She's a good person and I love her. And *she* loves *me*. That's what matters!"

Edith smiled. Her son didn't use that word frivolously. "Now, I don't think Kat is a bad person. I just don't think of her as a potential daughter-in-law who can elevate your status. What about Beatrice?"

"Trissy?" He got up and went to the sink for a glass of water. "What about her?"

"I always hoped you would marry *her*."

Jamie did a theatrical spit-take into the sink. "Are you having a laugh? Beatrice Aylesworth is a toffee-nosed snob! I can't stand her. I only put up with her gossip and self-centered prattling to please you. I wish you would stop pushing her at me. Compared to Kat, Trissy is Marie Antoinette. Besides, I don't need my status elevated."

He recognized the patronizing, 'You don't know what you're talking about' look his mother gave him. "Can you imagine Trissy giving up her job so someone else wouldn't be laid-off? Or helping a biscuit-arsed homeless person who's fallen down, or a stray cat? Kat would. She has. Not only do I love her, I like her. I admire and respect her. And she likes and respects me. I'm comfortable around her and never feel like I have to be careful about what I say, or suppress what I'm feeling, or be anything other than myself. Do you know how many people let me feel that way? Hardly any. Even the guys... I can count on one hand the number of people I feel that safe with—to say and do what I want, and know they won't criticize, reject, or tell me I shouldn't. Or worse, see it in the Globe, the next day."

Edith gave him a skeptical look. "Since when have you not said whatever you think? Do you censor yourself with your father and me?"

"No, of course not. But Kat is the only woman—besides you—I've ever felt completely safe with. I never feel like she's judging me. We don't always agree and sometimes we debate issues. That's another thing I love about her; we can be on opposite sides of something with no anger. She respects other people's right to their opinions, and I can persuade her that she didn't know all the facts about something. And sometimes she points out things that enlighten me, but it always comes from a kind, loving place, because she cares about how I feel. Not how I feel about *her*, but about *myself* and what I'm doing. That's rare. Has anyone ever made you feel that way?"

Edith sat down and folded her hands on the table. Thoughtfully, she said, "Your father always has."

Jamie sat down and put his hands on his mother's. "Mum, except for you and Dad, I've never felt that from anyone." He paused, then added, "I want that in my life. I want Kat in my life."

The following week, Jamie promoted *The Ivory Reel* on every medium known to man. He didn't have a minute to himself, yet Kat was on his mind much of the time. Throughout November, they talked or texted every day. He couldn't wait to see her at their December video shoot.

As the U.K. publicity campaign for *The Ivory Reel* slowed down before the big push in the U.S., Victor called Jamie. "I have a deal that will make you the happiest man in Britain."

"I'm already the happiest man in Britain," Jamie replied, beaming.

"This will make you happier. I've been talking with Warren McAvoy's rep. You know he directed the blockbuster John Crocker film. Well, Cliff Cotton had a stroke last month," Victor said, with ruthless joy in his voice, "and they're ready to start shooting the second book. He's been auditioning actors, looking for a new leading man, and I've convinced him to let you read for it before they make the final decision."

"Are you serious? That's fantastic! You're not just having a laugh, are you? That's a shame about Cliff Cotton, though! How bad is it?"

Victor ignored the question. "Pacific Studios have green-lighted a big budget with Leonard Goldman Exec. Producing. Get this job and you'll be an international star, with *years* of steady, multi-million-dollar film work ahead of you. We'll all be quids-in!"

"Brilliant, Victor! When? It'll be in L.A., right?"

"Yes. They want to decide soon, but I'll see if they'll hold off until you're there next month. Now, there's something else. I hear you proposed to that American—"

"Kat. That's right."

"That is *not* a good idea. You saw those dreadful pictures of her in the papers and what your fans wrote about her."

"People who have nothing better to do than snipe at others online don't concern me, and the tabloids make everyone look bad."

"Listen, Jamie, you're a rising star. You can't afford to be linked romantically to some sloppy, low-level, American government worker—"

Jamie bristled. "She is *not* low-level or sloppy. She's an award-winning spokesperson for California and a former radio presenter."

"Let her go, kid. Stick with the stylish, beautiful birds we've always seen you with."

"Sorry? You think physical beauty and designer wardrobes are what's important for your clients' wives? That's too shallow, even for you, Victor. Kat's beautiful to me—inside and out. She's the sort of person I want to share my life with."

Out of patience, Victor snapped. "Jesus Christ, Jamie, your career is on the line, here! We should see you with women who wear Alexander McQueen and Stella McCartney, not Levi Strauss and Keds!"

"She wears New Balance," Jamie corrected his shoe reference.

Victor ignored him. "Goldman and McAvoy want a sexy, *single*, jet-setting, Bond-like *ladies' man* who'll attract more female fans to these Crocker films. You want this job? Drop the American and go out with women who will *enhance* your image, like Tiffany."

Jamie stiffened at Victor's criticism and even more at the suggestion that he socialize with the talent agency slag. He hung up, livid. *I should fly to Sacramento and marry Kat right now, just to say, "screw you," and prove him wrong.* But he wasn't an impulsive man, so he merely fumed about it. Directors and producers shouldn't care who his wife was, as long as he did good work, was reliable, and behaved honorably.

* * *

When *The Ivory Reel* opened in the U.S., Kat took Jo, Molly, her husband and kids, Janet, and two other Scottish fiddlers to see it with her. Friends were happy to support Jamie on the all-important opening day. *The Ivory Reel* didn't break records, but it did well for a serious film with an environmental message. As soon as box office receipts were posted on the web, Kat phoned to congratulate him.

"Your *Tonight Show* interview was terrific," she said. "You're so good at deflecting the insults those guys throw at you!"

"Thanks. You have to do that. You know they're just going for laughs, and will do it at your expense. Hey, did you hear? They've nominated us for two People's Choice Awards."

"I'm not surprised. I hope BAFTA, SAG, and the Academy are as wise. You and the film deserve awards. The story was gut-wrenching, and you played that dedicated game warden perfectly!"

"You *saw* it?" he teased. "You risked humiliation, and went to the *cinema*? How many boxes of tissue did you need?"

"Very funny! Yes, and my heart stopped when the poachers kidnapped you. The elephant scenes made me cry, and that embarrassed me. But I can endure some tears and humiliation to support you. And the theater donated part of the opening day profits to the World Wildlife Fund's elephant protection program. God, I love you, Jamie. I'm proud of you, and I miss you, terribly. I can't wait to see you next month."

"I miss you, too, and I'm counting the days. You've changed my life, Kat. The house feels empty without you here. And you owe me a guitar lesson."

Chapter 31: Public Service, Private Pain

While flying to Los Angeles in mid-December, Jamie analyzed the scenes he would read in his audition. They were similar to scenes in the older James Bond films, full of intrigue, danger... and beautiful women whose characters were more set decoration than participants in the plot. At least in the scenes they sent him. That made the role a little less appealing. He'd rather not promote sexism, but this opportunity was too good pass up.

He wondered who else had read for the suave, chick-magnet role, and considered the possibility of losing it to another actor. That would disappoint him, but it would solve his engagement problem. If he won the role, could he tell the director he was engaged and ask if they couldn't promote the film without making him pretend he was a jet-setting playboy *off-screen?*

The wildlife PSA shoot was the day after he read to play John Crocker. Kat would want to know about the audition, and it would be wrong to hide things like that from his fiancée. But he didn't want to tell her they want him to remain unmarried. He could at least tell her about the opportunity. That might make it less of a shock if he won the role. And maybe he could talk them into a different publicity scheme.

* * *

In a small Los Angeles studio, Kat and Matt Ellison, a Department of Wildlife videographer, set-up to shoot the video. When Jamie arrived, Kat couldn't hide her enthusiasm for him. She bounced out of the control room, nearly running to embrace him. He picked her up and twirled around wearing a smile as wide as his slender face could hold. They kissed more passionately than Kat ever had, in front of anyone. Now she didn't care what anyone thought about it. She was in love, engaged, and this man was the center of her universe—the only person whose opinion mattered.

Jamie treated Kat like a professional director, bolstering her confidence. "How do you envision the overall look and tone of this?"

"Think of it as a video version of the radio spots you did last year."

They were shooting the PSA on a green-screen set, so later, Matt could superimpose Jamie onto two different backgrounds. In the sea otter part, he would appear to be at Elkhorn Slough Ecological Reserve, on Monterey Bay. In the endangered species segment, he would be in the mountains, not in a room featuring a bright green floor and wall, under hot lights.

"As in the radio spots," Kat said, "you're a friendly authority figure throughout the script. In tandem with that, express concern when you do the lines about the animals' problems, then transition to a more upbeat look and tone on the lines about how to help them.

"Start here." She pointed to a mark on the floor. "When you begin the third sentence, 'You can help wildlife,' I'll cue you to walk slowly and stop on your next mark, there." She pointed to a blue 'X' taped to the floor. "At 'Every dollar donated,' I'll cue you again to walk to this mark and finish the pitch." She pointed to another blue 'X' on the green floor, about twenty feet from Jamie, as he stepped to his starting mark.

"Speak to the camera most of the time, and occasionally look around at the incredible natural settings you're supposed to be in, so you're not always staring at the audience." Matt indicated he was ready to begin, and Kat put on the headset that connected her to the engineer in the control booth. "Are you ready? Okay. We're ready out here."

Standing next to the camera, she beamed at Jamie, held her right hand up with all fingers extended. "In five... four... three..." She curled her thumb, then each finger back into her fist as she said each number, silently mouthing the words "two... one." At zero she swung her hand forward to cue Jamie.

He performed the PSA perfectly on the first take. As they all watched the playback on a monitor, Matt shook his head. "Damn, you're good! It figures, 'One-Take Kat' would know 'One-Take Jamie'."

Jamie offered to do another one "for safety," and Kat agreed, but doubted she would need it. After a second perfect take, they helped Matt and the engineer straighten up the studio, then left to spend the rest of the day and evening at Bill's house, for an early Christmas together.

* * *

On the way, Jamie told Kat about the role he had auditioned for and how it could make him famous and make *them* rich. He kept the marketing plan and potential ramifications for her to himself. There was no point in causing her distress, since he might not get the job, and wouldn't take it if they insisted he jettison Kat for it. He and Bill had analyzed the situation the night before. Bill was a skilled listener who asked questions that usually led Jamie to his own best conclusions. But this time, the right answer eluded him.

Kat directed the conversation to *The Ivory Reel*. "I loved the scene where the female game warden fought off the poacher who, we assumed, intended to rape her. I wish we could all kick like that."

"She's very athletic. But if you're attacked, that's not the best thing to do."

Kat looked perplexed. "Why? What is?"

"Kicking someone with your foot puts you off-balance. Men who assault women probably expect that, and would grab your foot and push you onto the ground, on your back—precisely where they want you."

"Crap. So what can we do to defend ourselves?" Kat's eyebrows drew together, creating a vertical crease between them as she took a deep breath.

"Since a guy might expect a kick to the bollocks, kick the inside of his *knee* hard enough to dislocate it or tear a ligament. When he sees you're going to kick, he probably won't expect that, and will only protect his groin."

"Good idea. But if he's already got hold of me and I can't kick his knees, then what?"

"If you're facing him, stretch one foot back as far as you can. Make him think you're trying to get away—"

"I *am*!"

"Then with every ounce of strength you have, slam your *knee* into his crotch. He'll probably grab it and bend forward. Then you jam your fist or your elbow into his face and while he's off balance, push him down and run like hell, shouting 'fire.'"

"Fire?" Kat tilted her head and gave him a quizzical look.

"Fire." Jamie glanced at her. "Some people won't respond to cries of 'help' or 'rape,' but if someone yells 'fire,' *everyone* wants to know where it is, and they're more likely to come out where you'll see each other. It's hard to say 'no' to a victim who can see you."

In Bill's driveway, Jamie took Kat in his arms and held her. "I'm going to do my best to make sure you never need to use that advice." He kissed the top of her head and sighed.

A seven-foot Christmas tree that smelled like a boreal forest dominated Bill's living room. Just for grins, he grilled the steak dinner they had enjoyed for lunch at Lake Tahoe, more than a year earlier. "For old times' sake," he said, raising his glass toward Jamie and Kat. "Here's to the good things that day led to!"

"I'll drink to that," Kat said as they toasted the engagement.

"Have you decided when and where you'll have the wedding?" Bill asked.

"No," Jamie replied. "We'd like to do it sometime next year, but we need to work around my work schedule, moving Kat to London, and all the logistics that will entail. But we want you there if you can possibly make it."

"If you can't, we'll probably have a party afterward, in Sacramento, to celebrate with my friends and family," Kat added. "But we'd really like you to be at the wedding."

The following evening, the three exchanged Christmas gifts, as if they were a family. Jamie gave Kat diamond earrings with gold swirls that looked like waves to match her engagement ring.

For laughs, she gave him a royal blue T-shirt that said "Taken!" on both sides. For a moment, she acted as if that was her only gift for him; then she pulled a small box out from under the tree and handed it to him. He ripped the wrapping paper off to find tickets to an upcoming Cold Play concert at London's Wembley Stadium. They were superb seats, front and center, and—he knew—quite expensive for her. "You shouldn't have spent so much on me," he play-scolded after a hug and kiss.

"Yes, I should. I *want* to. You deserve a lot more than that."

* * *

Saturday, at an early morning hour Kat called "O-dark-thirty," she drove Jamie to LAX for his ten-hour flight home. She had a later flight to Sacramento, so stayed with him until the last minute at the security checkpoint. "I hate leaving

you," he said, "but it's a little easier now, knowing that—
someday soon—we won't have to do this anymore."

"I can't wait for that time." She squeezed his hand. "Or
to see you in February—"

"For the BAFTAs," Jamie exclaimed with another hug.

"Yes!" Her face lit up with contagious excitement. "And
let me know if you hear anything about your audition. I'll
keep my fingers crossed for you."

"Thanks. Sometimes they take forever to decide those
things. I may not even know until I hear *someone else* got
the part. You know, the next few weeks are going to be
terribly busy with that animation job and *Nigel* resuming
production. But you'll be in my heart all the time, and I'll call
you in a couple of days. I love you, Kat." He gave her a long,
tight hug and kiss.

"I love you, Jamie. I can't wait 'till we're together again,
permanently."

* * *

Jamie had to be in London to fulfill long-standing
commitments to visit terminally ill people—mostly
children—in hospitals at Christmas time. The Monday after,
he would begin a voice-over job for an animated film that—
the following week—overlapped the *Nigel Stone* shoot of
their last episode for the season. Kat would fly over in
February to join him at the BAFTA Film Awards, and return
to L.A. with him for the Academy Awards, two weeks later.
She couldn't remember ever being this excited.

Chapter 32: The Choice

Victor called and left messages several times while Jamie was in L.A., asking how the audition went, who was present, how long his read lasted, what Warren McAvoy said, and more. While he was with Kat, Jamie sent one text message to his agent, ending with, "I'll call you when I get home."

When he did, Victor snapped at him. "What the hell did you do in L.A., Jamie?"

"Sorry? What do you mean?"

"When you read for McAvoy! What do you think I mean?" Clearly, he was upset.

"I read the scenes you sent me, opposite an actor I don't know. Then we chatted a bit. Nothing out of the ordinary. Why? What happened?" Jamie was sure he must have failed.

"I don't know what you did," Victor snarled. Then he suddenly changed his tone. "But you blew them away. Congratulations, kid... *You're* the new John Crocker."

"What? Brilliant! That's fantastic, Victor, you git! You made me think I blew it."

"Sorry. This was way too off-the-wall to play it straight. I didn't expect to hear so soon. Did you know Pacific Studios' Vice President of Production was in the room? You were the umpteenth actor they saw, and she told McAvoy there was no need to audition anyone else, as far as the studio was concerned."

"Oh, my god... I'm gobsmacked! Now what?"

"Now we negotiate a star-worthy salary, a percentage of box office, foreign distribution... the usual details. They want to rehearse in February. We're in the money, now! Your mum will be so proud."

"Splendid. But remember, I will not disengage Kat. *She* is not negotiable."

"Everything's negotiable, Jamie. Your engagement could kill this deal, keep you off the A-List, out of the Academy, and cost you lucrative roles in the future. Goldman—the E.P.—says your *unmarried* status is a condition for you to get the part. Judy is working on P.R. tours with Pacific Studios' publicists. They're going to gin-up an affair between you and Ambrosia, the most beautiful 'Crocker Girl' in the film. The tabloids and gossip shows will go bonkers."

"Are you barmy? I can't do that! Kat would be gutted!"

Victor wasn't hearing it. "Don't blow this, kid! Stars don't have strokes every year and you may never get another shot like this one. We'll talk more, later." He hung up.

This was it. Jamie *really would* have to make this "Sophie's choice" between his ticket to stardom and a life with the woman he loved. *Damnit!* In a moment when he should've been bubbling over with joy, he felt numb.

Victor had always guided him in the right direction, gotten him good roles and money, making possible the success he now enjoyed. And this deal could make his acting dreams come true—the star status and income he had worked for all his adult life. But he had always intended to marry, too, and had finally found the right woman. He shouldn't have to break-off their engagement to hit the big-time in Hollywood.

Torn, Jamie told Peter Li, "I love Kat—truly! She's become such a part of me, my house has felt empty since she went home, and I wish she was here, right now." He paused. "But I love my work and want success, too. How can they tell me to discard her, merely to publicize some films?"

"For money," Peter replied. "You know that drives everything in the business. And the big-wigs are never satisfied, even with good box office. They always want more.

Are you sure she wouldn't be willing to hide or wait for a few years? If she really loves you..."

"Positive. Too many past rejections. Even *asking* her that would hurt her and make her doubt my commitment."

"Man... you're on a real sticky wicket. At least wait until Pacific signs your contract and the payoff is worth it before you do anything you might regret."

Jamie had considered telling Kat the situation, but knew it would break her heart to know he would *even consider* chucking her for a film role. She was ecstatic about their engagement. So was he, until Victor said he had to give up the *woman* of his dreams to get the *film deal* of his dreams.

But what if Victor was right? What if they wouldn't cast him if they knew he was engaged—or married? How would turning down this role affect his future opportunities? Would he be less attractive to producers if they knew he put his marriage ahead of work? Oh, yeah... *they would know* about it.

The uncertainty tormented him. He lost his appetite and his ability to focus on anything else. The media called Jamie a heart-breaker, but now *his* heart was breaking. And he couldn't sleep.

* * *

Christmas was the following week, and Kat had volunteered—as usual—to "hold down the fort" at work so her colleagues with families could spend the holidays at home. She wanted to be with Jamie, but they had enjoyed a nice early Christmas at Bill's. Next year, she would be in Jamie's—*her husband's*—arms. No matter where they were, that would make any holiday perfect.

After spending Christmas Eve and Day with her mother, Kat went to Janet's house for Christmas dinner. Janet lived alone, too, but she put up a tree, decorated her house, and invited single friends over for a "family-of choice" Christmas.

Most were musicians, so they sang and played well into the night. She and Jamie had agreed to talk the day after Christmas. She couldn't wait to spend every holiday—every *day and night*—with him.

The CDW Public Affairs Office was always quiet during the week between Christmas and New Year, so Kat could really get a lot of work done. Walking to her car alone in the dark was creepy, with most of the usual workforce absent. She held her keys between her fingers and remembered what Jamie had told her—just in case.

She wasn't one to go out and party on New Year's Eve. Too many drunks on the road. And *this* New Year's weekend, she had a lot to think about. Anticipating her move to London, she wanted to start purging the house of stuff she hadn't used in years. She and Jamie hadn't discussed when she should move, but she wanted to be ready when he was. It would probably depend on when she could get permission from the British government to immigrate. She hoped it would be that spring.

What should she do with her house? Sell it? Or make it a rental and employ a property management firm? She had owned a rental before, and none of the tenants took very good care of the old house. Her swimming pool would make neglect much more costly, so she would have to pay a pool service to care for it. Another item to discuss with Jamie.

And what about the wedding? The one time she had lived with a man, they never married and it ended badly for her. Should she move in with Jamie or wait until they were married? How would he react to that request?

But first, she needed to prepare to attend the BAFTA Film Awards and Academy Awards with Jamie, both in February. Talk about unfamiliar, high-stakes experiences... Kat had never been to any high-profile, formal event—and these were two of the *most* formal and high-profile events in the world.

Last year she had wished she'd been his date at the Emmys. Now, the reality of it was intimidating. Jamie was arranging for her to be outfitted, made-up, and have something fancy done with her hair on the day. She made him promise to put his foot down if anyone tried to make her wear high heels. It was hard enough to walk in pumps. She was sure she'd stumble and make a fool of herself in heels more than two inches high.

Friday, January eighth, the BAFTA Film Awards nominations included Jamie, in the Best Leading Actor category for *The Ivory Reel*! Excited, it took Kat three calls to reach him. His phone had been ringing constantly, ever since Stephen Fry had named him that morning. He was thrilled and happy to share the excitement with her. He said he couldn't wait to see her next month and take her to the awards ceremony at London's Royal Opera House.

A week later, Kat got up at the ungodly hour of 5:20 a.m. to hear the live nominations for Hollywood's Academy Awards. It seemed to take forever, but when they finally got to the Best Actor category and she heard "Jamie Knight," she whooped loud enough to wake her entire neighborhood. Jamie might achieve his greatest goal next month!

Her congratulatory call went straight to his voice mail. Everyone who knew him must have been phoning him that day. So she sent an email, a text, and snail-mailed a congratulations card. He would call her when he had a moment. Partly for laughs, she ordered an enormous bouquet of flowers delivered to his home. He would think that was funny.

But Jamie didn't call that day. Or the next. He must've been overwhelmed with congratulations. But the next day, Saturday... why hadn't he called? Or sent an email or even a brief text? Had he received the flowers? Had something bad happened? There must be a good reason. He would call. Now that they were engaged, she should stop feeling insecure about their relationship.

Finally, on Sunday, he phoned her. "I swear, everyone in the world I've ever met has tried to reach me, every possible way! I had to turn the phone off to get any sleep. I love the flowers and I'm sorry for taking this long to call you. Every time I tried, someone else got through first."

Kat was relieved, but still thought he could have found a way to contact her in a day or two. "I'm glad that's all it was. I was starting to wonder if something had gone wrong."

"No, but things are happening here, and I'm knackered. I'll call you later this week, okay?"

"Okay. Jamie, I'm so happy for you... You deserve these honors and I want to be there to support you. I wish I were there, hugging you right now."

"Thanks. I know you do and I appreciate that. We'll talk later."

"I love you, Jamie. Can't wait to see you."

He hung up—without saying goodbye. Something wasn't right. Or was she being overly sensitive? That was an awfully brief call, for them. And he didn't say "I love you," as he had every time they'd talked since last summer. Maybe he was overwhelmed by two major nominations and all the people contacting him since the announcements. Everyone he had ever met or worked with—old friends and girlfriends—must be coming out of the woodwork. That was not a comforting thought. *Don't get paranoid.*

The previous summer, Kat had set-up a Google alert for news clips about Jamie, and there had been dozens of them since the BAFTA announcement. The big Hollywood trade papers, *Variety* and *The Hollywood Reporter* featured stories about the awards' nominees, including Jamie. But another story that was about him wasn't what she expected.

Tues., Jan. 19, HOLLYWOOD, CALIF. — Pacific Studios has cast British actor Jamie Knight to replace Clifford Cotton in the *John Crocker* film series. Cotton suffered a stroke in October and is unable to work TFN. Production on the second film in the series (working title: *John Crocker II*) has been postponed until February. Warren McAvoy will direct. Leonard Goldman, EP on the first Crocker film, will exec produce again.

Knight, 45, well-known by audiences in the UK, is nominated for BAFTA and Academy Awards in the best leading actor categories for *The Ivory Reel*. The BAFTA Film Awards will be held Feb. 14 in London. The Oscars will be awarded in Hollywood on Feb. 28. Jamie Knight is repped by Victor Harrington of Actors Unlimited Worldwide in London.

Excited for Jamie, Kat checked her phone and voice mail, hoping he had left a message or text for her about his good news. He hadn't. Could they have notified the media before they told Jamie? That seemed unlikely. She called him and, again, landed in voice mail. After leaving a message, she sent a text: "Congratulations, 'John Crocker!' Saw the Variety story. Call me when you can, super-spy. I Love You!"

She wasn't normally obsessive about her phone or email. But this day, she checked both every hour or so. The day passed slowly and ended without a word from her fiancé. He must have been awfully busy. Surely he would call tomorrow. But he didn't. Kat felt left out again. Why wouldn't Jamie want to share his good news with her? Wondering made it hard to concentrate on work.

Finally on Thursday, she received a pithy text. He got the Crocker job and would call her this weekend. Hadn't he seen any of her messages? Had he skipped them? She replied with congratulations again and told him about her Scottish Quartet gig at a big, formal Burns Supper that coming Saturday. "Please call me, ANY TIME. I love and miss you Jamie; craving your touch and the sound of your voice."

* * *

Friday evening... this was going to be difficult. Jamie had put off what he had to do as long as he could. Table-reads for his film would begin the next week, then rehearsals and location shoots in February. He couldn't wait until Kat was packing for her trip to tell her not to come. Why would the Universe force him to make this excruciating choice? The opportunity of a lifetime *or* the marriage he had long desired—to the sort of woman he never thought he would meet, who was crazy about *him, too!*

He sighed, sat down with his phone and stared at her name, number, and photo in his contacts. His hands felt like fifty-pound weights. He couldn't lift them. Couldn't do it. As his eyes watered, he hurriedly put the phone and his watch on the coffee table, ran to the swimming pool, and in his jeans and shirt, dove in. He needed to swim laps until his heart beat hard and fast enough to stop aching for her.

Sunday evening... this was a better time to call. It would have been unkind to upset Kat right *before* she had to play a music gig. It was still going to be unpleasant, but he couldn't procrastinate any longer. It wasn't fair to her. Not that it was fair to him, either. But he had to set that aside long enough to get this over with.

Kat asked why he hadn't called her all week. "I'm sorry," Jamie said. "How was the Burns Supper, last night? You played, didn't you?"

"Yes. We had a good crowd and a good time," she replied. "I wish you could've been there. The haggis was delicious!" She laughed, as if expecting a wry comeback from him.

"Good, I'm glad you had a good night." Jamie paused. "Listen, I have to tell you something. You're not going to like it. I don't, either, and I'm terribly sorry." He took a deep breath. "I, uh... I've changed my mind. I can't get married now." The silence on the phone lasted so long, he wondered if she had hung up on him. "Kat?"

"You're joking, aren't you? Give me the punch line."

"There is no punch line, although I feel as bad as if I *had* punched you. It's not you, Kat. It's me. I can't be the husband you deserve right now."

"What? Of course you can. What do you think I expect of you?"

He wanted to stop but was afraid if he did, he wouldn't be able to go through with it. "I want you to take care of yourself and keep up with your music. You're much better than you think."

"Jamie! What's going on?" Her voice cracked.

"You'll find the right man for you." The words were getting harder to form and push from his mouth. "I'll always love you, Kat, and wish you all the best life has to offer."

"Jamie, no! You can't be serious! Stop it! This isn't funny." There were tears in her voice now. "Jamie? Talk to me. Are you *dumping* me? Why? Oh, god, *please don't—*"

"I'm sorry, Kat. I have to go." He had done it. Now they were both gutted. She must have heard the tears in his voice, too. No wonder she couldn't believe it. A moment later, his phone played a tune by Scottish guitarist Tony McManus. Kat's ring. Jamie knew she must be beside herself in pain. He turned the phone off and threw it onto a nearby chair. He sat there with his head in his hands for a few minutes, then curled up on the sofa and cried harder than he had since childhood.

* * *

A cocoon of cold air enveloped Kat as she pressed the call button under Jamie's picture on her phone. Voice mail. His last words were final. He wouldn't talk to her again. Ever. Losing her balance, she quickly sat on the living room rug. She pulled her knees up and hugged her legs, trying to stop shaking. This couldn't be happening. Aching all over, she fell onto her side and curled-up on the floor, sobbing uncontrollably. *Please... let me wake up from this nightmare!*

What had happened? Why had he changed his mind? She had never loved anyone as deeply as she loved Jamie. And *he* had said as much for her, too; that's why he wanted to marry her. Why was he ending their engagement? What did she do wrong? A long, plaintive meow told her Kellye had sensed her despair and come to sit with her.

The pain Kat had avoided by not getting involved with anyone for ten years was back in spades. It kept her awake all night and made her physically ill. There was no point in going to work the next day. She couldn't think about anything but Jamie and the pain in her chest, where her heart used to live.

Monday morning she called Ron to tell him she was sick and to cancel all the vacation time-off she had requested for her trips to London and L.A. He was kind enough to not ask why. How on earth was she going to tell her friends Jamie had dumped her with no plausible explanation? And Barbara... Kat could hear her saying, "What made you think a *TV star* would want to marry you, when no one else has?"

Spending all of Monday alone with her thoughts was hell. Tuesday she needed Jo's kind of wisdom and a hug. News that Jamie backed out of his engagement surprised Jo as much as it had Kat. She had to think for some time before saying, "You know, I believe everything happens for a reason, even if we can't see it. Maybe you shouldn't assume this is the end of things with Jamie. His world is so different from ours, maybe there's a bump in the road—a problem he has to solve—before he can follow through with the plans you made together."

Kat shook her head. "You're such an optimist, Jo. I hope you're right. But I can't imagine breaking off your engagement for a 'bump in the road.' And if it's merely a temporary glitch, why wouldn't he tell me about it?"

Neither could think of a reasonable answer for that one, but spending the afternoon with Jo and her elder wisdom helped Kat get through the day.

She had to tell Janet and get her act together that week. The Scottish Quartet had one more Burns Supper to play. As they drove to the venue, Janet turned up the radio to sing along with a Beatles love song. Kat could only stare out the side window. Janet stopped singing. "Come on, Kat. You always sing Beatles tunes. It'll make you feel better."

Kat glanced at the radio, then looked away again and swallowed hard. "Just another pop music lie." Was that where men learned to lie about love? All those songs she had listened to when she was a teenager? Her grief over losing Jamie and their relationship was slowly turning to anger—not only at him, but at all the social cues that taught boys and men that girls and women were disposable.

Chapter 33: Hot Awards

The BAFTA Film Awards ceremony was coming up February 14—Valentine's Day—and Kat hadn't heard from Jamie since January twenty-four, the day he had eviscerated her by ending their engagement and her optimism about the future. This was the awards show he was going to take her to, and introduce her to the public as his fiancée.

She hadn't intended to, but the day of the BAFTAs, she turned the TV on early, hoping to see Jamie navigate the red carpet gauntlet of cheering fans, photographers, and entertainment media. She was dying to see him. When she spotted him holding a beautiful young blonde's hand, her heart sank. They both looked fabulous and got loads of compliments from the interviewers. He deserved every kind word. She knew nothing of the girl standing next to him, but she looked like a date. Jealousy, an old nemesis Kat had defeated long ago, returned right before the doorbell rang.

"Have I missed anything good?" Jo asked with her usual smile.

"No, you're just in time." Kat gave Jo the happiest look she could fake and went into the kitchen to get the popcorn and tea. Kellye, who had been perched atop the back of the sofa, stepped down the throw pillows to take advantage of Jo's lap.

Kat brought out two cups of cinnamon-spice tea and fell into her rocker-recliner.

"Did you watch the silly stuff?" Jo asked.

"Yeah."

"Did you see Jamie?"

"Yeah." Kat's tone stung with bitterness. "He's got a date."

"Oh." Jo paused a moment and looked at the TV. "Well, you can't expect an actor to go to a big awards ceremony alone, can you?"

"He was *going* to take *me*." Kat couldn't completely hide the anger she felt, even though she didn't want to express it to anyone—not even Jo.

She usually enjoyed BAFTA host Stephen Fry, but this time nothing could make her laugh. It took forever to get to the awards that would affect Jamie. Despite her hurt feelings, Kat wanted him and *The Ivory Reel* to win everything they could.

When the cameras cut to celebrities in the audience, they couldn't show him often enough, and when they did, she was as excited for him as she had been before he broke off their engagement. He seemed especially handsome that evening. The guy who could be a playful cut-up and a sweet, tender lover moved like the next James Bond. Perfect for his new role. Everyone there was dressed to the nines, but not all carried themselves as gracefully as Jamie did.

After what seemed like an eternity, Fry introduced Maureen McGovern and Michael Caine to present the award for Best Actor in a Leading Role. Kat glanced at Jo, who crossed her fingers. Michael did the introduction and Maureen read the nominees' names. Since Jamie had done spot-on impersonations of Michael on chat shows, he added, "If Knight wins, I can leave. He can present himself the award in my voice and accept it in his own."

The audience laughed, and the camera cut to a close-up of Jamie, laughing and modestly shaking his head.

"And the Best Actor in a Leading Role is... Jamie Knight!"

Kat leaped from her chair, cheering with her arms up, like a referee signaling a touchdown. The cats, curled up on each side of Jo, jumped as if a dog had run into the room.

Upon hearing his name, he leaned over and kissed his date before getting up and trotting to the stage. Kat's joy and excitement for him died in an instant, replaced by bitter resentment. She sat down slowly, in silence, as her eyes drowned in tears.

As Jamie made his way to the stage, Jo said, "Don't assume that means anything. This is his career, not a social event. You've never been in his shoes. There may be a reason you and I can't even imagine."

Jamie's acceptance speech displayed his professional humility and appreciation for the luck that had opened doors for him. He honored the other nominees and thanked his parents, agent, everyone who worked on *The Ivory Reel,* and BAFTA members—the people winners *should* thank. And all too quickly, a "winner wrangler" ushered him off the stage.

Kat felt the pain of isolation that always hit her when she got left out of something important. "He acted like he loved me, for months," she told Jo. "*He* was the one who turned up the heat between us. He asked me to marry him and said he wanted me with him forever! Why did he break off our engagement, right before these important events in his life?"

Jo shook her head and looked sympathetically at her friend.

After Jo went home, Kat punched the stuffing out of a pillow. A few hours later, she couldn't resist congratulating Jamie, as a kind of peace offering. Maybe whatever led him to break up was temporary. Maybe it wasn't really *over*-over. Maybe the kiss was an act. Grasping at straws, she phoned and left a cheery message, and said she missed him. She sent both real and digital congratulations cards. He didn't respond to any of it. Had he even seen or heard them? Had he told Danny to delete everything from her? *Frickin' men!*

* * *

Sadness engulfed Jamie when he listened to Kat's congratulatory voice mail. His heart ached every time he looked at the guitar he'd bought for her. He couldn't bring himself to take it out of the case and try to play it.

Pushing food around his dinner plate, he told Leigh and Bob, "I miss her so much... I wish *she* had been with me at the BAFTAs. I want to talk with her and don't like being unkind. But what can I tell her? 'I'm sorry, but an executive producer made me choose between you and the biggest professional opportunity of my life?'"

"Yes, if that's the truth," Bob replied.

Jamie shook his head. "I've started to ring her, but hung up, afraid the sound of her voice would make me say sod it and tell Goldman the deal is off. It kills me to ignore someone I love. I haven't slept properly since the last night she slept in my arms. What if this film *isn't* a big hit, and I've lost the love of my life for nothing?"

"Then stop it, and call her," Leigh advised, with more than a hint of anger in her voice. "To end your engagement and not tell her why is cruel, Jamie. It was obvious she loves you. I promise, she's suffering more now than you can imagine!"

Jamie gave a slight nod of agreement. "But what if... We all know you have to sacrifice to make it in this business, and this film is my shot at the big time. I could lose everything I've worked for." He paused and stared at his plate. "I have to stay single, play the fake affair for publicity... and know Kat is mature enough to get over it... eventually."

* * *

In a Sacramento nursing home, Kat held her mother's hand and poured her heart out, knowing Lidia would forget it all within the hour.

"I can't believe Jamie dumped me—after those wonderful times last summer—and in London, when he proposed and said wanted me with him forever. Why do men do that?"

"I don't know," Lidia replied. She relaxed her hand and closed her eyes. When Kat was sure her mother was asleep, she quietly got up and went home to Kellye and Jeremy, the two furry loves she could always count on.

She tried to get Jamie off her mind and accept reality, but couldn't. As she usually did in a situation like this, Kat doubted herself. "What could I have done wrong that made him change his mind?" she asked Molly.

"You did nothing wrong. Maybe it has something to do with work," Molly suggested. "You said he works constantly."

"Maybe. He did say once that our careers have to be our top priorities." She halted. "Wait. Maybe that's it."

"What?"

"They cast him to play John Crocker. You know, the handsome, sexy hero who's supposed to be the next James Bond? Maybe it had something to do with that. But why wouldn't he have told me?"

The night of the Academy Awards ceremony in L.A., Kat planned to leave the TV off. Jo was at her daughter's that evening, so Kat didn't have to watch. She knew it would hurt to see Jamie again. But she couldn't stand to *not* watch. She craved the sight and sound of him—and his touch. When he appeared, he was with the stunning young blonde he had taken to the BAFTAs.

The Ivory Reel won Best Cinematography, and Jamie won the Best Actor award—his dream. Again, he kissed his date before going to the stage. Another gut-punch to Kat.

That he took someone else as his date to something right there in California eliminated any doubt. Jamie didn't love her. Still, he had called her every time he had been in L.A. since they met. The Oscar was the big award that meant the most to him, and she wanted to congratulate him. Grasping for a sliver of hope, she prayed he would call this time. That sliver pierced her heart.

The now-undeniable fact that their relationship was dead overwhelmed her. Her body went limp and fell back into the recliner. There wasn't enough air in the room. She pulled her knees up to her chest and sobbed uncontrollably into them. She couldn't stop it, no matter how she tried to steer her mind toward logic. Thank god, Jo wasn't there to see her fall apart.

Losing Jamie was bad enough, but that resurrected the long-buried memories of *all* her failed relationships. Why did this keep happening? Why had they acted like they loved her for a few months or years, then dumped her?

Of all the times men had walked into, then out of her life, this was the worst. Every time she watched the TV or used anything else Jamie had given her, the pain intensified and life seemed colder, darker, and more solitary than ever.

The whole world had seen him with his arm around the other woman, holding her hand, and kissing her when he won. To Kat—and every other viewer—he had made it clear she was nothing to him. Add humiliation to heartache. She reluctantly removed her engagement ring and placed it gently in her jewelry box as her anger turned to melancholy.

Poor concentration—a common symptom of depression—plagued her. Sometimes her mind would go blank, leaving her staring at nothing, seeing nothing, thinking nothing. Once, when she regained focus, her twelve-string was the first thing she saw. Kat flopped onto the couch with it and began mindlessly picking, then strumming chords. Not a song... only some uncommon chords she liked. A chord pattern and rhythm developed on their own. Then words that fit the rhythm came into her head.

I wake up every morning, just can't get you out of my mind.

You don't know what you did to me when you left me behind...

* * *

Jamie had stayed at Bill's house in the Hollywood Hills for the Academy Awards. When they got home after the show and parties, he dropped his key on the dining table and went straight to his room. Despite being surrounded all night by well-wishers, happy colleagues, and beautiful women who would have gladly taken him home, he felt isolated. He had won the grand prize Oscar he had always wanted, but he had sacrificed something dear.

Bill noticed him, sitting on the bed with his head in his hands. "You don't look like the guy who just won Best Actor."

"I don't feel like that guy." Jamie stared at the floor.

"It's Kat, isn't it?"

Jamie nodded. "I wanted her with me for this. She loved *The Ivory Reel*. And I feel bad about being in California and not calling her. It's like being in her home and not speaking to her."

"Then call her. You can get her back if you want to. I think it's illegal for an employer to require a specific marital status—or even *ask* if you're married. You could fight that and win. And you know your agent's only interested in his share of your salary."

Jamie didn't move or speak.

"You're an excellent actor, Jamie! You will not lose good roles for loving a normal woman. And why would you *want* to work for a director who wouldn't hire you just because you're married, or because your wife didn't give him a hard-on?"

Chapter 34: John Crocker

Production of *John Crocker II* had begun before the BAFTAs. It was already two months behind schedule, and Goldman, the executive producer, was anxious to get started as soon as the title role was re-cast.

Jamie wanted to call Kat and tell her about the film. Since he couldn't do that, he called Leigh. She wouldn't tell anyone about it.

"The storyline reminds me of the 1960s James Bond films. The free world is shifting to solar and other sustainable power sources. As traditional energy producers shut down, the film's bad guy—who must be wealthier than God—purchased the largest fossil fuel power plants in the western world for pennies on the dollar. Once we're dependent on sustainable energy, he launches massive solar "curtains" into space, to block the sunlight we need to turn solar rays into electricity. When he's deprived us of the energy we need to function, he'll offer to provide it—for a price that would bankrupt most and enslave us all. So I get to save democracies from the world's worst electric bill."

Leigh had made it clear she thought less of Jamie for breaking off his engagement to land a job, but she was supportive, anyway. "Brilliant. People will love you for that."

The first location shoot was in St. Andrews, Scotland, where there were both solar collection arrays and wind turbine farms, as well as lovely green farmland where Crocker could run for his life from the baddie's henchmen. The owner made more money renting his land to the film studio than he would have made farming it, that season.

The cast and crew Jamie met in Scotland welcomed him and were glad to finally get production under way. His reputation as a friendly, easy-going, but hard-working team player had preceded him and served him well there.

Warren McAvoy turned out to be Jamie's kind of director. He knew what he wanted in a shot and gave clear directions. He was open to occasional suggestions, but once he decided what he wanted, the discussion was over.

One evening a gaffer drove three of the actors down the coast to a restaurant in the fishing village of Anstruther that had won the "Best Fish and Chips in Britain" award. Getting to know each other after hours made working together easier and more fun.

Another night Jamie and some of the cast and crew went out to a pub that featured live music. It was fun until he recognized tunes Kat had played with Allan's band in London, and his mind took him to a place he didn't want to be. When his emotions threatened to betray him, he excused himself to the loo and splashed water on his face. After that, he politely declined invitations to go hear traditional Scottish music. He could drink at the hotel.

The company had taken a break for the Academy Awards after a week of outdoor work in Scotland. Jamie wasn't the only person working on *John Crocker II* who had been nominated. McAvoy took advantage of their location, scheduling outdoor scenes to be shot at a solar power plant in California's Mojave Desert, right after the Oscars.

One of the world's largest solar collection arrays, the Ivanpah solar thermal plant was an impressive sight, sure to get audiences' attention. Three-thousand, five-hundred acres of mirrors focused solar energy on three giant towers. They covered what looked to Jamie like barren land. But a story in the local paper about lawsuits indicated that land was wildlife habitat—home to endangered desert tortoises—and that the intensely focused light rays had burned thousands of birds and bats to death as they flew through them.

CDW biologists were working on the problems with U.S. Fish and Wildlife scientists. Kat probably arranged the paper's interviews with the state scientists. It seemed Jamie couldn't go anywhere without being reminded of her.

The second day of the desert shoot, Judy and Pacific Studios' PR team planted their rumours of an affair between Jamie and Ambrosia, the twenty-something blonde co-star he had taken to the awards ceremonies. It was on the air that night and in the British tabloids over the next few days. Ambrosia seemed pleased at all the attention. Jamie could only take their colleagues' teasing in stride and hide his resentment of the publicity scheme that forced him to back out of his engagement.

Inside Show Biz merged the actors' names and began referring to the couple as "Jambrosia." Irritated, Jamie tried not to think about how Kat would feel if she heard that.

The film company returned to London after a few days to shoot interior scenes at Warner Brothers Studios, Leavesden—north of London. Several sleepless nights robbed Jamie of energy for the days' work.

He sometimes arrived late on the set and forgot his lines. But so what? He wasn't the only one, and it usually wasn't his fault. After all, he couldn't control traffic. When he began blaming others for his mistakes, the friendly banter with his colleagues disappeared.

Warren McAvoy asked him, "What's the matter, Jamie? You've changed since we came to London. You've been bolshy, resisting direction."

Another day, a line producer remarked, "That Oscar has given you an attitude, kid. I hope you get over it, soon— before it hurts all of us." Their mild reprimands annoyed Jamie, but he stuffed his feelings deep inside.

Mairi McMillan had landed a minor role in the film and worked in some scenes shot at Leavesden. Feeling rather smug, Jamie decided to make her day. "Mairi... join me for dinner after we wrap, tonight?"

"Why? You planning some prank to make me look foolish?"

"No. Why would you think that?"

"Because I'm not thick."

"Look, I know I haven't always been warm toward you, but things that were in my way, then, are gone. Let me make it up to you."

Mairi studied his face, as though she wasn't sure she could trust him. But he knew he was the star of her fantasies, and she wanted to be seen with him.

Jamie took her to a nice restaurant near Hyde Park and watched her push her food around the plate, seldom taking a bite. An image of Kat enjoying a good meal popped into his mind. He banished it. He and Mairi talked about work. It turned out that was all they *could* talk about—the only interest they had in common. Still, when he invited her to his house for a drink she jumped at the chance.

The drinks went down as quickly as Mairi did. Neither of them bothered to pretend they were there for anything but sex. She was a beauty, with full, child-like lips, a model's body, and long, thick, ginger hair.

As they groped and undressed each other, Jamie noticed Mairi's breasts felt abnormally hard. Were they real? As he caressed one of them, Mairi pushed his hand down, as though having her breasts touched did nothing for her.

He lifted her frock and slip over her head. She pulled her pantyhose off, exposing the most prominent pelvic bones he had ever seen. *Bloody hell... Thin is in, but she could hurt a guy with those.* Her ribcage protruded, too—as they would on a starving Prisoner of War. Turning his attention back to her breasts, he felt scars. Implants, like her chin! What else is fake?

As Mairi was fondling and kissing Jamie, he lost his erection. She tried all the usual methods to fix that, but nothing worked. By then, Jamie was so disgusted, even the prospect of a one-night-stand repelled him. He had previously sensed phoniness, that she was always acting, even offstage. Now it seemed her body was fake, too. An image of Kat's soft, comfortable body came to mind.

"This is no good," he said, gently pushing Mairi away. "I'm sorry. This was a mistake."

"What's no good?" She glared at him and stood up. "What are you talkin' about?"

"I'm sorry, Mairi... I can't do this." He began putting his clothes back on.

Mairi's face turned red and her nostrils flared. "You can't... What's the matter with you? You're supposed to be the hot, randy stallion of the stage, and you can't even get it up."

"I could, until I realized I was holding a mannequin."

"You're callin' *me* plastic? You're a fuckin' phony, Jamie Knight! All that P.R. about you bein' a nice guy is bollocks. You're an egotistical cock!"

"All right; get out." His arm muscles flexed as he waved her away. "I'm not taking that shit from you."

"You just can't handle a real woman! Maybe that American didn't want a real man, and now you don't know what to do with a woman who does!"

Incensed, Jamie picked up Mairi's clothes and threw them at her. "Real? A *real* woman? You've had your nose done, a chin implant, your lips injected with god-knows-what, you starve yourself, and your tits are fake. You're about as 'real' as the wax figures at Madam Tussaud's. Even your mind is empty. Get your phony arse out of my house. And stay away from me, or I'll have your character killed!"

"Oh, I'll stay away from *you,* all right," Mairi shouted as she dressed. "You're all mouth and trousers. You'll regret making a fool of *me,* Jamie Knight!"

She made good on her promise. Two days later, The Globe featured poor little Mairi McMillan, telling doleful tales of all the times she had been with "Jamie Knight, who couldn't perform, off-stage." She made herself sound like a heroine who tried to save this pathetic man whose public image was a sham.

To make things worse, she got someone on the *John Crocker* film crew to confirm that Jamie couldn't remember his lines and was being "difficult" at work.

Jamie clenched his fists and threw the paper on the floor. But instead of proving them wrong with his old work ethic and easy-going manner, he continued to show up late and act like a spoiled rich kid. By April, he had earned notoriety for being a jerk, and the media were eating it up.

That kind of reputation made an actor hard to represent. "What the hell has gotten into you, Knight?" Victor demanded. "Have you lost the plot? Your reputation used to be stellar, but now I hear you're stroppy, showing up late for your calls, unprepared, bitching about everything from your wardrobe to the temperature, not knowing your lines, arguing the toss with McAvoy and doing things the way *you* think they should be—"

"Listen, Victor, I've read the Crocker books and I know my character better than anyone. If a director tells me to do something Crocker wouldn't do, I'm not doing it!"

"Yes, you are, or you're going to find yourself sacked and without an agent. You just cost both of us a lot of money! Two directors who were interested in you now say they won't work with the arrogant wanker you've become. If you ever become a director, you can call the shots. Until then, you do it *their* way. Get your arse into makeup on time, to the set on time, prepared for work, and remember you're part of an ensemble!"

"Oh, spare me—"

"God damn it, Jamie, get off your high horse! That Oscar has gone to your head, and your head is up your arse. Stop acting like you're the bleedin' queen, or you'll go for an early bath!"

Victor slammed the phone, leaving Jamie steaming. Winning the top honor had turned the world against him and made him a target.

After the Mairi fiasco, Jamie stayed home most of the time that he wasn't working. There, he could get trollied to drown both anger and pain—in private. He had no desire to go out and socialize, but he needed to talk with someone. Over drinks with cinematographer Paul Anderson, Jamie spoke bitterly of his new public image.

"They love you as long as you're an underdog," he groused. "As soon as someone says you're the best, they want to tear you down."

Paul, who had been a year ahead of Jamie at university, had studied psychology as well as film production. He was the kind of friend who could help a buddy solve a problem he had brought on himself without frustrating him further. "I've heard some of that. Is any of it true? Have you been less prepared, or less cooperative than usual? Losing your temper?"

"No."

Paul quietly stared into his drink.

After a few moments of silence, Jamie took a slug of Scotch whisky and began to open up. "Well... maybe a little."

"That's not like you. What's going on?"

Jamie stared into his glass for a long moment. "I can't sleep."

"Is something bothering you? Making you angry?"

"I don't know," Jamie lied. He knew, and he knew that Paul did, too. Pretending was pointless. He took another drink, followed by a deep breath. "Remember Kat? The American I was in love with?"

"Yeah, you were mad for her."

"I still am. But to get the John Crocker role, I had to be unattached, so they could fake an affair between Ambrosia and me for publicity. So, I dropped her." Jamie swallowed hard.

"Paul, we were engaged, and I broke it off for this job. Victor said it would propel my career and make me a star. I know I hurt her... *gutted her*! I can still hear the shock and pain in her voice when I did it, and now I can't get her out of my head."

"Hmm... And... what's happening to your career now?"

Jamie looked down. Then his eyes opened wider, and he leaned forward. "It's going pear-shaped. Bloody hell... I've lost *her*, and now I may lose everything I've worked for, too. I'm buggered!"

"Maybe," Paul replied. "You're the only one who can decide what's most important to you, and how to make your life what you want it to be. You're a smart guy, Jamie... and a damned good, successful actor. Your career isn't dependent on your marital status. And you know, most people will forgive almost anything if you ask them, apologize, and honestly share your feelings. Why don't you try to get inside your own head and heart? The answers will come to you."

Chapter 35: Cold Spring

Kat hadn't spoken with Barbara since December. She had put off telling her judgmental sister Jamie had broken off their engagement, knowing Barb's reaction would be some form of "I told you so." Yes, she *had* cautioned that the relationship Kat believed she had with Jamie was too good to be real, but who wants to hear that?

Barbara called *her* one late Sunday afternoon. "How are things going? Have you decided what you're going to do with your house when you move away?"

"I'm not moving, after all." She paused. "Jamie broke off our engagement." Damn, it hurt to say that aloud.

"Oh, no. I'm sorry. Why? Did he have a good reason?"

"No. He said he couldn't be the good husband he wanted to be, right now. Whatever *that* means. Sounds like bullshit to me."

"Typical man," Barbara said. "And they accuse *us* of beating around the bush. I know I wasn't enthusiastic about you getting involved with him, but you were so excited... I'm sorry your big dream fell through. That's got to hurt. How are you holding up?"

"Barely. After the initial shock & sadness, I was mad as hell at him and would have punched him if I'd seen him. Then I missed him and got depressed. I've lost interest in everything, don't want to do anything but sleep—and usually *can't* sleep when I need to."

"Well," Barbara advised, "try to focus on something that'll take your mind off him and what might have been. I know that's hard; that's how getting divorced felt. But at least you don't have kids to take care of. You were doing well before you met him, and you don't need a husband to keep having a good life. Especially one who would propose, then break up with you."

"Thanks, I'll try." Kat sighed. "Right now, it's hard to concentrate, and I'm forgetting things like never before. So I'm just trying to do my job well enough to keep from getting into trouble there."

"You'll do it. You've overcome break-ups before. You'll do it again. Call me if there's anything I can do to help."

There was nothing anyone could do for a broken heart, but it was nice of Barbara to call. Even nicer that she didn't say "I told you so." Kat hoped that meant their relationship could improve.

In late March, California's tax agency posted the total amount of money contributed to the Endangered Species and Sea Otter Funds the previous year. They had received record-breaking donations, and Kat was sure Jamie's PSAs were the reason.

Even though she had lost hope for their relationship, she wanted to thank him again for doing them and share the results of his work. She also wanted to stay on his radar in case he might change his mind. When she called, Jamie didn't answer. The enthusiastic, upbeat message she left was worthy of an acting award. He didn't respond.

After that, Kat gave up and stopped watching or reading any entertainment news, knowing Jamie and his new girlfriend—who looked young enough to be his daughter— could show up any time.

She slipped into apathy, her mind didn't work the way it used to, and she had no energy. Sometimes even the cats couldn't get her attention. She felt half-dead and once supposed she might as well be. *No one would miss me, except Kellye and Jeremy. And maybe Jo.*

That reminded her she needed to visit her mother. She hadn't gone as often as she used to, and that wasn't right.

The hardest part was putting on a "happy face" for her mom and the nursing home staff.

The thought of food made her nauseous, and she struggled to do her job. All her musical activities and the Scottish Games publicity team went by the wayside. After believing she would spend the rest of her life with Jamie, the renewed certainty that she would spend it alone was sometimes more than she could bear.

One evening, Janet called her. "You need to get out and have some fun. We're going to a musical!"

"No, thanks," Kat mumbled.

"Kat, you can't sit around being miserable, alone! It'll only get worse. I will not let you waste your life because some man led you on, then disappeared. He's just another selfish jerk. I'll get the tickets and pick you up Saturday at six-thirty."

"No, really..."

"Don't argue with me," Janet commanded. "We're going to see *South Pacific,* even if I have to bring Big Dave to drag you out of your house." Dave, another fiddler, *was* big, and strong enough to pick Kat up and carry her out to Janet's car.

"No, Janet! I *mean* it!" Kat immediately regretted speaking so forcefully to a friend and softened her tone. "I'm sorry. Listen... I'm trying to get over him, change my perspective... get back to my old life and forget about love. It's not easy, but I know I can do it, eventually. But a play about a nurse who gets her heart broken would *not* help. I'd probably fall apart in the theater. Give me some time to work through this."

"Okay. Listen—if you love him, let him go. Then he's someone else's problem."

Kat had to chuckle. "I'll get over him. It takes time. Remember? Time wounds all heels?"

She wasn't as sure as she sounded, but she convinced Janet. The emotional pain was paralyzing, and she had to get past it, forget Jamie, and regain her self-confidence—especially at work.

As a supervisor, Molly McKenna heard managers say things they wouldn't tell their employees. As Kat's friend, Molly told her Ron had groused about her always looking miserable and being late with a project. His boss, Susan, said Kat needed to hide her feelings and focus on work.

One of her college psychology professors had said it's impossible to intentionally *not* think of something. "Don't think about the pink elephant." Instead, intentionally thinking of something *else* was the way to go. So Kat made a list of things she *should* think about and taped it to the wall near her computer monitor. To her surprise, it worked!

Thinking about purging the junk in the garage, and actually starting the task, kept her mind off Jamie for a while. Weeds were emerging around the house, so when she started feeling down again, she focused on pulling them. She found an online cooking course that she could study at her own pace, and that worked better than anything. Her aversion to wasting food kept her mind from wandering while carefully reading and following instructions.

She hadn't purged Jamie from her mind—or heart—but attention to other things had made her think of him less and feel better as time passed.

When a neighborhood owl called for a mate, she felt sorry for it. Things like that could bring her down, but now she had a way back up. She was on her way back to normal life—the pretty good life she had before Jamie Knight barged into it.

Chapter 36: Jamie's Lament

"Dad... If you had to choose between success and the woman you loved, which would you choose?" Jamie sat on a lawn chair in his parents' garden.

Reggie Knight focused on his roses. "Is this a riddle?"

Jamie swallowed, blinked, and looked down. "No. I'm serious."

Reggie stopped trimming the rose bush and turned toward him. "Where am I in my career when I allegedly have to make this choice?"

Jamie took a deep breath. "About twenty years in." He gazed off into the distance and spoke slowly. "You're popular... and successful enough that you don't *have* to work. But you haven't reached the top yet. And you love your work as much as you love this woman. You can't live without either... but you have to drop her for a chance at stardom... or, in your case, the Supreme Court."

His father leaned back and deliberated for a moment. Then he looked closely at Jamie and, in a softer tone, asked, "Is this about Kat?"

"Yes. I was too embarrassed to tell you, but Leonard Goldman wouldn't cast me as John Crocker if I had any romantic attachments. This role could make me an A-Lister. He made me choose between her and the things I've wanted all my life. It was the hardest choice I've ever had to make. It killed me to do it, but I chose the job. Now I have this 'star-making' role, and I'm miserable. Not about the work, but missing Kat, and guilt for breaking my promise to her."

"That was unkind." Reggie let that sink in and looked at his son the way he might look at someone recently convicted in his courtroom. "I had a feeling something happened. You used to talk about her all the time, then suddenly stopped, and began dating..."—he paused, as if searching for the right word—"...other women again. Your mother told me you broke off your engagement. She seemed rather pleased, and I wondered why you hadn't mentioned it to me. Now I understand."

"We haven't spoken in three months, and I miss her more than I imagined possible. I love her. Mum and Christy think Kat's not what she seems. Victor thinks she was bad for my career. But they're wrong."

"Harrington? Your agent? What did he say?"

"He said I can't afford to be linked to a common, unattractive American, and that being seen with her could keep me from being offered good roles in the future. He and Mum both said marrying her could ruin me, professionally. Do you think that's true?"

"Certainly not. And you're a fool to let anyone tell you who you should love or marry, or to think it would affect your career. You're a skilled, gifted actor, Jamie. Your associates like you and your fans treat you like a rock star. That won't end, simply because you marry, or because the woman you love isn't a fashion model. And I think she *is* pretty."

"So do I."

"You're forty-five, son. Follow your heart and your mind. Do you know how many people told me I shouldn't marry your mother because she was much older than me? That's not important. Honesty, love, loyalty, and common sense... those are worth much more than a beautiful face or a perfect body—which you all will lose, someday." He pointed at Jamie. "Even you. Look at your mum and I. *We* used to be a handsome couple!" He smiled, perhaps hoping Jamie would laugh at his self-deprecating humor. It didn't work.

"You look first-rate to me, Dad. I know Kat's older than I am, but Mum thinks she's a lot older than she looks."

"So what? If she is, that may be the reason you like her this much. Maybe she's lived enough to have experiences and depth, and learned things many people your age haven't, yet. And she could be twenty years older and still *outlive* you."

With his elbows on his knees Jamie put his head in his hands and stared at the bricks between his feet.

His father went on. "I'm not sure about the States, but marital status can not be a condition of employment, here. Are you sure you love her?"

"Yes."

"More than the other women you thought you loved?

"Oh, god, yes." His lower lip quivered as he watched a tear fall on his shoe.

"Do you think she loves *you*?"

"Yes. Or at least, she *did*." Jamie's voice faltered. As he stared at the ground, another tear slid off his cheek. "After I broke up with her, I don't know." His voice cracked, he swallowed hard, sniffed, and tried to blink back tears he couldn't stop.

Reggie put his hand on his son's shoulder. "Then stop being a git, and call her. Apologize. Tell her the truth... and hope she still loves you. If she's as good a woman as you think, and she loves you, she'll understand and forgive you. Maybe not in a tick, if she's had unpleasant experiences with men—divorce or if they've left her for someone else. Too much of that makes it hard to trust anyone again. But if she really loves you she'll give you another chance, in time."

"Is that... unconditional love?"

"It can be. You won't know you have unconditional love until you're in the sort of situation that could end a relationship. When you do something hurtful to someone and she continues to love and support you..."

Jamie recalled Kat's supportive messages, even after he ditched her.

307

"If you were black-listed or disabled," his father said, "couldn't get work, or lost all your money, a wife who loved you unconditionally would do everything she could to support you and get help for you, without making you feel bad about yourself. She would show that she loves and respects you, and defend you against anyone who didn't. That's what unconditional love would be like. And the reverse is true, too. Would you do that for her?"

"Yes, but—damn—I hope life never gets *that* bad!" Jamie gave his father an uncomfortable half-laugh, hoping for some reassurance. Then he went quiet, thinking about all his father had said. They had never had a conversation like this before, and it felt good to open up to him and listen to his wisdom. He should have done it, years ago.

"Yes, I love her that much. At least, I think I do." Jamie reflected on a past relationship. History was repeating itself. He didn't realize how much he loved Leigh when they were young until he lost her to Bob. All because he wanted fame more than he wanted her. Or so he had thought. It had killed him to watch her with Bob at their wedding. Now, here he was, doing it again.

Jamie thought about his last phone call to Kat. The confusion and pain in her voice haunted him. He got very little sleep that night, thinking about his father's advice. Goldman's demand that he be unattached was illegal, and now Jamie wanted Kat in his life more than ever. But after all this time, she may not want him anymore.

The next day, he asked Bill Bleuchel to do some reconnaissance for him—see if he could learn whether she still cared, or had moved on.

* * *

The last Bill had heard from Kat was a thank you note for the early Christmas at his house. He contrived an excuse to call her colleague, Molly McKenna. Saying he was interested in using a state wildlife area for movie scenes, he asked the necessary questions about that, then casually asked, "How's Kat?"

Molly lit into him. "How do you think? Your friend *destroyed* her! She knew better than to fall for him, but he convinced her he loved her. Her heart overruled her head, and now she's miserable. She's lost interest in everything—even music!"

"I'm sorry, Molly. I didn't know. Do you think she still loves him?"

"Yes, unfortunately. But since he dumped her—like every other man she's loved—she thinks she's terminally unlovable. How could he do that? He asked her to *marry him*, for Pete's sake. Now she's so depressed, she won't even confide in *me*, anymore. "

"Damn... I'm sorry to hear that. Jamie didn't *want* to break up with her. He had to be unattached to get the John Crocker role he needs to make his professional dreams possible. He agonized over it. And he didn't think she—"

"Give me his phone number. I'll tell him! How could he think such a demand was legal? I'd like to kick his butt. Why didn't he tell her *why* he broke off their engagement?"

"I don't know. But he loves her so much, he cried about her, the night he won an Oscar. Listen, don't tell anyone—especially Kat—that I called you, okay? I don't know what Jamie will do, but... can I give him your phone number?"

"Please do. And tell Mister Hot-Shot-Movie-Star that he ripped the heart out of someone who didn't deserve it. She's the most loyal, supportive partner he could ever hope for."

* * *

Bill relayed what Molly had said, to Jamie, who was surprised to learn how hard Kat had taken his sudden exit from her life. "How could I be that important to someone as independent and self-sufficient as Kat?"

"According to Molly, you're not the first man to love her and leave her. I think you blew off the marriage you've always wanted, for an illegal demand."

"Oh, god... How can I face her now?"

"Do you have the courage to apologize and take whatever reaction you get?"

"What do you think she'll do?"

"I don't know, but if you don't, I will. There aren't a lot of women like her around."

"No! Don't you dare. I want her back in *my* life!"

An unfamiliar discomfort came over Jamie. He stared out the window, twisting his watch while deciding what to do next, as rain drenched his garden. At once he felt sad, guilty, lonely, desirous, excited, and afraid. Was this anxiety? It even upset his stomach. For a man who told others to listen to their bodies, it took him a while to hear what his own was telling him.

Chapter 37: The Lion Sleeps Tonight

In April, Kat ran a news conference in a remote part of the central Sierra foothills, where a mountain lion had attacked a boy, early that morning. It was one of those no-frills news conferences in a dusty clearing surrounded by oaks, manzanita, and large boulders. Reporters from the Sacramento Bee, two small local newspapers and a news website, one radio station, two TV stations, and one from The Collegian—San Joaquin Delta College's student newspaper—drove out to get the story.

A lieutenant game warden stood on a small boulder so all the reporters could see and hear his situation report. Kat moderated the Q&A session and helped reporters and photographers get the interviews and video they wanted. It was late Monday afternoon before the last one had left. The sheriff's deputies, wardens and biologist who had taken part had also left to join the search for the lion.

Returning to her state pool vehicle, hot and tired, she couldn't find her keys. *Oh, no!* In her rush to assist people who had arrived early, she had left them inside. She tried each door and the back hatch; every one of them was locked. The windows were all shut to keep dust out. As she tapped the numbers to call for help, the battery in her phone died. Alone in mountain lion habitat, where the one that attacked the boy still ran free, she couldn't get into the old SUV.

A chill ran through her as she grasped her situation. Her options included a walk of at least twelve miles to the last house she had seen on the narrow dirt road to the news conference site. But California mountain lion attacks had occurred on dirt roads and trails. If it was still in the area, the lion that had attacked the boy could easily see, hear, and attack *her* on the road. All she had for self defense were her pen, news releases, and clipboard. She imagined the headline: "Cougar Scared Off by Government News Release." Maybe, if Isabel—CDW's wanna-be PIO with no relevant experience—wrote it.

Kat stayed put, thinking the searchers would circle back to that clearing again. As twilight made it hard to see things, what sounded like a cougar snarled in the distance. The hair on her arms stood up, and her heart pounded so hard she could hear her pulse in her ears. She climbed atop the SUV, hoping if a puma saw her, she could see it, too, and make herself look big enough up there to discourage it. It had been a long day. Tired, she sat on the hood and leaned back against the windshield.

Twilight had turned to darkness—when lions hunt. Rustling in the nearby brush made her jump up and hold her pen as she would a knife. Realizing how ridiculous that was, she would have laughed if she hadn't been so nervous. Out here, the pen was *not* mightier than the sword. Nothing came out of the brush, but her muscles tightened, and she was haunted by that familiar, painful feeling that they had forgotten her.

The roof of an SUV was a short leap for a mountain lion, so she might have a better chance if she looked for the wardens who were looking for the lion. She knew which direction they had gone, but far from the lights of civilization, she couldn't see much under a quarter moon. She couldn't see foot- or horseshoe prints, or tracks from the all-terrain vehicles used in the search. She would have given anything for a good flashlight. And a spare key.

In daylight, Kat had an uncanny sense of direction, but not at night, especially outside a town. Following a fire road that narrowed into a trail, turning here and there to get around boulders or thick brush, it didn't take long to lose her bearings. She wanted to go back to the SUV, but by then, didn't know which way to go. Fatigue set in and she was getting cold. Her right knee ached.

She wished she had taken CDW's wilderness survival course, so she'd know how to stay safe out there. Mountain lions could go anywhere she could. She thought it best to climb a tree, anyway, and hope if she got high enough and sat still, she'd be a little less obvious than she would on the ground. Maybe a lion could walk by and not notice her, if the wind didn't give her away.

She put some golf ball-sized rocks in her pockets—pathetic weapons against an apex predator. It took some time to find a tree she could climb with three or four large limbs that formed a crotch high on the trunk, where she could sit securely. Climbing reminded her of the day Jamie pushed her to climb rocks. That day, she'd had a choice.

She was wide awake and alert at first, but her eyelids grew heavier and heavier as the night dragged on. The sounds of insects and small prey scurrying through leaves and the occasional call of an owl hunting them became the soundtrack of the night. Many times her eyes closed, and she jerked her head up and blinked madly to keep from falling asleep. Eventually, she couldn't keep them open any longer.

* * *

Tuesday morning in the public affairs office, Ron asked if anyone knew where Kat was. It wasn't like her to not show up without calling.

"Maybe she got back too late and couldn't get up early this morning," Molly said. She and Ron had both seen her on the news the night before. At noon, Kat still hadn't called. Had something happened on the way back from the news conference? Molly phoned, texted and emailed Kat's work and personal accounts, asking her to call the office ASAP. She hadn't posted anything relevant on social media.

When they hadn't heard from her by two o'clock, Molly called the California Highway Patrol to ask if Kat had been in a traffic accident. Neither her name nor the state vehicle she drove appeared on any CHP reports.

She drove to Kat's house, but no one answered the door, and the shades were all drawn. She knew her neighbor, Jo, from Kat's summer luaus, and asked her if she had seen or heard from her.

"Not since Sunday," she said. Jo had keys to Kat's house, so they went inside where two hungry kitties gave them what-for. Their "MomCat" was still absent. The women agreed they should call Kat's sister.

Barbara hadn't spoken with Kat in a month, but didn't seem concerned. "You know how independent she is... not inclined to 'report' to anyone."

"Yes," Molly said, "but she's never failed to show up for work without calling-in. And she was in a remote location yesterday. This isn't normal."

Back in the office, Roni Jorgensen wondered if depression might have gotten the best of her.

"What do you mean?"

Roni closed the door. "You know." Molly didn't respond. "Come on, do I have to say it?" Again Molly was silent, fearing what Roni implied. "I hate to think it, but... she's been so miserable... she might have gone off in the hills to kill herself."

"No, she would never do that." *Please don't let it be that!*

Molly called Lieutenant Nate Freeman, who had been at Monday's news conference. "That's the last time I saw her, talking with the last two reporters. I'll drive back up there to see if she had car trouble or ran off the road."

Lt. Freeman reported that he found Kat's locked vehicle, but no sign of her. He had two wardens search for her that afternoon, and when they hadn't found her by dark, he organized a full search-and-rescue operation to begin at daylight.

Seeing an opportunity to make Kat look stupid, Isabel Lorenzo leaked to the news media that Kat "got lost" in the foothills and was missing. It was a slow news day, so the Sacramento Bee and two radio stations carried the story. One even sensationalized it. Then the Associated Press picked it up, and it went statewide.

* * *

Half-listening to the news while reading his mail, Bill Bleuchel heard Kat's name. He went to the TV to see why, in time to hear the reporter say, "...searching the area, hoping *they* find the missing spokeswoman before a hungry mountain lion does." Startled, he searched the internet to find the complete story.

After reading it, he phoned Jamie, despite the late hour in London.

* * *

Tuesday dragged on forever, as Kat trudged up and down hillsides, sometimes using animal trails that dead-ended at thick brush. Star thistle and other thorny plants—all invasive species—pierced her skin through her long-sleeved uniform. The heat made her wish she'd worn short sleeves, but she'd be more scratched-up and colder at night if she had.

With her mouth as dry as the hillsides, she would have given anything for a running stream. And an antihistamine. When a turkey vulture circled overhead, she shuddered to think she'd be on the menu, if she didn't find a road or some hikers.

An image of her mother popped into her mind. Two days had passed since Kat had visited her. Did Mom miss her? Was she lonely? She wondered if Barbara would visit her often enough if Kat died out here. And the kitties! They hadn't been fed since Monday morning. What if they had drunk all their water or gotten food in it? Worry about her mother, Kellye, and Jeremy brought tears to her eyes. She *couldn't* stay lost or die. Who would take care of them?

Another night in a tree... without brushing her teeth. *Yuck!* But this time she carried a club-like section of a dead branch with her, as well as rocks in her pockets. Despite being agnostic, she prayed to a God she wasn't sure of. "If you do exist, I apologize. Some of your followers are giving you a bad name."

Wednesday morning, asleep in the large, three-limb crotch of another tree, Kat awoke to the crack of a rifle shot, not far away. "Oh, shit!" *Some poacher could mistake me for an animal!* She stood on a branch, clung to the trunk, and yelled, "Hey! Can you see me? I'm not game!" She waited a minute. "Hello! Can you hear me?" She heard something coming through the brush about twenty feet away.

A woman's voice finally called out, "Kat? Where are you?"

As two game wardens emerged on horseback, Kat yelled, "Up here! Oh, man, am I glad to see *you!*" She didn't know either of them, but any human was a welcome sight.

Abruptly, both wardens aimed their rifles at the ground beneath her.

Kat looked down. A large, adult mountain lion lay still. She gasped. "Holy *shit!*"

"Didn't you see it before I shot it?" one asked.

"No! I was asleep." She carefully climbed down from her perch, shaking like a leaf.

The wardens had never met her, but her dirty CDW uniform made it obvious she was their missing colleague. "Well, it saw *you.* You're lucky you didn't fall! What are you doing in a tree?"

"Trying not to be anyone's dinner."

"You know cats can climb trees, don't you?" the other asked.

"Of course. I just hoped I'd be less noticeable and harder to attack up there than on the ground." She pulled six golf ball-sized rocks from her pockets. "If one came up toward me, I hoped I could discourage it with these and a makeshift club wedged in the branches up there. What else could I do?"

Wardens Billy Yeaman and Patricia Travers introduced themselves. With the dead lion draped behind one saddle and Kat seated behind the other, she told them what had happened as they rode a few miles to the wardens' trucks. She gratefully gulped an entire bottle of water from Patricia's cooler as put the horses in their trailers and Billy took the cougar to the Wildlife Investigations Lab.

Pat drove Kat to her SUV, jimmied the lock, then followed her to the nearest town. She desperately wanted to shower and brush her teeth. She also wanted to phone the wardens and biologist who left her alone at the attack site and say, "Thanks a lot!" But they would undoubtedly point out that she was the fool who locked herself out of her own vehicle.

Around 9:50 a.m., Kat used Pat's phone to call Ron. She needed the day off to sleep. "Okay," Ron said, "but we need you here tomorrow. The media know you got lost. We're getting a lot of calls and you need to handle them." He sounded irate.

On the two-hour drive home, the events of the prior three months all hit her, and tears filled her eyes. Exhaustion, being abandoned by her colleagues, abandoned by Jamie, Ron's callousness, and nearly becoming Cougar Chow that morning were more than she could handle calmly.

Before day's end, Wardens Yeaman and Travers had told the story of the lion and the PIO to enough people in their region for details to have gotten back to the public affairs office. Someone told the environment reporter at the Sacramento Bee, who left three messages on Kat's phone. He wanted her first interview. Roni had told Kat's friend, Alexia Bennett, a news anchor at the NBC-TV affiliate, and Alexia's message made Kat feel better. She had asked, "Are you okay?" rather than for an interview.

"A PIO's nights with a mountain lion," as one station's promo exaggerated, was one of the top stories on a few California TV stations that evening. NPR carried it in their afternoon news and CBS ran it in the evening newscast. One news anchor introduced the story as "A harrowing night for one government spokeswoman." When she learned of it Thursday morning, Kat felt humiliated. *Locked myself out of a car... how stupid!*

Chapter 38: Got to Get You Into My Life

Jamie had taken a red-eye flight to San Francisco, then a commuter plane to Sacramento, Thursday morning. Relieved when Bill told him CDW had found Kat unharmed, he still wanted to see her as soon as possible. While waiting for a shuttle to the car rental office, he thought about the coming conversation at her house, until Bill sent another text saying he had heard her on the radio, and she was at work.

Jamie texted back:

> At work? After what she's been through? That's bollocks!

He drove faster than he should have to the small office building where he and Bill had surprised Kat a year and a half earlier. Screeching to a stop in the car park, he rushed toward the entry, where a man on a scaffold was replacing the words "Department of Wildlife" on an outside wall.

"Isn't this the wildlife office?" he asked the man bolting an "S" to the wall.

"Nope. They must have moved out."

Unbelievable. He had flown five-thousand miles, psyched himself up to apologize to the woman he loved, and she wasn't there. "Do you know where they are, now?"

"No. Someone inside might."

Jamie ran inside the building to the double doors that once led to Kat's office. They were locked. Through a small window he could see the hall and other doors, all closed, but no people. He went back to the entry and up the stairs, two at a time. The doors were locked on that floor, too, but there was a phone with instructions on the wall. The woman who answered said the CDW office was at Ninth and Q streets.

Jamie hurried back and typed "9th and Q" into the car's navigation system, then realized he didn't need to. The Capitol business district was a grid. To find a vacant parking space near that intersection took two aggravating trips around three blocks of one-way streets, and a credit card for the parking meter.

There were two nondescript office buildings on the corners, but neither showed who occupied them—only street numbers on the front walls. The glass doors into one building were locked. He bolted down one side of the building, then the other, searching for another door, an intercom, any way to communicate with people inside. *What is this, the CIA?*

As he started crossing the street to the other building, the door behind him clicked and a tall man sporting a long, gray ponytail came out. He looked familiar. Had they met at Kat's old office? Jamie rushed back.

"Pardon me... you know Kat Mancini, don't you?"

Brian Galway smiled with a look of recognition. "Yes. I'm Brian. Kat introduced us at our old building."

Jamie anxiously twisted his watch back and forth. "Yes. I need to see her. Please... would you let me in and tell me where her office is?"

"She's not here. The public affairs staff are at headquarters now. Didn't she tell you?"

"No." Another detour? He ran his hand through his hair. "Where's headquarters?"

"Not far. Are you all right?"

"No," Jamie confessed. "I've been so thick I made the worst mistake of my life, and I have to see Kat to make things right."

Brian pointed north. "Her office is in that big, dark-greenish building, two blocks down. Good luck."

"Thank you!" Jamie sprinted, stopping only to avoid getting hit by traffic on the cross streets. At the sixteen-story Natural Resources Building, he tried to enter the doors on O Street, but they were—like the others—locked. His blood pressure escalated.

A woman waiting for the light rail called out, "You can't get in there, anymore. You have to go around the corner."

Jamie darted to the front of the building and rushed into the large, recessed entry, perspiring, panting, looking for a directory.

The security guards couldn't have missed him. As he followed some employees toward the elevators, one guard—a large woman Jamie's height, in a navy-blue uniform—stopped him in front of Slow Sam's snack shop and challenged him with a less-than-friendly, "May I help you?"

Jamie was agitated, out of place, and he didn't know their procedures. "Please," he panted, wiping perspiration from his face. "I need to see Katerina Mancini, in public relations. Can you tell me how to get there?"

"Which agency?"

"Minist—I mean, Wildlife."

"Is she expecting you?"

"No... but she knows me. I'm her—we're good friends." Why was the universe throwing all these obstacles in his way?

After twelve hours on planes, not finding Kat where he expected her, having to drive on the wrong side of the road while searching for her new office, find a parking space, get to another building, and now deal with government security guards—on top of his anxiety about what he was there to do—Jamie knew his exasperation showed in his body language, his voice, and on his face. His shirt was damp with sweat and his breath came like a marathoner's.

Both guards gave him more attention than he would have liked. One said, "Let's talk outside," as he took hold of Jamie's elbow and turned him toward the exit.

Jamie jerked his arm from the guard's grip and glared at him. "What the hell? You want I.D.? Just ask for it!" He reached for the wallet in his back pocket, but before he could touch it, the first guard took his wrist and pulled it up behind his back in a terribly uncomfortable control hold.

"Outside." Her volume was normal, but indisputably a command.

Now Jamie was fuming—incredulous at being treated like a criminal. He tried to pull his arms from the guards' hands, but they tightened their grips as six people in the lobby watched. Knowing people saw him being escorted out of a building by security added to the volatile mix of emotions boiling over.

One guard spoke discreetly into his cell phone as Jamie complained about being restrained. In less than a minute, a black and white Ford Crown Victoria pulled up to the quad in front of the building. A khaki-uniformed California Highway Patrol officer joined them and listened to the guards' story, with Jamie objecting and correcting them throughout.

His emotions now overwhelmed him. Lack of sleep on the red-eye flight didn't help. Not knowing his immediate fate, and mindful of the fact that he was a foreigner here, his anxiety turned to desperation to contact Kat. "If I could only call Kat, she'll straighten this out." *I think... won't she?*

The no-nonsense CHP officer wasn't hearing any of it. "Calm down," he said, as he cuffed Jamie's hands behind his back and guided him onto the hard back seat of his patrol car. Jamie's emotions overcame him. Feeling tears dampen his eyes, he flopped his head back on the seat, closed his eyes, and whispered, "Oh, God... please..."

A short, elderly man who walked past the patrol car and toward the building stopped to talk to the guards, who appeared to know him. He looked at Jamie, sitting awkwardly on his hands. "Hey!" He bent down and squinted. "Are you who I think you are?"

Oh, bugger... no, wait... Jamie forced a smile. "I hope so."

The man with a New York accent stepped closer to the car and bent down to Jamie's eye level. "Nigel Stone?"

"Yes." His shoulder muscle automatically moved to extend his right hand, but the handcuffs stopped him. "Jamie Knight. Nice to meet you. Do you know Katerina Mancini?"

"Not by name. She work here? I'd know her if she comes into my shop, Slow Sam's. I recognize a lot of my customers, but don't know their names. What are *you* doing *here*?" He turned to the officers. "Do you know who this is? Jamie Knight's an actor. Why are you arresting him?" He turned back to Jamie. "Where does this lady work?"

"The wildlife department... public relations." The anger in Jamie's voice had turned into a plea for a liberator. Grateful for the help, he took a deep breath and exhaled slowly. The CHP car reeked of everything recent detainees had brought into it— tobacco, marijuana, beer, vomit... He leaned close to the open window for air.

One guard fiddled with his phone.

"Why don't you call that office," Sam asked the guards. "I bet you they say he's okay." He turned to Jamie and grinned, as the CHP officer nodded to the guards and one went into the building to make the call.

"I love your show," Sam said. "I wish it was on more often. You people don't make enough episodes."

"No, British telly doesn't work like yours." Jamie breathed more normally, despite his physical and emotional discomfort. "Thank you... Sam, is it? I appreciate your help."

The guard came back out, wearing an amused look. "They say to check his I.D., and if he really *is* Jamie Knight, send him up." At the security desk, she had Jamie sign-in and gave him a visitor badge and directions to the Wildlife public affairs office. "I'm sorry, but you looked like a man about to go postal. Return the badge and sign-out when you leave."

It took forever for an elevator door to open. People came and waited with Jamie. He kept his head down, trying to be inconspicuous, but two people stared, as though they recognized him. He hoped he didn't smell like the patrol car he'd just been in. The elevator stopped three times before reaching the right floor, and when he stepped out, a woman getting out with him said, "Excuse me, but are you Jamie Knight?"

"Yes. Sorry I can't chat now." Running down the hall, he called, "I'm late to a meeting."

The Public Affairs suite had no receptionist, and nothing on the blank, beige walls indicated staff's office locations. He rushed from door to door, past two small, unoccupied offices. Isabel Lorenzo was in the third.

Short of breath, Jamie said, "Excuse me... I'm looking for Kat Mancini."

The young woman got up and strolled to the door. "Really? Why?" Her sarcasm irritated and her low-cut blouse was wasted on him. She smelled of cheap perfume. He frowned at her. Finally, she pointed, "Down there and to the right."

Jamie hurried past the next two offices and took the right turn. Kat's name and posters for the wildlife funds were on the open door. He stepped inside and closed it.

The walls in Kat's small office were the same dull beige as the outer office, but hers were covered with animal photos, posters, and award plaques. Sitting with her forehead in her palms and her elbows on a desk facing the left wall, she stared at a thick document. She raised her head. Her face was pale, with dark circles under her eyes. Her hair didn't shine the way he remembered, and she had lost weight. Judging from the rest of her appearance, he guessed it wasn't intentional.

* * *

Kat's mind went blank. She hadn't thought she would ever see this man again. A tsunami of emotions hit her at once: surprise, love, excitement, pain, desire, indignation, anger, fear, love (again)... like the sound of a dozen musicians playing different tunes on different instruments, all at the same time. She stood to face Jamie and tried to appear strong so he couldn't hurt her again.

"What are you doing here?" she demanded.

Jamie couldn't miss the fury in her eyes, voice, and posture, as her hands closed into tight fists. He took a deep breath.

"Apologizing. Kat, I'm sorry for ending our engagement and for shutting you out. I'm sorry I hurt you. I took unscrupulous advice from people I trusted, when I should have listened to my heart." He pulled the guest chair up and sat, so he wouldn't tower over her.

"Someone offered me the role of a lifetime, a romantic-hero part working for one of Hollywood's most successful directors, in a film that was sure to be a blockbuster and the first of a series. Everyone said it was my ticket to the A-List. You know how much I wanted that. The catch was, I had to remain single—completely unattached—to get the job, for a stupid publicity campaign cooked up by the studio."

Kat stared silently at him, not moving or showing any feelings.

"I've always put my career first, Kat, as you have. I didn't want to break up with you, but I wanted stardom *so badly*... I've been an utter twat." He paused, then in what sounded like the voice of a prisoner begging for mercy, said, "I got scared, Kat. My priorities were out of order, and... and..." he held his hands out to her. "I wasn't thinking properly!"

This didn't sound like the self-confident Jamie Kat knew. His eyes were wet, as though he had been crying, or was about to. He stood, stepped toward her, and pleaded as he put his hands on her upper arms. "I know I hurt you terribly, and I'm so sorry! I want us together again, the way we were last October. Can you please forgive me?"

That October had been the happiest time of Kat's life. She was in love with a man who she believed loved her. She had thought she was finally in the long-term relationship she had always wanted, and about to be married. But the pain of love's end was every bit as powerful as the joy that love created.

"No. Damn you... get out of here!" She jerked her arms out of his hands and backed up to the wall, shaking. The past three days in the foothills had been bad enough; Jamie's unexpected appearance pushed her off an emotional ledge. "I mean it, Jamie! Get out, now, or I'll call security!" Tears rolled down her cheeks.

"Kat, please—"

Reaching for the phone and pointing at the door, she shouted, "Out! Now!" loud enough for other staff to hear.

A few of Kat's colleagues watched from their offices as Jamie reluctantly left.

Chapter 39: A Walk in the Park

Jamie sat in the rental car and, with his head resting on the steering wheel, finally let the tears flow. This day had been too much for him, and it wasn't even noon yet. The depth of Kat's angersurprised him. He needed a drink. It may be nearly lunchtime here, but it was evening as far as his body was concerned, still on London time.

Driving up R Street, he recognized The Fox & Goose Public House where she had taken him to breakfast. Sitting alone in a corner, a pint in front of him, his feelings fluctuated between sadness and anger as he tried to decide whether to give up and go home. He phoned Bill, but got voice mail.

As he gazed without focus into his Guinness, a man's voice said, "Jamie, did you find Kat?" It was Brian Galway, the older man who had helped him earlier.

"Yes." Jamie looked into his glass. "She kicked me out."

Brian took a deep breath. "I'm sorry. Anything I can do to help?"

"How well do you know her?" Jamie looked up at him with some hope.

"Better than most colleagues. We're not too close, but we both work at the Scottish Games as well as CDW, so we're pretty friendly. I know you're engaged."

"*We were* engaged. I wouldn't share this if she hadn't introduced you as her friend." Jamie summarized his situation and what had happened in Kat's office. "Do you know her well enough to guess how she'd react if I try to apologize, again? If I go to her home?"

Brian sat down. "I'm not sure, but I wouldn't give up, yet. She must be hurt, angry... and she's just been through a dangerous ordeal—"

"Lost and almost attacked by a mountain lion. I heard. Jesus..." He shook his head.

"She couldn't have slept much, and if she's at work today, someone must've *made* her come in. She's probably angry about that, on top of what you did."

Jamie's body stiffened. "What I *did*—" He stopped and sighed. Oh, hell, I'd be angry, too. I just... I love her, and I need to convince her..."

"Why don't you take a walk around Capitol Park to clear your head before you do anything? It's four blocks down Tenth Street." He pointed north, then gave Jamie his card. "Don't give up, yet. If you need other help while you're here, you can call me. Good luck."

* * *

Several minutes after Jamie left CDW, Molly insisted Kat go walk with her. She refused at first, then relented. She cursed Jamie repeatedly as they walked the mile-long rectangle around the State Capitol and park. Gradually, her anger subsided and turned to talk of how much she loved and missed him. When the pain overpowered her pride, she sat down.

On a bench in a secluded grove of trees, Molly tried to comfort her. "You're right to be angry. The way he ended your engagement was heartless."

"He thought he had to protect his career. He wanted to win an Academy Award and be an A-Lister more than anything in the world, and someone offered him a chance, if he'd stay single. His mother or sister probably told him I was bad for him. And they were right, because as soon as he got rid of me..." Her voice cracked and she could barely finish, "he won the Oscar."

Molly gave Kat a one-armed hug. "That's not why he won it. And he obviously loves you, even after choosing stardom over marriage. He knows that was the wrong choice."

"Oh, god, I miss him! I kept thinking about him when I was lost. The little time that I slept, I dreamed he rescued me. It reversed our running joke that I'd protect *him* from aggressive fans. But when I saw him in my office, I wanted to beat the sh—"

Molly's phone beeped. "Shoot... I have to go pick up Jennie."

"I can't go back to the office," Kat said, looking down and shaking her head.

"Will you be okay?"

"Do I *look* okay? I can't face the office. And I'm out of Kleenex!"

"Well... keep your phone on. If I don't see you within an hour, I'll call, and if you don't answer, expect another search party!" Molly smiled and hugged her again.

"Tell 'em to bring Kleenex."

Molly put her hand on Kat's shoulder, then turned to leave. She was the best kind of friend Kat could have right now.

"Molly? Thank you."

* * *

As he walked into Capitol Park, Jamie imagined things he might say to convince Kat to give him another chance, and her likely reactions.

While walking, he heard a familiar voice. It was Kat, with Molly at her side. Should he go speak to them, or keep walking until he'd made a rational decision? This could be a golden opportunity—or terrible timing.

Neither woman seemed to notice him standing in the shade, about thirty feet away. Molly left, and Kat leaned forward and stared at the ground, her head in her hands. When he was sure Molly was out of earshot, he walked toward Kat, slowly, and held a handkerchief out to her. "Here... take this."

Kat seemed shocked to see him there and dried her eyes with her sleeve. "No. Go away."

"I'm sorry," Jamie said, still offering the handkerchief.

Tears welled up in her eyes. As he sat down about a foot away from her, she turned her back on him, pulled her knees up to her chin, with her feet on the bench. Shaking, she wrapped her arms around her legs and pressed her face against her knees. "Damn you. Leave me alone."

Her reaction surprised him. "Kat, I'm sorry." He hadn't expected this self-sufficient, strong woman to be this distraught over him. Her powerful emotions were contagious, and Jamie teared up, too. "I didn't want to hurt you... and I feel awful about it. I made a dreadful mistake. It won't happen again."

* * *

Yes, it will," Kat sobbed into her knees. "It always does. Every frickin' time!" By now, the emotional pain had become physical. Her chest hurt, as though her heart was actually breaking apart. The asthma that had been under control now made her work to breathe, and she coughed intermittently.

Jamie placed one hand on her upper back. When she didn't react, he slowly moved closer, wrapped his arms around her, and held her. She remained curled up like a frightened hedgehog. He kissed the top of her head and spoke softly.

"Breathe, Kat. I know the last few months have been hard for you—and the last few days, even worse. It's been hard for me, too, knowing what an arsehole I'd been to hurt you—like all the other guys who've hurt you. They were fools to let you get away, and I almost made the same mistake. But I want you in my life."

"Oh, sure!" she sobbed. "For how long, *this* time?" She tried to take slow, deep breaths and stop crying as Jamie held her, but she couldn't.

The sound of horse hooves on concrete distracted them both. As each turned to look, an older CHP officer on horseback, just a few feet away, asked, "Is everything all right here?"

Jamie let go of Kat, and she turned to put her feet on the ground. The state was working to intervene in domestic violence cases, and the officer probably suspected she might be in trouble. "No. He's broken my heart—but nothing else. I doubt you can help with that."

The officer, who reminded Kat of Helen Mirren—if she had played a ranch-owning matriarch—gave her an empathetic look. "No. That's not illegal." Taking a deep breath, she looked out across the park, then at Jamie and said, in a kind tone, "Think carefully before you do anything you might regret later, son."

Kat watched the equestrian officer ride away. "Jamie, I've missed you so much." She looked down and, after a few silent moments, with a soft, shaky voice, she added, "But you made me wish I was dead. Please... go away." Still trembling, she must have looked awful. Why isn't there a box of Kleenex around when you need one?

"I've missed you, too." Jamie put his arm around her again and pressed his cheek against the side of her head. "More than you can imagine. I feel terrible for hurting you. I didn't realize you cared this much... or how empty I'd feel without you in my life. Do you still love me at all? Or have I lost you forever?"

Kat didn't speak. It surprised her to feel his warm tears fall into her hair. Her occasional coughs broke the long silence.

Finally, she took a deep breath. "Of course I love you... more than *you* can imagine." Looking at the ground, she added, "But I hate you, too. A little. And I'm afraid."

"What are you afraid of?" His voice was calm, not challenging.

"That you'll dump me again. I can't take this again. I can't even handle it, now." She leaned forward, elbows on her thighs, face in her hands—wishing she could stop crying and be stronger. She hated looking weak.

"No. I won't." He spoke softly and stroked her back with one hand. "I want you with me... always. I will *not* make that mistake again."

Kat wanted to believe and trust him, but she had heard that before. And worse, she still had to reveal something about herself. This was the moment she had avoided for two years.

"You won't want me when you know how old I am."

"No." Jamie straightened up. "I know you're older than I am."

"You do?" Kat straightened up and at last made blurred eye contact with him.

"Of course. That's probably one reason I like you so much. You have the sort of personality I like that most younger women don't have." He pulled her into a hug and held her. "You've been there and done that enough to relax and just be yourself, and give others room to do the same."

Kat weighed that for a minute. "How old do you think I am?"

"Oh, no!" He pulled away enough to look into her eyes and smile. "I wouldn't touch that with a bargepole! I've seen what's on the internet, and I think it's rubbish. You can tell me."

After a long pause, he pulled her close again. She quietly said, "Fifty-five." Another long pause as she waited for a reaction. "I'm ten years older than you." She bit her lip and closed her eyes, expecting a negative reaction. What seemed like a long time passed. She must have lost him again, this time forever. She trembled, more tears flowed onto his shirt, and it was harder to breathe. But... he was still holding her.

Finally Jamie spoke. "No. No way. Not that fifty-five is old, but..." he pulled away from her body to look at her carefully. "You look *my* age. You could even pass for thirty-something."

"Not naked."

"Well, no one else will ever get to see you naked." Jamie smiled and pulled her in to hold her close again. "You're mine... if you'll forgive me. Please?" His voice was quieter now, as though he wasn't sure she would.

Kat jerked herself away and glared at him. "What do you mean, I'm yours? Your *what*? What *am* I to you? A friend with benefits you keep in the closet while you take pretty little girls to the important events in your life?"

"Oh, Kat... I'm sorry. The studio insisted I take Ambrosia and play along with their stupid publicity scheme for the film. And last year, my agent asked me to take those young actors to the awards ceremonies. They were new clients, and he knew that would get them some free publicity. Being their 'date' was just another acting job. I don't even remember their names."

"But you acted with *them* the same way you did with *me*. And you *kissed* her—on network TV! How can I know you're not acting with me, too?" Saying that hurt her. Drowning in an emotional flood, she turned away.

"Kat, look at me... please?" His soft, emotional voice had an almost pleading quality she hadn't heard before.

"No. I look awful. And I need Kleenex."

Jamie pulled the handkerchief from his pocket and put it into her hand, then took hold of her shoulders and tried to squeeze the tension out of her muscles. They were solid as rocks. She dried her eyes and blew her nose, but still wouldn't face him. He reached for her chin, gently turned her head in his direction, and kissed her.

His warm, soft lips, pressed against hers brought a rush of good feelings. Jamie's cheeks were wet and his eyes bloodshot. His expression was encouraging, and Kat wanted to believe he meant what he said.

"I don't care how you look... and you're beautiful, even now. I love what you *are*, and I want to spend the rest of my life with you." He kissed her again, this time longer. "Will you please take me back and marry me?"

Kat didn't answer right away. She wanted to say yes. Before he ditched her, she had believed Jamie wanted to marry her. Now, if he changed his mind in a few years, it would be easy enough to divorce her. Then, she might not have a right to work in Britain, much less get a job that paid enough to support herself. Getting back to California and starting over would be extremely difficult, especially now that she was over fifty.

She leaned into Jamie's chest and they hugged as well as they could, sitting on the park bench. Jamie stood and helped her up, kissed her, and held her against him. He grinned when her cell phone played the *Nigel Stone* hero theme. It was Molly, exactly one hour after she had left Kat alone in the park.

"I'm okay." Kat walked away from Jamie.

"Where are you?" Molly asked.

"Same place. Guess who found me after you left?"

"Who? Not Jamie..."

"Yep." Kat smiled, unintentionally.

"Oh, god... What happened? You didn't slug him, did you? Do you need me?"

"Actually, I do. We need to go home and talk, but my purse is in my office, and I don't want to be seen there, now. Could you please bring it down to the quad in about ten minutes?"

"Sure. What about Ron? Have you spoken to him? He wanted you here, today."

"Oh, screw Ron! No... I'm sorry. I'll call him. If he wants to fire me, let him try. Will you take media calls for me? You know the story."

"Sure," Molly replied. "Can you do interviews, tomorrow, if they want to talk with you?"

"Yes, of course..." She looked at Jamie. "I think. Thanks. See you in ten."

Kat put her phone back in her purse and walked back to Jamie without answering his question. "What's wrong?" he asked.

She didn't want to tell him about the possibilities that had run through her mind. It would sound like his apology and proposal weren't enough. Were they?

"I'm afraid." She pressed her palms together in front of her mouth. "We need to talk, but not here."

As she walked, Jamie took her hand and held it tightly. "Bill told me what happened to you, with the mountain lion. I was so relieved to hear they found you, safe! You have to tell me what it was like, being lost out there overnight."

Chapter 40: Possibilities

Following her home, Jamie wondered what Kat needed to talk about before she could respond to his re-proposal. She didn't appear happy, but she didn't say no. How could he regain her trust? The song on the radio couldn't have been more pertinent: Chicago's 1982 hit, "Hard to Say I'm Sorry."

As they entered Kat's house, Jamie noticed spider webs around the door. Inside, there were dishes in the sink, papers, magazines and unopened mail scattered atop her dining table, and dust on the furniture. So unlike her. Standing in the living room, he pulled her close and held her. "What are you thinking?"

"Oh, god, Jamie... you'll never know how much I've missed you. I love you, dearly. Didn't want to... *tried not to.* I've kept men at arm's length for a long time to prevent pain like this. But you were so... so..." Her tears fell again on his shirt.

"If you missed me as much as I missed you, I do know," he whispered. "I am so sorry. Dad called me a git for not listening to my heart, and he was right. I know, now, you're more important to me than any job. There'll be other acting jobs, but there's only one you. I made an atrocious mistake and want to make things right again. Please, Kat... tell me..."

She pulled away from him, turned, and moved slowly to the sofa. *My god, she walks as if she weighs three-hundred pounds!* She sat down and leaned forward with her elbows on her thighs and her head in her hands. Jamie sat down beside her and put one hand on her back.

"When I was in my twenties, I lived with a man I loved, who said he loved me. For four years I let *my* radio career

slide to move around with him and promote *his*. Right after
we moved to Ottawa—where he had lived before we met—he
started seeing an ex-girlfriend. He stopped coming home,
some nights, and a month later, he said he didn't love me
and I should go back to California."

"I was alone in a foreign country, two-thousand miles
from friends and family, emotionally broken, with no way to
support myself. It took years to get back on my feet,
financially, and my career never completely recovered."

She told him how living out of a suitcase in friends'
homes and struggling to survive left scars on her self-esteem
as well as her heart. The following parade of short-term
boyfriends, who apparently just wanted to be seen with a
disc jockey, hadn't helped.

Jamie gently stroked her back as she described that life-
altering experience. The memory obviously revived long-
lived pain and fear of rejection, poverty, and failure.

"What a dreadful situation. I'm sorry you went through
that. You deserve better. And I'll make sure you're never
again vulnerable to anything like that."

Kat straightened up, faced him, and took his hand.
"How can I know *you* won't want a younger woman, and
dump me when my hair turns gray and my face—and
everything else— wrinkles and sags?" She searched his eyes
for honest answers.

"I can't bear to lose you again, Jamie. On top of having a
broken heart, I'd be alone, with no way to support myself, in
a foreign country, thousands of miles from home and
friends, again. And from England, I couldn't even drive
home! That's an emotional and financial train wreck I
couldn't survive."

Staring at Jamie's knees, she put her hand on his thigh.
"I love you and want you so much, Jamie... I do want to
marry you. I want to be with you, every day and night of our
lives."

Jamie relaxed a little as she took a deep breath, then her sad voice turned angry. "But you hurt me, damn it! You ditched me when someone said it *might* make you a star. I know, you said your career was your top priority. Except for those years with Mike, it's been mine, too.

But you didn't have enough respect for me to *talk with me* about it. You decided for both of us, fed me a bullshit line, and left me wondering what *really* happened... what *I did wrong!* Then I wanted to see you so badly, I watched those damned awards shows."

Jamie looked down as Kat continued. "When I saw you with that gorgeous young woman on your arm, holding her hand, acting the same way you had with me—even kissing her, in front of the whole w-world..." Her voice cracked as tears streamed down her cheeks, again. "It was obvious then why you didn't want the public to know we were engaged."

Jamie said nothing, still leaning forward with slouched shoulders, looking at the floor.

"You'll have to prove yourself to me before I'll risk this pain again. Putting a ring on my finger doesn't mean you'll never move me to the background, or cheat on me, or dump me again. I don't even know *what you see in me.* And I'm afraid in a few years, *you* won't either."

Jamie put his arm around her and pulled her back into the sofa cushions with him. With her head on his chest, he stroked her soft hair.

"What I see in you is an intelligent, beautiful, strong, successful woman who can take care of herself, and remind me I'm only human when others tell me I'm something more. A kind, loving woman who cares about most of the same things I do, and knows things that I don't. An unselfish, talented woman who has a kind of beauty cosmetics can't fake, who loves the real me, not the actor. I even think you would support me if I couldn't work and we were in financial trouble."

"Of course I would... if your government would let me. And if they wouldn't, I'd drag your ass back here, where I could!"

Jamie chuckled, then his voice turned serious again. "I will never abandon you or ask you to take a back-seat to anything; not even my career." He kissed her forehead and squeezed her to emphasize his words.

"We can go to the magistrate—or whoever does it here—and get married right now. Would Molly be our witness?" He sat up straight to face her and hold both her hands. "Or maybe invite Barbara and your friends, and get married here, or in a park, Saturday. Bill could come up to marry us. I'll even move here, if you want me to. Please, Kat..."

* * *

It was hard for Kat to believe anyone would want her that much—especially an award-winning actor. "Seriously? You really mean all that?"

"I do. With all my heart."

Still afraid, she had to think about it for a few minutes. But more than anything else, she wanted to believe and be with him. "I wouldn't ask you to move into my little house. Will you tell the world we're engaged, now? And get married this year?"

"Absolutely!" Jamie leaned forward and pressed his soft, warm lips to hers.

She paused to think. "Okay. I'll take one last chance on you... and love." She closed her eyes. *Please don't let this be another mistake!*

Jamie hugged her. "Kat, look at me." She did, as he wiped a tear from her cheek. "When it hurts to look back, and you're afraid to look forward, look beside you. I'll be there. Always." She hugged him, and he lifted her chin up to look into her eyes. "Tell your boss you're going to the BAFTA

Awards with me, next month—and everywhere else I go, from now on."

The cats appeared in front of the TV, watching their mom and the man. Kat smiled, let go of fear, and hoped that this time, love for life wouldn't only be in her dreams.

ACKNOWLEDGMENTS

Editing: Alicia Dean
Cover Design: 100 Covers

I am grateful to many people who have helped and encouraged me, including award-winning author Lizbeth Selvig; my friend and first editor Alexia Retallack, and developmental editor Cate Hogan. Author Jemma Heritage, University of Sussex Professor of Linguistics Lynne Murphy, TV production designer Arwel Wyn Jones; producer Sara Feilden, Rod Harper, director Tom Harper; and Michael Sicilia.

My sister Laura Wallan and my brother and sister-in-law, Ed and Diana Wallan.

My webmaster Win Day; Contemporary Romance Writers brainstormers Malinda Childers, Dotti Enderly, Donna Mortenson, and Amy Abramowitz; the late CSUS Professor Leigh Stephens; Patti Kishel, Sunny Magdaug, and Amanda Scott; Janet Kurnick, John Taylor, Jim Malcolm, Ed Miller, Karen Terrill, Kirsten Macintyre, Bruce Forman, Jane Lamborn, Don Elliot, Jo Evans, and Troy Swauger; Roni Java, John Turner, Vikke and Chuck Phalen, Sherry Slatten, and Maria Barrs.

This story began as a romantic comedy film screenplay. Thanks to TV comedy writer/playwright Ken Levine for reminding me that no production company or studio would even *look* at a screenplay from an unknown writer, and suggesting I write it first as a book.

—*Dana*

ABOUT THE AUTHOR

Originally from the San Francisco Bay Area, Dana Michaels is a former West Coast radio personality, news director and program director. She has also done public and media relations work for non-profit organizations, the California Department of Fish and Wildlife, and California State Parks. She still occasionally plays guitar with friends and a traditional Scottish quartet.

* * *

Thank you for reading my first novel! If you enjoyed reading ***In Your Dreams!***, would you please post a review on your favorite retailers' websites? Thank you.

In Your Dreams! is the first book in my ***Dreams*** series. Want to know about Kat's and Jamie's future? Stay tuned for Book 2, ***Dream On!***. Visit my website at https://DanaMichaels.com and sign-up for a quarterly newsletter. You can also see some of the settings and inspirations for this story in the photo gallery there. I'll let you know of special sales and when ***Dream On!*** and ***A Dream Come True*** will be released. I won't share or sell your email address or annoy you with frequent mail.

Made in the USA
Monee, IL
07 May 2022

96013642R00193